SILENCED

The doctor removed his glasses and mopped perspiration from his brow. What was wrong with the air conditioners? He made a note to call maintenance in the morning. He failed to notice a small orange metal cylinder behind a bank of file cabinets.

What he did notice was a feeling of drowsiness. He shook his head to clear it, but his muscles relaxed and against his will he found himself slumping in his chair. He was dimly aware of a telephone ringing and he thought to rouse himself to answer it.

Before he could transfer the will to action, his brain exploded into nothingness . . .

SYNDROME

BARBARA PRONIN

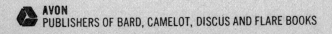
AVON
PUBLISHERS OF BARD, CAMELOT, DISCUS AND FLARE BOOKS

AVON BOOKS
A division of
The Hearst Corporation
1790 Broadway
New York, New York 10019

Copyright © 1986 by Barbara Pronin
Published by arrangement with the author
Library of Congress Catalog Card Number: 85-90800
ISBN: 0-380-89623-0

First Avon Printing, May 1986

AVON TRADEMARK REG. U. S. PAT. OFF. AND IN
OTHER COUNTRIES, MARCA REGISTRADA, HECHO EN
U. S. A.

Printed in the U. S. A.

K-R 10 9 8 7 6 5 4 3 2 1

For David . . .
and for Ely

For their friendship and their expertise and for sharing both with me, I am indebted to Dale Files, David Solinger, Ben Shwachman, MD, Rabbi Elisha Nattiv and—most especially—Barbara Greenberg, MD.

SYNDROME

REESE FOWLER MEDICAL CENTER, LOS ANGELES

"Dammit!"

Dr. Jeff Kohner's boyish face came very near to a scowl. Only hours before the Camthon grant committee invaded the basement lab, and he had to have butterfingers!

Quickly, he swept up the shards of broken glass, deposited them in a wastebin. With a soiled lab coat from the linen cart, he mopped up what remained of the chemical and threw the soggy coat back in the cart. Glancing up at the clock, he pulled the formula from the file and wondered how fast he could replace what had just been spilled. It was the second time this had happened. Damn, he'd have to be more careful.

With a wry grin Jeff recalled that the last accident—Tuesday morning—had also occurred after a nocturnal visit by the insatiable Alana McNeil. Pulling graveyard RN duty, Alana had latched onto Jeff one unlikely three A.M. in the near-deserted hospital cafeteria. "Lousy time for a dinner break, isn't it?" she had asked, slipping across from Jeff at the small Formica table. "Are you an ER resident, Dr.—?"

"Uh, research intern," Jeff had stammered, staring at her blue eyes and the tousled blond curls tumbling from

beneath the white cap. "I run the lab nights for the ubiq-
uitous Dr. Pederson. The name's Jeff. Jeff Kohner. Hi."

"Alana McNeil." God, she was gorgeous! "Eleven to
seven on five. Nice to meet you, Dr. Kohner."

"My pleasure. And it's Jeff," he'd managed to mumble,
noting how her breasts strained against the white nylon as
she reached back to straighten her sweater. She caught him
staring, and he looked swiftly at her tray. "Aren't you
eating? It's your dinner hour."

Alana'd regarded him with a hint of mischief over the
rim of her coffee cup—appraised him from the shaggy mop
of red hair and the candid brown eyes to the tips of his
long fingers, like a farmer appraising a prize steer. "There
are things," she told him finally, "I'd much rather see
going down at three A.M. than a few hundred calories on
my hips."

Jeff had nearly choked on a lump of congealed scrambled eggs. A first-year resident thanks to a scholarship and
a series of part-time jobs, he'd come to Reese Fowler with
glowing recommendations, a suitcase full of frayed shirts
and a grind's-eye view of the world. Even now, with his
crazy hours, he found little time for girls. But there was
no mistaking the invitation in the nurse's cornflower-blue
eyes.

"Are you . . . alone in that lab every night?"

Jeff needed no more urging. "Uh, mostly. I rotate day
and night shifts with a guy named Roger Howell. This is
my month on nights."

"Well . . ." Alana's eyes were fixed on his. "Would
you mind a little company now and then?"

Jeff had grinned and hoped he wasn't blushing. Worse,
he wondered if this whole thing wasn't a big, fat setup;
that old Rog himself wouldn't come charging out from behind the coffee urns in a minute, laughing himself silly.

But Roger never made his appearance, and Jeff didn't
have to wonder long. On Tuesday morning at precisely
three A.M. Alana had appeared in the doorway of the lab
and peeled down quickly to her enigmatic smile. She pro-

ceeded to demonstrate just what it was she preferred to her dinner, purring at him in tremulous tones.

"Oh, Jeffie," she'd shivered on the narrow little cot, "doesn't this beat the hell out of scrambled eggs?"

Smiling up at her from the V of her shapely legs, he had to agree that it did.

At 3:55, a scant ten minutes after her unceremonious departure, Dr. Jeff Kohner walked on rubbery legs to the steel work counter of the lab where, from trembling fingers, the first ampule of Pederson's chemical descended into white-tiled oblivion.

Pederson kept a careful control on the ampules, his latest efforts in the area of viral research. With this latest synthetic compound, Dr. Pedantic—as the interns ungraciously dubbed him—hoped to halt the spread of virus without the dubious accuracy and unwanted side effects of previously employed medications. The formula, increasingly effective in controlled testing with mice, was to be presented to the visiting Camthon pharmaceutical team this morning in the hope of eliciting a grant. "If you can get on with it, Kohner!" Jeff moaned.

Still ruminating on the remarkable effectiveness and unwanted side effects of Alana McNeil, Jeff hurried through the predawn routine, replacing the second ampule with a fresh one as he had done the other morning.

With wearied but determined skill, he then analyzed the latest data on the debilitated mice. He had inoculated the control group by six A.M. when Carmina Valdez sailed in from housekeeping to collect the soiled linens for the laundry. "Hey, Carmina! *Buenos dias, amiga!* What did you bring me? I'm starved!"

Cheerful and talkative, the buxom housekeeper often brought homemade treats for Jeff, whose boyish charm and slim physique brought out her motherly instincts. This morning, she proudly held out a foil-covered parcel that Jeff, having passed up dinner in favor of Alana, seized with relish.

"You're in luck, Dr. Kohner. *Pan de dulce.*" Carmina

smiled broadly, her several chins undulating. "But you
gotta make 'em last. That's it for a while. I'm taking my
two weeks vacation."

"Hey, Carmina, these are great. Thanks. What would I
ever do without you?" Jeff munched happily on the sugary-
sweet rolls. "Lucky you. Two weeks vacation!"

"Not so lucky," Carmina replied. "I gotta go to Albuquerque and take care of my baby sister. She's got that—
what do you call it? Mono something . . ."

"Mononuclcosis?"

"Yeah, that's it. Doctor says she's gotta have bed rest.
But she's got this little baby. What can you do? No family
there, so I go out and help her."

Jeff wiped crumbs from his mouth and the countertop.
"You're an angel of mercy, you know that, Carmina? If
you weren't married, I'd marry you."

"Come on, Dr. Kohner. You love me for my *dulces*.
Now take off that messy coat. I got work to do."

Obediently, Jeff threw the soiled coat into the cart,
reached for a fresh one from the shelf.

Carmina held up the wrinkled coat with which Jeff had
earlier mopped the floor. "This blood?" she asked, sniff-
ing at the stains.

"Chemicals. I had a little accident."

"The housekeeper rubbed at the darkened stains. "Okay.
We get 'em out," she assured him, wheeling out the cart.
"See you in two weeks, Dr. Kohner."

"I'll be back on the day shift by then." His face registered regret. Would Roger now inherit sweet Alana?

"Hey, that's good!" Carmina's dark eyes danced.
"You'll find better things to do with your nights!"

"Yeah." The young doctor looked decidedly glum. His
midnight snacks would never be the same.

PART ONE

Miracles

Chapter One

In the sudden flash of intense, hot light, Nancy Rafferty composed her even features into what she hoped was just the right mix of seductiveness and studied poise. She needn't have worried. In her wide, green eyes it was impossible to miss the alert vivacity, and in the curve of her full lower lip, half of Los Angeles' male population saw ripe, succulent strawberries begging to be nibbled and sucked.

Nevertheless, the promise of a smile had been artfully practiced since the start of her career in Omaha, and now, as she looked out into the blackness beyond the glare, it was as much a part of her face as the small tilted nose and the tiny cleft in her chin. When the red light came on above the camera, her eyes flicked to the sweep second hand of the big clock to her right. It was nearing twelve. Deftly, she fluffed her froth of chestnut curls, wet her lips and widened the promise of a smile just the tiniest fraction.

In the booth, as the sum total filled the small monitor, film editor Jack Henley felt a familiar lurch in his gut. How could anybody be so breathtaking?

On the floor, Sam gave the cue. Nancy Rafferty spoke.

"Hello, Los Angeles. This is Nancy Rafferty at KBLA News Central." A brief pause underscored the impact as her face lit up a million television screens. But Nancy, incredibly unmindful of her beauty, had more important things on her mind.

"In Syria tonight, Moslem leaders are marshaling their

forces for what may be the largest Israeli-Moslem conflict
since Lebanon four years ago. . . . In Washington, econ-
omists tell us we may be facing the largest surge of American inflation in this decade. . . . Fire breaks out in a
hillside area just above San Francisco—and in Los Angeles, police continue the search for a five-year-old girl missing from her home since Sunday.

"Details on these and other stories in a moment. But
first—" Now the awesome face registered childlike delight.
"First—the good news."

In the booth, Jack Henley wiped a thin coating of perspiration from his brow as he marveled again at the authority in the clear voice and the sheer charisma with which
Nancy Rafferty was able to charm her viewers away from
the latest calamities for this moment of spontaneous pleasure. Somehow, in this moment, relating a story with an
old-fashioned happy ending, something happened between
Nancy and her fans. It was as though her own enthusiasm
were transmitted through the screen. For an instant there
was hope for the world—and the weirdest feeling that you
wanted to reach out and take somebody by the hand.

Sure, it was corny. Jack shook his grizzled head. So
were family picnics and homemade ice cream. But it
worked—at least in Nancy's hands—if the increased ratings
were the measure of its success. Hell, even Ty Callahan,
the producer, who had nearly laughed Nancy out of his
office when she made the suggestion for this segment of
the news, now had to admit that, if nothing else, the girl's
own openness made it work. The viewers lapped it up and
begged for more.

The camera focused on a black-and-white photograph of
a white-faced, obviously frightened young family. "This
is the Rudy Penskov family," continued Nancy. "Recent
émigrés from the Soviet Union. After six years of unsuc-
cessful attempts to obtain exit visas, battling against personal and professional harassment, the Penskovs were one
of fourteen Jewish families allowed to leave the Soviet
Union this year.

"But the Penskovs, who planned to settle near relatives in Ridgefield, New Jersey, were forced to leave all their assets behind. They were penniless when they arrived in this country. Rudy had no promise of a job.

"So Ridgefield residents, alerted to the Penskovs' needs by relatives and the local press, geared up for American-type action." A neat, frame house now filled the television screen. The door opened and a gleeful young man waved the minicamera inside, where a happy crowd embraced and shook hands.

"This house," Nancy explained, "was offered by a local realtor rent-free for six months. Neighbors held a huge garage sale whose proceeds augmented secondhand furniture with everything from crib sheets to canned goods in the cupboard."

The camera zoomed in on the gleeful young man shaking hands with an elderly, smiling chap. A buxom young woman with a baby on her hip beamed at them from the sidelines.

"Best of all"—Nancy's pride in humanity was genuine—"local dairyman Louis Roszenski provided Rudy with a job in the émigré's field of microbiology, complete with a ready-made car pool. 'My father was a refugee who came here with absolutely nothing,' admitted an earnest Roszenski. 'I know how he struggled, but this country was good to us. Now I have the chance to do something to help repay my father's debt to America.' "

Jack Henley wiped the foolish grin from his face as the cameras switched to a commercial. "Damn," he muttered, his throat full of the same love and pride felt by every other immigrant's child who had seen the broadcast tonight. "Damn, damn, damn, damn, damn. . . ."

During the commercial break, Nancy daubed at her forehead with a powder puff and straightened the collar of her modestly cut pale blue suit. She reached for a mirror in which to check the effect. Judd Rohrbach's cool hand came to rest lightly on hers. The co-anchorman regarded her with a wry smile. "Gotta hand it to you, kiddo"—his voice was ice—"you did it again."

Nancy removed her hand and looked directly at his tanned, smooth face. He was a golden boy, a California Adonis, casually combed blond hair framing a perfect movie-star face. The magnetic sensuality in his deep-set blue eyes had left Nancy weak-kneed and terrified when she'd auditioned for this job a year ago. For all her bravado and her determination to succeed, she'd been a green kid from Nebraska with limited reporting experience on a local station. But she'd quickly responded to Judd's sureness, to his gentle coaxing, with an innate sensuality of her own that had not been missed by the producer, Ty Callahan.

She could not have known—did not know until later—that the golden boy had begun to bore the Los Angeles viewers; that Callahan had been looking for a new spark. She knew only that she'd gotten the job, and her elation was mixed with gratitude to Judd and, ultimately, something more.

She'd been flattered by his attention, completely swept up in his glamour, eager to prove herself worthy of it. Her inexperience was no match for his ardor, for the compelling lure of his eyes. She had given herself to him with starry-eyed innocence. Now she saw only smug conceit in those eyes, and the touch of his hand made her skin crawl. "Thanks . . . kiddo," she answered coolly and turned her attention back to the camera.

She carefully composed herself so that her face, springing to life on the TV monitor, registered only grave concern. "Los Angeles police are still stymied over the mysterious disappearance of little Jenny Ortiz, who vanished from her home last Sunday. Judd, what's the latest on this?"

The cameras switched to Judd's chiseled face as his smooth voice picked up the cue. "Well, Nancy, as you know, five-year-old Jenny was last seen . . ."

Nancy sat back and relaxed in her chair, knowing she was a full five minutes away from her next appearance.

From the booth, Jack Henley caught her eye and formed a victory sign with his fingers. Nancy smiled her thanks. She knew Jack meant it.

Listening to Judd's theatrical voice as he related the details of the Ortiz case, Nancy was struck anew with wonder that she had ever heard anything in it but duplicity and guile. How could she ever have been so naive, so charmed by this polished shell of a man? She had been betrayed by her own newly awakened needs and expertly played upon by Judd. Had she grown up that night in his high-rise apartment only a month ago? She reluctantly let her memory return her to that one night with Judd.

He had made love to her gently, his hands and his lips feathering her body, wresting from her the most exquisite longings. Then, when she clutched at him, wild with her need, he plunged into her deeply, thrusting quickly, slowly, leading her through hills and valleys of sensation until finally they crested the final peak.

She had never ceased to marvel that her body was capable of such a crashing symphony or that his was capable of conducting it. Yet even as she clung to him, she felt him slip away, as though he had orchestrated the final clash of cymbals without ever really being part of it.

She'd brushed away the jarring thought, nestling closer to him. His fingers absently played on her skin. They were silent for a long moment.

"You were good tonight," he'd told her finally. She'd lifted her green eyes to his, winking broadly. He chuckled. "No, you silly goose, I meant on the air."

"Oh," she yawned, resting her head on his chest. She loved to feel the resonance when he spoke.

"The good-news spot, though . . ." his voice was casual, sleepy. "Don't you think it's getting kind of—I don't know—not maudlin, I suppose, but . . . well, maybe a little sticky-sweet for a late news broadcast?"

"People like it," Nancy murmured, wanting sleep. "Callahan's happy. The ratings are up. It's kind of fun— the good news with the bad."

"I don't know that I like it. It detracts from the professionalism—the tone I've worked for years to build up with an audience."

"It doesn't affect you, Judd. You're still giving the news the same professional gloss as always. All I get is the sob-sister stuff and the local ballyhoo."

Judd was painfully silent.

"That's true, isn't it?" she persisted. "I've asked for some of the international stories, and Callahan pats me on the head and tells me, 'Later.' And the ratings *are* up."

"That's the point," said Judd, tracing circles on her breast. "It's as though every night I've not only got to compete against your gorgeous puss, but against the sentimentalism you're dishing out up front. All of a sudden, the world news is secondary."

"Well," Nancy faltered, surprised at the petulance in his voice, "maybe we could think about moving my spot to a later point in the telecast." Even as she said it, she knew Callahan would never buy it. It was the opening spot that brought in the viewers.

"I don't think so. I'm afraid the idea was a big mistake. Makes me wonder if you're—if the whole thing is working out."

Nancy was fully awake now, not quite believing what she had heard. True, Judd himself had suggested a female co-host to boost slipping ratings. He had had a say in her selection, and she supposed he had a right to criticize the result. But not working out? "You mean, besides the good-news spot? You just said I was good tonight."

"You're always good, you know that." Judd nuzzled her neck, pushing aside her chestnut curls, his voice soothing. "I don't know that I deserve such a paragon on my show."

Nancy jerked away. "You mean, maybe you're not up to the competition!"

"Now, wait a minute, kiddo." The cobalt eyes grew narrow. "I carried that show for years before you came on board."

"Yes. Long enough to watch the ratings slide into the cellar. You owe me a debt of gratitude . . . kiddo! It was me—and my idea—that kept you on top!"

Judd's lithe body coaxed her down. He grazed the silky skin of her inner thigh. "I like being on top," he murmured, moving skillfully above her. "On the air—and off. Let's not be hasty."

"Hasty, my foot!" Nancy struggled to free herself. "You said what you had to say. Now go tell Callahan!" Leaping from the bed, she had dressed hurriedly, refusing to be budged by what she now saw as placating oiliness.

She had slammed out of the apartment, driven home in a rage and showered viciously, shouting curses at Judd Rohrbach. Only later, after the anger wore off and the doubt set in—after she'd mentally rehearsed the showdown she was bound to have with Callahan—did she dissolve into piteous tears. Not because she'd been used—and now stood to be discarded if Judd had his way—but because it occurred to her, as she wrestled with the sheets in the predawn light, that this time the cymbals had indeed clashed for the last time. She had seen—and heard them—with bruising finality. This particular symphony was over. She wondered if the missing chords would ever sound for her again.

Now, breaking for another commercial interlude, it was Judd's turn to reach for the powder puff. The hot lights were murder on makeup. "I'm going to reverse the Syrian story and the Israeli," he stated crisply. "We gave the Israelis top billing yesterday. You'll come back with the parade story after the weather and sports."

Nancy nodded coolly, wondering for the umpteenth time whether their mutual animosity ever came off on the screen. Apparently, it did not. Surely, Callahan would have said something long before this. But then, Callahan had never confronted her with Judd's outburst after that night either— though she knew for a fact they'd been behind closed doors for nearly an hour.

In any case, she had never had to give the carefully re-

hearsed defense she'd worked out for herself. The status quo
was kept. If anything, Callahan was warmer toward her than
ever. Only Judd, with his closed silence and thinly veiled
sarcasm, spoiled the pleasure of her growing popularity.

Inevitably, the telecast drew to a close. Judd gave a detailed, if somewhat imperious overview of the new peace
talks scheduled to begin tomorrow. "We'll be back tomorrow night with all the headlines and all the news. Nancy?"

She knew how it irritated him to turn the final spot back
to her. "Thank you, Judd. All the headlines and all the
details. But first—" She wore her most engaging grin.
"First, the good news!" The screen went dark.

In a Westwood condominium, Miriam Phillips yawned
wearily, turned off the set and delayed her preparations for
what she knew would be another sleepless night.

In a house precariously perched on stilts high in Beverly
Glen Canyon, Ruthie Hillman hit the Off button on the
remote control by her bedside, wondering if the unexpected
cesarean would keep Louis at the hospital past midnight—
and what possible difference it could make if it did.

In St. Agatha's Convent, Sister Althea Rose switched
off her small set, paced once about her tiny room and,
knowing she would not sleep anyway, decided to go back
to the chapel.

And in the staff room at Reese Fowler Medical Center,
Dr. Jeff Kohner stared balefully at the fabulous face fading
from the screen, sighed once and prepared to go to work.

Chapter Two

For Zan Phillips the long vigil in Room 542 at Reese Fowler Medical Center had become routine. His tired gray eyes rested on the small form of his seven-year-old son, pale under the plastic tent, half hidden by a tangle of wires, tubes and bottles. Zan was filled with an aching weariness—a grudging acknowledgment that death was so imminent as to be palpable in the room.

What was missing, Zan realized, bearing down with both hands on the top of his own blond head, was the rage—the all-consuming, helpless pain—which had wracked him in the first days of Stevie's illness. What remained in its place was a bitter, futile acceptance of defeat—not unlike the final moments of a losing football game, when hope is gone and all that remains is to stumble from the field, lick the wounds and gear up for the next battle.

He felt vaguely ashamed, in the droning, blipping presence of these life-supporting machines, to compare the ebbing of his son's life with the loss of a football game. Yet, stirring uncomfortably in the green plastic chair in which he'd spent every night of the last three weeks, he could no longer deny the gnawing urge to be finished with this waiting for death and get on with the business of living.

He could never admit that to Miriam, of course—not to that wraithlike caricature of his once bubbly wife who prayed by day in this very chair and tossed, wide-eyed, in their bed each night while Zan took over the vigil. Miriam, who had not been inside a temple *or* a church in the ten years they'd been married, now prayed daily for some personal miracle—for Stevie's life to be spared.

She haunted the doctors for a shred of hope, became manic over the real or imagined flutter of a comatose eyelid. Above all, she was convinced that if Stevie were to cross the tenuous line to one side of life or the other, he could no more be permitted to cross it alone than he had been allowed to traverse the few short blocks to Wheatley School by himself only weeks ago.

When Stevie had complained that "the other guys" got to walk by themselves, Miriam had grudgingly allowed him to join the group. But she observed them, from an acceptable half-block distance away, each morning and each afternoon.

If Zan felt secretly that she babied their son, he kept his suspicion to himself. At least, he was sure that Stevie's illness was not the result of neglect.

He'd awakened slowly when Miriam panicked over the boy's sudden fever and stiff neck, and, although Stevie had been snuffling with a cold for days, they'd made the frenzied two A.M. drive to the hospital. Dr. Hillman—God bless Dr. Lou—had clearly indicated that their prompt reaction might have saved the child's life.

The viral meningitis had been assaulted with antibiotics, to which Stevie seemed to respond early on. Frantic, Zan and Miriam had clung to every sign of the boy's return to health. But slowly, the rally had ceased. Stevie's vital signs became weaker and weaker until finally he slipped into coma.

Beset with pain and unaccountable guilt, Zan had acceded to Miriam's insistence that the two of them share a twenty-four-hour vigil. Requesting an emergency leave from his job as a high-school teacher and football coach, Zan had assumed the night rotation.

He had opted for nights, convinced that if Stevie died in the early morning hours, when so many hospital deaths occurred, he would be better able to handle the moment than Miriam—though he did not tell her this. Their relationship was strained as it was. He saw no point in making things more difficult. Instead, he had sat here in the eerie semi-darkness night after night for two weeks, a victim of his own dark thoughts.

For the first two weeks he had listened for Stevie's every shallow breath, his own big body tensed and alert, tuned to the blips on the monitors. Occasionally, he allowed himself a ten-minute break when the nurses offered coffee or ice cream. The nurses, for the most part, had been supportive and warm, though they studiously avoided encouragement. In the past week, as Miriam's obsession deepened, Zan had wandered out to the nurses' station more and more frequently, eager for company—any company— and no longer looking for a miracle.

He was thinking about a break now, to keep himself from nearly dozing off. Three to five A.M. were the hardest. Zan's daytime sleeping had been fitful at best, pierced by every shriek and lawn mower in the active young neighborhood. As his mind balked, his body rebelled against the topsy-turvy change in its habits and lying awake, he would fantasize Miriam's lithe body moving on his until he was hard with desire, overcome with despair and frustration. He could not remember the last time they'd made love, had shared a joke—or even a meal!

Accustomed to putting Stevie's needs first, Miriam had often been tired and distracted. But if their love life had been less than Zan wished for, she had at least been warm, smiling, caring. Now, she was a ghost—an unreachable stranger—and Zan wondered, not without bitterness, what it would be like after . . .

From deep in his reverie Zan was suddenly conscious of what sounded like a moan from the still, blond form in the bed. Imagination, surely. He sat forward, massaging his face to force it to come awake. Once or twice in the last hour he thought he had detected a change in the steady blip-blip of the monitor.

Throwing off his drowsiness, his mutinous digressions, Zan now riveted his attention on the boy. Was it his imagination, or did Stevie's color seem better through the plastic of the oxygen tent? The translucent skin stretched over the fragile face—was it a more lifelike hue?

Zan gripped the arms of his chair as he scanned the monitors for some change in their incessant patterns. But the greenish screens yielded up nothing that he could hope to interpret. Certainly no irregularity in the droning output had brought Miss McNeil—or any of the nurses—running for a look.

For a long moment, Zan gazed fixedly at his son, scarcely breathing himself. Then, with a taste like gall in his mouth, he slowly leaned back in the chair and closed his eyes. "God," he whispered, "I'm getting as bad as Miriam. . . ." He guessed he'd better go for some coffee.

In the first-floor chapel of the Medical Center, a slim girl knelt at the altar, hands clasped at the railing before her. Head bowed, copper hair burnished in the glow of the stained glass, she did not notice the column of harsh light as the chapel doors opened wide.

RN Vera Presti, buxom and dough-faced, cleared her throat in the doorway, hesitant to break in on a prayer. The slight young woman kneeling at the altar might have been taken for a schoolgirl. But even had it not been for the small veil pinned atop the copper hair, Presti knew her well from St. Agatha's parish. "Sister Althea," she called.

The girl jumped at the sound of her name, turned quickly toward the door.

"Dr. Fairfield is with your mother, Sister. He asks that you come up at once."

The nun's dark eyes widened in alarm at the no-nonsense tone in Presti's voice. It was nearly four A.M. Why would Dr. Fairfield be with her mother now, unless—

"It's all right, I think," Presti added. "She's conscious. She was asking for you."

Sister Althea scrambled to her feet. Moving with light

grace, she followed the lumbering stride of the broad-hipped nurse, a prayer still on her lips. She had not quite finished her communion with God, but perhaps . . . perhaps, she'd said enough.

The silver-haired doctor was leaving her mother's room when the young nun emerged from the sixth-floor elevator followed by the starched Miss Presti. Althea read nothing in his smooth, tanned face, no clue in his elegant demeanor.

"Sister," he announced, hardly seeming to notice her, "your mother was conscious for a few minutes. She was asking for you, but I'm sorry to say she appears to have lapsed again."

Althea nodded, white-faced and solemn. "Thank you, Dr. Fairfield. May I go in?"

"I don't see the point. Just a temporary rally. We're monitoring her closely, of course."

"Yes," said the nun, "I understand." But there was stubbornness in the square Irish jaw.

"Five minutes," the doctor relented. "No more. And if she drifts back again, nothing to upset her." He accepted a chart from Presti, carefully avoiding her doting gaze.

Again, the nun nodded. With a wordless sigh, she entered her mother's room. No matter what Dr. Fairfield thought, this was not just a temporary rally. She, Althea, had traded heavily for it. Her mother, at least, would be fine.

The first thing Dr. Louis Hillman noted as he woke in the predawn chill was the distinct and somehow startling absence of pain. He lay in the wide bed, absently stroking his wife's left leg, which, as usual, was flung against his hip.

He watched the first pale fingers of light creep up the blue silk draperies. He heard the vague hum of the Seth Thomas clock on the opposite wall, became increasingly aroused at the faint answering in Ruthie's limbs, and con-

tinued to stroke her gently—all the time strangely aware
that he was a man waking in the predawn chill without the
damning, obstinate, unrelenting pain that had come to be
a part of his every waking.

Ruthie raised her tousled dark head, opening one eye
with reluctance. "What time is it?" she mumbled.

Louis did not look at the clock. He'd had no need of
them since his first days as a resident at Reese Fowler
nearly twenty years ago. He read, instead, the precise
amount of light in the morning sky and relied on the alert
system in his brain. "Six o'clock," he decided. He continued to graze Ruthie's still supple skin with the tips of his
probing fingers.

Ruthie's brown eyes now snapped open. "Louis?" The
question was tentative.

In answer, Louis turned over on his side, drawing his
wife's hand to his groin. His mouth sought the moist hol-
low of her neck. Ruthie stroked and fondled him, returned
his kisses almost shyly—until she herself could wait no
longer. It had been a long wait.

Afterward, she drowsed against him, the planes of her
face smooth and relaxed. He stroked her hair. It was good
to see her like this.

Almost absently, with his free hand he began to palpate
his abdomen. It was foolish, of course. He could tell nothing that way. Yet somehow he was sure the mass was
smaller. And there was no hint of pain. Knitting his thick
brows, he saw, in his mind's eye, the lab report sent up a
week ago. Under the pseudonym "Carl Sanders" was the
indisputable evidence of carcinoma that Louis himself had
suspected and ignored for more than three months.

At first he'd thought it was an ulcer. The burning pain,
the nausea and occasional vomiting seemed to indicate that
possibility. By then he had begun to feel light-headed from
time to time, and the pain increased in direct proportion to
his chronic feeling of weariness. Still, it was not until
Ruthie began to tease him about his loss of weight that he

decided to do anything besides swallowing an inordinate amount of Maalox.

At that point, he'd swallowed barium instead and paid a young technician to run an upper GI and keep his mouth shut. The test result was obvious. The startling irregularity of the barium's path indicated not only a mass, a tumor, but very likely a malignant one. Had "Carl Sanders" been anyone else, Louis would have urged him for an EGD biopsy stat. So why was it he'd sat on his own X ray for weeks while the pain increased, he worried himself sick, and his sex life went out the window?

He closed his eyes, shaking his head slowly. Again, it had been Ruthie's reaction, her silent questioning, which had ultimately sent him to Bernie Greenspan's offices— away from Reese Fowler—where he'd sworn his old friend to secrecy. But knowing the truth had not made it easier; Louis still had not told Ruthie, he simply had buried himself in his work.

It hadn't been difficult to do that. The flu epidemic—and then little Stevie Phillips, whose flu had been viral meningitis. God, what a world. What utter helplessness.

Ruthie stirred. It was nearly seven. Silently, Louis slipped from the bed, intending to shower and dress without waking her. But Ruthie, who, since the children had gone, rarely rose before nine, flung her short legs out of bed at the first sound he made and insisted upon fixing him breakfast.

They ate French toast and scrambled eggs in the sunny breakfast room overlooking the canyon. It was a ritual generally reserved for Sundays and holidays and only if Louis wasn't on call.

Ruthie poured fresh orange juice. "Louis," she ventured, "tell me, is it—over?"

"Over? What's over? What are you talking about?"

"Whatever the problem was. You know. I mean, why you—why we—" She broke off, blushing. "Well, I did some reading . . ."

Louis laughed aloud, his gray eyes clear and youthful

under scraggly brows. He could not remember the last time
he had laughed so heartily. God, it felt good. It felt good
to be sitting across the table from Ruthie, his raven-haired
Jewish princess who, at fifty, still looked like his bride. It
felt good that in a world where people took divorce as
much for granted as tomorrow's dinner, he and his wife
could look at each other with love in their eyes and care
whether they ever made love again.

"It's all right," said Louis; and with some second sight,
he knew, somehow, that it would be. He would be all
right. Unlikely as it seemed, he would be fine. He was
glad he had not told Ruthie. She would have worried herself sick. "I love you," he told her solemnly now.

"I love you, too." Ruthie squeezed his hand and kissed
the top of his balding head as she bustled out to make fresh
coffee. By the time he maneuvered his way down the wind-
ing canyon road and made the twenty-minute drive to Reese
Fowler, it was well past eight o'clock.

He was not prepared for what greeted him.

Chapter Three

"One cream, two sugars, right?" Alana McNeil placed the steaming cup before Zan and slid into a chair across from him at the tidy little desk in the nurses' station.

Zan nodded gratefully. "You saved my life."

Alana laughed, a throaty ripple strangely out of place in the sterile corridor. "I don't know that I'd go that far, Mr. Phillips."

"It's Zan."

"Zan. Must be short for something."

"Alexander. My mother had visions of greatness."

The blond nurse laughed again, and Zan wondered, not for the first time, why a gorgeous girl like this would choose to spend her nights in an eerie hospital corridor. Probably her boyfriend worked nights, too. He began to imagine the nurse and her unknown lover coming home from their night shifts, making love slowly with the shades drawn against the morning light. Then the daydream ended as he realized it was a far cry from the lonely bed Zan himself would fall into an hour or so from now. Miriam would have taken up her day watch by then, their only exchange a brief greeting. He felt guilty even thinking about sex while his son's life was in peril. But how he longed for the warmth of Miriam's embrace—for some clue that his strength was a comfort to her.

Alana seemed to read his thoughts. "It's a bummer, this

night shift. What do you do later? Go home and punch the pillows?''

Zan shrugged. ''It's not so bad,'' he lied. ''I manage to sleep most of the morning. He closed his eyes, passed his big hands over them. ''It doesn't look too hopeful, does it?''

Alana touched his shoulder, a gesture of sympathy that caused Zan to shudder deeply. ''I don't know,'' she said. ''Nobody does. All we can do is hope.''

The elevator bell dinged, the doors slid noisily open. Zan sat up straighter, saw the morning nurse emerge smiling, and noted by the clock above the nurses' station that it was nearly seven A.M.

''Good morning!'' The rubber soles of Miss Keating's white brogues squeaked across the polished tile. ''How is Stevie today?''

''The same, I guess.'' Zan heaved himself up, drained the last of his coffee. ''I guess I'll go back and sit with him awhile—until my wife arrives.'' The women watched him move down the hall, a big man with an athlete's grace.

''Too bad,'' clucked Keating. ''Quiet night?''

''Yes,'' responded Alana. ''No admissions. Mrs. Hanrahan goes on digitalis this morning. DC the Foley on Mr. Varese. . . .''

In Room 542, early spring sunlight had begun to dapple the walls. Zan tilted the blinds and, hands stuffed in his pockets, turned to gaze at his son. With a jolt, he saw that Stevie's eyes were open, flicking around the room. Now they rested on him. ''Dad?'' came a feeble voice.

Zan grappled for his own voice. ''Stevie? Yes, it's Dad.'' He was oddly afraid to move.

''Hi, Dad.'' The stirrings of a smile played on the boy's pale lips. He shifted restlessly, becoming aware of the tangle of tubes and the oxygen tent.

''Don't move, Stevie.'' Zan's pulse pounded in his ears. He bolted forward. ''Mrs. Keating! . . . Everything's fine, son. Hold real still— Where the hell is she? Mrs. Keating!''

Mrs. Keating, pouring coffee, jumped at the shout and scalded her thumb. By the time she arrived in 542, Alana McNeil, who'd been going off duty, had raised the O_2 tent. The blond nurse told the winded veteran, "Call Dr. Hillman—stat."

Miriam Phillips rode up in the elevator long before her usual time. She had wakened from a fitful sleep at five. It had seemed pointless to thrash around in bed. She wondered if Zan was sleeping better. She must remember to ask.

A stranger, noting Miriam's drawn, white face, might have assumed she was forty. Drab blond hair was pulled back in a rubber band hastily yanked from the morning newspaper. She wore no makeup. Dark blue shadows under her eyes were the only color in a grim and taut-lipped face. Her eyes, once described as electric blue, were as pale and worn-looking as the gray of her sweatshirt.

In fact, she was twenty-nine, and her best friends were openly dismayed at the toll this ordeal had taken on her. The worst of it was, Miriam reflected, she didn't give a damn what she looked like. Her own well-being was the farthest thing from her mind, even if Zan had gently suggested more than once that she might improve her bleak perspective if she took better care of herself.

Fat chance, she thought bitterly, stepping off the elevator into the familiar world of the fifth floor. There was no one at the nurses' desk, and while there was nothing unusual in that, she was suddenly seized with panic. She hurried her pace to Stevie's room—where the nurses clustered around the bed only sharpened her alarm. "Oh God," she whispered, slumping in the doorway. "Dear God, please, don't let it . . ."

Strong hands gripped her, shook her roughly, Zan's face inches from her own. "Miriam, he's conscious. I tried to call. Do you hear me, Miriam? He's awake!"

Miriam struggled up against the blackness like a swimmer under water too long. She searched Zan's face for a hint of a lie, but she found none and at last she caught her breath.

"Mommy?" The small voice pierced her numbness. She broke into great, racking sobs.

"Let her through," Zan directed the bustling assemblage. He propelled his wife gently across the room.

Dr. Louis Hillman chided himself as he crossed the expanse of the doctors' parking lot and headed for the staff entrance. It was eight-twenty; he hated being late, even if this morning had been special. He allowed himself a rakish grin, recalling his lovemaking with Ruthie.

His gaze swept the massive Reese Fowler complex, gray and stolid, unchanging. It had been a part of his daily life through most of the years of his marriage—his *shiksa* mistress, Ruthie called it, luring him with stately foreign contours. Yet, Ruthie would be surprised to learn how little he actually saw it. It was a shell, a maze of rooms and equipment, a place to do what he did. He would be hard pressed to describe its physical appearance. It was the *people* he saw, the patients who came here, their infinite mystery and challenge. Did they notice the crumbling Gothic arches, the chiseled mottoes in the stone?

Thinking again of "Sanders," the fictitious fellow who had borne the stigma of Louis's carcinoma, he determined to phone his own doctor and arrange for a new set of X rays. Perhaps it was too early even for cautious optimism. Still, he felt so well this morning. . . .

In the pristine whiteness of the doctors' entrance, the page clerk broke in on his thoughts. "Doctor Hillman! I've been trying to reach you at home. You're wanted on five—right away."

Fifth floor. Stevie Phillips. Louis frowned, grabbed a ward coat and hastened to the elevators. The boy's meningitis, his descent into coma had been frustrating and dazzlingly swift. Louis dreaded facing Zan and Miriam if the boy had taken a turn for the worse.

Nurse Keating met Louis as he stepped from the elevator. "They told me you were on your way up. Stevie Phillips has regained consciousness, doctor. He's alert and his responses are appropriate. Vital signs are stable." She grinned somewhat sheepishly. "It's all we can do to keep him down!"

In 542, Stevie sat propped against his pillows like a young rajah holding court. Miriam sat on the edge of the bed; Zan stood behind her, beaming. An LVN was checking the boy's pulse, but on sight of the doctor, Stevie wiggled from her grasp. "Hi, Dr. Lou! Hey, guess what? I'm gonna get a two-wheeler!"

"That so?" replied Louis, ignoring the chart Keating held out. He scrutinized Stevie. He noted the color in the boy's face and the alert energy in his eyes. "Well, I must say you look a lot readier to ride one than you did when I saw you last."

Stevie grinned, exposing a gap in his teeth. "Mommy says I slept a whole lot."

The doctor chuckled. "So you did. You certainly did do that." He turned to view the exuberant faces of the boy's parents.

"Stevie's come back to us." Miriam's eyes shone. "Look, Dr. Lou. It's like a miracle." Zan wrapped his arms around his wife.

Louis slowly straightened from his customary slouch, pulled a stethoscope from his pocket. More cautious optimism. What a morning. What in hell was going on here?

"Come on, Miriam," Zan whispered to his wife. "Let's leave these two fellows alone."

Miriam rose and kissed Stevie on the forehead. "We'll be waiting right outside."

Louis approached his perky young patient. "Let's have a good look, shall we?" Stevie grinned again, and Louis marveled at his bright and healthy demeanor. Somehow he knew, before he examined him, what he was going to find. . . .

* * *

Sister Althea sat in a pink plastic booth in the rear of a coffee shop across the street from Reese Fowler and tried to make herself inconspicuous. She was small-boned and slim, not quite five feet tall, but she found herself wishing she could make herself invisible. She caught her reflection in the dusty window glass, dark eyes enormous in a small, pinched face, springy copper hair impossible to hide under the short, starched veil; and she lowered her eyes and turned away.

She was exhausted, drained, and less from lack of sleep, she knew, than from her anguish of the night before. Just as the cancer had ravaged her mother's body, so did the pact Althea had made with God last night now tear at the fabric of her soul. But she had made the commitment. Her mother was better. Althea must keep to her bargain.

It had taken every shred of her will to telephone Michael Kelly this morning—to ask him to meet her here at the coffee shop while her purpose remained clear in her mind. But now, as his familiar blond head peered around a partition—and as he strode toward her in that jaunty way that never failed to elate her—she felt that purpose slipping away to leave her mute and confused.

"Breakfast!" He grinned as he sat across from her. "What a great idea! How's your mother? Better, isn't she? Good, we'll celebrate!"

Althea forced herself to meet his warm brown eyes. "Michael. This isn't a celebration."

Michael's brow furrowed with concern. "What is it? Is something the matter?"

She gazed at his shock of wheat-colored hair as though to memorize its whorls. How many times had she checked her hand from reaching out to tame a stubborn cowlick? She saw his snub nose, the bushy blond mustache, the full lips whose warmth she would never know. How could she have been so vain, so thoughtless, as to lead them both to this moment?

In the months they'd worked together in a foster-home program, they had found an easy camaraderie. He worked for the county social-services office, she on behalf of the parish. But no matter the difference in their daily lives, they shared an equal dedication. They cried together at the wrenching of families, laughed at the same silly jokes.

Yet, always in the easiness was a hint of intimacy, of passion the more alluring for its absurdity. Like an iridescent bubble it hovered between them, daring them to reach out and touch its elusive sheen.

In her lighter moments, Althea was intrigued, like a child with a new sense of power. She had entered the convent on her eighteenth birthday, just as her mother had intended, never questioning the role she was bred for or regretting what she might have left behind. In her banter with Michael, this innocent flirtation, she knew her first taste of frivolity. It was heady and sweet, tantalizingly sweet and, she believed, quite safe.

But in moments of reflection, she knew it for a sin and she trembled with guilt and remorse. Althea was well versed in the wages of sin, and though she could never bring herself to confess it, she prayed for the strength to resist. And the bubble shimmered, a forbidden plaything, a test of her piety and her will. Only last night, in the hospital chapel, had she been inspired to trade it. *Let my mother get well,* she had promised the Lord, *and I will give up my folly. I will never see Michael Kelly again. I will serve You with all my heart.*

Then she had seen the miracle wrought. Even Dr. Fairfield, the distinguished parish doctor, had seen the improvement in her mother. The pact was sealed and it remained for Althea to say good-bye to Michael.

She studied the beads of moisture on her water glass, the ring pooled on the chipped Formica table. "I'm going to ask to leave Saint Agatha's Convent."

Michael stared. She saw the dawning of hope flicker in his eyes. She cursed her stupidity, for in her confusion she'd given him precisely the wrong impression. "No," she blurted, "I'm not leaving the order. I meant I will ask for a change of diocese."

"Why, Althea?"

"Sister Althea. And that, Michael, is why. When I'm with you I almost—forget I'm a nun. I'm guilty of the worst kind of sin."

"But I've never—"

"I know. It's nothing you've done. The sin is within myself. Last night I prayed, and though I don't deserve it, the Lord has shown his forgiveness. I must go away . . . away from you. And pray for strength and humility."

"Althea—" Michael rose from his seat, but she silenced him with a finger to her lips. "He has forgiven. He has answered my prayers. Now I know what I must do." It was she who rose now, preparing to leave, quickly, before she began to cry. But he took her hand and forced her to look at him, a long and searching look.

It was at that moment that RN Vera Presti, who liked to treat herself to a decent breakfast, came around the partition looking for a seat and stared at the table in the rear.

In the basement lab Dr. Rolf Pederson perspired lightly, a moist sheen extending upward from his smooth, pink cheeks into the balding scalp. His pale eyes squinted as he polished his glasses with a corner of the long white lab coat.

Jeff Kohner, with typical eagerness, had stayed past his night shift to observe the morning's proceedings. Roger Howell, the young black doctor who shared the lab duties with Kohner, lounged casually on a corner of the work counter while the Camthon team pored through the lab books. Pederson observed Roger's air of studied calm. He admired the haughty confidence in the aquiline nose, the jauntiness of the small, trim mustache. He wondered how a man developed that kind of poise—if, indeed, it was developed at all and not God-given like an orator's voice or a witty sense of humor. As for him, he knew he had none of these gifts. He tended to talk too much too fast. He sounded condescending in his efforts to inform; and though it smarted, he knew it was not without a reason that the staff had dubbed him "Dr. Pedantic."

In the lab, alone with his work, Pederson was confident and quick. He was brilliant in his estimates, unerring in judgment, sure in summation and procedure. But when, as now, he was called upon to interpret his work—to win the confidence and support of others—wit and grace deserted him. He was filled with self-doubt and further confounded by the easy camaraderie of his peers. He could only hope his findings could stand by themselves. His discovery would be lost if it fell to him to defend it.

Karl Fredericks, tall and portly, with the distinguished air for which Pederson would gladly have traded a year of his life, now clapped him soundly on the back. "Well, Pederson, it's all very interesting, this substance of yours, 6BW. It appears to have the capacity to attack the virus with less of the typical side effect."

The slight emphasis on the word *appears* made Pederson's heart sink. The results had not been graphic enough.

"If you continue to chart dramatic results over the next three to six months," Fredericks went on, "and particularly if you can demonstrate a more universal application for it, I would say there's every chance of a grant at some time in the future."

"But Dr. Fredericks," Pederson interjected, "the problem is that we can't continue without some outside funding. The Center provides me with some round-the-clock assistantships"—he pointed to Kohner and Howell—"and a minuscule budget, not nearly enough—"

"Come, come, Pederson," the big man chuckled, inviting the concurrence of his peers. "With round-the-clock assistance, I would send myself sailing off the coast of Catalina on a rather regular basis!"

Pederson smiled weakly. "But we haven't the wherewithal, in the face of routine lab work, to expand the project beyond—"

Again, Fredericks cut him off. "Camthon's research grants, as you know, Dr. Pederson, are generous though not downright unlimited. And then too, we have people in our own labs working diligently in viral research." The man's chin jutted forward; there was a noticeable change in his stance. "Of course, if you can document a broader application for 6BW, an area our own chemists haven't approached . . ."

Pederson heard the implicit challenge and decided to let it pass. He wondered, miserably, if Camthon's researchers were as close to a breakthrough as he.

Fredericks seized on Pederson's silence. "Well, then, there you are. Provide us with documented success ratios, doctor, over a protracted period of time. Give us a broader base of effectiveness, something we can really sink our teeth into. As a pharmaceutical company, Camthon is very anxious to stay in the forefront of viral research. But frankly, on the basis of what you've shown us, it's too early for us to get involved."

Fredericks straightened his tie and tugged at his vest, signaling the end of the meeting. There was a discreet shuffling of feet and papers as the others prepared to follow suit.

Pederson wanted to grasp the big man's arm, to fling the challenge back in his well-groomed face. Yes, there was a broader base! His 6BW was tantalizingly close to bridging the viral link to cancer. And Fredericks knew it; he had to surmise it from what he'd seen in the lab books.

The chemist was tempted to blurt it all, to pinpoint the threshold he stood upon. But Fredericks' face was already closed, and the film of perspiration in which Pederson felt himself bathed made him acutely aware of his ineptitude. Even if he were willing to divulge the possibility, this was neither the time nor the place.

Howell and Kohner rose slowly, followed the committee to the door. Kohner broke the silence. "May we call on you again if the results become more graphic?"

"Anytime," barked Fredericks with the mild annoyance of a busy man compelled to swat a fly. "We are as near as your telephone and at your disposal." He shook the proferred hand. Then, wondering how in hell he was going to make that flight to Hawaii, he followed his colleagues out the door.

Inside, Roger Howell made an inane comment about getting back to the drawing board. Jeff Kohner, recalling a bit of hospital gossip, asked to speak to Pederson. But the chemist, flustered, was in no mood to talk. "See me tomorrow, he mumbled.

Outside, in the corridor, a dapper little man took Karl Fredericks by the elbow. He asked, without wanting to appear disrespectful, if his colleague hadn't been a bit hasty.

Fredericks, whose mind already lolled on Waikiki's shores, brushed the man away with a wave of his hand. With customary efficiency he'd arranged to temper his business in the islands with a nubile and willing young secretary. He felt an anticipatory swelling in his groin.

Still, he could hardly be unaware of the implications in Pederson's work. He made a mental note to call Paul Fairfield at his earliest opportunity. Both he and Fairfield had a lot at stake in keeping research projects like 6BW in obscurity.

Chapter Four

Dr. Paul Fairfield tapped his left foot impatiently, waiting for Vera Presti. If she weren't so obese, she might move a little faster, he decided.

A tall man, fashionably slim and relatively young-looking, he took a seat on a nearby stool and smoothed back the sides of his impeccably groomed silver hair. He ran his manicured hands over his cheekbones in a manner calculated to suggest weariness but which was, in fact, a self-imposed exercise calculated to discourage wrinkles. He watched an unkempt orderly push a gurney down the hall, turn to ogle a nurse's aide and shove the gurney straight into a rickety wooden ladder. A workman atop the ladder, scraping paint from the hopelessly peeling walls, teetered, nearly fell, and descended to swear loudly at the hapless orderly in some strange but effective-sounding foreign language.

Fairfield turned away in disgust and wondered what in hell he was doing in the dilapidated wards of Reese Fowler at all. Thirty years ago, when he began his career here, he'd been forced to minister to the destitute. He'd soon become known as the unofficial parish doctor for the neighboring St. Agatha's, treating the nuns and the nearby downtrodden with skillful charm. And over the years his exclusive private practice had grown to awesome proportions. His prudent investments, first in Camthon Pharmaceuticals and later in the chemotherapy clinics, had propelled him to respectable wealth. So why did he bother to keep up appearances by spending time in these wards?

He supposed it was because the cloak of humanitarianism was an easy one to wear. And in some ways the challenge of ward medicine was a welcome relief from the whiny hypochondria he detested in his wealthy clientele. The Riley woman, for example, Sister Althea's mother. Who would have expected this sort of rally? A day or two ago he wouldn't have given her six weeks—but damn if she wasn't indicating some sort of spontaneous remission!

Presti lumbered up to him at last. He avoided her openly adoring eyes. He turned to study Mrs. Riley's chart, keeping his voice professionally bland. "Good morning, Miss Presti. Forgive me for adding to your overburdened work load, but would you kindly take a discharge summary on Mrs. Riley?"

In the doctor's honey-coated tone, Presti detected no sarcasm. If only the rest of the doctors who barked their demands were as pleasant and respectful of her abilities as he! Presti located the proper forms and happily settled herself at the counter.

"Mrs. Riley," Fairfield dictated, "exhibits satisfactory post-surgical responses which would indicate no further need for routine hospitalization. Patient is to be transferred to the Sunnyvale Clinic for treatment by radiation. Institute Metastaban, thirty milligrams daily, as a chemotherapeutic."

Presti paused in her scribbling. From her perusal of the surgical notes it seemed clear the poor woman was too riddled with cancer to be subjected to the rigor of chemotherapy. Yet, as the nurse thought more about it, the patient did seem to be responding well at the moment, and of course, Dr. Fairfield knew best. Presti chastised herself for questioning his judgment.

Fairfield, avoiding Presti's eyes, managed to find a sight line somewhere between the obese nurse's forehead and her ear. "Check with the patient's daughter, Presti. Sister Althea will need to file state forms. And have the Sister phone

for an appointment at my Wilshire office sometime this
afternoon. I want this transfer made by tomorrow.''

Presti returned the chart to its place with a fillip of brisk
efficiency. She debated ending the encounter on a personal
note, perhaps even with a juicy tidbit about the young nun's
apparent indiscretion in the coffee shop. But by the time
she had composed her fleshy features, Dr. Fairfield was
halfway down the hall.

In his cluttered hospital cubbyhole, Dr. Lou Hillman
completed some dictation of his own. "I am frankly at a
loss to explain the remarkable recovery of Stevie Phillips
after protracted coma induced by meningitis. Patient exhibits a mild rash of unknown origin that we will continue
to monitor, but vital signs are normal, and if lab results
bear out his visible condition, I will advise his return home
with suitable after-care. Patient appears to have suffered no
intellectual dysfunction . . ." Dr. Lou smiled, recalling
the boy's vivid description of the features his new bike
would boast. ". . . and is, at this moment, the picture of
robust seven-year-old good health." Having nothing to add,
he switched off the mike and set it down. He leaned back
in his chair and rubbed his belly absently.

After several moments he picked up the telephone,
squared his shoulders and dialed Bernie Greenspan's number. Stevie's were not the only tests that should be back by
this afternoon. "Dr. Greenspan, please. Lou Hillman calling." He was embarrassed by his own cautious optimism.

Sister Althea pushed open the door of the hospital chapel
and moved soundlessly down the aisle to the altar. As she
knelt, the small blond woman she had seen there so often
in the past few days looked up to smile at her tentatively.
Althea returned the smile, surprised and pleased that the
woman seemed to bear no sign of her previous anguish.
Once or twice, moved by her sobs, Althea had attempted
to speak to her. But the woman had shrunk from Althea's
touch, leaving the nun to her private communion.

This morning, however, the woman spoke in a hushed, shy whisper. "My name is Miriam Phillips—Sister. And I want to apologize for my past rudeness."

"Oh, please, there's no need. I should not have intruded. But I'm happy to meet you. I'm Sister Althea Rose."

"Well, I thank you for—caring, I suppose. Maybe your prayers have helped the miracle to happen."

Althea tilted her head to one side, her dark eyes soft and questioning.

"My son, Stevie, had viral meningitis. He was in coma. We thought . . . he might die." Tears sprang to the woman's eyes. "But he's fine now. He'll be fine, I know he will. The doctor can't explain it. It's like—we've had a personal miracle."

The woman's tears glistened, jewellike, in the pale glow of the altar light and Althea felt her own eyes grow moist. She felt drawn to the pale Mrs. Phillips whose miracle was so like that of her own.

"Do you come to the hospital chapel often, Sister?" Miriam felt awkward in her ignorance of Catholicism. It was strange to be talking to a nun.

"No, not really." Althea smiled ruefully. "I'm afraid this was a personal mission." She dropped her eyes to stare at the floor.

"Oh." Miriam didn't want to pry. Was it silly to tell a nun to have faith? "Well," she said finally, "God answers our prayers. I just learned that. He really does answer."

"Yes," murmured the nun. "He surely does. Even when we've—lost the right to ask—". Now tears welled in the Sister's dark eyes and her lips began to quiver. She looked like a small, lost child, terribly vulnerable and alone. Instinctively, as she would have done for her son, Miriam reached out to embrace her. The unexpected gesture crumbled Althea's wall of reserve. She wept freely, clinging and trembling, in the warmth of the simple embrace. Later, Miriam could not have said how long the two of them had remained so, huddled in the chapel. She held the nun gently until the sobs were spent, subsiding into ragged, awkward silence.

"You must think I'm an utter madwoman," Althea told her at last, attempting a smile that was more like a grimace.

"No," said Miriam, patting her hand. "Hugs do the strangest things. And I don't suppose," she added with a grin, "that nuns get too many of them in the normal course of things."

Althea looked at her new friend and laughed. "No, I suppose we don't. God bless you, Mrs. Phillips—"

"Miriam."

"Miriam. But I'm afraid I've kept you long enough." Althea rose unsteadily and began to smooth the folds of her short gray habit.

Miriam became aware of her own disreputable appearance, the rumpled jeans and sweatshirt worn now for some twenty-four hours. Neither she nor Zan had left the hospital yesterday after Stevie's amazing recovery. They had hovered over him as though the miracle might be snatched away and only their vigil could prevent it. Finally, after all the lab tests had been completed, after they'd fed their son some cereal and gelatin and watched him fall into a deep, peaceful slumber, she'd persuaded Zan to go home. "You must be exhausted. You've been here all night. Please go home and try to get some rest."

Zan had resisted, but finally gave in. "I'll be back in the morning. Early. Then you go home, and no argument, Miriam. You need to get some sleep, too."

Miriam had nodded and kissed him perfunctorily. She was far too keyed-up to sleep. She had passed the night quietly, watching the comforting rise and fall of Stevie's chest as he slept; then, as the first blush of morning came, she'd felt a need to go to the little chapel.

Now she was eager to see her son when he awoke and to run home for a shower and a change of clothes. "Listen," she urged Althea, "there'll be lots of hugging going on up on the fifth floor. Maybe you can stop by and see us."

The nun's smile was radiant thanks. "I just may do that. And God bless."

Zan's broad back was hunched over the sleeping child when Miriam slipped into the room. In his yellow sweater, jeans and running shoes, her husband looked to Miriam like the hulking, sensitive football captain he'd been at Glen Hills College when they'd met.

She watched him reach out to brush a lock of fine hair away from Stevie's face—gently and with practiced tenderness, aware of the brute strength he possessed.

So had he caressed Miriam, tentatively, exploring with care and wonder ever nuance of her slight body in the early days of their marriage. Once, she now remembered, in her need for him she had cried out, "Harder, Zan. Please, harder!" and he had crushed her to him, battering and thrusting until ribbons of white, hot light spun out before them and she lay panting in his arms. "You see, Zan," she had whispered then, her small breasts heaving, "I won't break. You don't need to treat me like a doll." And Zan had gazed at her, tracing the planes of her face, as though she had given him a gift. It had marked the beginning of a physical harmony that was both violent and tender. Miriam flushed, caught up in remembrance and aware of how long it had been . . .

"Zan?" The word was hardly a whisper, yet the tone was unmistakable. Her husband turned with awe in his face and folded her to his breast. To her amazement, he began to sob, softly, into her hair. "It's all right," she told him, holding him tightly. She knew now with certainty that it would be.

On the floor above them, Sister Althea held her mother's hand. It was frail and papery and very thin, but it gripped with surprising strength. "Good morning, Mama. How do you feel?"

"Much better, Althea. Really, I do."

"You will be fine, Mama, I know you will. God has assured me you'll be fine."

It was painful for the girl to see her mother so, a caricature of her once robust self. The buxom frame had shrunken by forty pounds, the once fleshy face was pale skin stretched tautly over bone. Only the eyes, black and piercing, remained as Althea remembered them: eyes that had withered her with unbending reproach through all the years of her childhood.

"You are His good servant, Althea, as I have always known you would be. He took your father from us so that I could raise you to be His servant. The Lord is wise in all things."

Althea winced at the reference to her father, though indeed she had heard it many times. She did not remember her father's face clearly. As a child she had often studied his photograph on the mantel, hoping to find a glimpse of herself in the laughing, carefree face. A lapsed Catholic, Tom Riley had objected mightily to his wife's sheltering of the child. "She'll be a nun over my dead body!" he had roared more than once. The Lord, according to Mrs. Riley, had then merely acceded to his wishes. And Althea had clung ever closer to her mother, fearful of losing her, too.

"Fix my pillow," commanded Mrs. Riley. Althea stepped forward to do her bidding.

Entering as briskly as her bulk would allow, Vera Presti smiled. "Well, Mrs. Riley, how are we today? Looking better, I see." The nurse plucked the pillow from Althea's grasp, leaving her to stare in consternation as Vera put it behind the sick woman. "Just checking up before I go off shift. Dr. Fairfield said to take special care. Oh, and Sister—" She barely glanced at the petite nun. "You are to call Dr. Fairfield's office and make an appointment to see him."

Althea nodded, looking perplexed, as the nurse marched stoically from the room. But breakfast arrived to distract her worry, and while Althea insisted upon pouring and stirring, she was gratified to see how well her mother was able to manage on her own.

Later, in the elevator, Althea paused, her hand poised

over the panel. She needed to sleep, and yet, somehow, she knew that she was too filled with turmoil for that. The small show of bravado she'd managed earlier for Michael in the coffee shop had now deserted her and she was not ready to face Mother Regina at the convent. As yet, she did not have the faintest idea on what basis she would request a change of service nor did she feel up to thinking about it. She needed to telephone Dr. Fairfield—but that, too, could wait for a while.

Impulsively, she pressed number five, the floor Stevie Phillips was on. Perhaps it would cheer her—bolster her resolve—if she saw the little boy for herself.

Hearing no sound from beyond the opened door, Althea tiptoed into 542. She blushed to see her new friend clasped in a passionate embrace. "Oh, excuse me!" she sputtered, backing out of the room. The couple separated quickly.

"Sister?" The big blond man peered at her. "Did you want Room 542?"

Miriam, seeing the young nun's uncertainty, spoke up. "Sister! Come in! This is my husband, Zan. Zan, this is Sister Althea. We met in the hospital chapel downstairs. I invited her up to see Stevie."

"If it isn't convenient—I won't interrupt—"

"No, come in, please." Zan straightened his sweater and smoothed his hair, embarrassed by his public display. "I'm happy to meet you, Sister," he said, shaking the tiny nun's hand.

Miriam gestured toward their sleeping son. "I'm afraid he's still asleep."

"No, I'm not!" Stevie sat up, grinning. "I was awake, but I didn't want to bother you and Daddy!"

Miriam laughed, a musical tinkle that filled her husband with joy. "Sister, this is Stevie." She sat by the bed. "Stevie, say hello to Sister Althea."

Stevie scrutinized his unexpected visitor, noting every detail of her short, gray, white-collared habit and the veil pinned atop her head. "Hi," he murmured shyly.

Althea extended her hand. "I'm very happy to meet you."

The boy shook her hand and began to fidget, a frown on his perky little face.

"It's okay, son." Zan leaned close to Stevie. "There's nothing to be nervous about."

"I'm not nervous," Stevie stage-whispered into Zan's ear, "I have to go to the bathroom."

Zan chuckled, ruffling the boy's fine hair. "If you'll excuse us, ladies, nature calls."

The women, realizing Stevie's dilemma, moved to the open doorway. The child slipped out of bed, clutching his hospital gown around him.

"Good-bye, Stevie," Althea called. "I'll come back and see you again." In the corridor, she took Miriam's hand in hers. "I can see the happiness in your eyes. You're very blessed. I rejoice with you." Her dark eyes filled suddenly with tears.

Miriam found herself oddly touched by the words of this troubled woman. "We're very fortunate, and very grateful. I pray you'll find peace of mind, too."

In that intimate moment, Althea wished that she could blurt out her misery to Miriam—her pact with God and her mother's amazing recovery. She felt somehow that Miriam would understand the deal she had made in the chapel last night and the price she now had to pay. But Stevie called and the moment was lost. She lowered her anguished gaze. "I'd better go."

"Please come back whenever you like. I have a feeling we're going to be friends."

Friends, thought Althea, stepping into the elevator. How nice to have Miriam for a friend. Someone to talk to, to laugh with, to care. It was hard to be alone so much of the time. The church still frowned on friendships between the sisters, and anyway, there wasn't a soul at St. Agatha's with whom Althea felt the slightest bond. Miriam was different. She had a life of her own.

Then she reluctantly remembered Michael was her

friend, and her friendship with him had brought her only pain. Althea felt the beginnings of a headache.

The basement lab was in perfect order, as Pederson insisted it be. In contrast to the decaying upper floors, it literally sparkled from the stainless steel countertops to the white-tiled walls to the pristine rows of beakers and equipment.

Roger Howell looked up from his microscope as Jeff Kohner entered through the swinging doors. "Hey, mah man, mah redheaded friend, welcome back to the cellar of the world!" He watched as Jeff silently unzipped his windbreaker, hung it on a peg and donned a lab coat. "Why the scowl, mah man? What y'all so uptight about? You the one goin' on days!"

Jeff hated it when the good-looking black man lapsed into stereotyped street talk. Roger was at least as well-educated as he was, and his act made Jeff feel pompous and tongue-tied. He didn't answer, knowing his friend would pry it out of him anyway.

"Come on, man"—Roger's speech returned to norman—"you know I like putting you on! Buck up, buddy. You've got your nights to yourself! You look like you lost your best girl!"

"You don't know how right you are . . . Did you have any visitors last night?"

"Visitors?" The light dawned in Roger's knowing eyes. A slow smile spread over his face. "You don't mean to say old straitlaced Kohner's gone and found himself some midnight diversion?"

Jeff smiled sheepishly.

"Well, I'll be damned. Who's the hot little nurse?"

Jeff busied himself checking the logbook. "No chance, man. You couldn't keep up with her."

Rog slapped playfully at the back of Jeff's head. "Shoot, I could give you lessons and you know it!"

"Yeah, well, I've been doing just fine, thanks, Junior. Go find your own midnight snacks."

"You better believe I will, nights or no nights. There's a whole lotta darkness before midnight!"

"Well, before you go out on the prowl, old buddy, tell me if you got any work done last night.

"Jeffie baby, you got no faith. Yeah, I got the work done last night! Took all the stats on Pederson's pet mice and wiped out the overflow lab work. Say, you know the Phillips kid upstairs? The kid with meningitis?"

"Yeah, I ran the CBC. What about him?"

"I did a repeat CSF profile ordered by Hillman. Spinal fluid's clean as a whistle. Damndest thing I ever saw. I would have sworn the kid was a goner."

Jeff looked up from a routine blood serum. "That's great, Rog. Good news. I know you've got a soft spot in that hard heart of yours for his dad—he was your coach, wasn't he?"

"Yeah, he's quite a guy. I played football for him in high school. I'd like to see his face when he gets the good word."

"Morning, gentlemen." Pederson came through the swinging doors, mopping an already perspiring brow. "And what good word is that, Roger?"

"Morning, Dr. Pederson. The meningitis on five. Spinal fluid's normal—no cells or protein. Looks like the kid's gonna make it. You know," added Roger, "that's the worst part of being stuck down here in the lab. You get the good news first, but you never get the chance to deliver it."

"On the other hand, Roger," Pederson added dryly, "you don't have to deliver the bad news, either, when the pathology report is grim."

"This must be the day for good news." Jeff looked up from his microscope. "Here's a Mrs. Riley whose bone marrow is normalizing. White-cell count's cut in half."

"Hey, that's great!" said Roger, shedding his white coat. "Well, I can see it's gonna be a good day. I'm gonna get me some shut-eye and find a lovely lady to while away the shank of the evening."

"Happy hunting," Jeff muttered glumly, peering back

into the scope. He wondered if he might get a message to
Alana—maybe meet her before she came on shift. On the
other hand, as Dr. Pedantic might say, maybe she wouldn't
dig him in the daylight. . . . "Shoot," he muttered, recording the data. "It's gonna be a long, long month."

"You say something, Jeff?" Pederson looked up from
his notes.

"No, sir. I was talking to myself."

"You said there was something you wanted to see me
about—yesterday, when the Camthon team left."

Jeff hesitated, caught between a wish to encourage the
old man and embarrassment over the humiliation Pederson
had suffered at the hands of that blowhard Fredericks.
"Well . . . yes, sir. That is . . . well, it's only hospital
scuttlebutt, sir, but the word is that Dr. Fairfield has a
powerful voice at Camthon Pharmaceuticals."

Jeff's ears reddened. He felt foolish after yesterday's de-
bacle, suggesting that the modest chemist sniff around a
snob like Paul Fairfield. There were many who thought that
the silver-haired society doctor only put in time at Reese
Fowler for his image.

Pederson did not respond except to peer at Jeff, squinting
myopically as he began to polish his glasses.

"I was thinking, Dr. Pederson." The words came in a
rush, as if the younger man were anxious to be through
with them. "If you could talk to Fairfield—show him how
effective 6BW's been in testing—maybe he'd go to bat for
you at Camthon."

Pederson grunted. He was damned if he was ready to
spill a hint of 6BW's effectiveness to the likes of Paul
Fairfield. The oily son-of-a-bitch didn't get involved with
anything that didn't line his own pockets. Like the chemotherapy clinics—Fairfield owned a string of them up and
down the coast. The word was he was branching out into
Hawaii—maybe even all across the country.

And pharmaceuticals. Damned right Fairfield was a
power at Camthon. He'd bailed them out when Fredericks,
as president of the company, had been struggling to stay

afloat—put them into chemotherapeutic chemicals. It was a cozy little setup Fairfield had working. Produce the drugs, sell them and push them in your own clinics. Scoop up the money at both ends.

At the moment, Camthon was pushing an overblown placebo—Metastaban, another chemotherapeutic. Why would Fairfield be interested in what Pederson had? It put him in direct competition. He grunted again as he put on his glasses and the world swam into focus. Though his young assistants considered him out of it, Pederson wasn't entirely unaware. He was happiest in his lab and not the least political, but he knew that his lack of participation curried him no favor. And much as it disgusted him, he managed to keep abreast of the political and financial wheeling and dealing in the medical community.

Jeff tried to interpret the grunt. He considered making a clean breast; telling Pederson that Fairfield had approached him about going to work for Camthon. Jeff had already turned down the offer because of his belief in what Pederson was doing.

Jeff hadn't mentioned 6BW specifically to Fairfield, he had only hinted that a project of major significance was going on in the hospital's own lab. Fairfield had been more than willing to hear about it—had even invited Jeff to lunch. But Jeff, fearful of betraying Pederson's trust, had said only that he'd mention Fairfield's interest. Now the opportunity had come up, but Pederson was apparently having none of it. In fact, the older man simply turned away and immersed himself in his notes.

Jeff shrugged. He had done what he could and he felt almost curiously relieved. If Dr. Pedantic chose to keep things to himself, he supposed it was the chemist's prerogative. He turned his attention to another blood sample—this one from a hepatitis on four. The decreased enzymes and improved liver function didn't jibe with the severity of the disease. He ran it again with the same results. More good news! What the hell was going on here?

Chapter Five

Ventura Boulevard was gorgeous. The shopping malls were beautiful, the bank buildings sleek monoliths, the entire San Fernando Valley sparkled like a jewel! How was it he had not noticed before, he wondered, his Celica snaking smoothly through the canyon, this exquisite panorama—the consummate beauty of light and shadow as the sunlight played through the foliage?

Perhaps, Lou Hillman chuckled, pulling into his rose-lined driveway, because he had rarely seen this particular panorama at three o'clock on a Thursday afternoon! Perhaps because, like a truant schoolboy, he savored this taste of unaccustomed freedom over the pangs of his guilt. In any case, he reflected, filling his senses with the sights and sounds and scents of the canyon, he was an inordinately lucky man!

The screen door banged behind him; he grabbed Ruthie around the waist before she had time to turn from the kitchen sink. He lifted her off her feet, swung her to and fro, deliriously aware of a burgeoning erection with the friction of her body against his groin.

"My God, Louis," she panted, struggling frantically to right herself, "you nearly scared me to death!"

"Scared you to death?" he sang in a Pavarotti-like tenor. "You were expecting someone else, perhaps?" He set her gently on her feet and drew back slowly, his fingertips

47

tracing the length of her arms so that she shuddered deliciously and smiled.

It seemed to Ruthie, in that brief instant their eyes met, that she was privileged to see inside his soul. So profound, so perfect was their union at that moment that she knew, with the instinct born of her love, what he had chosen not to tell her.

"So!" he whispered, dabbing at her tears, "this is how you greet a returning husband?"

Ruthie sniffled, and stuck out her chin. "Who told you to come home in the middle of the day without even telephoning first?"

"I'm entitled," he countered, tweaking her nose. "Why, was there someone leaving when I came in?"

Ruthie returned to her place at the sink, glad for the busywork, the distance. She was almost embarrassed, after so many years, to be so powerfully attracted to her husband. She had missed the sex during Louis's abstinence. She had known, intuitively, that he must be ill, that it wasn't just a passing phase of temporary, middle-age impotence. Now she was caught between elation at having him back and hurt that he had not shared his secret.

"Of course not," she retorted, scrubbing a pot in which she'd made rice pudding, his favorite. "But when you come home unannounced in the middle of the day, there has to be a reason. So tell me"—her voice became casual, bantering—"what are we celebrating, Louis?"

Louis considered, tempted to tell her the reason for his joy. But having spared her the anxiety of his illness, why complicate matters now? "Do we have to be celebrating?" he teased, finally. "I can't just come home to *shtupp* my wife?"

Ruthie, wanting yet fearing the revelation, realized it wasn't forthcoming. She dried the pot with elaborate care. "Tut, tut, such language," she said. "And here I just got my hair done!"

Louis took the pot from her hands, coaxed her gently

toward the bedroom. "I haven't heard such an excuse for twenty years. Come, Ruthie. My beautiful Ruthie. . . ."

They made love slowly, giving and receiving pleasure with the road map of a lifetime to guide them. But Ruthie sensed an elation, an urgency, that was not part of Louis's careful way. *"Nu,"* she said afterward, tweaking his flaccid penis. "You still say there's nothing to celebrate?"

Louis lay on his back, his hands under his head. "As a matter of act, there is. You remember Stevie Phillips—I told you about him—the seven-year-old viral meningitis case?"

"Of course I remember. For two nights you didn't sleep. You were prowling the house like a tiger."

"Well, I didn't do anything out of the ordinary, but somehow, miraculously, he's all right."

"You're a good doctor, Louis. What you consider 'not out of the ordinary,' is more than a lot of doctors do."

"No, Ruthie. Thank you for your unfailing confidence, but so help me, in this case it's a miracle. The boy was dying. Everybody knew it. And suddenly . . . well, you wouldn't believe it—he's up and around, bouncing out of a coma like nothing I've ever seen. I'll see the lab reports when I go back to make rounds, but I'm betting the spinal fluid is normal."

"Ah hah!" exclaimed Ruthie. "So I'm a nooner! You are planning to go back to the hospital."

"Just to see the lab reports and make rounds, I promise. Then I'll come home and take you out to dinner." He glanced over at his wife.

"You'll do nothing of the kind. I've got veal chops and rice pudding." She kissed him soundly and stroked his cheek. "But I'm happy your little Stevie is better."

"Amazing." Louis shook his head. "A truly happy ending."

"It sounds like a story on the eleven o'clock news." Ruthie snuggled into the curve of his arm. "Nancy Rafferty, you know? First the good news?"

"Good news, indeed," Louis murmured, his free hand

returning to his own abdomen. Again he was tempted to reveal his own miracle but instead he said, "Well, I'd better get back."

Ruthie curled up in her husband's place as he slipped out of bed. "You promise you'll be home in time for dinner?"

"Seven at the latest." He gently smoothed her hair. "Why don't you take a little nap?" He winked at her as he rolled out of bed.

A nap she wouldn't take, thought Ruthie drowsily. She felt decadent merely to be in bed in the afternoon. Maybe she would just close her eyes for a minute—till Louis was out of the shower. She pulled the covers up under her chin. Where did Nancy Rafferty get those good-news stories, she wondered. Perhaps she would call the newscaster at the station. . . .

Paul Fairfield drummed his manicured fingers on the glass-topped antique desk. Ten minutes to five, and he was expected at the club. Where the hell was that little nun? He leaned back into the gray crushed-velvet chair, hoping to be soothed, as he generally was, by the quiet opulence of his private office. Every detail from the Aubusson rug and the rich wood paneling to the Meissen vase on the side table had been chosen with care.

Indeed, sitting here he sometimes felt less like a practicing physician than an actor in an elegant stage set. Well, what the hell? His patients expected it, it was their whopping fees that paid for it. What good was success if one couldn't enjoy the advantages? Glancing at the sleek Cartier watch on his wrist, however, Fairfield felt himself becoming more and more eager for one of his club's excellent martinis. He toyed with a silver paperweight on his desk. A ward case. Why was he waiting?

He had started to rise when he heard the outer door open and a hushed exchange with his receptionist. Seating himself carefully, he smoothed back his hair, took up a gold pen and busied himself with some papers. A moment later his door was swung open, the receptionist retreating as the nun stood uncertainly in the doorway. "Sister Althea." He smiled. "Do come in. I hope I haven't inconvenienced you."

"On the contrary," said Althea, impressed by the opulence of the office. "It's good of you to see me so late."

"Please sit down, Sister." He indicated a gray velvet armchair. "There are matters we need to discuss. Your mother, at this point, is at a crossroads, one might say, in the long process of her recovery."

"She seems to be doing wonderfully, Dr. Fairfield. She was sitting up and able to eat this morning."

"Her immediate responses are encouraging, my dear." He paused and his voice became grave. "However—there is no easy way to say this, Sister—the surgery was less successful than we'd hoped."

Althea thought of her recent pact with God.

"There's no cause for alarm. I see your mother as an excellent candidate for chemotherapy. I want to try her on a marvelous new drug with an encouraging ratio of success. But since you are unable to transport her as an outpatient, I want to install Mother in a little place called Sunnyvale. It's a chemotherapy clinic not far from Reese Fowler where she'll be comfortable and very well cared for."

Althea, fearing how much her mother would hate that, was doubtful and concerned about the cost. She told him as much but Fairfield overcame her reluctance, insisting that she was not to allow financial concern to outweigh Mrs. Riley's best interests. In the end Althea agreed, bowing to the judgment of the eminent physician whose dedication was legendary in the parish. She assigned whatever insurance benefits there were, signed a request for Medi-Cal assistance and left his office more troubled than she had come, though unable to say why this was so.

In the silent elevator she told herself to be grateful for the doctor's intervention. If she were really going to leave the parish, her mother would be in good hands at the clinic.

Fairfield, by now almost tasting the frosty gin, shrugged as he rose from his desk. He would hardly get the fancy fee he could command from a private patient. But the old lady would fill the last empty bed in this newest of his clinics, Sunnyvale, until a more appropriate candidate came along. He wondered why it had become so important to him to keep Mrs. Riley under his care. Certainly not for the paltry fee the state would eventually pay him. Sighing, he chalked it up to instinct; and he had to admit he'd done very well by following his instincts so far.

If the woman died, his hands were clean, his course of treatment unassailable. Surgery. Chemotherapy. He'd done what he could, and it would not be his fault if it was to no avail. But if, as he suspected, she was in remission, he could claim the success for Metastaban. Camthon's newest product was faltering despite an arduous sales campaign. A paper in the medical journals documenting success would give it one hell of a boost.

Fredericks was in Hawaii now, touting the drug on the islands. Fairfield chuckled as he thought about his friend. The man was a fool about corporate business and a bigger fool about women. But he was a fine spokesman, and with Fairfield's guidance, he'd managed to get Camthon on top. With the cash Fairfield had already plowed into Camthon, and with the idea of diversifying into clinics, they had both become rich, and with careful management, Metastaban could make them a fortune.

Karl Fredericks picked his way between the well-oiled bodies around the Waikiki Sheraton's pool. He felt ridiculous in the orange flowered shirt and walking shorts Ginny had chosen for him in the lobby gift shop. But she had pointed out that it was the native costume, and he might have felt more ridiculous in the three-piece suit he'd arrived in. Besides, it paid to humor the girl. She was so deliciously responsive.

Fredericks knew that his presidency of Camthon was in name only, at best. In exchange for solvency, control of the company had passed, bit by bit, to Paul Fairfield. And he had to admit that Fairfield had steered them on a sound financial course. It galled him sometimes that his father-in-law's company had somehow slipped through his fingers. But at least he'd maintained his family's security and avoided a confrontation with his wife, Mary. As Mary had grown up with wealth, she would have been bitterly disappointed in a husband who could not manage to maintain her high standards.

In a sense, Fredericks was quite delighted to have been relieved of decision-making. He was, after all, a chemist by profession. He'd never pretended to be a businessman and he'd been as surprised as anyone else when his father-in-law left the company to him.

There were definite advantages in letting Paul Fairfield run the show while he remained titular head of it. First, of course, was financial freedom. Parlaying pharmaceuticals into a chain of chemotherapy clinics had been a stroke of genius on Fairfield's part. Fredericks could continue to provide for Mary in a way that would never disappoint her. Second, he'd discovered he had a flair for public relations he'd never known he possessed. It pleased him to know that he had a talent so vital to their success.

He spied Ginny, lean and shapely in a string bikini, on a chaise at the far end of the pool. Eyes closed, platinum head thrown back, she offered her body up to the sun with youthful and heedless abandon. It occurred to him then that another benefit of his present position was the amount of travel it entailed. There was always a secretary to see to his needs—whatever those needs might be. He knew that his little indiscretions would certainly disappoint Mary—perhaps even more than the bitter knowledge that he'd nearly brought the company to ruin. With luck, he thought, striding across the deck, she would never know about either.

He stood over Ginny, perspiring lightly, his bulk obscuring her in shadow. When she did not stir, he leaned forward and cupped his hand around her breast. He mas-

saged the nipple through the flimsy cloth until it rose obediently in his fingers. That caused him to recollect with
pleasure what he'd done with her the night before. He'd
made a good choice in this little Ginny. She was worth a
small promotion in the Camthon hierarchy.

Now, as he knelt, his fleshy face inches from hers, she
hissed at him through tightly clenched teeth, "Stop that,
Karl. Jeez, it's about time. You said you'd be two hours
at the most."

"Sorry, my dear. A slight delay in the inter island flight.
But I'm here now and you are altogether ravishing." He
playfully pinched the engorged nipple. "What say, a cozy
little nap?"

"Nap my ass, you horny toad. I haven't had lunch and
I'm starved!" She glared at him through narrowed eyes.

Fredericks raised a finger to his lips, glanced around him
at the sun worshipers. Alone, he loved her dirty talk; it
was one of the things that turned him on. But here, by the
pool, surrounded by people, he found it acutely embar-
rassing. "Now, Ginny." He coaxed her gently to her feet.
"Suppose I call Room Service for some *puu puus?* Champagne too, if you like the idea; I'll even scrub your back
in the shower."

Ginny pouted, but somewhat mollified, she followed him
gamely toward the lobby. In their room she shed the bikini,
paraded her naked body before him. But she steadfastly
eluded his grasping hands until after he'd called Room
Service.

Having done so, he quickly shed his flowered shorts and
knelt astride her on the bed. He groaned as her teeth grazed
his impatient member. The bedside telephone shrilled.
"Shit, I should have told them to hold my calls. He inched
his bulk toward the phone. Ginny giggled, and moved to
the far end of the bed. Angry, Fredericks lifted the offend-
ing receiver. He intended to dismiss the caller with dispatch. The caller, however, was his wife, Mary, who was
obviously unaware of his discomfort. He pressed backward

against the pillows and forced himself to modulate his voice.

Ginny, the vixen, played with him all the time he talked to his wife. When he'd finished and fairly flung himself on her, she giggled as the phone rang again. "Whoops!" she whispered with a maddening little tickle. "You still forgot to have them hold your calls."

This time the caller was the hospital administrator, the reason for his trip to Waikiki. "Good news, Fredericks. We're going with Camthon. Your presentation was convincing, to say the least. And by the way, if you should tire of pharmaceuticals, you might hire out as a healer."

Fredericks, by now a study in frustration, winced as Ginny sucked his toes. "A healer?" he barked. "What the hell does that mean?"

"Your friend, Senator Evanson," exclaimed the administrator. "You saw him here yesterday, flat on his back. You ought to see him today."

Evanson, poor devil, had been vacationing on the islands when he suffered what he thought was a heart attack. Turned out it was a viral myocarditis, and the senator was a very sick man. Fredericks, arriving at the hospital on business, had paid the man a perfunctory little visit. Personally, Fredericks could not have cared less, but it never hurt to pat the hand that fed you. Evanson was a Camthon stockholder.

"What about Evanson?" Fredericks asked shortly as the girl's practiced fingers slowly caressed his buttocks.

"By early last evening he sat up in bed, demanded a telephone and began to conduct business with the mainland. They tell me his pressure's down and his pulse is normal. You'd never know how sick the old boy's been."

Fredericks, his nerve ends twitching frantically as a result of Ginny's ministrations, had damn well had enough of conversation. "Clap him on the back for me. I'll try to see him again. And thanks for your support. You won't regret it.''

Disconnecting and quickly summoning the hotel switchboard to forestall any further interruption, Fredericks grabbed a handful of his companion's platinum curls and drew her facile, teasing tongue to the center of his considerable frustration.

Chapter Six

Nancy Rafferty replaced the receiver in its cradle and looked thoughtfully out the fifth-floor window of KBLA's newsroom. She did not hear Jack Henley come up behind her and pointedly clear his throat. He had to tap her on the shoulder and call her name before she focused her green eyes on him.

"I said, great footage on the Merriman story, Nance. Can you come on in and take a look at it?"

The Merriman story was tonight's good-news bit and it had yet to be edited before airtime. "Sure, Jack. I'm sorry. I was thinking of something else." She uncrossed her long legs and rose from the cluttered desk.

"Penny for your thoughts." The technician smiled as he led the way down the corridor.

"I just got a phone call from some doctor's wife in the Valley. It seems her husband has been treating a seven-year-old who's made some sort of miraculous recovery from viral meningitis. She thought I might like to check it out, use it on the air as a good-news story."

"It sounds to me like it's right up your alley."

"Mm, if there's anything to it. Somehow, I don't put a lot of faith in miracles, but I guess it's worth checking out. Soon as we're through here, I'll telephone the parents—see what else I can find out. Before I go charging out with a Minicam, I want to be sure it's for real."

* * *

In the basement lab of Reese Fowler Medical Center, Jeff Kohner slipped his pathology reports into their respective envelopes and prepared to ship them upstairs. He noted, as he did so, that it was nearly time to draw samples from the 6BW mice.

Pencil poised, he leaned forward to jot down the patient room numbers. He checked again, but there was no mistake. Stevie Phillips, 542; Kathleen Riley, 642. Odd, one floor after another with good news in the brown manila envelopes. He placed them in the Out basket and whistled tunelessly as he headed for the supply cabinets.

"Hey, Dr. Kohner! You're in a good mood today!" Carmina Valdez bustled into the lab pushing a cart full of clean linens. "You got a date tonight, maybe?"

"You better believe it, *muchacha!*" Jeff smiled at the thought of the accommodating curves of Alana McNeil. It had taken three phone calls and a lonely stint at the nurses' entrance, but she'd finally agreed to meet him. "Say, what are you doing here, Carmina? I thought you were supposed to be in Albuquerque."

"Well, I was for a couple of days, Dr. Kohner." She methodically stacked linens on the shelves. "But I guess I got the magic touch or something. My sister's all better. She don't need me no more, so I come back to L.A.—save my vacation."

"All right!" Jeff exclaimed as he prepared a syringe. "But I thought she had mononucleosis."

"She did. When I got there, she was so sick she couldn't lift her head off the pillow. Two days later, she's suddenly up doing laundry, carrying the baby on her hip."

"It was probably only a quickie case of flu."

Carmina planted her hands on broad hips. "No, it was mono, all right. They did all the tests. Doctor said he never saw nothin' like it, didn't know how she got better so fast. Like I say"—the cleaning woman blew on her knuckles and rubbed them against her bosom—"I got the magic touch. Guess it comes from hanging around you."

Laughing, Jeff approached the stainless steel cages and

noted with surprise the flurry of activity among the new test group of mice. "Hey, you guys. You've got viral pneumonia. Don't you know enough to lie down and be sick?"

Carmina wrinkled her bulbous nose. "Good thing we don't have to do their laundry!" She pushed the empty cart through the double doors of the lab. "See you later, Dr. Kohner. If I have time tonight, I make you fresh tortillas. You can have 'em for lunch tomorrow."

Jeff waved the syringe. "Great, Carmina, thanks. And welcome back." Then he turned back to study the mice.

Althea rapped softly on the door of Mother Regina's office on the main floor of St. Agatha's convent. The cheery "Come in!" from within did nothing to relieve her anxiety.

The Mother Superior stood behind the massive desk, glancing up over half-glasses to wave the young nun inside. She was dwarfed by the heavy, period furnishings, and as her birdlike hands darted about organizing papers on the desktop, Mother Superior looked more like a child at play in a grown-up's world than the ruling hand of a convent. "I noticed a little wooden desk plaque the other day," she began. "I think it said, 'Bless This Mess'!" Her blue eyes crinkled into a smile. "I think I shall have to purchase one, don't you? Please sit down, Sister. I'll be with you in a moment."

Althea nodded with a wan smile, grateful to sink into the well-worn chair, for now her knees were shaking badly. She watched the older woman stack a pile of manila folders, place one on top with an absent pat and sit, folding her small hands before her to smile at the young nun. Althea was not fooled by her superior's air of cheery inefficiency. She well knew the precise authority with which she ruled her domain.

"Well, child," Mother Regina began at last, "your mother is better, I understand. Praise God. You look as though you could use some rest yourself."

"I—haven't been sleeping well," Althea admitted. "But

yes, my mother is better. She's being moved to a private clinic for treatment by chemotherapy . . . Mother Regina— that isn't why I'm here.''

"Very well, Sister Althea. What may I do for you this morning?''

Althea drew a ragged breath. The speeches she'd rehearsed during the long, sleepless night seemed stiff and futile under the gaze of the Mother Superior. The older woman waited in the deepening silence until finally Althea blurted, "I want to be transferred from Saint Agatha's.''

For a moment, Mother Regina did not respond. When she did, she said simply, "I see.''

The girl searched her jumbled mind for the words she needed. To her mortification, tears welled in her eyes and she struggled to keep her composure.

Mother Regina produced some tissues and allowed Althea a moment. "You seemed so happy in your work here, Sister. You've been a godsend to our program of social services. In fact''—she rummaged on her desktop and held up several small telephone message sheets—"there have been three urgent messages for you in the past twenty-four hours from Michael Kelly. It would seem they could hardly manage without you.''

At this Althea started to speak, then stopped, and Mother Regina regarded her closely. "Child, do Michael Kelly or the Social Services Department have anything to do with your request?''

Althea swallowed and seized the opportunity. "Yes, I've become too involved in my work. It's too meaningful a part of my life.''

Her superior smiled at the rush of words. "Come, come. You may be justifiably proud. You've accomplished a great deal of necessary work here, Sister.''

"Yes, Mother, but please believe me, I have sinned.'' She floundered again for a way to go on. She felt somehow out of her depth.

Mother Regina sighed, pushed her glasses up on her nose and began to rummage in an overflowing wastebasket to one side of her desk. She held up the crumpled remains of what appeared to be a letter. "This came in this morning's mail, Sister. As you can see, I had chosen to discard it. It is from a parishioner who describes 'unseemly behavior' between Michael Kelly and you in a public eating establishment."

Althea's eyes widened in horror, her mouth working to form words.

"Before you say anything, I want you to know that I try to pay no mind to idle gossip. However, if this has anything to do with your sudden request, I must ask you to examine your innermost self and to be honest about whatever torments you."

"Mother, I assure you," Althea implored, "there has been absolutely nothing between us! You mustn't believe—"

"I do not believe it, Althea. That is why the letter is in my wastebin. Nonetheless, you are an attractive young woman and I can understand the nature of temptation."

Althea covered her face with her hands and began to sway gently back and forth in her chair.

"Sister, we are in the service of the Lord, but we must daily contend with human frailty; not only the frailty of those around us but also the frailty of our own devotion. Tests of our faith must strengthen our resolve to do His work unswervingly."

"But Mother, my faith is not the issue—"

"Then what is the issue, child? You are asking me to allow you to run from temptation, and that is something I cannot do. You must struggle against it, repent and find strength in the place where the Lord has called you."

Althea, immobilized, wept at last, tasting in the salt of her tears the acrid taste of guilt. But she found no comfort in the familiar flavor. She was simply not up to the task.

"I shall pray for your strength and for His loving hand to guide you in this difficult time of your life." Mother Regina, with customary dispatch, excused herself and quietly left the room.

* * *

When the telephone rang in Paul Fairfield's minuscule Reese Fowler office, the doctor was watering his plants. He continued directing a stream of vitamin-laced water into the base of a prized dieffenbachia. The lush greenery provided the only elegance in a drab and seedy atmosphere, as different from his Wilshire Boulevard surroundings as it was possible to be. Only when he had completed the task and meticulously swabbed the glossy leaves with a damp cloth did he turn his attention to the telephone. "Paul Fairfield here," he snapped.

Karl Fredericks, having passed a sybaritic if exhausting night with Ginny, stretched luxuriously in his hotel bed. He gazed with pleasure at the wide expanse of palm-studded beach visible through the open lanai doors, the receiver tucked loosely beneath his chin.

He jumped reflexively at the sudden bark of Fairfield's curt response. In his lassitude, he forced himself to smile. "Good morning, Paul. Karl Fredericks here. How are things in Los Angeles?"

"Just as you left them the other day. I trust your Polynesian mission has not proven terribly burdensome."

"On the contrary," Fredericks allowed, "I'm doing my best to enjoy it. The weather's steamy and the native pace is wearisome, but things have been going very well. Oahu General is backing Metastaban straight down the line and wants the full range of Camthon's products."

"Good. What else?"

"My presentation at the inter-island conference was very well received. Chemotherapy is big business here, too. I think they'll follow along in short order."

"Splendid. What about the new clinic?"

"Groundbreaking's tomorrow, right on schedule, and all the right people will be there. I'll stay of course, steamy weather or no, and board a five o'clock for the mainland."

Fairfield grimaced. Obsequious bastard. He wondered who his companion was this time. "Yes, well thanks for putting up with another day in paradise, old friend. I'll see you on Friday, first thing.''

"There's something else," added Fredericks, his voice lowering noticeably. "We may have a problem with Pederson."

"Oh?"

"He's getting good results with his viral antidote called 6BW. It wasn't easy to deny him a grant on the basis of what he's got."

"And what, exactly, is that?"

"A synthetic chemical that increases the body's natural ability to fight off foreign attackers. Not too far different from interferon, in a sense, and damned effective in killing virus in a consistent study with mice. The problem is not so much in what he claims it'll do but in what he leaves unsaid."

Fairfield waited for his colleague to get to the point.

Fredericks resumed. "It appears to kill cancer cells as well."

"He doesn't say that?"

"Not in so many words. But it's there in the lab books, nevertheless; a control group of mice with carcinoma of the liver was treated with successful results."

"And without the side effects of chemotherapy. Is that what you're inferring, Karl?"

Fredericks concluded. "It's very specific—at least, from what I could tell. Unlike Metastaban or other chemotherapeutics, there doesn't seem to be any evidence of destroyed surrounding tissue."

Fairfield recalled a conversation he'd had with the young lab assistant, Jeffrey Kohner. So this was the under-wraps experiment going on in the Reese Fowler lab. "Well," he said in a deadly calm voice. "And is our friend Pederson ready to announce his so-called cancer cure?"

"Apparently not. The data he presented to the grant committee detailed the effectiveness of 6BW against various strains of virus. Nowhere did it state conclusively its effect upon cancer cells."

"Then," decided Fairfield smoothly, "you're jumping the gun. You were right to deny him the grant. If he isn't ready to divulge success with cancer, one assumes it's because he isn't sure. Or because what he has is nothing more than a variation on interferon. In any case, we've too much invested in Metastaban and the chemo clinics to encourage him in that particular pursuit."

"What if he goes to another source? With financing, he'll surely step up the testing—perhaps substantiate an improvement over interferon. I don't have to tell you, if he succeeds with this thing, it could mean an end to chemotherapy." Fairfield could hear a note of panic in Fredericks' tone.

"Fortunately, Karl, much of modern medicine is steeped in old tradition. And chemotherapy is, traditionally, the foremost treatment for cancer. What we need," mused Fairfield aloud, "is some sort of breakthrough for Metastaban. A cure the public can sink its teeth into—a panacea against cancer." Kathleen Riley's timely remission floated into his consciousness. But he wasn't ready to discuss it with Karl—at least, not over the telephone. "Well, old boy, don't overdo. I'll see you on Friday."

As he hung up, Fairfield leaned back in the battered vinyl chair, fingered the leaves of the dieffenbachia. Kathleen Riley, he thought again, filled with rising excitement. If the remission held and if somehow he could prove that Metastaban was instrumental in her cure. . . .

No wonder he'd had her ensconced at his clinic! His instincts were seldom wrong. He'd have to alter the hospital charts to show earlier treatment with Metastaban. A minor risk in view of the rewards. It could provide just the "breakthrough" they needed. Of course, they'd also need a public forum—vast public exposure. Publication in medical journals was too slow. It would have to be something else. . . .

Chapter Seven

Stevie Phillips fidgeted under his mother's hand. Unperturbed, Miriam kissed the top of his blond head and continued to brush the fine hair into a semblance of order. "Hold still, Stevie. You'll want to look handsome when Miss Rafferty gets here."

Stevie shrugged. "Why?"

"Because Miss Rafferty wants to put you on television."

"Why does she wanna do that?"

"Well—because you're so healthy again after being terribly sick. She thinks people will want to hear about you on her news program."

"Will I get to see myself on TV?"

"Of course."

Stevie smiled his best gap-toothed smile, grinning up at her in a way that never failed to make her heart turn over. Overcome with a wave of thanksgiving, Miriam pulled the startled child to her breast and rocked him gently against her.

That was how Nancy Rafferty found them when she paused in the open doorway of Room 542. She cleared her throat. "Mrs. Phillips?"

Miriam blinked back tears, turned toward the voice. "Yes, I'm Miriam Phillips," she said. "And you're Nancy Rafferty. Please, come in."

"Thanks for letting me visit," said Nancy. "I've been looking forward to meeting you."

Miriam was immediately struck by the fact that the young newscaster was more vibrantly beautiful in person than she was on the screen. Dressed in a simple jade silk shirtdress that emphasized the brilliant green of her eyes, she made Miriam feel dowdy by comparison. Miriam, who had taken great pains this morning to brush her blond hair into soft waves, had nevertheless decided against makeup as she donned a pale blue sweater and jeans. She determined now to treat herself to a facial and to take more care with her appearance.

Nancy smiled and walked toward the boy. "Hi. You must be Stevie. I'm Nancy Rafferty."

Stevie peered up at her. "Am I really gonna be on TV?"

Nancy nodded. "If it's all right with you."

"Can I have a couple of friends be on with me?"

"Well, that depends. Who would you like?"

Stevie thought it over. "My dog, Cuddles. Only sometimes he pees when he gets excited, so I better have my friend Peter to mop up."

The women both laughed and Miriam hugged Stevie, who squirmed easily out of her grasp. "Hey, Dad!" he yelled, leaning toward the door. "Guess what? Me and Cuddles are gonna be on TV!"

Zan stood just inside the open doorway, flanked by a beaming Dr. Hillman. "That's great, son. And look who I met on the elevator. Dr. Lou says you're doing just fine."

Miriam, recovered, made the introductions. Nancy shook hands with each man. She listened with interest as the doctor confirmed that Stevie was indeed in excellent health.

"No surprise in the lab reports," he said. "The spinal fluid's clear as a bell. There's no evidence of any residual symptoms and, frankly, although I'm puzzled as can be, I can't see any reason for keeping him." He bent till his features were level with the boy's. "Stevie, how'd you like to go home?"

Stevie whooped and bounced on the bed. Zan squeezed

Miriam's hand. Nancy considered all that she'd heard. There certainly did seem to be a story. "If nobody minds," she stated, "I'll have a Minicam here to record Stevie leaving the hospital. I can follow you home to film some background and edit the footage later. And I'd like to interview you, too, Dr. Hillman. Would nine A.M. tomorrow in your office be all right?"

The doctor wondered briefly who had called in the story. While personally uncomfortable about the notoriety, he suspected that Ruthie would be thrilled. "That's fine," he mumbled, turning to Stevie. "And I'll be in to see you before you leave."

He nearly collided in the doorway with a fragile-looking young nun. "Excuse me," she said, looking for Miriam, "I didn't know you had company."

"Come in, Sister." Miriam moved to the door. "This is Nancy Rafferty. She's going to tell Stevie's story on her news program. Nancy, this is Sister Althea Rose."

The nun's dark eyes widened in recognition. She nodded. "I'm so pleased to meet you."

"And I, you," proclaimed Nancy, smiling. "Are you a friend of the family?"

"Sister can tell you another good-news story," Miriam explained to the newscaster. "We met in the chapel here at Reese Fowler. Her mother's recovering from cancer."

"Wonderful," said Nancy with genuine warmth. "Perhaps I could talk to her doctor." Another medical marvel in the same hospital, she knew, would only take the punch from Stevie's story. Still, she might file it for future use. Good news wasn't easy to come by.

"That would be Dr. Fairfield," the nun informed her. "I'm sure he'd be happy to speak to you. Forgive me for staring." She smiled at the newscaster. "It's just that you're so very beautiful!"

Nancy laughed, a rueful acknowledgment.

"I hope I haven't embarrassed you."

"No, Sister, thank you," Nancy said. "It's just that I

sometimes wonder why nobody ever tells me, 'My, you're one hell of a reporter!' ''

In the basement lab, Dr. Rolf Pederson paced the confines of his inner office. It had been a waste of time to approach Camthon. Karl Fredericks was a stuffed shirt and a philanderer, but he was not stupid. Pederson was certain the big man had fully comprehended the implications of the 6BW study. He could not have missed the evidence of the chemical's effectiveness against cancer, even if Pederson had elected to downplay the significance. If, as a representative of Camthon, Fredericks chose to overlook it, it could only be because the firm's own researchers were close to a similar breakthrough.

Or was it simply, Pederson wondered, mopping a film of perspiration from his pink face, that they were too heavily invested in Metastaban to encourage the sort of research that might ultimately replace the need for chemotherapy? The scientist exhaled softly. Yes, that could certainly be the case. Chemotherapy was big business. Why would they encourage its demise?

For the hundredth time, Pederson asked himself why he hesitated to reveal his latest findings. Interferon was now widely accepted within the medical profession, not only as a viral combatant but as a formidable weapon against cancer. There was no question that his own synthetic, 6BW, was a vast improvement upon the original. It was cheaper, faster and quite specific, not only attacking the afflicted cells without destroying healthy tissue but enhancing the body's own defense system for a broad spectrum of disease!

If Pederson were correct with what he had observed thus far in testing mice, 6BW might make it possible to treat cancer and viral infection long before the diseases even manifested themselves. It would not only seek and destroy affected tissue, it could be used like a vaccine to guard against disease by perfecting the body's own immune system. A revolutionary discovery.

But for the hundredth time, the scientist admitted miserably, he was unable to explain even to his own satisfaction why this should be true. What was it in his experiments with 6BW that triggered the amazing results? Was it light-sensitivity? A simple trick of dosage? And of what significance was the rash? Dammit, that's why he needed the money! There was so much yet to find out before he could be satisfied with his miracle drug.

He could level with administration here, in hopes of garnering more support. Perhaps if he could show them how close he was, they might be more receptive. But the upper echelon had clearly indicated a limited interest in his work. They obviously viewed it as a parallel to the interferon research now being carried on elsewhere. How, in his bumbling, inept way, would he ever convince them it was more? As it was, he'd been allowed to continue his research only if he did it in addition to fulfilling his responsibilities as head pathologist in the lab. Suppose they lost patience with his unsubstantiated claims and pulled the assistantship funding for Howell and Kohner?

Pederson glanced through the window of his office at Kohner hunched over a worktable. As yet, neither Kohner nor Howell was aware of 6BW's triumph over cancer. It was Pederson's secret—an accident of fate that cancer-bred mice had been delivered by error and Pederson had included them in his research.

How long would it be before Kohner made the inescapable connection? Even Howell, for all his air of carelessness, was capable of discovering this truth. Perhaps he should include them in his search for the answers, enlist their aid with administration. Could he trust them with this important discovery? If the funds were pulled, would they stick with the project or be lured away from the confines of the lab by a seductive giant like Camthon?

The beleaguered scientist mopped his brow. All he knew at this point was he had not come this far, this close to the answer, to be raped by a corporate machine. In the end, it was the grant that was imperative, the money to ensure continued research regardless of the obstacles he faced. If commercial funding was not the means, perhaps he'd try the National Cancer Institute. Could he parlay his personal conviction with enough documentation to make a persuasive appeal to Bethesda?

Through the window of the office, Pederson became aware of Kohner's glances in his direction. The older man generally made it a point to be available for consultation with his assistants at any time, and Kohner sorely looked as though he required one. But Pederson had excused himself today for an hour or two and made it clear he was not to be disturbed. He intended to follow his train of thought until he reached some sort of conclusion.

He turned his attention to the neatly penned lab books, the careful recording of his progress. Without a doubt, he was incapable of interpreting them in the form of a viable grant request. But now it occurred to him there were technical writers, professional writers, who specialized in formal grant proposals. Allowing himself a small surge of excitement, he reached for the telephone directory.

In the lab, Jeff Kohner scratched his head. All of this was simply not credible. In the past hour, he'd run three separate blood serums from patients within the walls of Reese Fowler, and in every case, he'd come up with a sample of a perfectly normal count. In itself, that was fine, not terribly unusual. But he wished Dr. Pederson would confirm. Because each of these normal, healthy specimens came from very unhealthy patients.

He checked the results against the patient lab slips: One leukemia. One A.I.D.S. One hepatitis . . .

Chapter Eight

The next morning, Nancy Rafferty swung her yellow Volkswagen into a tight spot in Reese Fowler's parking lot. There was a lot to be said for continuing to drive the battered little bug, regardless of what her coworkers thought! She smiled, remembering what a sore point it had been for Judd Rohrbach that Nancy persisted in keeping the car when her salary would easily have permitted her to drive almost any car on the road.

She patted the peeling dashboard fondly. No Cadillac would have zipped in here! Besides, the bug had carried her loyally from Omaha when all she'd had was a hope for the KBLA job. Consider it a mark of eccentricity, she wasn't giving up on it now.

She scooped up her notebook and purse and strode toward the marbled main entrance. There was so much to do, and she had only an hour before the camera crew arrived. Holy mackerel, what was that? Congregated on the hospital steps, in various poses of boisterous camaraderie, were seventy or eighty teenagers—maybe more!

She paused briefly, considered finding another entrance and finally approached a small knot of kids on the outer perimeter of the crowd. She half expected to find some youthful protest afoot, and news was news, after all. The boy whose shoulder she lightly tapped turned to face her squarely. She saw recognition dawn in his face and shushed him with a finger to her famous lips before he was able to shout. "Yes, I'm Nancy Rafferty. How do you do? And what on earth is going on here?"

The boy, more than happy to have the famous woman to himself for a moment, leaned toward her conspiratorially. "There's this coach from Mesa Oaks High, in the Valley? His kid is getting out of the hospital today and we're giving them a royal welcome home."

"You're all from Mesa Oaks?"

The boy nodded. "The whole football team, including the junior varsity, and half of Coach Phillips' regular classes."

"I take it Coach Phillips is a pretty popular guy."

The boy shrugged his bony shoulders. "Yeah, you could say that. He's something else. And anyway, Stevie's like a mascot. Hey! You know what, Miss Rafferty? You could use this on your good-news program."

Nancy winked. "I just might do that. But don't tell anyone you saw me." She put her finger to her lips again, patted him on the cheek and ducked around the corner to another entrance.

The boy stared after her, his hand poised wonderingly at his cheek.

In his Reese Fowler office, stacked with books and in comfortable disarray, Dr. Lou Hillman peered at Nancy through candid, deep-set gray eyes. His straight, shaggy brows lent a hint of a scowl, though in truth, Nancy realized, he was open and friendly and a little shy in her presence. He carefully downplayed his own part in the phenomena while outlining for her the details of Stevie's remarkable recovery.

If his manner was stilted, the reporter's warmth and gentle encouragement gradually put him at his ease. He soon began to punctuate his story with gestures and generous smiles so that, by the time the cameraman arrived, he was relaxed and amiable, the quintessential pediatrician, and the resulting footage was appealing.

Nancy, gratified and duly impressed, thanked him for sharing the phenomena. She would meet him in Room 542 at eleven, just before Stevie's release. Then, freeing her cameraman to get a cup of coffee, she decided to track down Dr. Paul Fairfield and check out the other little miracle.

Fairfield, paged, was stunned by her call. The timing could not have been more propitious. He would vastly have preferred to meet the reporter in the ambience of his own private office, but in deference to her schedule, he invited her into his Reese Fowler cubicle. If he was awed by the presence of the beautiful celebrity, he was careful not to reveal it. Urbane and sophisticated, the silver-haired physician was a striking contrast to Hillman.

"I'm interested in your patient Kathleen Riley, Dr. Fairfield. I understand her recovery has been unusual."

Fairfield permitted himself a modest smile. "Perhaps not, in light of her treatment."

"Mrs. Riley is a cancer patient. Was there something unusual in her treatment?"

"Mrs. Riley came to us with widespread and locally invasive cancer. Frankly, if it were not for a new drug, Metastaban, I doubt she would have had much of a chance."

"Metastaban," repeated Nancy, inviting explanation.

The doctor was happy to comply. "Metastaban is a recent addition to the Camthon Pharmaceutical line. It's a vastly effective and, more important, rather specific chemotherapeutic agent."

Nancy regarded the doctor thoughtfully. Was there a story here on a new wonder drug?

Fairfield correctly interpreted her interest, assumed an expository air. "Cancer," he explained carefully, leaning back in his chair, "is not a haphazard destroyer. It's a very orderly, progressive disease in which the afflicted cells reproduce themselves quickly, spreading the cancer throughout the body in a process we call metastasis."

He met her eyes directly: patient, forbearing, forgiving her her lack of medical knowledge. "Chemotherapy is, at present, a widely accepted form of treatment. And rightly so, for the fact of the matter is, chemotherapy does kill cancer cells. But until now, it's been a shotgun approach, killing not only the unwanted enemy cells but also any others unfortunate enough to be caught in the dangerous crossfire."

Nancy grew impatient with his tóne—he was patently patronizing. But she held her tongue and allowed him to continue, despite the unnecessary drama in his delivery.

"By that I mean," the doctor went on, "that chemotherapy kills the afflicted cancer cells but in doing so also kills surrounding healthy tissue. That is why the patient's hair falls out, for example. The hair follicles have been inadvertently poisoned in the attempt to kill off the cancer."

"And Metastaban is an improvement somehow," Nancy urged him forward.

"Metastaban," announced Fairfield, somewhat grandly, "is a whole new phase in chemotherapy. It immobilizes the afflicted cells and renders them incapable of reproduction. Moreover—and this is the marvel of the drug—it does it without the wanton destruction of healthy surrounding tissue."

"That's quite an assertion, Dr. Fairfield," prodded Nancy. "If it's true, then there is a cure for cancer."

He would have to be careful not to go too far. His handsome face was carefully composed. "It's possible in this early phase of testing."

"Let me be sure I understand you, doctor. Kathleen Riley was cured by Metastaban." She wanted a conclusive statement.

Fairfield leaned forward, brought his palms together under his chin. "Miss Rafferty, may I be frank?"

Nancy chafed under his maddening aplomb. She nodded curtly. "Please."

"My colleagues within this noble profession are notoriously slow to accept change. They tend to remain with the tried-and-true methods, rarely deviating from traditional forms of treatment until advances can no longer be ignored. And while I pride myself on keeping abreast of new advances, I dare not deviate too far from tradition without jeopardizing my professional reputation.''

"In other words, doctor, you treated Mrs. Riley traditionally as well as with Metastaban.''

"I did perform surgery to determine the extent of her condition, but as the disease had already spread far into the lymphatic system, it was impossible to excise the cancer surgically. I then prescribed massive doses of Metastaban, with the result that she is recovering rapidly. Now, in deference to medical tradition, she will be treated with radiation and chemotherapy.'' He straightened

"But if Metastaban has been so remarkably effective, why resort to more old-fashioned methods?''

Fairfield offered a rueful smile. "Self-protection in the event of inquiry. It's an unavoidable safeguard. In this age when malpractice is a household word, I must take every precaution. But my personal faith is in Metastaban, Miss Rafferty. Metastaban cured Kathleen Riley.''

Something was not ringing true, she decided. "Tell me, doctor, if the drug is so effective, why has it not been touted as a wonder drug?''

"Because, my dear,'' Fairfield said with a smile, "Camthon is conservative and responsible. They've been granted FDA approval for Metastaban to be used on an experimental basis. They have chosen not to capitalize on that privilege until proof of its effectiveness is conclusive. But believe me, Miss Rafferty, in my opinion the drug is the most important weapon against cancer yet to come forward in this century.''

Nancy was silent, weighing his words, trying to distill the essence of truth. She had the distinctly uncomfortable impression it was not to be found in this room.

Fairfield took the silence for assent and decided to press his advantage. "Perhaps it's time for you and I to get the good news to your viewers.''

In 542, dressed and combed, Stevie Phillips chafed with impatience. He was terribly excited by the Minicam present in his room and by the time Nancy Rafferty arrived, the youthful cameraman had the boy on his knee, allowing him to peer through the lens.

Miriam Phillips sat in a chair, nervously twisting her fingers. She smiled fleetingly and answered Nancy's questions, but she was visibly impatient to get it over with. Zan looked uncomfortable in a brown suit and tie, pacing about the small room and stopping, every now and then, to peer through the slats of the venetian blind at the milling students below.

"That's quite a fan club you have down there." Nancy followed his gaze.

"Yeah," muttered Zan, more embarrassed than pleased. "And every one of them is cutting classes."

With the arrival of Dr. Hillman, Stevie's excitement peaked. He lost his interest in the camera when a nurse brought in a wheelchair. Miriam hustled him into the chair, looking close to tears, and a collection of stuffed animals and picture books were quickly maneuvered onto a cart.

Finally, the well-wishers were cleared from the area and the mini-floodlights flashed on. The cameraman dodged the surrounding hubbub to focus in on Nancy. Amid a chorus of "Good luck's" and "Thank you's," she hunkered down with a microphone at her lips and winked at the bewildered little boy. "Time to go home, Stevie," she began with a grin. "What's the first thing you want to do when you get there?"

Chapter Nine

Nancy Rafferty closed the door to her small office, shoved aside the pile of telephone messages on her desk and tried to get started with her workday.

The KBLA switchboard had been besieged with calls since her airing of the Stevie Phillips story the night before. Scores of well-wishers demanded to know where the Phillips family could be reached and offered to deliver everything from model airplanes to stuffed zebras for the fortunate and appealing little boy. From what she was told, the gymnasium of Mesa Oaks High School was beginning to look like the receiving room of F. A. O. Schwarz.

All of that was wonderful and Nancy was delighted for the Phillipses, was happy for their miracle. She was proud to have been their spokeswoman. But while Callahan had been effusive at their staff meeting this morning, Judd Rohrbach was pointedly cool. Damn it, she decided as she sat down, yesterday's news was yesterday's news; and if nobody let her do her job, there would be no good news for tonight's spot or any other!

She ran a tired hand through her thick hair, sipped at her tepid coffee and reviewed the bits she had managed to scrounge from the wires earlier this morning.

From the AP: Senator John Evanson, rumored to have dropped his plans to make a third bid for office due to personal illness, had arrived in Washington looking fit, and called a press conference to reaffirm his bid.

Terrific. In the first place, Evanson was a pompous politician with well-lined pockets and a do-nothing record, and Nancy was damned if she was going to give him the barest modicum of free publicity. In the second place, the last thing she needed right now was another medical wonder.

UPI: A New York businessman had won a quarter of a million dollars in the latest drawing of the state lottery. A great story if the windfall were earmarked to provide bread for his starving family or college educations for his poor but brilliant kids. Unfortunately for her, the businessman was a top-flight executive for a major oil company who was probably, even now, beside himself worrying how in the hell he was going to write it off on next year's tax return.

UPI: An Albuquerque woman claimed her sister in Los Angeles held the secret to the art of healing. Not only had the Albuquerque woman been cured of acute mononucleosis, but her dog had been saved from cancer of the liver.

Nancy closed her eyes. "Now we have medical miracles in the animal kingdom too," she mumbled. Nothing, absolutely nothing, she could use. Draining the last of the bitter coffee, Nancy pushed away from the desk. If this was the week for medical marvels, her good-news spot was doomed to a week of monotony. Maybe she could pull out that Birmingham rescue story where the kid saved the mayor's cat. It was cutesy if not terribly inspiring.

The switchboard operator rang with a querulous request. Would Nancy kindly do something quickly about the Shetland pony tagged for Stevie Phillips which had taken up residence in the lobby? It seemed he was not only causing a traffic jam at the elevator banks but an odious problem for Maintenance. Nancy sighed. Maybe the best thing she could do would be to remove herself from this madhouse. She'd go with the Birmingham story tonight and use the afternoon to do some checking into Dr. Fairfield's wonder drug.

"For Pete's sake, Althea, this is no good!" In the conference room of the county social service office where they worked, Michael Kelly jammed a freckled fist against the cluttered desktop, sending a flurry of paperwork skittering through the air.

Althea flinched and looked away, clenching her hands into tight fists as the papers rained upon her feet. Michael was right. It was no good. Of that, Althea was sure.

Michael spun around and knelt before the nun, already regretting his outburst. "Look, Althea, it isn't my fault that Mother Regina refused to send you elsewhere. Whatever her reasons, we still have to work together and I'm not going to let you throw this project to the winds because you've got some crazy notion that—"

"Crazy notion?" Althea stared. "Michael, please, this isn't a crazy notion! This is my life that's being torn apart. I am fighting to hold it together!"

"Maybe you're fighting too hard, Althea. Why can't you just let it be?"

"And go back to the way it was before? Pretending that nothing is wrong?"

Michael rose and turned away, caught between love and pity. "What is it that's wrong, Althea? What is it you're fighting? Say it out loud. I want to hear it."

"I—can't," she murmured. "You know what it is."

"Do you love me? Is that what's so wrong? Because I love you. There, I said it—it's out. And I'm not so sure that it's wrong."

"How can you say that? You know what I am! How can you say it's not wrong?"

"Because I can't change what I feel, Althea. And if God saw fit to let you feel the same way, then maybe that isn't what's wrong."

Althea sat in stunned silence. The words, once out, seemed indelible. She was at once frightened and vastly relieved. Her shadowy dilemma had taken shape.

Michael went on, his voice gentle. "You took your vows at eighteen years old. Eighteen! An innocent child! Sometimes children make promises they can't keep. Maybe what you're fighting is a childish promise. Maybe that's really what's wrong."

"He gave me a sign, Michael. He made my mother well. I promised I—"

"Promised what?"

"I promised I would—give you up. Not dally in the path of temptation."

Michael's eyes were pools of sadness. "Another childish promise. Poor Althea. When will you let yourself grow up?"

The nun pressed her hands to her ears. She wouldn't allow him to go on. But Michael drew them gently to her sides, forced her to look at his face. "I'm only going to say this once. For whatever it's worth, you'll listen. I love you, Althea, right or wrong. But I'll never take advantage of that love. I'll never ask you to choose. The decision is yours alone."

Althea tried to twist from his grasp but he held her firmly and went on. "I'm a Catholic, too. But it isn't blasphemy to realize that you might have made a mistake. You'd hardly be the first to break your vows because you found that the life of a nun doesn't suit you. Get to the bottom of your deepest feelings, not only the way you feel about me, but how you feel about your calling."

"I feel—"

"No. Think first, Althea. Search for your deepest feelings. If you want to come out, I'll be here by your side. I love you and that will never change. But if you want to stay, for whatever reason, I promise I'll support you in that too. I will love you as the best friend you'll ever have and I promise—and this is not a childish promise—I will never let that love get out of hand." Michael looked deeply into her stunned eyes.

My true feelings, Althea thought. Mother Regina had asked the same thing. But she was almost too tired to care.

"Regards from our friend John Evanson," said Fredericks, sinking appreciatively into a pearl-gray armchair in the office overlooking Wilshire Boulevard.

"Evanson?" Fairfield arched a silver brow. "I thought he was at death's door with myocarditis."

"He was. I saw him myself in Hawaii. But the old buck's made a helluva comeback. He's fit as a fiddle and ready to throw his hat back in the ring for another go 'round in the senate. Why the frown? He's always been good to us. He can only help, as far as Camthon goes."

"I know that. It just seems a little odd."

"What's that?"

"This remarkable comeback. It's a phrase I'm getting damned tired of hearing." Fairfield fingered the sterling paperweight, an unfathomable expression on his face.

Fredericks was accustomed to his friend's somber musings. He chuckled. "What's that supposed to mean?"

"There seems to be an epidemic of remarkable recoveries right here at Reese Fowler. From what I hear, the lab is sending up reprieves from death sentences like a drunken governor."

"Really? Any common denominator?"

"Everything from hepatitis to lymphocytic leukemia. Damndest phenomenon I've ever seen."

"A run of luck. It goes in cycles. Is there any way we can use it?"

Fairfield nodded. "Perhaps. I've a patient, Kathleen Riley—spontaneous remission from cancer. I've already spoken to a newscaster about her. As I see it, it's an opening wedge for a nice little splash on Metastaban."

"How long has your patient been on the drug?"

"Long enough," Fairfield snapped, as his eyes narrowed. "I will document the case study myself, make it as dramatic as possible. What I want you to do, as a director of Camthon, is support me with a profile on Metastaban. The same sort of hogwash you used in Hawaii. But beef it up—it's going to Nancy Rafferty."

Fredericks whistled. "Nancy Rafferty?"

"Don't wet your pants, Karl. She's not your type."

"I'll forgive that remark in light of our long association. But do you know what in hell you are doing? Leaking the story of a miracle drug to a sleazy newspaper is one thing. Nobody expects them to be reliable. But sending it out over television news—Metastaban can't stand up to that kind of claim.''

"It's a one-shot exposure, Karl. A juicy little tidbit to roll off that pretty girl's tongue. If the public buys it, Metastaban will be bigger than laetrile overnight, and''—he smiled—''at least as effective.''

Fredericks leaned back, rubbed a hand at the nape of his beefy neck. Bigger than laetrile. Overnight. And with FDA sanction to boot. He nodded thoughtfully, the financial implications staggering. "I'll get busy on the profile," he agreed.

In her sunny kitchen, Miriam Phillips brushed toast crumbs from the counter, rinsed her sponge and rested her elbows on the edge of the kitchen sink. Through the window, she watched her son creep stealthily on hands and knees from behind a canvas pup tent. Then he paused, peeking around the front of the tent.

Cuddles appeared from out of nowhere, a ball of gray-white shag. He barked joyously and leaped, but the boy was quick and disappeared under the open flap just as the dog approached. Stevie sang out the dog's name in syllables and Miriam laughed as Cuddles splayed his legs and forced his fat little body, snakelike, under the flap.

Seeing Stevie so healthy, so normal, filled her with joy and energy. It was as though new life had been breathed into her with the safe return of her son. Even her relationship with Zan had changed. It was vibrant, new again, fun.

Except for the rash on his upper chest, Stevie was his old cheerful self. And even the rash was fading quickly. Soon, there'd be no reason to keep him home. Stevie had taken his publicized homecoming with remarkable equanimity. He had immediately inspected the contents of his room, Cuddles at his side. Satisfied that it was just as he'd left it, he joined the others in the living room where Nancy Rafferty and her camera crew were mercifully quick and efficient. In an hour they were gone, the house restored to order.

This morning, Stevie had appeared, fully dressed, his book bag slung over his shoulder.

"Whoa, tiger," Zan had told him. "No school for you this morning."

"Why not?" Stevie had stuck out his chin. "Dr. Lou said I was better."

"Well, you are," soothed a radiant Miriam, pouring his cereal. "But you still have that funny little rash. Besides, a few more days of rest won't hurt, before you go back to school."

Stevie had shrugged off the bright blue book bag, sat to eat his breakfast. "When I get my bike," he said through a mouthful, "can I ride to school by myself?"

Miriam had met Zan's steady gaze over the rim of her coffee cup. "Of course," she announced firmly. "Of course you can. As soon as you learn to ride it."

"Did you mean that?" Zan had asked her later as he prepared to leave for school. "The bike, I mean. Will you really let him ride by himself to school?"

Miriam had nodded, her eyes solemn. "He's not a baby anymore." And Zan had reached for her, drawing her to him until the telephone wrested them apart.

"You won't believe this," he said, hanging up. "There's a truck on its way here from KBLA and it's loaded with presents for Stevie."

"What?"

"Half of L.A. must have been watching Nancy Rafferty last night and they all want to welcome him home. The secretary says it'll take a warehouse to hold it all and they've already routed some to the high school."

"What'll we do with it?" Miriam sank wearily into a chair.

Zan shrugged, sitting too. "Keep a few things, I guess, and give the rest to charity. That's the only thing I can think of."

They sat for a moment, suddenly overwhelmed with the enormity of what they had been through. Stevie's gleeful shouts and Cuddles' answering barks seemed to underscore their return to normal.

No, thought Zan as Miriam reached for his hand, *this is better than it was before.* He had regained not only his son, but his wife. He would never let her slip away again. "Miriam," he said, "when Stevie's back in school, you and I are going away."

"Away? But Zan, we can't afford—"

"Oh, yes we can. Just the two of us. You and I."

"Stevie—" she began. She stopped herself instantly. "A trip. Just you and I? Oh, Zan, yes. . . ."

Chapter Ten

Later that morning, Nancy's heel tapped a quick stiletto on the tiled floor of the hospital corridor. There were days when nothing went right. "You're certain Mrs. Riley is no longer here at Reese Fowler."

The bored receptionist barely looked up. "I told you. She was discharged this morning."

"And you don't know where she's gone."

"We cannot give out the patient's home address. You might be able to locate her through her doctor—Dr. Fairfield."

Nancy had no wish to see Fairfield again just yet. Among the messages on her desk this morning had been two from the glib physician. Whatever the man was selling, she thought, she wasn't buying. Not until she knew something more about his drug. So now what was her next step? She pursed her lips. Who else might corroborate his story? The lab! It was certainly someplace to start. "Where is the lab?" she asked a passing orderly.

Jeff Kohner held the white mouse in his hand, ruffling its fur the wrong way. There was no doubt the animal had some kind of eczema—a coarse, reddened roughening of the thin skin extending down to its underbelly. He put the mouse into a small, clean cage and proceeded to examine the others. He had isolated two more and was murmuring soothingly to the last of the litter when he heard the musical, "Excuse me."

Nancy had been standing unnoticed in the doorway of the basement lab, entranced by the gentle ministrations of the tall, red-haired young doctor. "If this is the way you treat your mice," she said, "I'm checking in as your patient."

There was something familiar about the lilting voice. Jeff turned and felt his mouth drop open. Nancy Rafferty in the Reese Fowler lab? Roger would never believe him.

She extended a hand as she moved toward him, smiling. It felt cool and soft in his.

"I'm sorry if I startled you." Nancy laughed. "I really am. Are you all right?"

He nodded as he found his voice. "Not accustomed to celebrities in the lab."

She laughed again. "So you know who I am. But I don't know you, Dr.—"

"Kohner." He still held her hand, and though she looked down, he made no move to release it. "Jeff Kohner. Dr. Jeff Kohner. I'm very happy to meet you." Their eyes met and held for a moment.

She gently removed her hand from his firm grasp and peered down at the mice in their cages. "Cute little fellas, aren't they?" she said. "And you do have a wonderful bedside manner."

"Thanks. I'm afraid I can't practice it much down here. We don't get too many live patients."

"Why did you separate these three from the others? Are they part of a new experiment?"

"No, they're all part of the same control group, but they're all exhibiting an unusual response. See the little red patches on the skin?" He held one up for her inspection.

"I see. What will you do with them now?"

"Isolate them—away from the others. It may be unimportant, but you never know. I wouldn't want to take a chance on contaminating the whole group. They're part of a very important project."

Nancy nodded, glancing quickly around at the well-ordered lab, the complex paraphernalia. "It's a fascinating world you have down here. Surely you must never be bored.''

"No, never bored," agreed Jeff Kohner. "Lonely. Sometimes. A little."

Nancy met his frank, open smile and realized how she'd missed that kind of candor. A nice man, this Dr. Jeffrey Kohner. The kind of man she'd like to know better.

"Well," he said after a long moment, "as far as I'm concerned you can stay forever, but what brings you here to the lab?"

"I need some information." Her voice became brisk. "I think someone may be trying to sell me a bill of goods. Have you heard of a drug called Metastaban?"

"Metastaban? Sure. It's a chemotherapeutic. Still in the experimental stage."

"Can it cure cancer?"

Jeff blinked. "Cure it? I doubt it. Not all by itself. See, any chemotherapy works on cancer cells, but it leaves other problems to contend with."

"There was a patient here named Kathleen Riley. If I'm to believe what her physician tells me, she was cured of cancer by Mestataban."

"Riley." Jeff paused. "I remember the name. Her white count took a nosedive after surgery. I remember because it was one of the things that came at the beginning of the avalanche." He indicated a coffeepot on a hotplate in the corner. "Like some?"

Nancy nodded. "Avalanche?"

He poured the thickened brew, wishing it were fresher, agonized at having nothing else to offer his glamorous guest. Where were Carmina's *dulces* when he needed them?

"You were saying something about an avalanche?" Nancy prodded.

The young doctor seated himself on the edge of the counter, offered Nancy the stool. "Well, not an avalanche, maybe, but a series of—shall we say, unexpected recoveries. People who'd been deathly sick and then took a turn for the better. Actually, I guess it started with Stevie Phillips. You interviewed him on your show.''

Nancy inclined her head. "And then?"

"Then Kathleen Riley and, I don't know, maybe a dozen or more patients who all of a sudden got well. People with every reason to be at death's door just got up and got better." Jeff stopped, wondering suddenly why he was telling her all this. But Nancy's frank interest spurred him on.

"Tell me," she said with a curious frown, "did they all have the same sort of illness?"

"Nope." Jeff shook his head. "A whole spectrum of disease."

"So they weren't all treated with Metastaban."

"No way. I told you, Metastaban's a chemotherapeutic agent. You'd never prescribe it for, say, hepatitis. No, it just seemed like a lucky string of—I don't know, spontaneous recovery, I guess." He sipped the acrid coffee. "Jeez, I'm sorry about this stuff."

As if on cue, the lab doors swung open and Carmina Valdez bustled in. "Hey, I promised you tortillas, Dr. Kohner, and—oops, I didn't know you had company."

"It's okay, Carmina." Jeff edged off the counter. "I was just wishing for some of your homemade treats."

Carmina stared openly at the dark-haired visitor. "Say, aren't you the lady on TV?"

Nancy stood and offered her hand. "Nancy Rafferty. Happy to meet you."

"This is Carmina, my favorite housekeeper," Jeff said. "She keeps me from hospital food poisoning."

Smiling, the buxom housekeeper unwrapped a foil-covered parcel, revealing a stack of thick, homemade tortillas, and from the pocket of her apron, she produced a stick of butter.

Jeff made a face of rapturous gratitude. "Manna from the gods," he exclaimed. "Actually, Nancy—can I call you Nancy?—Carmina's being here is something of a coincidence." He busied himself hunting up a knife, his stream of chatter continuing. "Carmina has a kid sister in

Albuquerque who made the same kind of spontaneous recovery. One day she was prostrate with mononucleosis, and the next day she was up and feeling great.''

Nancy's eyes widened as she remembered the UPI report she'd read earlier. "The woman thinks," the reporter recited with surety, "that Carmina, here, is a faith healer."

"How you know that?" Carmina blinked.

But Nancy was too deep in thought to reply.

Jeff returned with a cafeteria-cadged knife and began to slather butter on a tortilla. He rolled it up and, with a fancy flourish, presented it to the reporter.

Nancy accepted it somewhat absently, her mind beginning to race. "Let me be sure I understand this. Beginning with the recovery of Stevie Phillips and right on through Kathleen Riley and a dozen other patients, you've observed a series of—medical miracles. Including Carmina's sister in Albuquerque."

"I don't know that *miracle* is the word for it, but certainly spontaneous recoveries."

"From various illnesses with no common treatment, just a kind of—serendipitous good fortune."

"Serendipitous." Jeff chuckled, running his hand through his hair. "I like the sound of that. Yeah, I guess you could call it serendipity."

The reporter took a bite of the soft and buttery tortilla. "Delicious, Carmina, thank you." She stood and faced her host. "And Dr. Jeff Kohner . . . I can't tell you what a pleasure it's been to meet you."

"You're not leaving?"

"I have to, I'm afraid. I have to get back to the station." She finished the tortilla in one bite, though a part of her was reluctant to leave.

Wordlessly, as if it were the most natural thing in the world to do, Jeff lifted the corner of his lab coat and daubed a glistening spot of butter from Nancy's chin. The gentle gesture left her speechless.

"Hey," she managed finally, her voice soft as velvet. "Have you ever been inside a TV studio?"

Jeff shook his head.

"There aren't any mice. But it's fascinating in its own way. If you're free sometime, give me a call. I'd be happy to show you around."

Jeff Kohner felt the startling presence of winging butterflies in his chest. By the time he recovered his power of speech, she had waved from the doorway and was gone.

Carmina clapped him soundly on the back. "Hey, Dr. Kohner! I think she likes you!"

A short time later, in the KBLA lobby, Nancy Rafferty jabbed at the elevator button. She was relieved to see that the pony was gone, presumably on its way to Stevie. She watched the floor indicator creep slowly down and cursed it for its maddening slowness. She was, she realized, alive with impatience—and filled with a heady anticipation.

It wasn't only that Dr. Jeff Kohner was intriguing to contemplate in himself. More than that, it was an intuitive feeling that he'd pointed her toward something really big.

In her office, she riffled through the clutter, extracting the notes she'd put aside. She rolled a fresh sheet of paper in the typewriter and typed as a heading for tonight's broadcast, THE SERENDIPITY SYNDROME. Yes, she nodded with satisfaction. She liked the sound of it.

The young man tapped his pencil on the desk, smiled his encouragement and listened to Rolf Pederson's halting drone. "In other words, Dr. Pederson," he said when he was able, "you wish to engage me to write a grant proposal in hopes of securing funds to continue your research."

Pederson mopped his perspiring forehead. The man was awfully young. Still, his credentials were impressive enough and he seemed to be intelligent. Pederson studied the alert blue eyes set wide in the clean-cut face belonging to Martin Jennings. "Yes," he said, "I think I do."

"Good." The writer reached for a yellow legal pad. "Let me take some preliminary notes."

"There's just one thing." Pederson hesitated. "The nature of my research is highly technical. How much experience have you had, Mr. Jennings, in the fields of chemistry or medicine?"

The young man set down his pencil. "Let me assure you, Dr. Pederson, that despite my youth, my experience—as I've shown you—is considerable. The success of a grant proposal, no matter how technical, lies less in my personal familiarity with the material than in my clear and concise reportage of your research."

Pederson nodded.

"Facts count. Salesmanship counts. Together, you and I will set forth a proposal both factual and riveting in its interest. To answer your question more specifically, yes, I have done proposals in your field. But where my expertise ends, I have you to guide me and I count on you to help me understand."

Pederson grimaced. "I have the damndest time, sometimes, getting my thoughts across clearly."

"And that's where I come in." The young man smiled candidly. "To help you to organize your thoughts." What he didn't add was that he had an uncle, a chemist, whose aid he might enlist.

Pederson was finally satisfied. "Let's get started," he said. "The chemical is called 6BW."

Althea approached the clinic slowly, hardly noticing the brilliant azaleas lining the red brick walkway. She felt hopelessly torn between her feelings for Michael and allegiance to the order, and she was tired of thinking. She shook her head as though to clear it and determined to focus on her mother.

Now she noticed that the clinic building was long and low, freshly stuccoed and fronted by a wide expanse of lawn. A discreet brass plaque above the doorbell read, "Sunnyvale. Visitors welcome." It was cheerful, at least, Althea decided, and steeling herself, she rang the bell.

A smartly tailored woman with the most perfectly arched eyebrows Althea had ever seen ushered her into the hall.

"You must be Sister Althea," she stated. "Dr. Fairfield told us to expect you. I'm Laura Norton, the administrator here, and I'm delighted to say your mother's doing splendidly."

She led the nun through a cheerful, sunny sitting room into a hallway sprigged with tiny flowers, brightly lit and lined with sleek, oak book racks. She chattered in a sprightly fashion about the importance of patient morale and the comforts of home, while Althea chewed her lower lip and worried anew about the cost of such enlightened convalescence.

"We've given Mother a patio room," said Miss Norton, gesturing toward a garden beyond a glass enclosure as though it were a very special prize. The room itself was done in crisp greens and whites, softly carpeted, furnished in natural oak and resembling less a clinic room than a smart and elegant salon. But its charm was evidently lost on Mrs. Riley, who sat straight up in bed at the sight of her daughter and demanded that Althea take her home.

"If you'll excuse me," announced the gracious Miss Norton, "I'm sure you two would like some privacy." She retreated hastily, patting Althea's arm. "Be sure to let us know if Mother needs something."

"What Mother needs," insisted a fiery Kathleen Riley, "is to be taken home at once so she can rest."

"Please, Mother." Althea approached the bed. "You ought to be able to rest here very comfortably. Dr. Fairfield says you need more treatment, though I'm happy to see you looking so much better." Indeed, the sallow color had left her mother's face, and though she still appeared shrunken and painfully thin, there was great vitality in her manner.

"I've been taking perfectly good care of myself for fifty-five years, Althea. I expect I ought to know when I'm sick. I need a little meat on my bones is all, and nothing can take care of that as well as my own cooking. Besides," she added, "this place must cost an absolute fortune."

Althea took her mother's hand and smiled gently. "You are not to be concerned about money. Dr. Fairfield assures me the fees will be covered between Medi-Cal and personal insurance. The important thing is for you to get well. After all, you haven't had just a simple cold."

Mrs. Riley looked up through watery eyes. "What will they do to me here?"

"Continue chemotherapy—a wonderful new drug. Dr. Fairfield says you're going to be just fine."

"Chemotherapy makes your hair fall out. Mrs. Laughlin's mother is bald!"

"You've been taking Metastaban for a very long time and look—your hair's as thick and pretty as ever."

Mrs. Riley continued to worry. "I just don't think I need it, that's all."

Althea sighed, suddenly fidgety. "You've always thought the world of Dr. Fairfield. This is a lovely place and they'll make you very comfortable. And I'll come back as often as I can."

"Lovely, indeed. I hate it. Well, go on then. I can see you don't want to be here with me."

"I have work to do, Mother—"

"I'm sure you do. You never did know your place. That's your trouble."

"My place is—" Althea stopped. It was exactly what she did not know. "Mother, I'm sorry. I have to go." She kissed the papery cheek and hastened from the room before the accusing eyes could see inside her head and force her to confess her indecision.

There was no sign of Miss Norton as she found her way out and hurried down the path to the bus stop. The afternoon sun had faded away, the darkening clouds heavy with a threat of rain. An omen, she thought, like her mother's admonition: "Althea," hurled through the years, "remember your place."

To boot, she felt the gnawings of doubt about the need for Dr. Fairfield's further treatment. Her mother was doing well because of Althea's pact with God. Why should she now require chemotherapy?

And what if she broke the pact—if for even one moment,

she allowed herself to think of a life with Michael? Would Mrs. Riley be stricken again? Was this treatment, then, a sensible precaution? It was all so confusing, this making of decisions. Why were they all at once being thrust upon her?

She boarded the number-six bus for the ride to the convent, and the driver, whom she had never seen, refused to allow her to pay. She forced herself to smile her thanks as he dropped coins from his own pocket into the change box. But the gesture angered her in some perverse way, as though it were further proof of her helpless dependence.

She felt, at that moment, a dizzying insight, and she groped to steady herself and sit. That was it! She was mired in a helpless dependence—first on her mother, and then on the order. She was not prepared to make decisions; she had never made a decision in her life.

She sat in the back of the bus, by the window, small and alone, and felt the stirrings of an old, familiar headache. She tried to pray, but the words wouldn't come. She watched the world go by through the grimy window. . . .

Chapter Eleven

Karl Fredericks poured himself a large snifter of brandy. Swirling it gently, he slipped off his shoes, eased his bulk into a leather recliner and hit the remote-control button for KBLA.

Nancy Rafferty's image filled the screen. Usually he watched the news purely for the pleasure of watching the newscaster's remarkable face, but tonight he saw her through different eyes. With luck, she might make him a fortune. He took a large swallow of brandy and settled back in his chair.

". . . which, for lack of a better explanation," she was saying, "I'll call 'The Serendipity Syndrome.' It appears to be happening right here in Los Angeles, in the huge complex called Reese Fowler Medical Center."

The camera dissolved to a shot of the massive rococo building, then refocused on the girl. "The other night I reported to you the good news about Stevie Phillips. Critically ill with viral meningitis, the youngster made a remarkable recovery, snapping out of coma with no visible ill effects and without a vestige of the serious illness which had threatened his life." This last was accompanied by a brief clip of the footage showing Stevie leaving the hospital.

"Today, this reporter learned that a series of unexplainable recoveries has been sweeping the twelve-story medical center, baffling doctors and emptying hospital beds at a surprising rate. Already, the facility is down to three-fourths capacity for the first time in its fifty-year history."

So this was what Paul Fairfield had referred to when he'd mentioned the spate of curious recoveries. Fredericks wondered if the suave physician had any idea of its magnitude. . . .

"Most baffling of all in this surprising syndrome," Rafferty continued, "is that patients who have recovered as a result of the serendipitous phenomenon have been the victims of a variety of illnesses . . . including cancer. The Reese Fowler staff is, therefore, hard put even to guess at the cause of the mysterious recoveries. . . ."

Fredericks leaned forward in his chair and reached for the control to turn up the volume when the shrill ring of the telephone split the air. "Goddammit." He turned the volume down. "Hello!" he snapped into the mouthpiece.

"Uncle Karl? It's Martin. Am I interrupting anything?"

"Martin! No, it's—all right, my boy. How the hell are you?"

"I'm fine, Uncle Karl. But if you've got a minute, I sure could use your help."

Fredericks, seeing that the picture had switched to Judd Rohrbach, turned off the television set and wondered briefly if Fairfield had seen the broadcast. "About a minute's what I've got, son," he replied. "There's a phone call I've got to make myself."

"I'll be brief, Uncle Karl. I'm on assignment for a grant proposal, and chemistry, as you know, is not my forte."

Fredericks chuckled. That, he thought, was putting it mildly.

"The fellow I'm working for's kind of a Milquetoast type. Getting words out of him is like pulling teeth. He's developed this substance—a synthetic protein, I guess. He calls it 6BW."

Fredericks felt a jolt and immediately reached for his drink.

"As near as I can tell, the stuff fights viruses by improving the body's natural defense system. I take it that's a departure from chemotherapy, which suppresses the immune system and kills everything in sight. Is that right?''

Fredericks took a swallow of brandy, swirled it reflectively in his mouth. ''That's a little simplistic, Martin, but basically you've got the idea. 'Course, there's nothing new about that. Interferon's been around for quite a while.''

''He mentioned interferon, as a matter of fact. But his stuff is supposedly an improvement. It's cheaper, for one thing. Faster and more accurate. 'Specific' is the word he used.''

''Specific against what?'' Fredericks asked cautiously.

''Cancer cells.''

''Well now,'' stalled his uncle. So Pederson damn well knew what he had—for all that he'd chosen to downplay it. Fredericks considered his strategy.

He was well aware of the powerful influence of big business on the American public—acutely aware that pharmaceuticals could alter the direction of medicine. With the proper advertising and enough giveaway samples, any drug could become a moneymaker.

As a director of Camthon, his responsibility to the public was to provide products that were effective and safe. The job of the grant committee was to sniff out advances in product development, back them with their resources and promote them as profitably as possible. At the same time he had a responsibility to his stockholders. Profit and loss was still the bottom line. To fly a drug as revolutionary as 6BW was to outmode most of Camthon's line. Was the projected profitability great enough to overcome that kind of loss?

Given the reluctance of the medical community to accept what was truly revolutionary, Fredericks was doubtful. Far better to give them what they expected. Besides, as Paul Fairfield had been quick to point out, they'd sunk a fortune into Metastaban. It was only now beginning to pay off. If Fairfield could deliver on his promise of publicity—if he could get Rafferty to tout Metastaban as an anti-cancer miracle drug and continue to open clinics in which to dispense it—the bottom line was inconceivable wealth.

He owed it to his stockholders to make Camthon a giant once and for all. Fredericks knew what he had to do.

"Martin," he began. "I know you want this grant-writing assignment. "But your client doesn't stand a chance."

"Really? Why?"

"I'm going to try to keep this simple. Basically, it boils down to this. Interferon has been effective against cancer. Possibly, this guy's stuff is, too. But that presupposes a viral link to cancer, and that link is tenuous, at best. There are many other known carcinogens that cause the disease to occur: chemicals, cigarette smoke, any number of things that can't be traced to a virus.

"The thrust of modern cancer research, Martin, is far beyond interferon. We're onto monoclonal antibodies that are truly specific, cell-fusion technology and the like. What your guy's developed might have been exciting ten years ago, but today it's a step in the wrong direction."

"Not as revolutionary as he seems to think it is, is that what you're saying, Uncle Karl?" came the expected response.

"Not only is it not revolutionary, Martin, I would say it's downright passé. Hell," he went on, feeling a bit carried away, "Camthon's got a new drug they're calling Metastaban that's going to revolutionize chemotherapy. Now, *that's* exciting, Martin. That's worthy of a grant. You're wasting your time on this fellow."

"Well," said his nephew, by now thoroughly confused, "I guess I owe him a shot at it. Thanks for your input. Talk to you soon. And give my love to Aunt Mary."

Fredericks felt guilty, double-talking the boy. Hell, he loved him like a son. Not that he'd lied, except to imply that chemotherapy is in any way superior. Chances were, Pederson would get his grant; it was only a matter of time. Had it not been for Metastaban and their investment in the clinics, Fredericks would have jumped to have Camthon back him. But the money was on the clinics, on chemo-

therapy, on Metastaban as the *pièce de résistance*. Time
was of the essence, Fairfield was right. Now was the time
to make their move. His glance fell upon the darkened TV
screen and he squirmed uncomfortably in his chair.

Serendipity syndrome. Jesus Christ, that was all they
needed. He wondered, idly, if 6BW might conceivably have
a part in it. . . . Preposterous, he concluded, slamming
down his snifter so that the amber liquid sloshed. The stuff
was locked up in the confines of the lab; there was no way
for it to . . . unless . . . With scalp-crawling clarity, a
palling thought surfaced as he watched the brandy in the
snifter. He dismissed it at once as utterly fantastic, reached
instead for the telephone. He dialed Paul Fairfield's private
number, listened to it ring eight times. Pompous prick was
probably out speaking at one of his innumerable banquets.
If that was so, then he hadn't heard the broadcast. They'd
better get together first thing in the morning. . . .

Karl Fredericks' estimate of Dr. Paul Fairfield's late-
night whereabouts could not have been farther from the
truth. While the phone rang unanswered in his sleek apartment, the doctor sat in a file room at Reese Fowler, meticulously appending his notes. It was a simple matter to
indicate on the patient's chart that Metastaban had been
administered from the inception of her illness, even prior
to her hospitalization. Since Kathleen Riley was not likely
to reenter the hospital, there would be no reason to activate
the chart.

Should Fairfield wish to produce the chart for his own
purposes at some future date, he felt sure that Vera Presti
would happily corroborate his newly chronicled course of
treatment. He grimaced with distaste at what that might
cost him in terms of currying to the old bag's favor if she
recalled with any certainty his order to initiate Metastaban
just before her discharge to Sunnyvale.

It occurred to him briefly as he altered the chart that what
he was doing was illegal. In his years of practice he could
not recall an act more blatantly so. Yet what bothered him

most, if he cared to examine it, was not the deed itself.
What bothered him was the need to perform it—to concede
an error in judgment.

He did not often question his medical judgment—nor
tolerate the questioning of others. His professional decisions were quick and sound and rarely open to inquiry. If
he'd erred with Riley, it was in not prescribing Metastaban
in the first place—not because he expected miracles, but
because he had a stake in the drug. Although he'd had no
way to foresee her remission, he'd missed an opportunity
nonetheless.

He paused in his writing to realize something he had
heretofore not considered. His interest in Camthon and in
the clinics overshadowed his interest in medicine! What an
odd phenomenon. He put down his pen. He never failed
to amaze himself!

The amassing of wealth had not been a challenge once
he'd established his practice. The challenge had really come
in using his wits to parlay it into a fortune. Not for him
the safety of real estate or stocks—or the risks of some
dubious oil well. He'd needed something he could control,
and he'd found it in the floundering Camthon. A short ar-
ticle in the L.A. *Times* business section about the company
had caused Fairfield's blood to race.

Karl Fredericks had been only too happy to give up the
faltering reins. Paul Fairfield had met the challenge and
turned the company around. His decisions had been fault-
less, his inspiration brilliant, and oh, the pleasure he had
discovered in power!

Even now, as he felt the familiar rush—an exquisite,
erotic surge of strength—he was damned if he'd give that
up! Not when Metastaban was so very close to making
him—and Camthon—number one! A giant among giants, a
power to be reckoned with! With renewed zeal, he completed his jottings and replaced the file as he'd found it.
The file drawer slammed shut with a satisfying click and
he leaned back, satisfied, in his chair. Now he had only to
convince Nancy Rafferty to air the news of his success.

He felt confident that once she nibbled at the bait, he could win her over with sheer persuasiveness. Why hadn't the bitch returned his phone calls? Riley, bless her, in total remission would make an excellent subject for an interview. With that pious little nun wringing her hands on the sidelines, anyone would be apt to buy the miracle bit. He had been right to keep Riley at Sunnyvale under his immediate control.

He could wish, of course, that the Rafferty woman hadn't stumbled onto Stevie Phillips. That broadcast had caused a mild sensation, and Fairfield had a vague notion that, in the interests of show business, one didn't follow one medical marvel with another.

He decided that was it. She'd had one coup and was enjoying the fruits of her performance. When the hullabaloo died down, she'd be ready for another little miracle to pull out of a hat. Fine. He'd give her a day or two, and then he would call her again. By then, she might have need of his magic wand. . . .

Chapter Twelve

Like a snowball rolling inexorably downhill, the newly dubbed syndrome swelled to undreamed-of proportions in the hours between midnight and dawn.

By nine A.M. on the sixteenth of April, ten hours after Nancy Rafferty's broadcast, KBLA-TV had added six temporary telephone operators to handle the overloaded switchboard. The harried operators had been deluged with some seven hundred phone calls from people, or kin of people, who claimed to have been part of the serendipitous syndrome or demanded to know how they could be.

From the farthest outreaches of the station's broadcast area came accounts of swift and miraculous recovery from an incredible number of diseases. It was as though, having been deemed plausible by the broadcast, the tales of spontaneous recovery could now be told.

Callahan, wary of oversensationalizing, had carefully checked Nancy's facts. Once mollified by the authenticity of her sources, the producer basked in her achievement. As telephoned reports continued to pour in, the credibility seemed established. The morning L.A. *Times* carried the story first page with a photo of a smiling Nancy Rafferty.

Judd Rohrbach was enraged. "Goddammit, Callahan, I've had it up to here!" The blond newscaster paced the producer's office, shirtsleeves rolled up and his tie uncustomarily askew. "That sanctimonious Pollyanna broad has upstaged me with her cockamamy bullshit for longer than

I care to remember. But this is it, Callahan, I draw the line. This one takes the cake!''

Callahan, his ruddy face complacent, bit into a cherry Danish.

''When a terrorist hijacking and an in-depth exposé on government spending take a backseat to that kind of vaporous, delusionary claptrap, it's time to reexamine this station's policy!''

Callahan chewed with slow deliberateness. ''Care to take a look at the ratings?''

''Ratings, my ass! I worked for weeks on that exposé! It was goddamned good and you know it!''

''Come on, Judd, it hardly ranked you for a Pulitzer. Give the girl credit where credit's due.''

Judd watched Callahan demolish the Danish. ''You wanna replace me, Callahan? You banging her or what? 'Cause I just can't compete if she's tickling your balls!''

Callahan crumpled the square of waxed paper, slam-dunked it into the wastebasket. ''All I know is that she's making us number one, and if you can't live with that unless the credit's all yours, then maybe you'd better look for another grandstand.''

Judd's clenched hands trembled in anger, his blue eyes slits of steely flint. ''Well, if that's the way it is, Mr. Hotshot Producer, then you better watch me move. I promise you this—before I'm through, you and Rafferty both will eat my dust!''

Rafferty, at that moment, sat hunched over the news wires, an expression of disbelief on her face. In her broadcast last evening she had studiously avoided any mention of Carmina's sister in Albuquerque. That, she felt—like the AP account of John Evanson's recovery—might have been coincidence only, without a tie-in to the syndrome. To report them as part of the mysterious phenomenon had seemed to her irresponsible. But the *Times* front-page story had been dispatched to all the news services, and responses from all over the country now clicked mechanically back to L.A. From New York and Philadelphia; from Helsinki,

Finland, for God's sake, reports of serendipitous recovery trickled in. And it now seemed possible that both Albuquerque and Hawaii were part of the sprawling reach of the syndrome.

But if it had started at Reese Fowler, then how had it spread with such rapidity? Could Carmina have carried it from the hospital to Albuquerque? Could someone have carried it to Hawaii? New York? Helsinki? There was always the chance that, like flies to the honey pot, people were clinging to good news; rallying to the syndrome in hope of salvation from whatever ailments plagued them. So perhaps the number of reported "miracles" was exaggerated to some degree. Yet, there was no denying that a certain percentage—like Stevie Phillips—were genuine. There could be no doubt that a serendipity of some extent was taking place.

How was it traveling from Honolulu to Helsinki, and more important, *what was it* that had materialized? Nancy ran her hands through her chestnut curls. What had been set off in the first place?

"Movie star, look what you started!" Ruthie Hillman jabbed at the newspaper. "A serendipity syndrome! When the word comes out it was your golden hands, the world will clamor for your attention." She playfully ruffled Louis's thinning hair. "Tell me, will you still have time for your adoring if slightly overweight wife?"

"I guarantee you will always be my number-one priority." Louis put down his newspaper and smiled at Ruthie, who thought he could do anything.

Since the airing of the Phillips interview on television, Ruthie had taken to calling Louis her movie star. It was an endearment he enjoyed in the privacy of their home, though he had been embarrassed by his sudden fame in the austere corridors of Reese Fowler. Further, he'd been chagrined to learn that it was Ruthie who had first called Nancy Rafferty.

In truth, he knew he had nothing to do with the wonderful recovery of Stevie Phillips. He was merely humbled by the miracle that had been bestowed upon the child. To be singled out, to be interviewed and adulated as a hero when it was not his due went against the very fabric of his nature. Too, he stood in awe of the very same mercy which had somehow restored his own health. He was unable to discuss it with Ruthie, though she teased him sometimes about the slight rash on his abdomen and chest. Ruthie was so innocently grateful for her husband's return to his old self that he did not wish to burden her with his own fanciful suspicions.

Yet there was no question that the innocuous rash was inescapably similar to the one he had observed on little Stevie's chest shortly after the boy's return to consciousness. Whether there was any connection was speculative. But reading this account of the so-called serendipity syndrome, he found himself faced with a dilemma. As a physician, he was loath to accept such an unsubstantiated phenomenon. But formerly sick patients were being discharged whole and healthy for reasons their doctors were unable to explain, and this he was unable to ignore. He supposed he might question some of his colleagues about the appearance of such a rash on their patients. . . .

He shook his head to Ruthie's offer of more coffee, took her face between his hands and kissed her soundly. Whether or not there existed such a syndrome, he was as puzzled by its origin as anyone else. And perhaps—to avoid further publicity—he need not come forward just yet. From the newspaper reports, there were plenty of vocal people more than happy to provide grist for the mill.

In the early-morning hubbub of Reese Fowler's cafeteria, there was little to indicate an undue interest in the phenomenon that had started in its midst. Nurses and residents chatted unhurriedly. Coffee breaks were less strenuously clocked because the work load was smaller than normal. But whether it was because their professional pragmatism overrode their curiosity or merely because the respite was so heartily welcomed, the snatches of conversation Jeff Kohner overheard had little to do with the headlined controversy Nancy Rafferty had started.

The red-haired doctor chewed his limp toast and watched Alana McNeil from across the room. She was telling a story which, judging by the attentive gales of laughter from her all-male audience, must have been hilariously funny.

Jeff observed this with no jealousy or rancor. He wished her well in her search for bliss. He recalled with fondness their few midnight trysts, but he thought it was just as well she had not returned his phone calls. He was obsessed with Nancy Rafferty.

For the hundredth time since she'd materialized in his lab, he rehearsed the call he wanted to make. She had asked him, for Pete's sake, to give her a call. Why couldn't he bring himself to pick up the phone? At the worst, she'd come up with some lame excuse, and he'd be no worse off for having tried. But the very thought of rejection by this woman froze him into helpless paralysis.

Damned if he wanted to be another Rolf Pederson, brilliant and dedicated and totally alone because he was tonguetied in a social situation. At the thought of Pederson, Jeff's mind switched gears. For the past three days Pederson had been gone, "on business," leaving Jeff responsible for the lab routine. It wasn't so bad, considering the sudden drop in lab work, but what puzzled Jeff was that his absent boss seemed to have lost all interest in his own pet project!

Kohner and Howell meticulously made their entries in the rapidly expanding lab books. Presumably, Pederson was keeping tabs on them during his own shift from four to midnight. But if he was, then he certainly wasn't sharing his interpretations with his junior associates. It bothered Jeff that Dr. Pedantic had stopped taking them into his confidence. It added to the mystery that the older man would say only that he planned a meeting "of extreme importance" to take place "within the next few days."

Jeff glanced at his watch. Slow or not, he'd better get

back to the lab. When Pederson relieved him this afternoon, he'd make that phone call to Nancy. . . .

Another meeting of extreme importance was, at that moment, taking place in Paul Fairfield's lush private office. The urbane doctor had been awakened at six by a rather agitated Karl Fredericks. An "urgent development," Fredericks had said, must be discussed at once.

Fairfield, never one to be bullied, declined to alter his routine: breakfast at his club, perusal of the financial pages and perfunctory hospital rounds. In deference to Fredericks' anxiety, however, he postponed a consultation with a Beverly Hills matron and agreed to meet Karl Fredericks at nine. It was an unruffled and indulgent Fairfield who faced his colleague now.

Fredericks began without preamble, rocking on the balls of his feet. "I don't suppose you happened to see the Rafferty woman's broadcast last night?"

Fairfield gazed with distaste at the other man's bulk. "No. I had business to attend to."

"Well, in the event you also missed the front page of this morning's *Times,* my friend, she's stirred up a hell of a hornet's nest. She's capitalized on that run of recoveries you mentioned and turned it into a goddamned phenomenon. A syndrome, she calls it—a serendipity syndrome—and every crackpot in town is jumping on her bandwagon."

Fairfield, having bypassed the headlines for the financial section, hardly saw cause for alarm. "Give Nancy Rafferty credit for showmanship. She saw an opportunity and she took it. The 'syndrome' of recoveries will pass in short order. As you pointed out yourself, it's just coincidence." He gave his companion a wintry smile. "What will escalate just as rapidly are her ratings. And that, Karl, can only help when she drops the bombshell about Metastaban."

"*If* she drops the bombshell about Metastaban. And if, in fact, there *is* no syndrome."

"Come now, Karl." Fairfield was impatient. "What on earth are you getting at?"

"Pederson," replied Fredericks. "There's an outside chance his goddamned chemical is behind it."

Fairfield emitted a genteel snort. "Surely you can't be serious."

"Apparently, he knows very well what he has: a virus-killer effective against cancer."

The physician's silver eyebrows rose. "Even if that's true, and it's doubtful at best, you were sure he wasn't ready to reveal it."

"Not to me. But when Camthon turned him down, he decided to go after another grant. He contacted a writer to do the proposal. The writer happens to be my nephew."

Fairfield hefted his sterling paperweight. "And he's ready to document his success."

The portly man nodded. "What worries me more is, it's possible that somehow he's already got the stuff in use. If there is such a thing as a mysterious syndrome of recovery, 6BW just may be responsible. Take a careful look at the patients who've been involved: their illnesses were viral in nature."

"But how could he possibly administer the stuff without permission from patients or physicians?"

"Possibly he didn't administer it at all—not in the standard fashion." With infinite if condescending patience, he began to theorize a way.

Fairfield listened with mounting incredulity. It was all too fantastic to be true. Yet something was happening, that much was clear—he didn't need the media to tell him that. And it posed a threat not only to Metastaban but to the chain of clinics as well. It posed a threat to everything he had worked so hard for. He rubbed the satiny surface of the paperweight as though it might yield up a genie. But no genie was needed. Only decisiveness. His only option was to stop 6BW and redouble his efforts with Rafferty.

It was Fredericks' turn to listen in amazement when the silver-haired doctor finally spoke. He outlined a plan that left his colleague aghast, his porcine eyes bulging from their sockets. "You've lost your mind," Fredericks said at length. "What in hell are you suggesting?"

"I'm suggesting," answered Fairfield without missing a beat, "that we've far too much at stake here in Camthon and the clinics to send it down the tubes without a whimper. Besides," he added, his own eyes strangely alight, "I feel a responsibility here for public safety. Metastaban is perfectly safe, a known, familiar quantity. What Pederson's let loose, if your theory is correct, is an untried drug which, for all we know, could carry with it devastating properties. Really, Karl, the solution is simple—and beneficial, in the long run, for all of us."

Fredericks watched his old friend's face, mesmerized by the simplicity of his conviction. "But I wouldn't have the faintest idea where to start. Something like this is—"

"Well, now." Fairfield put the paperweight down, aligning it carefully on his desk. "That shouldn't be too dreadfully difficult. Start with your friend John Evanson. I daresay the senator has a wide circle of friends—and his own vested interest in Camthon."

"Jesus," murmured Fredericks, "I don't know, it's—"

"Cool and steady. In the long run, you'll thank me for my foresight. You can do it, Karl, I know you can, and I don't want to know the details. My job is to elicit the assistance of our spokesman, Nancy Rafferty."

PART TWO

Mysteries

Chapter One

Sister Althea returned to St. Agatha's Convent at just after one in the afternoon. She hurried past Mother Regina's closed office door, slipped quietly up the stairs, thankful to meet no one, and let herself into her room. Inside, she collapsed on her bed and buried her face in the pillow. To her consternation, she found it impossible to cry. She supposed she was finally drained as all she could feel was the ceaseless pounding in her head. The nun removed her veil and began to knead her temples.

Her meeting with Michael in the morning had been brief and efficient. Michael had seen to that. True to his word, he'd been painstakingly casual and their conversation had been confined to casework. It was she who'd had to sit on her hands, to keep from reaching out, from touching his arm. She wanted so much to be warmed, to be comforted, and it filled her with fear and self-loathing.

From Michael's office she had gone to Sunnyvale, determined to keep her guilt concealed. But she needn't have worried that her mother would guess. Kathleen Riley was too absorbed in her own dilemma. "Take me home, Althea. Dr. Fairfield is wrong. I don't need to be in this place." And Althea had been shocked to note how well the woman looked. God had indeed wrought a miracle. But if He had, Althea's sins would be even greater if she failed to live up to her covenant.

Now, Althea moaned in her bed, curled her body in a

knot. How could she live with such duplicity? She could confess her guilt, her sins, to Father Rainey. She could beg. for penance, pray for strength. But suddenly she realized, with a sense of panic, that she had no faith in Father Rainey's penance.

The thought formed slowly in her tortured brain. It froze her, took her very breath away. What was she if she had no faith at all? She would be a sinner with no hope for redemption. She felt herself choking, gasping for breath. Althea knew she could no longer stay in this room. She flung herself up, swayed unsteadily on her feet, and grabbed her purse as she fled.

Miriam Phillips stood distractedly amid a clutter of toys and cardboard boxes. At least she had it inventoried. That was the first step. She sighed and scanned the long list on her clipboard.

Zan had already left for school when the KBLA truck pulled into the driveway. She and Stevie had watched, dazed, as two burly young men unloaded cargo. They chattered good-naturedly as they blocked the entrance from her hallway into the living room with gifts; and, handing Stevie a big caramel lollipop, they pumped her hand copiously and left. She stared with dismay at the trail of toys snaking out of the laundry room into the garage.

Tethered securely to the backyard swing set was a living, breathing, whinnying Shetland pony. Stevie, wide-eyed and licking the lollipop, paced a cautious circle around the horse. Cuddles, hunkering at his master's feet, emitted a series of anxious yelps to keep the boy from venturing too close. It had seemed as likely a place to start as any, and Miriam had quickly galvanized her senses. She located a stable from the Yellow Pages and requested that the animal be collected. She was flabbergasted at the boarding fees and said as much to Stevie. Fearful that the magnificent prize might be lost to him, Stevie readily agreed to sort through his booty and part with anything else his mother wished, as long as he could keep the pony.

Doggedly settling down to their task, they sorted through the toys. They selected a bicycle and some books and games and stacked the rest by category against the walls. Sometime later, the Westwood condominium was reasonably restored to order. It had been decided that the anonymous well-wishers could be thanked via Nancy and the largesse distributed to charity.

Stevie begged to ride his bike. "Tomorrow can I ride it to school? I know how. You know I do. You saw me ride Petey's, remember?"

Miriam looked at his earnest face. Yes, she had seen him ride Petey's. The stubborn rash was gone at last. There was nothing to keep him from school. It took every ounce of Miriam's will not to renege on her promise. But she watched him mount his new blue Schwinn and careen into the world beyond their block. Zan, she knew, would applaud her decision. She could picture his enthusiastic grin.

She walked back slowly into the house, quiet save for Cuddles' querulous moping. "He's gone for a ride," she told him sternly. "He'll be back soon and he'll be fine." She busied herself as best she could, listening for Stevie's return. She jumped when the phone rang, answered it quickly, chiding herself for her fears.

"Miriam? This is Sister Althea. I hope I'm not disturbing you." The voice was tight and close to a sob.

"Sister! How are you? I'm so glad you called." And, apart from her relief, she really was. She had thought several times of the sad little nun since they'd brought Stevie home from Reese Fowler. But now she heard desperation in the voice. "Sister Althea, please come right over! There's a bus . . ." She gave her directions.

Paul Fairfield dialed for an outside line, jabbing at the pushbuttons to reach a number he had, by now, quite committed to memory.

"KBLA. Good afternoon. Can I help you?"

"Nancy Rafferty, please. Paul Fairfield calling."

"I'm sorry, sir. Miss Rafferty is on another line. Would you care to hold?"

The woman was always on another line or out of the office. "No," he snapped, drawing himself up. "But I would appreciate her showing the courtesy of returning my call as soon as possible." He gave the number of his Wilshire office. "I can be reached here all afternoon."

It was the third message the physician had left, and his patience was wearing thin. Obviously, Miss Rafferty was none too anxious to hear what he had to say. But then, why would she be? he reflected bitterly. Her vanity had been piqued quite enough.

He scanned again the *Times'* front page, nearly devoted to her "syndrome." Serendipitous recoveries, Jesus Christ! And the clinics were beginning to empty. Fairfield massaged the supple skin just above his cheekbones. Now was the time to break the story on Metastaban; make the thing work for him, not against him. Perhaps he was taking the wrong tack with Rafferty. A little subtle charm might be in order.

Of course, if Fredericks managed his end, the "syndrome" would be yesterday's news. Rafferty's publicity would be at a standstill. She'd return his calls then, all right! And if she didn't—his manicured hands slowly twirled the sterling silver paperweight—there were other ways to break his story. She wasn't the only newscaster in L.A.

The caller tying up Nancy Rafferty's line was Dr. Jeffrey Kohner, who found himself, at one in the afternoon, with unaccustomed time on his hands. With admissions down, the routine lab work in the Reese Fowler lab was down as well. For the first time in his memory, there wasn't enough work to keep him busy on his eight-to-four shift. He continued to be baffled by the apparent well-being of the 6BW mice. The three he had isolated, while still showing signs of a reddened eczema, were otherwise in very fine fettle.

With Pederson unavailable for consultation, there was precious little Kohner could do.

Pederson was calling his long-awaited staff meeting for eight o'clock tomorrow night. Jeff had found a note from him when he came on shift this morning. Roger Howell, who'd been similarly informed, was less than enthusiastic. "Man, that's four hours before my shift's supposed to start."

"So what? It's four hours after mine ends."

"Well, I got a date I don't plan to cancel. Maybe we could make it a little later."

"Okay by me." Jeff shrugged his shoulders. "Give Pederson a call and let me know."

The meeting was to be held in Pederson's office in the lab. It was, according to the scientist's note, "of great significance" and "highly confidential."

Roger, noting Pederson's frequent absences of late, quipped that perhaps the old man had abandoned 6BW in favor of a newly discovered aphrodisiac. But despite his offhandedness, he, like Jeff, was eager to hear what Pederson had to say. The conference could only have to do with new developments in their research.

Still, until the scheduled meeting, conjecture was all Jeff had to go on. His thoughts, allowed to wander on this April afternoon, returned and finally fastened on Nancy Rafferty. He had watched her broadcasts for the past two nights as she updated the reports of a serendipity syndrome. New case histories continued to drift in, lending credence to the unsolved mystery of the strangely curative phenomenon. If the statistics at Reese Fowler were any indication, there was more to the theory than hype.

Jeff was as stymied as anyone else as to the cause of the curious happenstance. And, like most of the rest of Los Angeles, he was warmed by Nancy's spirited reportage. But apart from his admiration of her professionalism, he was transfixed by her image on the screen. Breathtaking under ordinary circumstances, the reporter now positively glowed. She was vibrant with enthusiasm, radiant with conviction, and the result turned Jeff's legs into jelly.

"You jerk!" he exclaimed to himself; and in a burst of resolve, he dialed the busy KBLA newsroom.

Her voice on the phone was warm and encouraging. "Jeff! I've been meaning to call you!"

"As your most ardent fan, I called to congratulate you. Your series on the syndrome is terrific."

"I appreciate that. But it's all thanks to you. That's why I've been meaning to call."

"Me? What did I do?"

"Oh, nothing. Nothing much. Just clued me in at the beginning. If it hadn't been for you, I might not have put it together."

Jeff was puzzled. "Put what together?"

"The whole serendipity syndrome. I'd had a few reports about isolated recoveries—including the one in Albuquerque—Carmina's sister. But it wasn't until you told me about all those recoveries at Reese Fowler that the whole thing came together as a syndrome."

"Sort of the opposite of a disastrous epidemic. I still like your word. Serendipity."

A note of wistfulness crept into Nancy's voice. "But there's got to be more to it than that. I'd give anything if I could just zero in on the source. I don't suppose you'd care to venture a guess."

"I wish I had a clue. I'd like to help—"

"Well, you can. By letting me take you to dinner. I'm ashamed of myself for not calling you first. It's the least I can do to say thanks."

"Actually, that's the real reason I called. I was going to ask you to dinner."

"Then it's settled. But it's my treat, I owe you that much. What would you say to tomorrow night?"

"Sounds fine. Oh, wait!" There was Pederson's meeting. "How about the following night instead?"

"Great. Can I meet you at Scandia?"

"Sure."

"Eight o'clock. And Jeff—I'm looking forward to it."

"Me too," murmured Jeff. He hung up the phone. Why had he waited so long?

Senator John Evanson took the call from Karl Fredericks at a very inopportune time. His newest aide, a curvaceous brunette, was expounding her theories on his campaign. He appreciated her loyalty and her lucid insights almost as much as her nakedness.

She had slowly undressed him, talking all the while, and clucked sympathetically at the vestige of a rash on his upper chest. She was just beginning to disrobe herself with a tantalizing lack of haste when the telephone shrilled at his side.

Evanson listened to Fredericks' request for a connection of less-than-sterling repute. He heard it with the ear of a seasoned politician but with the impatience of a man about to be laid. In the end, his impatience won over his judgment as Fredericks rattled on about what he needed. The senator blurted a phone number and quickly hung up. He had pressing needs of his own.

Chapter Two

Miriam Phillips brushed her blond hair, coaxed it into flattering waves. She applied some blue shadow to accent her eyes, and to her lips a pale rose color. Then she stepped back to see the effect and she smiled at what she saw.

The ghostly pallor was gone from her skin. She had no need of rouge. And the warmth and sparkle was back in her eyes. She looked as she felt—young, alive. She redraped the cowl collar of her favorite pink sweater and patted it in place over her jeans. She was no Nancy Rafferty—alas, alas—but she didn't look half bad!

She checked her watch and went to the window. Stevie was nowhere in sight. But the afternoon had clouded, threatening rain, and wind buffeted the limbs of the budding crepe myrtles, hunching them forward in surprised displeasure at the late arrival of spring.

She fought an urge to get into the car, to drive the streets and find Stevie. His friends were home from school by now. He was probably showing off his bike. He would be upset with her to be so babied on his first day out with his prize. But he wore only a nylon windbreaker over his T-shirt and jeans; he was not prepared for rain.

"Miriam Phillips!" she chastised herself. "When will you ever learn? He's not a baby. He has enough sense to come in out of the rain!"

Besides, she had promised to be there waiting when Sister Althea arrived. The bus would be there anytime.

She was pleased that Sister Althea had thought to call. She had instinctively liked the young nun. Too, the girl had seemed so . . . frightened, so alone, and Miriam felt sure there had been distress in her voice when they'd talked briefly on the telephone.

She felt for a moment the niggling of doubt—that same sort of upside-down, something's-wrong feeling she'd had when they spoke in the chapel. A nun was . . . an island all to herself. What could Miriam offer her? What did she know about her problems, her rules? For that matter, even about her religion?

An RTD bus glided smoothly to the curb, disgorged its passengers and went on. It was easy to pick out the nun's slender form—dressed as she was in the short gray habit—crossing the street against the wind. She saw Althea pause to check the house numbers and hurry, head bent, down the street.

She opened the door as the nun strode up the path, drew Althea to her and hugged her close. "It's good to see you, Sister. Please come in. You must be cold without a coat."

"I—left in a hurry," the nun explained. "I didn't realize it was getting so cold. Thank you for letting me visit."

"I'll make some tea," Miriam soothed, leading the way past the neatly stacked cartons into the small yellow kitchen. "Excuse the mess." She gestured around her. "You wouldn't believe where all this came from."

Putting a kettle on to boil, she told Althea how the gifts had poured in after the broadcast about Stevie. "It's incredible," she said. "Even a pony! We'll have to give most of it away. It's hard to believe, in this day and age, that people can be so kindhearted."

"It is," agreed Althea, sitting at the table and looking a little more relaxed. "Where is Stevie? Is he here?"

Miriam's glance strayed to the clock. "He's out for a ride on his new bike. He should be back . . ." Her voice trailed off. "I was thinking I might go and look for him."

"Oh, please, if you like. Go ahead, I can wait—"

But Miriam shook her head firmly. "No. He'll be fine. He'll be home anytime. Tell me, Althea, how are you?"

"I'm—fine," said Althea, looking down at her clasped hands. "Busy. I try to keep busy."

Miriam poured spiced tea into earthenware mugs, carried them to the table. She sat across from her visitor, watching her while breathing in the fragrant steam. "And what about your mother? How is she?"

"She's doing well. So well, it's amazing. But Dr. Fairfield is keeping her at Sunnyvale. It's a clinic, you know—not far from Reese Fowler. They're giving her chemotherapy."

"Oh. Well, I suppose he knows best. Apparently, she still requires treatment." She wasn't sure quite what to say.

Althea shook her head. "If you saw her . . . I don't know. . . . I prayed for a miracle. And the miracle seems to be happening."

"I prayed for a miracle for Stevie, too. To this day, we don't really understand it. Now there's this syndrome they're talking about. So many people getting well again."

Althea was adamant. "This was God's miracle. We made a bargain, the Lord and I."

"A bargain?" asked Miriam. But then her attention was diverted by the loud and sudden slam of the front door.

"I put the bike in the garage, Mommy! It's raining!"

"Is it?" answered Miriam. "Are you very wet? I'm here, in the kitchen. Let's see you."

Stevie bounded into the kitchen, followed closely by Cuddles, who had come out of hiding at the sound of his master's voice. The boy looked at his mother. "I thought you might come after me. After it started to rain."

"Did you? Now, why would I do that?"

Stevie shrugged.

"You're a big boy now. You know enough to come in when it rains. Stevie, you remember Sister Althea."

"Sure. Hi."

"Hello, Stevie. It's nice to see you again."

"Did you tell her about my pony? And my bike?" the boy asked, shaking the wet sleeves of his windbreaker.

His mother nodded. "Go and put on dry clothes. Then you can have some hot chocolate."

"What a wonderful boy." Althea watched him leave. "And he looks just fine, he really does."

Miriam smiled. "We're very fortunate. For whatever caused the miracle, we're grateful. Sister," she added, "if you have doubts about your mother, you could seek another opinion."

"I couldn't do that." The nun was firm. "Dr. Fairfield is a legend at Saint Agatha's. He's a wonderful doctor, I'm sure of that. He just doesn't know about—the bargain. . . ."

Miriam regarded her in thoughtful silence. "The bargain you made with God."

Althea nodded.

"You traded something in return for a miracle that would make your mother well."

"How did you know?" The nun's eyes were wide.

"Because I thought of the very same thing. When Stevie was so sick, I would have given anything—even traded my own life for his. Only somehow, I didn't think God would trade. . . . But look at me, telling you about God."

Althea was transfixed. "No, please. Tell me why. Why didn't you think God would trade?"

"Because," said Miriam, "I think that God treats each of us on his own merits. If He spared Stevie's life, it was for Stevie's sake, not mine. My life was worthless in trade." She began to get nervous. "Sister, I'm sorry. I have no right to—"

"Please!" Althea worked to find the words. "What if you had sinned? And you promised to repent? Would God have traded for that?"

Miriam sighed, brought her hand to her face. "I'm sorry. I don't believe in sin. Not in the sense that it's a stain on our souls like the mud on Stevie's jeans—that can be washed away with tears of repentance or thrown in the washing machine. I can throw Stevie's jeans in the washer every day and they come out looking clean. But until Stevie learns to stay out of the mud, they're going to get stained again. Does that make sense? There's no permanent clean. We must learn through our mistakes and keep growing.''

Althea frowned. ''But playing in the mud—''

''Is a no-no, and Stevie knows that. If he makes a mistake, it makes him feel bad. He'll try harder not to do it again. That's all I can ask—that he try his best to live up to my expectations.''

The nun was thoughtful. ''God expects us to do our best as well. . . .''

''But He knows we're human. We make mistakes. That's okay if we admit them and learn from them. You know, Althea, in the Hebrew language there is no word that translates as 'sin.' The closest is a word—the word is *chet*— which literally means 'missing the mark.' ''

Althea repeated the guttural sound. ''*Chet*,'' she murmered. ''Please go on.''

''I believe that God expects us to be good—to follow His laws and do our best. But if we miss the mark, He's less concerned with our guilt than with our efforts to improve ourselves. One noble deed, the Torah says, is more meaningful to God than our *chet*.''

Althea was mesmerized. ''*Chet*,'' she repeated, the sound far back in her throat. ''If I make a mistake, I must learn from it. I can't trade my guilt for a miracle. . . .''

Miriam smiled. ''I've made my share of mistakes. They nearly destroyed my marriage. They haunted me when Stevie was so sick. I wanted so badly to trade them away— to swear I'd try harder if Stevie lived. But believing as I do, I knew that was useless. I couldn't presume to intercede for my son. . . . Oh look, the tea is cold and you've hardly touched it. I'll make some fresh. Here's Stevie.''

She made hot tea and chocolate for her son while the boy showed off his new bike. Zan soon came home. ''Stopped raining,'' he called. ''But it's colder than a— well, hello, Sister.''

Miriam pleaded with the nun to stay for dinner, but Althea insisted upon getting back to the convent.

"I'll drive you," offered Zan.

"Please don't bother. The bus leaves me right at my door. I'll be perfectly safe, you may be sure." And at the door she turned to Miriam. "Does Zan believe the same way you do?"

"Zan doesn't believe in much of anything, I'm afraid. I have to believe enough for both of us." She reached into a coat closet. "Please borrow this, Sister. It's much too cold to be without a coat."

"I couldn't possibly—"

"Of course you can." She smiled broadly and helped Althea into the light beige coat, drawing the fur collar close under her chin.

"Thank you," said Althea. "It will give me a reason to come back very soon and return it."

"You don't need a reason. I'd really like to see you soon. Please let me know about your mother. Zan will walk you to the bus."

At the doorway to the bus, Zan shook her hand gravely. " 'Night, Sister. Take care. And God bless."

She nodded, watched him stride away and settled back in her seat, her hands in the pockets of the coat. She became aware of the satiny lining, of the tickle of the fur under her chin. She looked down at the soft beige fabric, so different from the stiff wool of her own. How lovely, she thought, stroking the fur. Then, embarrassed, she glanced quickly around her. But no one paid the slightest attention. She was left alone with her thoughts.

Judd Rohrbach took a last look at himself in the full-length mirror in his hallway. He grabbed up his trenchcoat and prepared to leave for the studio. Not that anyone would notice whether I get there or not, he thought bitterly.

For the past three days, he had observed with mounting anger that Rafferty's three-minute good-news spot had been the focal point of the eleven o'clock broadcast. Hell, even in her straight reportage her personality had taken on such authority and vigor that she commanded the whole god-damn program. Judd felt like a two-bit pitchman filling in between her appearances. It was obvious he could expect no help from that prick Callahan; the producer was having orgasms over the KBLA ratings. He had as much as told Judd to go peddle his papers elsewhere if he wasn't willing to take a backseat. Well, goddammit, Judd Rohrbach wasn't taking a backseat to anybody—particularly not to a broad from Omaha, Nebraska, who hadn't known shit when he found her.

Serendipity syndrome! Jesus Christ, what the public wouldn't buy! Goddamn press was eating it up, people falling all over themselves to yell hallelujah; and there probably was no more substance to it than there was in a fluffy wad of cotton candy! Not one physician, not one scientific authority—nobody in the midst of this whole as-inine circus had come forward to substantiate, never mind explain, the whole frigging thing.

Judd sank into the plush blue interior of his sleek 280Z. He turned the key and gunned the engine to a satisfying roar. If he could only find somebody to punch holes in the theory—find statistics to prove that a certain number of spontaneous recoveries were made, unpublicized, every year—then maybe he could let the air out of Rafferty's high-flying balloon. . . .

Chapter Three

Dr. Rolf Pederson, in the early evening of April 18, was filled with unaccustomed resolve. Having turned the writing of the grant proposal over into more capable hands than his own, he was prepared to take his associates into his confidence.

He suspected that Kohner, at least, was already asking himself the proper questions and that even Howell, whose careless charm belied a brilliant mind, could not be far from partial comprehension. It annoyed Pederson that Howell had requested an hour's delay of their meeting. But he supposed that in the long haul it could not make much of a difference.

His two assistants had, from the start, been totally absorbed in the 6BW project. Despite Karl Fredericks' offhanded dismissal of its importance, the chemical had proven itself a powerful anti-virus since the inception of Pederson's extra-curricular project. And Howell and Kohner had been encouraged early on by their phenomenal success with specially bred mice.

They had adjusted and readjusted dosages, computed the relative quantities necessary for effectiveness without side effect (based on weight and degree of debilitation) and calculated that, based on their findings, 6BW ought to be similarly effective on human beings with equivalent viral debilitation.

The mild skin rash which Pederson knew Kohner had

observed when he isolated three of the cancer-bred mice
was the only unwanted, if seemingly random, side effect
of the chemical's success—and the reasons for it must
surely be addressed in the next stage of their research.

But his two assistants would be more than a little surprised to learn that 6BW was equally effective against certain strains of cancer. Pederson had not yet shared with
them his discovery of the cancerous mice in the newest
control-group specimens. He had yet to apprise them that
they had crossed the line between conjecture and certainty
of a viral link to cancer.

He now felt it was time for them to realize that 6BW
had the intrinsic ability to locate and destroy malignant
cells—and to commit themselves to staying with him long
enough to solve the riddle of the eczema, the one idiopathic
reaction to treatment with 6BW. Random and harmless
though it appeared to be, it was something that needed to
be dealt with.

Pederson carried the lab books to his office and closed
the glass-paneled door. He was eager to apologize to Kohner and Howell for his intermittent absences from the lab.
Kohner, especially, had probably missed their daily con-
sultations; and it went against the grain of Pederson's tu-
torial nature not to be available when he was needed. He
would correct that tonight and share his optimism about
securing a grant that would allow them all to continue regardless of what hospital administration did.

Only one thing disturbed the scientist as he moved a
newspaper from the top of his desk to make room for the
bulky lab books. It was something he hesitated to broach
to his colleagues, for it implied that his trust in them was
less than total. Yet it niggled at him with stony persistence,
flared again each time he read a paper or noted the drop in
routine lab work requested in the half-empty hospital.

The serendipity syndrome. That was the tag they'd given
to it, this escalating series of unexplainable recoveries
which reportedly had begun here at Reese Fowler. Mired
though he'd been in his own concerns, Pederson could

hardly have missed the media ballyhoo regarding the mysterious phenomenon. And although Pederson had had neither the time nor the inclination to research those first stunning recoveries, he was plagued by an unsettling thought. A drug like 6BW could cause such recovery if administered under the proper circumstances. Since Camthon had refused his grant for reasons undisclosed, could it be that the pharmaceutical company was already experimenting with a similar drug of its own?

He thought he knew both Howell and Kohner well enough to count on their discretion. It pained him to think that either one of them might possibly have leaked a hint of 6BW outside the confines of the lab. Could a very special case—a girl friend, a sick relative—have tempted either of his assistants to experiment with 6BW on human patients?

Pederson removed his glasses, polished them absently and mopped perspiration from his brow. It was warm in his office, unusually warm. What was wrong with the air conditioners? He made a note to call Maintenance the next morning, and continued with his somber speculations.

He failed to notice a small, orange metal cylinder, partially opened and well concealed behind a bank of file cabinets. And he did not detect the odor of escaping gas, for the leaking cyclopropane was absolutely odorless.

What he did notice as the minutes passed was a gradual but distinct feeling of drowsiness. This he passed off as delayed reaction to the sleepless hours he'd recently spent in preparation for this meeting. He glanced at his watch and wondered sleepily if there was time for a nap before his associates arrived. He decided there was not, and he shook his head to clear the languorous waves that threatened to engulf him. But the anaesthetic which invaded his consciousness was not to be warded off. His muscles relaxed, and against his will he found himself slumping in his chair.

He was dimly aware of a telephone ringing and he thought to rouse himself to answer it. But before he could transfer the will to the action, his brain exploded into nothingness. As the man who initiated that phone call knew, at the instant the solenoid sparked to activate the bell, a blast rocked the bowels of Reese Fowler.

Had the perpetrator been present to view his handiwork, he would have been pleased at its force. Walls and glass and woodwork convulsed, propelled into a ghastly, showering maelstrom. Blue flames erupted in the explosion's wake, precisely as he'd planned. But he would have been equally pleased to note that he'd demolished only that which he'd intended. Like a skillful surgeon, he'd excised only that which he'd been paid to destroy. The huge concrete structure, though unavoidably maimed, was far from totally disabled. When the flames were extinguished and the rubble cleared, his "patient" would continue to function.

That he had just destroyed a lab and a man's life which had inestimable value did not trouble him. He had done his job with professional dispatch, and in this he took a measure of pride. Pleased with himself, he replaced the receiver, then lifted it and dialed again.

Moments after the carefully timed phone call ended Rolf Pederson's life and turned a portion of the basement of Reese Fowler into wreckage, the telephone rang in Karl Fredericks' wood-paneled study. An anxious Fredericks picked up quickly.

"Is this Fred?" an unidentified caller asked.

"Yes, yes," rasped Fredericks, his edginess compounded by a feeling of foolishness at his weak attempt to mask his identity. The caller knew him only as Fred.

The man on the line spoke a brief, toneless message. "It's done," he said, and hung up.

Fredericks sank heavily into a wing-back chair, closed his eyes and shuddered. Then, the receiver still to his ear, he disconnected and dialed. The message he spoke was even more cryptic. It consisted of one word: "Done."

There was a brief pause at the other end of the line. "Good," murmured Paul Fairfield.

* * *

By the time Jeff Kohner walked the three short blocks from his apartment to Reese Fowler for the long-awaited meeting with Pederson and Howell, the night sky was awash with smoke and flame. The red-haired young doctor stopped and stared, unbelieving, at the scene before him. From where he stood, at the entrance to the parking lot, the entire left front side of the hospital appeared to be a gaping hole. Flames like iridescent fingers clawed at the charred and jagged concrete with nimble if maniacal grace.

He heard the scream of sirens, felt the ground beneath him tremble as massive fire engines careened through the lot and lurched to a stop before the building. He jammed his shaking hands into the pockets of his windbreaker and watched in horrified fascination as men shouted and scurried about and giant hoses unfurled into the debris. "Jesus Christ," he exclaimed into the wind and madness. "Holy Mother of God, Jesus Christ . . ."

The phone was ringing as Jeff let himself, stupefied, into his darkened apartment. Without bothering to turn on a light, he picked up the receiver, seeing as he did that the smoke and the eerie orange light were visible through his window. "Yeah," he said. He licked his lips. "Hello."

Roger Howell's breathless excitement forced its way into his consciousness. "Jesus, man, did you see it? Did you see it? What the fuck! I don't believe it!"

"Yeah, I saw it. See it, I'm looking at it. I don't believe it either. . . ."

"What the hell happened? Was Pederson in there?"

Jeff felt a shiver curl up his spine. "I don't know. It started before I got there."

Silence fell, heavy and palpable. Neither man could bring himself to speak. Finally, Roger, his voice barely audible, murmured, "Probably be on the news . . ."

"Yeah," said Jeff, thinking of Nancy. "Well, there's no point going back there—not till morning."

"Back where, my man? Ain't no lab to go to. We are temporarily out of business."

"No," said Jeff. "They'll set us up someplace. Hospital can't be without a lab."

"Nothin' much doin' anyway," said Roger. "Place has been half-empty for a week. Besides, it's got to take a day or two just to set up some temporary equipment."

Jeff nodded. "You may be right. Well, it's my shift in the morning. I'll go on over."

"Jesus, up in smoke. Pederson, the lab— Look, I'll catch you tomorrow." Roger hung up.

Jeff sat for a long time, looking out the window as the color faded from the sky. At last even the smoke was dissipated; the night once more was prosaic, inky black.

Jeff switched on a lamp, rose unsteadily to his feet and punched on the TV with the back of his hand. Judd Rohrbach's handsome face looked at him from the screen. "At Reese Fowler Medical Center," Rohrbach was saying, "allegedly the springboard for the so-called serendipity syndrome we've been hearing about, an explosion and fire of unknown origin tonight caused an estimated half-million dollars' worth of damage, destroying most of the basement laboratory and a portion of the laundry facilities next door."

The picture dissolved to a graphic view of the morbid conflagration Jeff had witnessed hours ago. "Flames rose dozens of feet into the air," the anchorman continued gravely, "until the blaze was contained by an efficient team of city firefighters. Hospital officials commended the firefighters, stating that another half-million dollars might have been lost if the flames had been allowed to reach the radiology or X-ray facilities nearby."

Jeff watched, scarcely breathing, as the anchorman's smooth features sobered into hard, grim lines. "While no lives have yet officially been claimed as a result of the incident, a hospital spokesman fears the loss of Dr. Rolf Pederson, chief pathologist, who may have been in the lab at the time the explosion occurred.

"Firemen investigating the cause of the tragedy are without an answer at this hour. While they have thus far failed to locate a body, they are doubtful that anyone in the lab could have escaped the spontaneous and forceful blast.

"In other news tonight," Judd Rohrbach continued—but Jeff hit the Off button, overcome with nausea, and turned from the instantly darkened screen. He sprinted for the bathroom, retched repeatedly into the bowl and let himself sink slowly to his knees. He rested his head against the cool porcelain of the tub. It was too much of an effort to get to his feet. . . . He must have dozed. When the telephone jolted Jeff awake, he found himself on the tiled floor of his bathroom, an acrid taste in his mouth. Sickened, he splashed cold water on his face, rinsed his mouth and walked unsteadily to the phone.

"Jeff?" It was Nancy Rafferty. "Jeff, it's Nancy. Are you all right? I mean—you've heard the news."

"Yeah. I'm all right. What time is it?"

Nancy hesitated. "It's nearly midnight. I couldn't reach you earlier. I was worried sick when the news came in. I thought—you might have been in the lab."

Jeff closed his eyes. "I was on my way. The meeting was delayed. Nancy, have you heard anything more?"

The girl drew in her breath. "They found a body. Pederson's. What was left of it. My God, Jeff, you might have been there too."

Jeff swallowed. "I'm all right. Look, maybe I should go down there to see if I can help somehow."

"There's no point tonight. There's nothing you can do. The police have the area cordoned off. No one gets in till morning, at least. . . . Jeff, can I see you? Tonight?"

"Sure," he said, and realized all of a sudden it was the only thing he wanted. "Listen, my place isn't really fit for company."

"I understand. I just got home. Eleven-seventy West Franklin. In Hollywood, not far from the Freeway."

"Give me half an hour," he said. "And Nancy . . . thanks. For calling."

"See you soon." He heard a click, replaced the receiver in its cradle. Galvanized with a sense of purpose, he stripped as he headed for the bathroom. He flushed the toilet and sprayed the room with Lysol. Then he turned on the shower, stepped under the jets and, face-up, let the water sluice over him.

In twenty minutes he was in his old Chevy, skirting the hospital area to pick up the Hollywood Freeway. He did not look toward the charred and blackened hole. He had had enough for one night.

Nancy opened the door of her apartment as Jeff stepped off the elevator. "I've been watching from my window," she confessed, strangely shy. Her gaze rested firmly on his face.

It seemed to Jeff as he crossed the hall that he'd waited all his life for this moment. She was dressed in a caftan, green and silky, belted at the waist. Lamplight from behind her cast an aura about her hair, and her eyes were luminous, large in a pale oval face. Her full lips parted as though to speak, but she held out a hand to show him in. He would never be able to remember with certainty whose lips sought first to breach their distance. He knew only that from the time they touched, he was engulfed in a timeless, spaceless sea.

How or when they moved from the doorway to the darkened bedroom was another mystery neither would ever answer nor seek to understand. All that mattered was an overwhelming need, a desire to touch, to taste, to succor. When Nancy cried out from the height of fulfillment, Jeff found himself filled with a pure elation that froze the breath in his body.

Afterward, drowsily clasped in his arms, Nancy became embarrassed by her ardor. She reached up and traced the curve of his jaw. "This isn't why I asked you here, you know."

"It isn't?" Jeff murmured, sinking his teeth softly into the ripened morsel of her lower lip. "Well, I guess I misunderstood. I could come in again and we could start over."

Nancy laughed, pushing him away. "You're a better man than I am, Gunga Din."

Jeff sat up, drank in the sight of her lying amid the rumpled bedclothes. "God, you're beautiful. You're all I ever wanted. What could I ever do to deserve you?"

"Feed me," she promptly decided, her green eyes wide and playful. "I'm starved. Are you hungry, Dr. Kohner?"

"Ravenous. Insatiable. I'll never get enough of you. Not if I live for a hundred years."

"Well, you might as well know I am totally useless unless I get regular nourishment." She bounded out of bed and searched for her caftan. "I didn't stop to eat when I left the studio, and now we'll have to settle for scrambled eggs."

He followed her gamely into the kitchen, dressing hurriedly and for the first time seeing the charm of her immaculate apartment. "I like your place," he told her, kissing the back of her neck. "It's bright and sophisticated. Like you."

"And largely furnished with whims and fancies. I tend to be a slave to my impulses." She flushed at the grin on his face, sat him firmly in a cane-back chair and turned her attention to the refrigerator.

"I'll follow your impulses anywhere," he said, leaning back to stretch his long legs, content to watch as she busied herself, her every move a repast for his senses.

"Make yourself useful." She tossed him a bag of bagels. "Toast a couple of these. Over there."

They ate cheese omelets and slathered the toasted bagels with butter and raspberry jam. They kissed away the crumbs, feeling silly and serene, giggling like ill-behaved children.

"This is ridiculous," Nancy said at last. "It's four in the morning. We really should get some sleep."

"You haven't told me why you asked me here," prompted Jeff. "If it wasn't only my body you craved, what did you have in mind?"

Nancy smiled, her gaze traveling deliberately down his frame. "Your body's irresistible. You made me forget whatever it was."

Jeff's face took on a look of blasé irritation. "God, a man gets tired of being used!" But then he became serious and sat forward, putting a hand over hers. "No. You had a reason. . . . Was it—the accident?"

"Don't call it an accident." She looked at him levelly. "I don't think it was an accident at all—but a well-planned act of violence and murder."

Jeff blinked. "Are you serious? What are you saying?" He leaned forward to meet her gaze.

Nancy went on. "What would you say if I told you that whoever did it set out to destroy the lab. And everything that was in it. Including Pederson."

"Poor old Pedantic." Pain clouded his face. "I still can't believe it."

"Believe it. He's gone." Her voice became softer. "You might have been there too. For the meeting."

"An hour later . . . Jesus Christ . . ."

"Jeff, what was the reason for that meeting?"

Jeff willed himself to force out words. "Pederson, Howell and I work the lab in shifts. There are others too, but we three share the major responsibility. Rog and I rotate days and nights, so there's always coverage for Pederson's project. The old man's always there from four to midnight—that's his choice, so he can see us each briefly."

"So anyone who wanted to kill Pederson would know those were his hours in the lab."

"I guess so, sure. But because of the way we work, there isn't always time for consultation. The 6BW project was coming to a head and I think that's what Pederson wanted to tell us."

"The 6BW."

"That's the generic term for the chemical anti-virus we've been working on."

Nancy's questions were crisp and terse. "The meeting that was scheduled. Was it common knowledge?"

"It wasn't a secret, if that's what you mean. Though I don't know who might have known or cared. It was slated for eight o'clock, but Roger had a date. At the last minute, it was put off till nine.''

"Jeff, the explosion occurred at eight-fifteen precisely. If the meeting had been on schedule—'' She didn't finish.

Jeff blanched and turned dull eyes to Nancy. "You really think that blast was set off on purpose?''

Nancy's eyes never left his face. "I do. And so do the investigating officers.''

"Why, for God's sake?'' Jeff's eyes were wild. "Why the hell would anybody do that?''

"You may know more about that than anyone else. What, exactly, is 6BW?'' She reached for his hand.

"I told you, it's a chemical. A synthetic protein. A powerful and effective anti-virus. In testing, it's overcome a lot of viral strains. Why the hell would anybody want to sabotage it?''

"Think about this carefully before you answer, Jeff. Could 6BW possibly be the answer to this puzzling serendipity syndrome?''

Jeff shook his head. "Impossible. No way. It's never been administered to human patients. And anyway, it's a virus killer, not likely to cure cancer—or a lot of the other diseases people are claiming to have recovered from.''

"You're sure of that?'' asked Nancy. "That it's never been administered to human patients in or out of Reese Fowler?''

"Absolutely certain. I'd stake my life on that. Pederson is—was—too ethical to have treated patients without a special protocol procedure. The use of a protocol waives responsibility in the event of any unforeseen side effects. No such protocol existed for 6BW. It wasn't ready for human experimentation.''

"I see,'' said Nancy. But her skepticism was clear.

"Believe me, only the mice got 6BW.''

Nancy decided to try another tack. She began to clear the dishes from the table. "Jeff, doesn't it strike you as too coincidental that the first serendipitous recoveries happened at Reese Fowler? That the place where the miracle started to happen is suddenly blown sky-high?''

"You don't know that that's where it started. We may only have noticed it first. And you've got to admit, after all that publicity, that some of these so-called recoveries may not be for real.''

Nancy stiffened at the implication that she might have overreacted to the syndrome. That it had occurred to her—and to Callahan—was one thing, but it hurt to hear it from Jeff.

He saw her wince and he touched her arm. "Nance, I'm not saying that's so. Something's going on, people are recovering. But I don't think 6BW is responsible. And even if it were,'' he added as she nestled closer, "I can't think why anyone would want to destroy it. For Pete's sake, Pederson should be in line for the Nobel Prize if 6BW's more than what it seems.''

Nancy decided it was too late to argue—and anyway, she felt herself on shaky ground. She did believe that Pederson's chemical was the reason for the syndrome—and the explosion. But how and why it had begun to spread was a question she could not yet answer. And as for who had wished to destroy it . . . she couldn't even venture a guess.

There was work to be done—research, follow-up. Ideas began to form in her head. But even to her, they sounded outlandish, maybe because she was so tired. Only one thing seemed clear: what she felt for Jeff and what she knew he felt for her.

She held his face between her hands, kissed him gently, felt his warmth. "Come to bed. Please stay the night. I need you near me while I sleep.''

Jeff, whose whole being was suffused with love, was thinking the very same thing.

Chapter Four

Jeff awoke in the unfamiliar room, breathing in the scent of Nancy Rafferty. But when he reached for her, he found her gone. He sat up, disoriented. It was 7:20.

He pulled on his pants hurriedly, knowing he'd be late to the lab. Then he remembered there was no lab to go to, and he sat down heavily on the bed. The long night kaleidoscoped in his brain. He'd go to the hospital anyway. There might be something he could do.

He found a new toothbrush, still in its package, propped on the bathroom sink along with a note from Nancy: "Good morning, love. I had to leave but I couldn't bear to wake you. Help yourself to whatever you need and try to have the best day you can. I have lots to do but I still owe you dinner tonight. Meet you at Scandia at eight."

By the time Jeff Kohner found the note, Nancy was already at her desk. She found two messages from Paul Fairfield, which she laid aside with annoyance. The man was entirely too anxious, she thought. On the other hand, it occurred to her, she had never checked out his patient Kathleen Riley. If there was a possibility she was part of the syndrome, Nancy wanted to know. She made a mental note to call the woman's daughter, the nun—Sister Althea—and arrange to see Mrs. Riley for herself.

She began making a list of the things she needed to do, wondering how she'd cram them into the day. She checked the news wires and noted, without surprise, that the syndrome still appeared to be escalating. A rock star in Liverpool, a famed American designer of women's fashions and a score of nameless, faceless men, women and children from an astoundingly large geographical area claimed to have rejoined the ranks of the healthy, cured of their various illnesses presumably through the same serendipity.

She telephoned a friend at police headquarters to see if there was anything more on the Reese Fowler investigation. She learned two things. The explosive was an anaesthetic, a gas called cyclopropane that was rarely used in the O.R. now because it was so sensitive it could be set off by the ripping of surgical tape. A cylinder of the stuff had been located amid the debris, and there was no reason for it to have been in the lab. A hospital switchboard operator confirmed a phone call to the lab seconds before the explosion occurred. Under the right circumstances the sparking of the solenoid could have provided the impetus.

The second thing she learned began a train of thought that caused her to add something to her list. The escaping gas had been contained in the basement area because the air vents in there had been closed. Had the gas been allowed to travel through the vents into the upper stories of the hospital, the explosion would have been even more catastrophic.

When the main branch of the public library opened at nine A.M., Nancy was the first through the massive doors. When she emerged, at just past eleven, she was flushed with mounting excitement. She found a phone booth, made one brief call and sprinted down the street to her yellow Volkswagen.

Paul Fairfield, seated at the scarred wooden desk in his small office at Reese Fowler, studiously massaged the area beneath his eyes and perused a disquieting report. Population in the chemotherapy clinics was down by nearly half. He needed no financial accounting to assess the resulting implications. If the goddamned syndrome wasn't brought to a halt, the loss of revenue would be disastrous.

But the task before him, he reflected now, was not merely to slow down the syndrome. If Fredericks was correct in his assumptions about 6BW, that much had been accomplished by the explosion. With the chemical destroyed, along with its founders and its formulae, its potency would surely be dissipated. The greater triumph would be to capitalize on its success by turning it to the advantage of Metastaban. With this in mind, his ire was aroused at the constant rebuff of Nancy Rafferty. The bitch was avoiding him, that much was clear. She had yet to return his calls. Well, why not? She was riding the crest of success by prolonging the mystery of the syndrome. He simply could not afford to sit idly by waiting for her to respond.

What about her co-host—Rohrbach, wasn't it?—a showman if ever there was one. What was his stand on Rafferty's coup? Was he ripe for a miracle of his own? There was nothing to lose, he decided finally, by tossing out the bait. If Rohrbach was less than enthusiastic, there were other avenues to consider. But how gratifying it would be to break the story while upstaging Rafferty on her own show. And trusting again to his unerring instincts, he reached at once for the telephone.

In moments he was speaking to Judd Rohrbach in the newsroom. The anchorman's interest pleased him. "Perhaps we could meet," Rohrbach suggested. "There's a French restaurant on Sunset. The Taix."

"I know it," agreed Fairfield. "Shall we say, half an hour? I think you'll agree it's worth your time."

He was halfway to his silver Mercedes in the doctors' parking lot when he spied a young man poking amid the rubble in the roped-off area. Shoulders hunched forward in a light windbreaker, the man's hands were jammed into his pockets, his face grim as he kicked desultorily at bits of pipe and broken glass, the remains of the Reese Fowler lab.

There was none of the jauntiness Fairfield had associated with this figure. Yet, there was no mistaking the carrot-red hair or the youthful planes of his face. It was Kohner, without doubt, and for a moment Fairfield paled. It was as near as he had come to seeing a ghost. Scowling, he hurried to his car. Couldn't anyone be trusted to do things right?

He was still weighing the impact of Jeff Kohner's well-being when he drew up to the entrance of the Taix. But this was not the time to debate the alternatives. He had a more pressing task at hand.

The restaurant was a landmark, one of the few original Los Angeles restaurants to successfully flee the downtown area. It had reappeared in a burgeoning if not quite fashionable section of Hollywood's Sunset Boulevard. It was a popular meeting place for junior executives and lesser-known personalities. At this early hour it was reasonably empty, and Fairfield had no difficulty in recognizing the newscaster who sat in a booth toward the rear. "Mr. Rohrbach," he said, striding purposefully toward him. "Paul Fairfield. Good of you to meet me."

"My pleasure." Rohrbach rose to shake hands. "You made this sound important."

"So it is," replied Fairfield evenly, regarding the man across the table. Close up, the face which, on television, seemed authoritative was bland and lacking in character. The blue eyes were vacuous, the chin weak and the mouth a petulant bow. Surprised but pleased to see such weaknesses, Fairfield ordered a Perrier and turned his attention to the menu.

Judd Rohrbach, for his part, saw the silver-haired physician as distinguished almost to the point of caricature. He belonged on the cover of a gentleman's magazine, urbane, sophisticated, solvent. There was no escaping the air of confidence. He was a man who commanded respect.

Indeed, in the space of those initial judgments, an invisible bond sprang up between them. Each recognized in the other a potential ally, a man of inconstant scruples. It remained only to ascertain what each might be worth to the other. Their orders given, Fairfield spoke first. "You're a busy man, Judd. I'll get to the point. I have an announcement of great medical significance. I'd like you to be my spokesman to the media and the public at large.''

"Medical significance." Judd was wary. "Relating to the serendipity syndrome?"

Fairfield laughed, throwing his head back. "My boy, there's no such thing as serendipity.''

"Well," smiled Judd, "it seems that you and I are part of a shrinking minority of disbelievers.''

"Perhaps," agreed Fairfield. "I'm a man of science. There is no room in science for whims. There is no illness without its cause, and cure is not effected through chance.''

"Then all these recoveries we're hearing about . . . you don't believe they are fact.''

"Some of them are," conceded the doctor. "A very small percentage. You see, if there's one true variable in medicine, it's the outlook, the sheer will of a patient. Given a reason to think himself well, many a patient can convince himself it's so.''

"Then the syndrome is providing an easy out—an impetus to strengthen his will.''

"In some cases, yes. A sugar pill could achieve the same result. It's human nature to believe in miracles—to want to believe you'll recover. With the media hoopla sweeping the populace, I should think it would be easy to succumb: to jump on the bandwagon and proclaim yourself cured whether or not you really are.''

"If that's the situation, then hospital beds may empty but the cemeteries shortly may be full," Judd concluded.

Fairfield smiled. "A morbid thought. A high price to pay for gullibility.''

"But there have been cases," Judd interjected, "in which the recovery has been documented.''

"Early on. Isolated remissions. Perhaps successful medical treatment. When the media got hold of it and whipped the public into a frenzy, the supposed cures were too numerous to be documented.''

"I take it," said the newsman, smiling again, "you think my colleague was a bit—irresponsible.''

Fairfield could hardly miss the sarcasm in Judd's voice. He shrugged. "Women tend to be hysterical."

The waiter brought their lunch to the table. Judd inspected his French onion soup. "Dr. Fairfield," he said, looking up at the doctor, "would you be willing to repeat that on television? To help the public understand that hysteria will not cure illness?"

"Of course," answered Fairfield, forking tuna from his salad. "Though I doubt it would do any good."

"Why is that?" asked Judd.

Fairfield put down his fork. "To refute the theory might only serve to fan the fire. Right now, the whole thing's blown out of proportion. The public is blissful in its ignorance. For me, or anyone, to raise a voice in protest could make them rise up in its support."

"Then where does it stop?" Judd was puzzled. "The media will continue to play it up."

"Every phenomenon peters out." Fairfield resumed his eating. "You're a newsman. Remember the pyramid schemes? They were headlines for weeks a few years back. No amount of warning kept the suckers from trying to get rich. Until a few caught on and the media tired of it, and in no time the phenomenon died out."

"Then you're advocating silence." Judd stirred his soup. "Downplaying the new reports of recovery." He laughed derisively. "I know one thing. We'd have to put a muzzle on Nancy."

Fairfield looked up sharply at Rohrbach's choice of words.

"Metaphorically speaking," added Judd.

"Of course," said Fairfield blandly. "But more important, divert public attention to something else."

"Your announcement of medical significance," smiled Judd. "You've found a cure for cancer."

Fairfield allowed himself the hint of a smile. "As a matter of fact, I think I have."

It was Judd's turn for an incredulous snicker. "Dr. Fairfield, your timing is superb."

"Indeed," agreed Fairfield, raising the glass of Perrier to his lips. "Though in this case, not merely coincidental. Serendipity may be hogwash, but Metastaban is not. It may, in fact, have started the so-called syndrome." He reached into a briefcase and placed before Judd a folder with the single word emblazoned on it.

"Metastaban," the newscaster read aloud. "All right, I'll bite. What's Metastaban?"

"It's a natural substance derived from fruit pulp, developed by Camthon Pharmaceuticals. Like laetrile, it markedly reduces cancer's symptoms without resorting to drugs. Unlike laetrile," the doctor smiled, "it's been given FDA approval. Because, unlike laetrile, it's been proven in testing to reverse the process of metastasis."

Judd was silent, digesting the words. "Are you saying it actually cures cancer?"

"When combined with a program of chemotherapy, yes." Fairfield's gaze was candid. "It's only just come into use, and that's where the timing is superb. One of my own patients, successfully treated with Metastaban, made one of those supposedly serendipitous recoveries. I'm sure there were others, in other parts of the world, who were treated successfully as well. With the result, as I hinted earlier, that the media whipped up a 'syndrome.' "

Judd's mind reeled with the impact of such a story. "How many cases can you document?"

"Enough," said Fairfield smoothly, "to give the thing credence. It's all here." He patted the folder. "Read it at your leisure. I think you'll agree it's worthy of public announcement. And if I were you," he added conspiratorially, "I'd keep it away from Miss Rafferty. She's done enough harm with her massive hysteria. I'm trusting you to treat this with more professionalism."

There were questions Judd Rohrbach could have asked as a responsible, probing journalist. Why, for example, was Fairfield representing Camthon? Did he have a vested interest in the product? And why, if Metastaban was all that he said, did Camthon not break the story through scientific channels?

But Rohrbach was nourished by desire for a coup as much as by the food he'd just eaten. Ethics aside, wasn't he just as responsible as Nancy had been in fomenting the goddamned serendipity? This was not conjecture he would air, it was based on medical corroboration. His pulses quickened. It would not be merely a rebuttal, but an *answer!* It was better than anything he might have hoped for.

Fairfield, sipping coffee, watched the machinations of Judd Rohrbach's mind exactly as if they'd appeared on a computer screen. His judgment had been infallible; the man was a glory-seeker. He decided to feed in the final data. "You needn't concern yourself with opposition to the facts you're about to disclose. You're providing an important public service, not only by dispelling the myth of serendipity but by offering help to the helpless."

Rohrbach stared at Paul Fairfield through eyes already glazed by power and revenge.

Chapter Five

Sister Althea, in St. Agatha's Convent, stared at the paperwork before her. But try as she might, she could not rouse herself from her stalemate of confusion. Miriam's philosophical words had seemed to her a revelation. Over and over, she played the catchphrases in her head, and their meaning was always the same: human frailty permitted mistakes. One needed to learn from them and grow.

It was frightening to think she might have made a mistake in entering the convent. It was just as frightening to imagine her life without the presence of Michael Kelly. But whether she had erred more in following her mother's dictates or in following the dictates of her own heart was difficult to know. In either case, she had not sinned, so what had she to trade for her mother's life?

There was no denying Kathleen Riley was better. Althea needed no one to tell her that. The woman grew stronger every day, gaining weight and irritability. "Look!" she would shout, gripping her daughter's arm. "My hair is falling out in patches! I don't need this awful chemotherapy. You can see that I'm better. Take me home!"

Dr. Fairfield persisted in pulling at her too, as surely as if he'd gripped her other arm. "Your mother's recovery is encouraging," he said. "Thanks to the miracle of Metastaban. But we dare not take a chance on incomplete therapy. We must be sure she stays in remission."

Althea hoped it was the doctor's drugs and treatments

that were making her mother well. It proved that Althea's "bargain" was invalid—and it gave her strength to stand up to her mother. "You tell me," she would say, "to remember my place. Is it my place to question Dr. Fairfield?"

And now, of course, there was this syndrome in the news. So many people were getting better. Was her mother's new health just an odd twist of fate? Another unsettling question. Althea sighed and put the forms back on their folders. She would not get much work done today. She had too many questions, too much to resolve, and it left her with bewildering, restless energy. She could go for a walk. It might clear her head and help her to put things into focus. . . .

Nancy Rafferty crossed her long legs and faced Dr. Louis Hillman squarely. "Thanks for seeing me on short notice," she began. "I'm afraid reporters have a well-earned reputation for barging in on other people's time."

"No problem, Miss Rafferty—"

"Nancy."

"Nancy. As you know, I'm far from overworked these days. In all my years here at Reese Fowler, I've never seen so many empty beds."

"Then you'll agree there's a syndrome of wellness going on. It hasn't just been blown up out of proportion."

The physician's face remained maddeningly bland. "I don't know. But I'll bet that's why you're here. How can I help? Why don't you tell me what you're thinking? Frankly, I'm as puzzled as the next guy."

Nancy smiled, encouraged by his willingness to listen to her theories. "Thanks, Dr. Hillman. I'll start at the beginning. Maybe you can help me sort things out. I've been trying to research this syndrome of recoveries. I'm convinced something real is taking place. And furthermore, though I have no proof, I believe it began at Reese Fowler."

"Stevie Phillips."

"Not just Stevie. There've been many others. As you said yourself, you're hardly overworked. The rate of recovery here over the past ten days has been nothing short of remarkable. And the rate of new admissions is at an alltime low. No one can argue that."

"Agreed," said Hillman. "It is unusual. And possibly cause for concern. There may be people in need of treatment who've talked themselves out of seeking it."

"You're referring," countered Nancy, with a trace of uneasiness, "to all the optimistic publicity. Well, I can't be held accountable for what's happened elsewhere. In Los Angeles, I reported what I saw. The greatest concentration of reported recoveries seems to be happening here."

Hillman said nothing, but Nancy didn't stop to interpret the reason for his silence. "Look, Dr. Hillman, I'm not so naive as to count every reported recovery as a genuine part of the syndrome. I realize there's some sort of psychological factor in play as a result of all the publicity. But as a physician you cannot deny that a certain percentage *are* genuine. Patients who had every reason to die have genuinely had their health restored."

"No," responded Hillman quietly, "I can't deny that. There are those who have, indeed, recovered."

"If only there were a way," Nancy went on, "to separate the fact from the fiction. To identify those people who've truly been affected by means of a common link." The reporter laughed. "I'm not asking for much. A brand on the forehead would do."

Hillman laughed and considered the earnest face in front of him. To date, he'd told no one of his personal triumph over cancer. His doctor knew, but even he was unaware of the rash, the rash on his chest startlingly similar to the one he'd observed in little Stevie. Was that the link, the common link, that Nancy Rafferty was looking for? It was tenuous at best . . . and he, a physician . . . but perhaps he should share what he'd seen.

"Nancy . . ." he began, and something in his tone arrested the reporter's attention. "The morning after Stevie came out of coma, he developed a mild, reddish rash. It centered on his upper torso, but apart from causing some discomfort and itching, it had no visible effect. It faded away in a matter of days; and now, as you know, Stevie's fine.''

Nancy listened, waiting for more. Hillman did not disappoint her. ''Now I will tell you in the strictest of confidence something even my wife doesn't know. Not long ago, I was diagnosed as having cancer—a rather large, malignant tumor. The tumor is gone.'' He leaned forward in his chair. ''It simply disappeared. Shortly after Stevie's recovery, new X rays confirmed that for me. And the strange thing—the thing I know you'll be interested in—is that for several days afterward I exhibited the same kind of inexplicable rash I had observed on Stevie Phillips.'' He raised his hands in a helpless gesture. ''Make of that what you will.''

Nancy was shaken. A mild, reddish rash. Where had she heard the phrase before? In the lab, with Jeff, the day she'd met him. His mice had a mild, reddish rash! What had happened to those three white mice? Had they too recovered from disease?

''Dr. Hillman,'' she said, ''I can't thank you enough for your honesty in sharing that with me. It's off the record if that's what you want, but it's certainly worth looking into. And I'm happy for you—for your own recovery. You're a very special person.'' She reached over to touch his hand.

Hillman barely suppressed a smile. ''If you'll pardon the pun, I'm glad it's off my chest. I've been stewing about the coincidence for days. There may be no connection at all—but as you say, it's worth looking into.''

''Yes. Dr. Hillman, if I'm not imposing, could I bounce some crazy theories off you?''

''Why not?'' The physician leaned back in his chair. ''So far, the whole thing is crazy.''

''As I went back over the reports of the first recoveries,'' explained Nancy, ''I discovered an interesting thing. Many of the earliest were from viral disease, at least the ones that were documented. A few—like you—recovered from cancer. And even that may have a viral connection."

Hillman nodded. "There's a school of research that believes cancer may be virally caused." His bushy brows furrowed as he thought.

"I read about it in the library this morning. And something else as well. A virus is transmitted by floating through the air. It travels until it finds a victim."

"In a sense that's true," the doctor agreed. "There are viruses in the air all around us."

"Well, here comes the crazy part." Nancy sat forward eagerly. "Suppose that an antidote existed. Might it not be capable of floating as well, attacking and killing virus in the very same way that a virus itself is transmitted?"

Hillman raised his eyebrows and scratched his head thoughtfully. "It seems a little farfetched. But then, there's a lot we don't know about the virus—and a lot we don't know about curing it. Are you suggesting something floated through the air at Reese Fowler: some unknown but powerful viral antidote?"

"Yes," replied Nancy. "I think it came from the lab. And I think someone wanted it stopped."

Understanding dawned on Hillman's face. "The explosion. Is that what you mean?"

"Dr. Pederson and his team in the lab were working on an anti-viral project. It may have been more successful than even Pederson knew—especially in light of our conversation. I saw some white mice who'd been exposed to 6BW as part of Pederson's project. They exhibited the same kind of mild, reddish rash you described in Stevie Phillips and yourself. If they recovered in all other respects, as you and Stevie did, then is it preposterous to make the assumption that 6BW started the syndrome?"

"Those mice," said Hillman, "were probably injected with this—6BW. Certainly I never was, or Stevie."

"That's what Jeff said. I mean, Dr. Kohner." I've discussed my theory with him. But allow me this one flight of fancy. What if the molecules floated on the air, out through the vents of the lab and into the atmosphere at Reese Fowler? What if they were able to attack a virus in the same way that a virus attacks?''

As she spoke, Nancy was steeled by the validity of her growing conviction. According to her police sources, the vents in the lab had been closed, presumably by the perpetrator of the explosion, to keep the cyclopropane gas from escaping into the upper reaches of the hospital. At all other times, those vents were open so that heat and air conditioning could circulate. If molecules of 6BW had floated up through those vents . . .

But Hillman's face was suffused with doubt. "It does seem a little incredible. And even if it happened just as you suggest, what about recoveries outside the hospital? Surely you aren't implying that those molecules had the ability to float clear across the country—or the world?''

"No." The reporter shook her head. "Bear with me for just another minute. Suppose there are carriers who, like Typhoid Mary—or A.I.D.S. carriers—harbor the molecules and unknowingly spread them through contact with victims of the virus?''

At this the physician expelled a deep breath. Nancy grinned sheepishly. "Too far out?''

"Let's say," admitted Hillman, "it's asking a lot to accept this particular flight of fancy. But then, a month ago, I would not have been receptive to the idea of unexplainable recoveries. . . .''

Nancy, having blurted her whole crazy theory, suddenly ran out of words. She shifted in her chair, feeling slightly foolish and uncomfortably aware of Lou Hillman's steady gaze.

"Another thing bothers me," Hillman said. "Suppose— just suppose—this were possible. Why would anyone want to destroy such a potent enemy of disease? Who would see this 6BW as anything but a boon to mankind?''

"Someone," said Nancy, her face expressionless, "with a heavy stake in human illness.''

Hillman chuckled. "All physicians have a stake in human illness."

"Touché." Nancy smiled. "So what do I do? Attack the entire AMA?"

"Not unless," the doctor said, "you've got some pretty heavy ammunition."

"Well." Nancy rose and extended her hand. "I can't thank you enough just for listening. Not to mention the clue about the rash. I've still got something to go on."

Hillman took her hand in his. "I didn't imagine this tumor, Nancy. It was here and now it's gone. Outlandish as your theory seems to be . . . if there's anything I can do, let me know."

"I've a feeling if I persist with this crazy stuff, I may need you to certify my sanity."

"Glad to, my dear. Until someone comes up with a better idea, your theory's as viable as any."

"Thanks, Dr. Hillman. I appreciate that. Now, all I have to do is prove it."

Paul Fairfield had required no proof. The very possibility was enough. From the moment Karl Fredericks broached the outlandish theory, Fairfield was inclined to consider it. Somehow, whatever was contained in 6BW had been floating in the corridors of Reese Fowler. Whether it had, in fact, filtered through the air vents or had been dispersed by more conventional means was of little concern to him. What concerned him was this damned epidemic recovery. The confounded syndrome had to stop. That his carefully built empire of chemotherapy clinics might crumble was in itself cause for alarm. But the fortunes inherent in distributing Metastaban simply must not be put in jeopardy.

Nor did the silver-haired doctor even wonder what 6BW contained. He saw the formula as an enemy, counter to his goals; and as such, it warranted destruction. The "accident" in the lab had been necessary to destroy it, along with its formula and its founders.

But Kohner was alive. How much did he know? Enough to reproduce the potent chemical? Damn that Fredericks and his incompetent hirelings! And the time had come to silence Rafferty. With Judd Rohrbach waiting to tap-dance in the wings, it was up to Fairfield to clear the stage. He was beginning to enjoy the intricate game. It was at once a threat and a challenge. He reached for the phone. "Fredericks?" he said. "Meet me on Wilshire just as fast as you can get there."

Miriam Phillips held up a blue silk evening dress. Body-skimming and cut low, its only ornamentation were two thin, glittery shoulder straps. It had cost too much at Saks, even on sale, but it made her feel daring and sexy and free, and that was exactly how she wanted to feel on this upcoming second honeymoon.

Zan had presented her with last-minute cruise ship tickets with unabashed excitement, prepared to brook her resistance. "It's Easter vacation," he'd said. "I have a week off from school and I can't think of a better way to spend it. Mom will stay with Stevie, it's all arranged. And you can't say no, it's all paid for."

"Then I guess we'll go." She'd smiled sweetly, enjoying her husband's astonishment. "I can't think of a reason in the world not to."

They'd had only a day to prepare for the trip, but that was, perhaps, the best part. The whole adventure was heady and romantic, as much a departure from the routine of their days as it was possible for it to be.

Carefully, Miriam folded the blue wisp of silk in her suitcase and turned her attention to shoes. At the back of her closet she found a pair of silver sandals purchased for a long-ago New Year's Eve. She was wrapping them in tissue when the telephone rang. Damn! She was so short of time!

It was Nancy Rafferty. "How's Stevie?" she greeted Miriam.

"Fine! You'd never know he's been sick!"

"Is his rash gone?"

"His rash? Oh, yes, it disappeared days ago. How did you know about the rash?"

"I had a long talk with Dr. Hillman this afternoon," Nancy said. "Miriam, I'd like to see you, too."

"Well." Miriam hesitated. "If it's really important I might be able to drop by. Zan and I are leaving on a trip."

"A trip? Where to?"

"The Caribbean. On a cruise. It's kind of a . . . second honeymoon."

Nancy could almost see her grin. "Oh, that's wonderful! You surely deserve it. Listen, Miriam, have a good time and I'll call you when you get back."

"Nancy, if you really need to see me—"

Nancy was firm. "It can wait. Bon voyage. And give my love to Stevie."

Moments later the telephone rang in the common room at St. Agatha's convent. Sister Althea was summoned to the phone. "Hello?" Her voice was barely audible.

"Sister Althea, it's Nancy Rafferty. We met in Stevie Phillips' room at Reese Fowler."

"Yes, of course," recalled the nun, becoming flustered. "I watch you all the time on the news."

"Thank you, Sister. That's why I called. I'm sort of working on a story. I tried to see your mother at the hospital to get some information but I understand she's been moved."

"Yes, she's in a chemotherapy clinic called Sunnyvale. She's still under Dr. Fairfield's treatment."

"Oh. Then she isn't fully recovered, after all."

"Well, I'm not sure . . ." The nun's voice trailed off.

"I'd like to see her if you think she's up to it," Nancy said. "Is she well enough for visitors, do you think?"

"Oh, I think so, yes! I know she'll be thrilled. A celebrity and all, my goodness!"

"Thank you, Sister. It may be important. . . . Sister, may I ask you a question?"

Althea paused while the reporter continued. "This may seem silly, but it could be important. At some time during your mother's illness—has she ever suffered a mild red rash?"

"A rash?" Althea blinked. "I don't know. I don't think so. Why would she have had a rash?"

"She may have been exposed to a chemical, 6BW. It could account for part of her recovery. Sister, is it likely she had this rash and didn't tell you?"

"I doubt it. She's—quick to complain."

"Oh," said Nancy, disappointment in her voice. "Well, perhaps I can ask her when I see her. How about tomorrow? About noon? At Sunnyvale."

Althea agreed and hung up slowly. She felt a bit better than she had for days. Now she had something exciting to tell her mother when she saw her this evening at the clinic. A real celebrity coming to see her might even take her mind off her complaints.

Nancy drummed her fingers on the desk. So Kathleen Riley was still sick. And she'd had no rash that her daughter knew of. Here was one less triumph for 6BW.

Still, she'd keep her promise and see the woman tomorrow. She gathered up her things and prepared to go. There were a few things yet to do before meeting Jeff at Scandia. Nancy smiled with pleasure at the thought of seeing him. She had so much now to tell him—and to ask! What a pity she had to be back at the studio by eleven. But she would make sure they got together again after the telecast.

Walking quickly, she practically bumped into Judd Rohrbach as she turned the corner toward the elevator. Her co-host was cordial, smiling grandly. "In a hurry as usual, I see."

Nancy returned the smile with candor. "I'll be back in plenty of time."

Chapter Six

For the second time that day Jeff Kohner stood under a needle spray, relishing the hot water as it sluiced over his body. It had been a long day.

He had been unprepared for the tumultuous feelings that rocked him as he poked amid the rubble of the lab. Pederson was gone. Jeff had dealt with that fact in the eerie half-light of the hours after the fire. And he had dealt with the fact that but for the capriciousness of Roger Howell and the last-minute change in plans, he and Jeff too might have been ashes in the ruins.

What he had not dealt with and could not reconcile was that the work of a man's lifetime was gone. Every vestige of the work Pederson had devoted himself to and which had seemed so near to completion was lost, destroyed, literally up in smoke.

Meaningless adages had flitted through Jeff's brain as he kicked at the lumps of twisted metal and shards of glass and talked with an endless stream of investigators. Old sayings like "putting all your eggs in one basket" and "locking the barn door after the horse is stolen" came to mind time and time again. Stupid, maybe; trite definitely; but pitifully apt in the growing realization that Pederson's lifelong project was finished.

And it was, Jeff knew, finished. There was no way he or Howell could hope to reproduce what had died in the flames last night. Sure, he'd been privy to it, even formu-

lated 6BW himself on at least two occasions when he'd
had to, to save his clumsy skin. But his mind had been
elsewhere after those encounters with Alana, far from the
ratios before him. Even as collaborators, he thought, he
and Rog would be futile in an attempt to try to recreate
6BW.

Jeff toweled himself vigorously, splashed cologne on his
torso and inspected himself in the mirror. He was tall and
lean, broad-shouldered, slim-hipped. He tried to see himself through Nancy's eyes. Not bad, he decided. A certain
symmetry in the dark red mat of hair on his chest and in
the muscles of his thighs.

Now, as thoughts of Nancy caused a growing and swelling in the middle region of his mirrored image, Jeff was
thankful for this proof he was pulsingly alive. Damned if
he would die as Rolf Pederson had died, empty and, worst
of all, alone. They had a life to live, Jeff Kohner and his
Nancy. His work was just a part of his life.

He rummaged through the closet for his one gray suit,
his med-school graduation suit long neglected. He hoped
it would measure up to Scandia's elegance, and he promised himself on his next day off he would definitely shop
for new clothes. The least he could do was look reasonably
prosperous in the presence of the glamorous woman he
adored. Maybe, now that Pederson was gone, Jeff should
reconsider Fairfield's offer. Regular hours and decent pay.
What better way to start off a marriage? The eminent young
chemist and his famous bride. Jeff could almost see the
caption in the newspaper. Knotting his tie, he felt suddenly
foolish. He hadn't even asked her. He didn't really know
her. But soon . . .

While Jeff Kohner ruminated on his premature wedding
plans, Nancy fought her way through crosstown traffic. Zan
and Miriam Phillips prepared for their cruise, and in the
voice of Sister Althea there was a certain buoyant fillip as
she announced the impending visit by a TV personality to
an almost enthusiastic Kathleen Riley.

But when Karl Fredericks stepped into the balmy April

evening onto Wilshire Boulevard, there was nothing buoyant in his step. Jee*zus,* he muttered, Paul Fairfield's gone
crazy! Why in hell did I let myself go along this far?

He was hardly averse to a little business strategy when
necessary. He was well versed in financial chicanery, not
a stranger to bribery, and the phrase "conflict of interest"
never disturbed him. There was no doubt Paul Fairfield had
made him a wealthy man and a certain amount of loyalty
was called for. He had sweated through the blowup in the
Reese Fowler lab, before finally accepting it as necessary.
He could hardly stand by while his interests were threatened. In the end, he had even taken some satisfaction from
his ability to contract out the job. But now it seemed his
contacts had been sloppy. Pederson had been alone in the
lab when the blast occurred and Paul Fairfield was livid
with rage.

Fredericks had half expected the silver-haired doctor to
demand that Fredericks finish the job. Strangely enough,
Fairfield had demanded no such thing. To go after Howell
and Kohner was tempting fate.

"How much do they know, Karl?" asked the doctor as
his colleague sat, sweating, in a nest of crushed gray velvet. "You saw them in the lab that morning with Pederson.
Can they reproduce the stuff with the formula gone? How
much did they know about its properties?"

Fredericks racked his brain to remember. "I don't think
they knew—all there was to know about 6BW," he stammered finally. "They were overseers, recording test data.
I don't think they were collaborators in the true sense. I've
no idea whether either of them has ever actually formulated
the chemical."

He recalled something he had thought strange that morning with the grant committee in the lab. "When I brushed
off the significance of his project, Pederson could have
stopped me if he'd wanted to. He knew the conclusions I
would draw from his lab books. But he never mentioned
the word *cancer.* It was as though he didn't want to reveal
too much in front of his underlings." Fredericks grew em-

boldened by his own recollections. "I would swear they weren't privy to what Pederson knew."

Fairfield had nodded, pacing, lithe as a cat. "There's too much at stake here to gamble. We must proceed with caution—" He shot a look at Fredericks. "And with unfailing accuracy."

Fredericks had waited, hesitant to speak. There was a glint in Fairfield's eye he'd never seen before. No more murders, he pleaded in silence. I haven't the stomach for any more. The doctor smiled frostily at him, as though he were reading his thoughts. "It may not be necessary to kill them at all. Provided we keep tabs on their every move. Can you *handle* that, Karl? Can you inform your *friends* that every move they make must be reported?"

Fredericks nodded. "I think so," he said. "We'll know about it every time they pee."

"Not only every time they pee," retorted Fairfield. "But the color, the white-cell count and the alkalinity."

Fredericks nodded again. "I'll take care of it. No problem." He was grateful. He wanted to get out quickly.

But Fairfield stopped him. "One more thing."

Fredericks had closed his eyes and listened as the doctor had related with thinly veiled triumph his tentative deal with Judd Rohrbach. The newsman could be counted on to break the Metastaban story, but Rafferty must be removed from the public arena. Fredericks had broken out in new waves of sweat. Jesus! He couldn't mean permanently!

And once again, Fairfield had smiled at him coldly. "No, Karl. I'm not talking about murder." He outlined a plan that left Fredericks speechless. It required great speed and special skill. "I know I can rely upon your utmost efficiency and your talent for getting things done."

"I can't do that, it's impossible," Fredericks muttered at last. "I have neither the contacts nor the will."

"May I remind you," threatened his colleague smoothly, "that your skill in finding contacts has been admirable. And that should they be called upon to identify their employer, it is your name which will spring to their lips."

Fredericks paled with the realization that, in fact, the culpability was his. Nowhere in his dealings with the explosives expert had the name Paul Fairfield come up. The physician was right. Granted, the contact knew him as Fred. But Fred was disturbingly close to Fredericks. Should names be named, it was he, Karl Fredericks, who'd arranged the "accident." The stout man stood and stared at his mentor, trying to interpret his expression. But Fairfield's face was closed and there seemed no point in prolonging the awkward confrontation.

His choice was clear, thought Fredericks, lightheaded, as he walked a block up Wilshire to his car. He could go to the police and tell them what he'd done, implicating Fairfield in the scheme. With luck he might be able to secure some immunity in return for fingering Fairfield and the perpetrator. Or he could, as he knew Paul Fairfield expected, follow through in the hope they'd prevail. If the run on Metastaban were quickly engineered, the financial rewards would be staggering.

He slid his bulk behind the wheel of his cream-colored El Dorado. He hadn't come this far to contemplate prison as a final destination in his life. Better, he thought, to go for the prize—total freedom and financial security for the rest of his days. But time was short. He'd have to work fast. Christ, where the hell did he start?

The subject of Karl Fredericks' newest assignment fidgeted in a plush booth at Scandia. It was 7:55. Jeff wouldn't be late. Nancy knew that, but she chafed nonetheless.

She remembered how he'd looked as she left him this morning, asleep in her bed, red hair tousled. He'd looked innocent, vulnerable, yet he'd shown her his strength and his infinite capacity for tenderness. She needed to see him, to see in his eyes that their coming together as they had last night was more than just the frightened coupling of children blocking out the horrors of the night; that the healing they'd found in each other's arms was an affirmation of love.

More than that, she realized, sipping white wine, she was desperate to share with him what she'd learned; to test out her wild-eyed theories on him and to ask him some very pointed questions. She shifted in her seat, brushed a speck from her taupe knit dress and looked up to find Jeff smiling down at her. "Good morning," he greeted her, brushing warm lips against hers. "I didn't get to say that when the sun rose."

"Good morning." She smiled. "I'm sorry about that. You were dead to the world and I couldn't wake you."

"I probably should've stayed in bed. What a lousy day. The lab is a garbage heap. I couldn't salvage much of anything from it. God! I kept thinking about Pederson— what a way to end a life."

Nancy reached for his hand as he slid in beside her. "I know. Oh, Jeff, I know how you must feel."

"Thank God for you. The thought of you got me through the day." He grinned. "Not to mention the night."

"I think I must love you, Dr. Jeffrey Kohner. I simply had to see you last night. When it dawned on me you might have been in that lab—" She shuddered. "I had to see you, touch you." She leaned closer and kissed him thoroughly.

"I hope that's true. I want it to be true. I believe I've loved you from that first minute I saw you in the lab."

"Cocktail, sir?" The waiter appeared, setting menus before them.

"Champagne!" Jeff decided. "To celebrate . . . beginnings. Treasures from the rubble. Serendipity."

"Serendipity," murmured Nancy. "I'll drink to that. Good fortune when you least expect to find it."

They pored over the menu, teasing, debating, lovers needing to know each other's tastes. They both loved veal. She hated scallops. He was crazy about Roquefort dressing. Small things, unimportant things, catalogued and neatly filed away.

Once their orders were taken, Nancy became serious. "Jeff, there's so much I have to tell you! But first, a question: Do you remember the mice? The ones you isolated

from the control group? You showed me a rash—an eczema, you called it—that morning I met you in the lab.''

Jeff, gazing raptly into Nancy's green eyes, did his best
to seem attentive and intelligent. "I remember." He nodded. "They're the only survivors. They were in a holding
cage in another wing when the explosion—anyway, what
about them?''

"I know this seems silly, but it could be important. Did
you ever find a reason for the rash?''

"Not really. Reaction to the treatment, I guess. The eczema faded and the mice are fine.''

"You don't seem surprised that the mice are fine. What
were you treating them for, anyway?''

"Viral pneumonia. It was a routine experiment. The
6BW was, after all, a viral combatant.''

"And it killed the virus but it left a rash.''

Jeff shrugged. "Some sort of idiopathic reaction.''

Nancy's eyes were fixed on Jeff. "Did you ever test
6BW against cancer cells?''

"Cancer cells?" Jeff was puzzled. "Not that I know of.
Nancy, what on earth is all this about?''

"I discovered something interesting. Stevie Phillips had
a rash when he recovered from his bout with meningitis.
So did Maria Torres, Carmina's sister in Albuquerque—I
telephoned her this afternoon. She developed a rash when
the mono disappeared. And there were others who had the
same reaction. One of them is a doctor who recovered from
cancer—''

Jeff stopped her. "Nancy, what are you getting at?''

"All of these patients, at least the ones I've checked out,
made exactly the same kind of miraculous recovery as those
white mice in the lab. And all of them were left with the
same kind of rash: a mild, reddish eczema that soon
faded.''

Jeff shook his head. "I don't understand.''

Nancy fairly trembled with impatience. "It's as though
all these patients were treated identically—and reacted in

the same way as those mice. I'm asking if it's possible that 6BW was in some way responsible for their recoveries.''

"No," said Jeff. "Absolutely impossible. No patient ever had access to 6BW."

"The mice were injected."

"Yes," stated Jeff.

"And the patients weren't."

"No."

"But suppose the chemical was transmitted somehow without being injected?"

Jeff threw up his hands. "Nancy, what are you talking about?"

"I'm talking about Typhoid Mary!"

The waiter brought their salads. Nancy pushed hers aside. "Jeff, listen. Don't say anything. Just listen." She brought her hands up to her forehead as though to capture her thoughts, to make them gel. Finally she began, her face earnest, her voice barely above a whisper. "Point one," she said. "The 6BW is a synthetic protein not unlike interferon. Interferon, apart from its ability to attack a virus, is in the forefront as a tool against cancer. Therefore, it's possible—theoretically possible—that 6BW could cure cancer as well as a host of other diseases."

"Theoretically, yes," Jeff began, "but—"

Nancy put a finger to his lips. "Point two," she said. "A virus can travel in the atmosphere, attacking its victims haphazardly. If a virus can do that, why not its antidote? Let's assume 6BW can float as well, randomly attacking the virus—in some cases, even cancer cells."

Jeff started to speak but Nancy silenced him again. "Please, Jeff, just let me finish. Afterward, you can tell me I'm crazy as a loon, but right now . . . just hear me out. Point three," she continued without a pause, "there are many known carriers of disease. A.I.D.S. is an extreme example, but certainly many people who never show signs of disease are capable of transmitting it to others. If we accept that as proven medical fact, then it is equally feasible that some healthy people could be carriers of the antidote 6BW. That would explain how the serendipitous cure found its way all over the world.''

Jeff found himself intrigued against his will. Nancy's theory almost began to make sense. His awe of this unpredictable woman grew.

"Point four," said Nancy, growing more confident. "Epileptic patients who are treated with anti-convulsants often suffer similar side effects. If we find that a substantial number of those patients who recovered as a result of exposure to 6BW exhibited a similar side effect—in this case a mild, reddish rash—then we have to accept the remote possibility that they were treated with the very same drug.'' She drew back and smiled at Jeff, a lopsided grin. "Granting that all of this is purely theoretical, are you with me, at least so far?''

Jeff stared at her, fascinated. "I guess so, sure. Though how the stuff would float is beyond me.'' He gazed at her with new respect. "How you got this far is amazing.''

"Easy," she said, reaching for her salad. "I spent all morning in the library. Now, I'm hungry.'' She picked up a fork. "So you don't think I'm certifiably crazy?''

"Not crazy." He kissed her. "A little far out. But no more so than this whole crazy syndrome.''

"That's exactly what Dr. Hillman said. That it's possible. But he didn't kiss me.''

"I'm glad." Jeff paused as a new thought struck. "I wonder if Pederson suspected.''

"Suspected what?''

"That 6BW is conceivably effective against cancer.'' Frowning, he looked at her and set down his fork.

"What?''

"Nah, forget it. It's crazy.''

"We just decided nothing's crazy. What flitted through your handsome head just then?''

"That shortly after the last stage of the experiment was begun, Pederson began acting funny. He'd shut himself up in his office for hours, poring over the lab books. I wonder

if he'd proven something that he hadn't let Rog and me in
on.''

"Such as?" asked Nancy.

"Such as the salient fact that 6BW was effective against
cancer cells.''

"How would he know that?''

"From studying the mice. Some might have recovered
from cancer.''

"But,'' said Nancy, "you just told me you were treating
them for viral pneumonia.''

"We were. But possibly for cancer too—even if Rog and
I didn't know it. See, when mice are bred for lab experiments, they're bred for a variety of diseases. If you're testing a measles vaccine, you buy mice who are infected with
measles. To test a polio vaccine, you order mice bred for
polio. It's easy enough to check whether Pederson ever
requested cancerous mice. All I have to do is call the
breeder.'' He ran his hand quickly through his hair as he
realized the implications of the tests he'd been conducting
for so long.

"Do it," said Nancy. "If Pederson knew what he had
in 6BW, there's a chance someone else knew it, too.''

"You mean,'' said Jeff, after a long moment, "whoever
blew up the lab.''

Nancy nodded, her face grave. "Whoever blew up the
lab.''

The salads were replaced by veal *cordon bleu.* Jeff stared
at it as though it were a foreign substance. "I still don't
understand why anyone would set out to destroy what could
be a cure for cancer.''

"That's because you're too noble, love. Noble and
idealistic. There are those who'd see it as an incalculable
threat.'' Nancy tasted the veal. "Don't you know what a
cancer cure would mean?''

"Of course. A lot of saved lives.''

"And a lot of lost revenue to doctors. Hospitals. Even
Dr. Hillman sees that. Everyone connected with the treatment of cancer stands to lose a whole lot of income. That

includes pharmaceuticals, chemotherapy—'' Nancy stopped, cocked her head.

"What's the matter?"

"Hm? Nothing, just thinking. . . ."

Jeff grimaced. "So I'm idealistic, among my other failings. What do you see in a guy like me?"

"Only the most caring human being I ever met. I cherish that. Don't ever change." A long moment passed, each drinking in the other. "God, I love you, Nancy," Jeff said softly.

"Then order dessert. I hate to say this, but I have to be back at the studio in half an hour. . . . Jeff, will you wait for me back at my place?"

"For lack of a better offer, I will wait for you forever. Or till midnight, whichever comes first."

Nancy spooned up chocolate mousse. "Yummy. But I really have to go."

"I'll watch the broadcast, then. At your place. Don't waste a minute getting home."

"I won't." She gave him a key. "Jeff—be careful."

"What on earth is that supposed to mean?"

"I don't know. Just that I love you." And then she insisted on paying the check. "Please, just this once, my treat. After all, it was I who made this date."

She rose quickly, kissed him on the forehead, smoothed back his hair, and strode through the crowded restaurant. How could she tell him what she feared most of all? That whoever blew up the lab might come back for him. It would never occur to him. But perhaps she was being too dramatic. . . .

Chapter Seven

For Judd Rohrbach, the evening had gone as smoothly as if it had played from a script. He had spent the better part of the afternoon culling through the material on Metastaban. By early evening he had put together a dynamic narrative on the drug. It bordered on the sensational, he was well aware, but it was guaranteed to arouse interest. At ten P.M., fully made up, he forced himself to concentrate on the hard news stories slated for the late-night broadcast.

By ten-thirty Nancy Rafferty had not yet checked into the building. From his cubicle across the hall, Judd could see Callahan pacing his glass-enclosed office, peering distractedly out the fifth-floor window and chewing on antacid tablets. Once or twice he picked up the telephone and then resumed his pacing.

Finally at ten-forty, a pimply-faced kid in a jogging suit and a battered Dodgers cap knocked on Callahan's door. He handed the producer a yellow envelope and trotted down the hall toward the elevators. Without knowing why, Judd grew excited. Moments later, as Judd bent studiously over his script, Callahan appeared in his doorway. The producer did not look happy. "Jesus," he said, "I don't believe this." He tossed a flimsy sheet of yellow paper onto the anchorman's desk. "Nancy's on vacation. As of now."

Judd read the cryptic telegraphed message. "Too much pressure. Need few days off. Don't worry. Will phone. Rafferty."

Judd suppressed a smile. "Sounds just like her. She always was impulsive."

"Maybe," muttered Callahan. "But hardly irresponsible." He ran a hand through his thinning hair. "I don't know what the hell it's all about, but can you handle the eleven o'clock alone?"

"Oh, I'll try." Judd fought to keep the sarcasm from his voice. "Actually, it may be prophetic. I've a bit of good news to present myself tonight." He extracted a thin folder from a file drawer. "An announcement about a cancer drug. Could be big. Here— Care to check it out?"

"No time." The producer jammed his fists in his pockets. "You're due in the studio. Forget it."

The newscaster shrugged, returned to the files and began to replace the folder.

"Did you check it out?"

"What am I, an amateur?"

Callahan paused. "Use it."

The phone was ringing in Nancy's apartment as Jeff Kohner let himself in. By the time he found it and picked up the receiver, he only heard a disconnecting click. Shrugging, he turned on the television set and settled himself on the sofa. He counted four commercials and a public-service announcement before Rohrbach's face flashed on the screen. Jeff frowned, puzzled. Where was Nancy? She always opened the broadcast.

The anchorman's face was customarily smooth, his expression both earnest and appealing. "Good evening, Los Angeles. This is Judd Rohrbach speaking. Welcome to KBLA News."

Jeff sat through the headlines, leaning forward in his seat until finally the announcement came. It was brief, almost glib, and the impact sent Jeff's heart plunging to his shoes. "Nancy Rafferty's on vacation tonight, but don't despair of good news. I'll be back in a moment with tonight's top stories—and hope for the end of an age-old killer."

The picture dissolved to a commercial for beer. Jeff,

galvanized, sprinted for the phone. In minutes, he was connected to the KBLA newsroom. The receiver was picked up at once. "Newsroom, Callahan," came the response.

"Where's Nancy Rafferty?" Jeff blurted.

A slight pause. "Who's calling, please?"

"Jeff Kohner. A friend. Where's Nancy?"

Disappointment came through in the man's voice. "On vacation." The syllables were clipped.

"Wait!" Jeff shouted. "Don't hang up. She can't be on vacation. I just left her."

A small hesitation. "When was that?"

"I had dinner with her an hour ago."

The disembodied voice held a note of uncertainty. "An hour ago. Who'd you say this is?"

"Jeff Kohner, dammit, I'm a doctor and a friend and I just had dinner with her at Scandia!" There was no response. "Who is this, anyway? Who the hell am I talking to?"

"Ty Callahan, the producer. And in my hand is a telegram from Nancy saying that she needs a few days off. Now, if you can—"

"Hold on. I'll be right there."

Callahan heard a click at the other end.

Judd Rohrbach had decided, with a showman's instinct, to save the Metastaban story for the end of the broadcast. In the first place, he had no wish to emulate Rafferty. Hard news belonged at the top. In the second place, he reasoned, Metastaban as a tag story would assuredly have greater impact. The phones would be ringing before he was off the air. He wanted to be there to answer them.

Karl Fredericks, his face florid, refilled his guest's brandy snifter. "I've been assured the matter will be handled," he said. "Let's hope your friend Rohrbach comes through." He seated himself in his favorite chair. For a moment, the onus was not on him.

Paul Fairfield, his eyes never leaving the small screen,

inhaled the bouquet of the brandy. He began to relax at the moment when Judd Rohrbach's face became the first to appear on the screen. He smiled broadly at the brief announcement of Nancy Rafferty's vacation. At 11:23, when Rohrbach promised to be back in a moment with a medical breakthrough of unparalleled significance, Fairfield slapped his knee and stood up.

His face was inches from the screen when the Metastaban story broke. It was perfect. He could not have done it better. He allowed himself a triumphant shout. "By God, I've got to give the man credit!"

"Professional," Karl Fredericks agreed and stared at Fairfield in wonder. The man was positively manic.

"We're on our way," said Fairfield, his eyes blazing. "Provided your friends follow through. We'll come in tomorrow night with Kathleen Riley's case history; and before anyone can question the validity of Metastaban, there'll be a run on it the likes of which you've never seen! A fortune!" He smoothed back his silver hair.

"A fortune," murmured Fredericks, feeling a little ill.

"Cheers!" Paul Fairfield lifted his glass. "Now you can keep a goddamned harem in the south-sea isles!"

Mary Fredericks chose that moment to tap lightly on the door of the study. "Karl?" she asked. "May I interrupt?"

Karl Fredericks opened the door.

"I just heard the news," she said from the doorway, her plain face registering wonder. "Metastaban. Isn't that one of Camthon's?"

"It is," answered her husband, surprising her with a hug. "Please forgive me for letting you hear about it this way. You know how the pharmaceutical industry is. There are more secrets stolen from within each house than there are from Balenciaga's drawing boards. I didn't dare leak the news—even to you—until the thing had gone public."

"I quite understand." His wife smiled sweetly. "How wonderful you've been able to have a hand in it! Well"— she retreated back into the hall—"I just wanted to congratulate you. I'll leave you alone."

"Notice the awe in your own wife's face, Karl." Fairfield clapped his friend on the back. "Multiply that by a millionfold. That's the response this will cause. By tomorrow, Metastaban will be a household word."

A prickle of fear pierced the ebullience Karl Fredericks was beginning to share. "Of course— Well, hell, we've been over this before. . . ."

"What?" mocked Fairfield, his blue eyes glinting. "That Metastaban isn't all that it could be? Come now, Karl, it's a new hope for cancer—the drug that started the syndrome! It's offered in good faith on the basis of limited success. No one's been promised a panacea. And I'll tell you something, Karl. You want to see serendipity? You watch gullibility in action!"

Fredericks flinched at the mention of the word, but his mentor plunged ahead. "You'll see serendipity like Nancy Rafferty never dreamed. People will fall all over themselves to believe they're cured. Perhaps a few of them will be, at that. After all, Metastaban is chemotherapeutic."

"One thing's certain," Fredericks mused. "They'll never trace the syndrome to 6BW." He felt a little better. Only one thing niggled at him. He hesitated now to bring it up.

Fairfield cannily did it for him. "What's past is past," he said. "It had to be done to get this far—and you've handled your end splendidly."

"There was that slipup," Fredericks said.

"If you're right about Kohner's ignorance, it shouldn't matter. So long as there are no further slipups . . ." The physician pointedly stopped in mid-sentence.

Fredericks lifted his brandy with a trembling hand. For the first time in years, he prayed.

Jeff Kohner didn't hear the Metastaban story break. While Judd Rohrbach, with restrained excitement, recounted the unveiling of a wonder drug, the red-haired young doctor was breaking speed limits as he raced to KBLA.

Inside the building, it took every bit of restraint Jeff could muster to keep himself from punching the security guard. The elderly guard was not about to admit him without an okay from upstairs, and Callahan, flooded with incoming phone calls, could not be reached to give the okay.

When he finally bolted into the newsroom, it was minutes before he could speak. Callahan, or someone he assumed to be Callahan, spoke into two phones at once. The only other man in the newsroom was Rohrbach—who was similarly occupied.

Jeff approached the older man. "Callahan? I'm Jeff Kohner."

The harried producer glanced at Kohner and continued his dual conversation. "Yeah," he bellowed into the mouthpiece on his right. "Just remember you heard it here first." He slammed down the receiver, waved a beefy hand at Kohner and spoke into the mouthpiece on his left. "Yes, you heard it right. It'll be released through Associated Press by morning. Yeah, well, it pays to have sources." He hung up the phone, extended a hand. "Callahan," he managed to say as the phone rang.

"Jesus, Rohrbach, handle it, will ya? I gotta see this guy—it won't take long. Call Sarah. Tell her we need a few extra bodies. And Rohrbach—you better have this straight."

Callahan ushered Jeff out the door, pointed to an office across the hall. Neither he nor Jeff saw the look of venom which passed across the anchorman's face.

"Now, what the hell is this?" Callahan began without preamble. "Here's the wire. Read it yourself." He seated himself in a worn leather chair and watched the young man read the message.

Jeff shook his head. "I don't know who sent this. It wasn't Nancy. She was on her way back here at ten."

"What makes you so sure?" Callahan indicated a chair. "How do you know? Did she tell you?"

"Christ!" Jeff exploded, ignoring the chair. "I told you we had dinner at Scandia!"

"So you said. What'd she say when she left?"

"She was on her way here to the studio! She gave me her key!" He tossed it on the desk. "She asked me to wait for her at her apartment! She was coming here to do the show and then she was coming home!"

Callahan looked skeptical. New boyfriend? Since when? "She gave you the key to her apartment?"

"Yeah," said Jeff, color rising in his cheeks, "we're—good friends. She asked me to wait for her."

"So you turned on the TV and made yourself comfy, and then you found out that she split."

"She didn't split, goddammit, Callahan! I'm telling you she was on her way here!"

"What the hell are you yelling at me for? I'm just as bamboozled as you are!"

"Then do something, dammit!" Jeff paced the small room. "Maybe she had an accident."

"She carries ID. We would have heard. She's not exactly unknown."

"Check with the hospitals anyway," Jeff suggested. "Maybe we ought to call the cops."

"For what? To report her as a missing person? I got a wire here says she's on vacation!"

"She didn't send it!"

"That's what you say. No cop's gonna take a report. And I'll tell you something—" Callahan paused. "It's not like her, but I can almost buy it. She has been under a lot of pressure; she's been putting in long hours ever since this serendipity thing; she's tired. She needed a rest."

"She loves every minute of it, Callahan, don't you know that? She thrives on the challenge—and the pressure! She's been knocking her brains out to put this syndrome mystery together. She'd never run off! Not now!" He turned away to compose his face, but the older man saw his expression.

Callahan sighed, rubbed a hand over his eyes. Outside, the phones kept ringing. "Look," he said finally, "I don't know anything about your relationship with Nancy. But it wouldn't be the first time a girl decided to split before she got in over her head.''

Jeff turned back with such worry in his eyes that the producer reconsidered. ''Hey,'' he said a little more sympathetically. ''I got work to do out there. Maybe she'll call in by morning.''

''Yeah,'' said Jeff. He was unconvinced. ''Call me if you hear something, will you?'' He scribbled his home number and the hospital's on a scratch pad.

''Same here. Jesus Christ, whatta night. . . .''

Chapter Eight

Zan Phillips lay back on his deck chair and gazed up into the sky. Azure, he thought. No, maybe cerulean. He watched a cloud scud across his line of vision. Opalescence on aquamarine, he decided, and it did not surprise him that he lay in the sunlight seeing through the eyes of a poet.

He felt whole, he realized, as finely wrought as that scudding cloud and all of a piece with the sun and the sky and the air and the mist that formed it. He turned his head to look at Miriam, asleep beside him at the edge of the saltwater swimming pool. Her skin seemed iridescent where a fine salt sheen clung, sundried, to her limbs. She was happy, he knew. But he wondered if she felt the same suffusion of perfect peace that threatened to spill from his pores. He hoped she did. He could never explain how he felt, even with the voice of a poet.

He shifted his weight, the better to memorize the long, slim form of her body. He wanted to make love to her here on the deck, to taste the salt on her skin. But he could wait, he decided, smiling, with a pleasurable surge of anticipation. Their lovemaking now was better than it had been even in the first flush of their youth. They had somehow lost touch—and now had regained it, the more precious for its having eluded them. It was as though, having come separately through this miracle with Stevie, they yearned to share the deepest parts of themselves.

Zan raised one shoulder and gazed out to sea. What color

would he call it? Sapphire. Then he lay back and closed his eyes. He felt he knew the meaning of bliss.

Sister Althea rose from her seat as the crowded bus rolled to a stop. The people in the aisle parted to make way for her and she stifled her annoyance. It was the habit, of course, that set her apart. As if she needed a reminder! She stepped down gingerly, smiling her thanks, color rising in her cheeks. She felt like a fraud, a compliant puppet. She did not deserve their respect.

Lately, she moved about like a stranger at the convent, acutely uncomfortable among the Sisters. Surely they read in her eyes, in her voice, the pain that had come to haunt her. Yet, they kept to themselves as she went through the motions, and she felt herself slipping away.

Michael, dear Michael, remained true to his word at their regular casework conferences. If he sensed her turmoil—and she knew he must—he was careful not to tip the balance. In fact, he had moved all their conferences from his office to the all-purpose coffee room. There, in the presence of chatting coworkers, it was easy to maintain a neutral atmosphere. But his presence was at once a comfort and a threat. She needed his warmth and yet she feared it. And in being with the others at the office, she'd realized something else: a part of her longed for their world.

What was so wrong with wanting to be like them, those others who flirted and laughed? They gave to each other a sense of worth, of encouragement and commitment to their work. There was no one at the convent to argue with Althea, nor to understand her failures and her triumphs. Only there, with Michael and his friends, did she feel that special sense of belonging.

She had not sinned in her feeling for Michael. She knew that now with certainty. And she'd gone to confession with a curious absence of guilt. She found herself asking questions she had every right to ask about who she really was and what it was she wanted. If she'd missed the mark at all, it was in waiting so long before she'd ever forced herself to ask them. Not that this made the burden any lighter. She was trapped in a sea of indecision. She had rarely made a choice in her life, and she was light-years away from making this one.

The crepe myrtle trees along the avenue where she walked were starbursts of pink and white blossoms. But Althea felt none of the pure, childlike joy she once might have found in their beauty. Michael was right. She had been a child when she took her vows at the convent. She had been a child just days ago when she offered to bargain with God. It had always been so easy to trust others to wash away the stains of her guilt—and such a comfort to feel new and clean like Stevie in his just-washed jeans. But someday, even little Stevie would learn to stay out of the mud. Althea wondered if she'd ever learn to trust herself to do what was right.

She paused at the entrance to Sunnyvale Clinic and tried to clear her head. It took every ounce of her strength to endure these daily visits with her mother. The older woman was a source of constant complaint. But today, Althea remembered, there was company coming. She hoped that Nancy Rafferty's visit would provide a pleasant change.

What was it Miss Rafferty had said about a rash? Althea must remember to ask her mother.

She continued up the red brick walkway. The door was opened as she neared it. Miss Norton greeted her with a dazzling smile, her perfect brows more highly arched than ever. "Sister Althea." Her voice was a song. "I was hoping you'd be right on time today!"

"I'm here at this same time every afternoon. Is my mother— Is everything all right?"

"Oh, yes," chirped Miss Norton, her dark eyes glittering. "Mother's just fine. I'm so sorry. I didn't mean to alarm you. It's just that Mother's going to have a visitor. She's going to be on television! Isn't that exciting?"

"Television? You mean Nancy Rafferty? She didn't say a word about filming her."

"Not Nancy Rafferty. The other one, Judd Rohrbach. Dr. Fairfield was going to try to reach you."

Althea frowned. "Judd Rohrbach? Why? What does Dr. Fairfield have to do with it?"

Miss Norton beamed. "It seems he's cured your mother with a wonderful new drug! You haven't heard? Mr. Rohrbach announced it on his show last night."

"No," said the nun. "I didn't hear. What's the name of this drug?" She regarded Miss Norton suspiciously.

"Metastaban!" The word rolled grandly off Miss Norton's tongue. "It's a wonder drug. Finally, a cure for cancer!"

Metastaban. Althea recalled Dr. Fairfield's mentioning that. But it wasn't what Miss Rafferty had referred to. Where was Miss Rafferty? She'd said she would be here. Althea began to feel uneasy.

She walked past Miss Norton into the elegant foyer. "How does Mother feel about all this?"

"Well," crooned the woman, "you know how she can be. I'm afraid she's been—a little testy."

"Then," said the nun, "I'll see her right away. Please don't admit anyone unless I tell you to."

Mrs. Riley was more than testy. She shrieked at the sight of her daughter. "Althea, thank the Lord! I thought you'd never come! What is this nonsense about television?"

Althea sighed. "Please, Mother, stay calm. I'm here, and we'll sort it all out."

Mrs. Riley was not to be calmed. "I simply don't understand it! First Dr. Fairfield tells me I'm sick; that I have to stay in this place. Now he tells me I am cured after all and he wants me to say so on television! I don't want to go on television. I look horrid, simply horrid! If I'm well, then why can't I just go home?"

"You don't have to go on television if you don't want to. I can promise you that much," soothed Althea.

"My hair's falling out. I told you it would!" Mrs. Riley lay back, pouting, on her pillows. "It's all that radiation and chemotherapy. Please, I just want to go home."

Althea looked at her mother's ravaged face, at the patchy bald spots on her scalp. In some ways, she looked worse than she had when she'd come here. "Mother," she said, "I want to ask you something. Have you ever, either here or when you were at Reese Fowler, had any kind of a rash?"

"A rash?" Mrs. Riley's tone was wary. "Why are you asking me that?"

"Because," explained her daughter, "it could be important. Have you had any kind of a rash?"

"Well . . . yes." Her mother's voice was small. "I suppose you could call it that. It was very itchy and I didn't want to tell you or you'd never have agreed to take me home. It only lasted a day or two anyway. Dr. Fairfield said it was nothing."

"I'm sure it wasn't anything," Althea said. But her growing uneasiness startled her.

Miss Norton knocked twice and held the door ajar. "Excuse me, ladies. Time to get ready. Mr. Rohrbach and his camera crew are here."

Mrs. Riley burrowed under the covers. "Make them go away. I won't see them!" she shouted.

Miss Norton approached the side of the bed. "Come now, Mrs. Riley, I'll get you all fixed up. You're going to look just fine!"

"No!" came the muffled response from underneath the sheets.

Althea heard voices out in the corridor, the impatient shuffling of feet. When a loud knock sounded at the door, she clenched her fists tightly. She wavered for a moment, but only for a moment. She didn't want to make Dr. Fairfield angry; still, there had been something urgent in Miss Rafferty's tone—she had promised her mother.

Steeling herself, she went to the door, opened it and faced Judd Rohrbach. "I'm sorry," she told him as forthrightly as she could manage. "There will be no pictures today."

Rohrbach smiled his most ingratiating smile. "You're mistaken. Dr. Fairfield arranged it."

"Dr. Fairfield made a mistake. He should have checked with me first."

Rohrbach chuckled. "Excuse me, Sister." He tried to edge his way past her.

Althea stood her ground. She placed her hands firmly on the door frame. "I'm afraid it is you who doesn't understand. I'm Mrs. Riley's daughter and I forbid it."

Rohrbach hesitated, his face mottling. "I think you will regret this, Sister."

"We'll see," replied the nun, pulse thundering in her ears. She closed the door firmly and leaned against it.

"I don't think that was a wise idea," Miss Norton broke the silence.

Althea turned to glare at her. Her mother stared, shocked at the display of strength she had just seen in her daughter. Althea had stood her ground, though she had half expected the six-foot Rohrbach to lift her up and set her aside.

I did it, Althea thought. She stifled a giggle. I actually threw him out!

Jeff Kohner paced the makeshift lab. He slammed a fist against a countertop. A stack of glass slides jumped and scattered with an oddly musical sound.

"Hey, man." Roger Howell looked up from his microscope. "No need to take it out on me."

"Sorry," said Jeff. He continued to pace. "Goddammit, what the hell do I do?"

Roger placed a new slide on the stage of the scope. "Nothin' you can do. The Man said wait."

"Wait!" Jeff spat. "That's a hell of a note. She's missing and nobody cares!"

"The law's the law," responded Roger, peering down. "Nobody's a missing person for forty-eight hours. Then, of course, there's that wire she sent."

"That wire's full of shit! She didn't send it!"

"Maybe, maybe not," Roger allowed. "If she didn't, you got any idea who did?"

"No. Wait a minute. Maybe . . . I don't know." Jeff

picked up Roger's copy of the *Times*. "Hell of a coincidence this Metastaban story breaks on the same night Nancy disappears. . . ."

"Metastaban story? What's that got to do with anything?"

Jeff hesitated. "Rog, I'm gonna level with you." He pulled up a stool alongside his colleague's. "See, Nancy had this crazy idea. She was working on the angle that the serendipity syndrome was started by Pederson's 6BW."

Roger looked squarely at his friend. "You're right, man, that's a crazy idea."

"Maybe not so crazy. Listen to this." Slowly, painstakingly, Jeff outlined to Roger the four points Nancy made that night at Scandia. He finished with the most important point: Nancy'd found a common side effect in patients who may have been affected—a benign reddish rash, probably idiopathic, that surfaced after exposure to 6BW.

Jeff watched his friend's guarded expression change from boredom to incredulity to speculation. "No shit," exclaimed Roger at last.

"No shit." Jeff smiled. "Think it over. Okay, I admit it's a little far out, but there's so much we don't know about the virus. Granting that, it's not so tough to accept this as a theoretical possibility."

Roger put his elbows on the counter, cupped his chin in his hands. "Theoretical is right, my friend."

"There's more. Listen to this. Nancy thinks that somebody else came up with the very same theory. That whoever it is has a lot to lose if 6BW is a wonder drug. And that somebody—somebody with a lot on the line—blew up the Reese Fowler lab."

"Aw, come on, man! What the hell is this, some kind of Ludlum thriller?"

Jeff ignored that. "Listen, Rog. Something started the syndrome. The lab blows sky-high, Pederson is gone and so is the formula for 6BW. On top of that, Nancy disappears—and suddenly, up pops a cancer killer. Metastaban, Rog! You know what that is—a lousy little chemotherapeutic! But if all this publicity about it being a cancer killer flies, Camthon is gonna make a fortune!''

"Camthon," said Roger. "That's your suspect. Good, man, that's really good. You charging out there in your Superman suit, accusing a giant like Camthon of a few indiscretions like arson? Murder? Maybe kidnapping? Not to mention fraud?''

"Maybe," said Jeff. "Yeah, it occurred to me. If I can find a way to prove it.''

"Prove it. Right. How you gonna do that? With the magic wand or the crystal ball?''

"Neither. We'll take it a step at a time." He grabbed a notepad and began to make a list. "But not here. My place. Can you be there at seven?''

Roger deliberated. "Yeah.''

Judd Rohrbach phoned Fairfield from the privacy of Miss Norton's office. "Goddamned nun won't let us in the room.''

"Really?" replied Fairfield, mildly annoyed. "What happened to your unfailing charm?''

"Screw charm," said Rohrbach. "She's a nun for Chrissakes. What do you want me to do? Seduce her?''

"Hardly," replied the doctor. "Leave it to me. Mrs. Riley is my patient, not the Sister.''

"Yeah, well, you'll have to get past the Sister first. And that is one tough little nun.''

The description hardly fit the twittering little nun Fairfield had dealt with more than once. He could undoubtedly overcome her resistance but time, of course, was of the essence. "Listen," he commanded. "I want Riley's story to be aired on *your* broadcast tonight. We need living proof that Metastaban works. Run it without the film footage.''

Chapter Nine

Nancy Rafferty had no idea when the night had ended and the day had begun. It disgusted her to realize that she must have blacked out at some point after it happened. She, the intrepid big-city reporter, had swooned at the sight of a gun! She must have fainted, because she had no recollection of the journey from Sunset Boulevard to—wherever she was. She faced her captors filled with self-loathing at how much trouble she had saved them.

Last night the parking attendant had brought her car around while she waited at the entrance to Scandia. She had climbed into the yellow bug, maneuvered onto the crowded boulevard and turned right at her first opportunity to avoid the bulk of traffic. She had barely come to a halt at the Stop sign when she felt herself grasped from behind. Big hands clamped over her eyes and she'd been dragged backward over the seat.

Her head smacked the roof, and the steering wheel grazed a painful path over her abdomen and thighs. She felt breathless and weightless like an old rag doll, too stunned and frightened to scream. Then she found herself plunged into the minuscule rear seat, her face buried deep in the upholstery. Doors slammed; there was a jerking shift of gears; and the Volkswagen bucked forward. By the time she'd recovered her senses enough to struggle, powerful arms pinned her motionless. Cramped and pinioned, she remembered wondering how two grown people could possibly have concealed themselves in the ridiculously small backseat.

She ceased her struggle, suddenly fearful that she might suffocate in her own upholstery. She let herself go limp, turned her head and tried to concentrate on breathing. The big hands relaxed their grip and helped her to a sitting position. "That's better," she heard a growling voice. "Take it easy and you won't get hurt."

She looked at last at her assailant but his face, in the darkness, was grotesque. He was wearing a stocking mask, she realized. "Who are you?" she managed to ask.

"A friend of a friend."

"What do you want?"

The voice lapsed into silence.

She tried to peer over the seat at the driver. Surely, he wasn't wearing a mask. She felt something jab sharply at her side. She looked down and saw the revolver. Her eyes widened, she tried to speak, saw the gun lifted slowly to her face. It was at that point that she'd fainted, she supposed.

When she came to, she was tightly blindfolded, propped up in the backseat of a car. She moaned. Her head hurt, her body felt bruised, and visions of the terrifying incident flooded back to her. She had no idea how long they'd been driving. She was ashamed of herself for passing out. If she'd been able to keep her wits about her, she might have some idea where she was.

"What time is it?" she ventured finally.

"Sorry. You missed your telecast."

So they knew who she was! She was not a random victim. "They'll be looking for me, then. Don't you know that?"

"Maybe." The voice was noncommittal. "Doesn't matter, you won't be gone long."

The information was welcome relief. "How long? What do you want? Ransom?"

A cold laugh. "Long enough. And no, Miss Rafferty, no ransom."

Nancy frowned a painful grimace, the blindfold taut against her skin. If not for ransom, then why? she wondered. But she knew it was pointless to ask. She eventually must have dozed, lulled into sleep by the motion of the car. She was jolted awake when they rolled to a stop. The engine stopped with a familiar shudder. She knew they were still in her car. Then she heard a thumping behind her. It sounded for all the world like a garage door closing, and it now seemed darker through her blindfold. "Home, sweet home?" she mused aloud. There was, as she expected, no answer.

She was led from the car up two short steps, felt her way along with a free hand. Was that a washer? Cold, square porcelain. A laundry room? A few more steps. Her hand flailed, felt nothing. She felt herself backed into a chair. The blindfold came off. The light hurt her eyes and she was amazed to realize it was daylight.

She found herself in a sunny kitchen, not unlike her mother's in Omaha. It was very clean, cheerfully wallpapered and there was a bowl of silk flowers on the table. She squinted at the still blurred faces of the two men in stocking masks.

"Where are we?" she asked.

"Home, sweet home, as you said."

She scrutinized her captors. The taller one, barrel-chested and slim-hipped, was the one who had spoken. She knew from his voice he'd also been the one who'd sat with her in the backseat of the car. The other one, the driver, was no taller than she. He was poking around in the refrigerator. He gestured at her with a can of orange juice. Nancy shook her head. The gesture and her response were so typically domestic, it almost made Nancy want to laugh.

"Make yourself at home," the shorter one said, as though she were there by choice. "Bathroom's down the hall if you want to use it—second door on the left."

Nancy sat for a moment, attuning her ear to the sound of the garbled words. She wondered if she were going to be allowed to go alone or whether one of them would accompany her down the hall. But when she rose and took her first unsteady steps, neither of them made a move to come after her.

The bathroom, too, had the look of home: pink-tiled, and stocked with fresh towels. She tried the window. It wouldn't budge. She used the facilities and washed her hands and face, the traces of makeup she left on the towels strangely reassuring her this was real. She returned to the kitchen and, not knowing what else to do, took her place at the table.

The smaller man nodded at her as though she'd done well. "There's grapefruit juice too," he offered. "And Coke." His casual tone and polite hospitality served to heighten Nancy's feeling of absurdity. "Thanks," she muttered, and, playing along, "What are the chances for some coffee?"

"Of course!" the little man replied at once and busied himself with a percolator. It was clear he knew his way around the kitchen. "Do you live here?" Nancy asked.

"The house belongs to a friend. Coffee will be ready in a jiffy."

"You know my name, but I don't know yours." Nancy paused. "What am I supposed to call you?"

The taller man, lounging against a counter, said, "Why don't you call me Bonnie? My friend here, you can call him Clyde. That's it. Bonnie and Clyde." Neither man laughed, and it was impossible to tell, through the stocking masks, whether they were smiling.

"Well then, Bonnie," Nancy pushed on, "thank you for your gunpoint hospitality."

"Sorry about the gun. It was just to keep you quiet. If you behave, you won't need to see it again."

"Thanks. That's comforting." She tried to sound confident. "How, exactly, shall I behave?"

Clyde lowered the flame under the coffeepot. "Just enjoy yourself and relax. Be our guest."

Nancy was exasperated. "Enjoy myself? How can I?

I'm your captive! I wasn't exactly invited here, and I certainly didn't come because I wanted to!''

"No, you didn't," Clyde replied. "But it will be my pleasure to make you comfortable.''

Nancy's confusion was now complete. She struggled to reconcile the manner of these men with the brutes who had accosted her in her car. "Why am I here?" she blurted. "When can I go home? What is it you want if not ransom?''

"Kind of silly to ask for ransom," said Bonnie, "when nobody even knows you're missing." He calmly flipped through the magazine he was holding.

"How can you say that? I missed my telecast last night. And I won't be at the studio today. Plenty of people will know I'm missing. They're probably looking for me now.''

"You're on vacation," Clyde said simply, as though she had somehow forgotten. "You're tired and you need a few days' rest. You explained all that in your telegram.''

"Telegram?" Nancy rose from her seat. "What are you talking about?''

"The telegram you sent your boss." Clyde took a mug from a cupboard and carefully poured her coffee. "You told him you'd call—and so you shall—as soon as we think you can handle it.''

Nancy sat tongue-tied, the comforting smell of the coffee overpowering her anger and confusion. The whole thing was obviously well thought out and she decided to try to stay calm. "If you don't want ransom, then you want something else. Why don't you tell me what it is, and if it's something I can do, I promise you I will. Then maybe we can all go home.''

"Wrong," growled Bonnie, sitting across from her. "We don't want you to do a thing. That's why you're here. No more questions. Drink your coffee. Okay?''

Nancy took the steaming cup and sipped gratefully while she thought. Who in the world would want her kidnapped and why, without ransom or demands? Who had the foresight to send a telegram to cover up the fact that she was missing?

She wondered if Callahan would buy the idea that she'd sent him a wire and taken off. Could he possibly think she was that unprofessional? That she thought so little of her work? And what about Jeff? Where did he think she was? He'd been waiting last night at her apartment! Unless, of course—the thought was chilling—he'd had visitors waiting for him outside of Scandia, too!

She sipped the coffee, trying hard to keep her features expressionless. But her brain was electrified with the growing realization that she was here because of what she'd told Jeff. Someone else shared her hypothesis, her "theoretical possibilities." Whoever had blown up the lab now wanted her silenced as well. And Jeff . . . dear God, by rattling off to him, had she put him in even greater danger?

Clyde must have sensed her turmoil. He reached over and patted her hand. "As long as you do precisely as you're asked, no one will be hurt. That's a promise."

She stared at his distorted features, focused on the misshapen face. "Why are you wearing those stupid masks? Take them off! Let me see who you are!"

"I'm afraid," said Clyde, "we can't do that. They're for your own protection, you see." His voice was gentle, almost apologetic. "If you could recognize our faces, at any time in the future—we might have no choice but to kill you."

Dr. Lou Hillman completed his rounds. It didn't take him long. He had two young patients at Reese Fowler these days, a broken leg in traction and a second-degree burn, a cheerful four-year-old, healing nicely. Nothing contagious, nothing viral, nothing requiring his immediate attention. He checked his watch and decided he had time to make the phone call before reporting to his office.

He closed the door of his hospital cubicle and consulted a telephone directory. KBLA. He jotted the number, dialed for an outside line. After his visit by Nancy Rafferty, he'd done some checking on his own. He was not surprised to learn that four of his patients, in the course of their serendipitous recoveries, had exhibited the odd, reddish rash. He was sure Nancy would want to know, and he had become intrigued with her theory.

As a pediatrician, he was accustomed to the epidemic spread of childhood diseases. It seemed as if one day there wasn't a case of chicken pox around; and then, out of the blue, it descended on some hapless child and quickly spread, infecting half the neighborhood. The more he thought about it, the more credible it seemed that, just as Nancy suggested, an antidote might do the same thing: attacking the virus with epidemic speed. He wanted to lend his support to the reporter and offer assistance if he could.

He might even, he thought as he was connected to the newsroom, invite her to dinner to discuss it. Ruthie would be thrilled to meet the young woman and would enjoy the excuse to cook an elaborate meal without feeling guilty about the calories! "Nancy Rafferty," he said into the phone. "Dr. Louis Hillman calling."

"One moment, please."

He waited. Finally, a male voice spoke. "Callahan here. Can I help you?"

"I wanted to speak to Nancy Rafferty."

"I'm her producer. She's on vacation."

"Vacation?" The pediatrician was puzzled. "But I spoke to her yesterday. Are you sure?"

The man said shortly, "It was a last-minute decision."

"I see," said Hillman, though he didn't. "Well, will you leave a message that I called? Dr. Hillman at Reese Fowler Medical Center. When do you expect her back?"

"Don't know, exactly," Callahan said. "She didn't tell you yesterday that she was leaving?"

"No, she didn't. I'm a little surprised. She seemed to be in the midst of something important."

"Yeah. Well, a last-minute thing. I'll give her the message that you called."

Hillman hung up, rubbed his chin. So much for Ruthie's

fancy dinner. But it did seem strange. The reporter had been so intent! Why, suddenly, a vacation? He recalled her reference to Jeffrey Kohner. On impulse, he dialed the hospital lab.

"Kohner, lab." The phone had hardly rung.

"Dr. Kohner, this is Lou Hillman. I was trying to locate Nancy Rafferty and I wondered if you know where she is."

"I wish I did. She told me she spoke to you. Did she mention anything about a vacation?"

"No, she didn't. What do you think—"

Jeff broke in. "I don't know. But I'm trying to find out. I'd like to talk to you. But not here at the hospital. Could you possibly come to my place tonight?"

Hillman considered. "I suppose so," he conceded.

Jeff told him the time and the address.

Chapter Ten

Exhilaration coursed through Judd Rohrbach's veins. He felt back on top, going full throttle. Last night's telecast had unleashed a furor which began with the overloaded KBLA switchboard, swept through the front pages of the morning dailies, gathered momentum in the nation's wire services and culminated in a veritable stampede into hospitals, clinics and physicians' offices across the country. So much for serendipity, Judd reflected with satisfaction. Everybody and his cat had cancer, it seemed, and now they were screaming for the cure-all—Metastaban.

Even Fairfield had been unprepared for the cataclysmic reaction. Already this morning he had conferred with Camthon management, been assured that production could be stepped up to meet the demand and been filmed by Rohrbach's crew in his Wilshire Boulevard office in lieu of the cantankerous Mrs. Riley. And in the end, thought Judd, the sincere testimonial of the silver-haired doctor would do more to promote public acceptance of the drug than the word of a sickly-looking old lady. Even Callahan had grudgingly conceded that what Judd had introduced was breaking news—not Pollyanna speculation on a syndrome of unknown veracity.

Thinking of Nancy, Judd found himself wondering where she had gone—and why. He felt the ghost of the uneasy feeling he'd had when he'd spoken to Fairfield. It was tough to accept this vacation business—he knew Nancy better than

192

that. But he wasn't about to ask questions now. He knew when to keep his mouth shut and when to seize an opportunity. It paid to know where the hell you were going and how you were planning to get there!

Roger Howell hadn't the faintest idea what he was doing in Jeff Kohner's apartment. He watched his friend and the older man, Hillman, talking animatedly and shook his head. The more he reflected on the outlandishness of the 6BW theory, the more he wished he'd never agreed to be a part of it. "I don't know, man," he drawled from his perch on the sofa. "The whole thing don't make a lot of sense."

Jeff looked up in exasperation. *"Doesn't,* for Chrissakes, Rog, get off it! You're an MD, man, educated—act like it!"

"All right, I'm educated! Scientifically oriented! And I'm telling you the theory won't fly! Floating antidotes, carriers, for Pete's sake, a syndrome of epidemic recovery!" He shook his head in disbelief.

"There *has* been an epidemic of recovery, Rog—Jesus, you can see it at Reese Fowler!" The red-haired doctor gestured wildly. "Why couldn't 6BW have started it?"

"I tend to agree," stated Lou Hillman quietly. "Stranger things have been known to happen. I don't have to tell you that new strains of virus make themselves known all the time. Nobody knows for sure where they originated—they just seem to descend out of the blue! And in many cases, our only clue in diagnosing them is a similarity in their symptoms."

"Right," conceded Roger. "Okay so far, if all we're dealing with is virus. But you're asking me to believe that Pederson's virus killer is not only floating around killing viruses, it's chewing up cancer cells, too!"

"Yes," Jeff argued. "Because the clue is the symptom. And the symptom—the unifying factor in these recoveries—is the appearance of this mild, benign rash."

"Nancy came to me," said Hillman, "looking for that clue, for that common side effect of exposure to 6BW. I mentioned the rash Stevie Phillips developed, and the same rash on a recovered cancer patient. She apparently related that to the rash on the mice in your lab.''

"The mice," added Jeff, "who had been cured of cancer along with the viral pneumonia. I checked with the breeder." He looked straight at Roger. "There were cancerous mice in that control group. When the error was discovered, they called Pederson right away. He told them that was fine—he'd use them anyway. I think Pederson knew that 6BW was a cancer fighter. He hadn't gotten around to letting us know that yet, but that may have been the reason he called that meeting."

"But those mice had been directly injected as part of the 6BW experiment," Roger pointed out. "You try and find that cancer patient who recovered out of sheer exposure."

"That's easy," Hillman murmured. "I am that patient. There was a large, fibrous tumor in my abdomen. It's simply disappeared. I can vouch for that, gentlemen, and there are X rays and confirmation by another physician to prove it. I believe I was exposed to 6BW at the very same time that Stevie Phillips was. We both recovered and we both exhibited that common side effect: the rash."

Jeff was surprised and encouraged by his colleague's revelation. "If we can document that, along with other case histories, we may be able to establish that 6BW is, in fact, the basis for the cures." He looked expectantly at both Roger and the physician.

"Perhaps," said Hillman, "we could set up a special-studies unit to investigate and document such recoveries. With luck, we may learn whether there are carriers and how the antidote travels in the atmosphere."

Roger listened with stubborn skepticism until he could no longer contain himself. "Gentlemen, I hate to burst your bubble, but it seems to me you're forgetting two things. The first is that it won't be easy to find the genuine recoveries. The syndrome, or whatever it is, is too far out of hand. And trying to do it in the face of this Metastaban publicity is like swimming against the tide."

"Metastaban," barked Hillman, "did not cure these people."

"Spare me. I know what Metastaban is. But it's here," said Roger. "It's available. The second thing you're forgetting, gentlemen, is that 6BW is not. Whether or not you can make a case for it, 6BW no longer exists."

"Then," decided Jeff in the deepening silence, "I guess it's up to us to reproduce it."

Roger bestowed on him a pitying look, but Jeff felt the bile rise in his throat. "Look, somebody knew what 6BW was and succeeded in blowing it off the earth. And somebody knew Nancy'd figured it out. Goddammit, that's why Nancy's missing!"

"Camthon," said Roger. "I know, you made that clear. Camthon blew up the lab and kidnapped Nancy. Try that out on the LAPD, man. Try it out and see how far you get."

"Fredericks." Jeff shoved his hands into his pockets. "Fredericks knew about 6BW. Maybe he knew more than we did that morning when his grant committee turned us down."

"Good." Roger's head bobbed up and down. "Lay it on Fredericks, file a complaint. Even if you're right, by the time the cops start investigating, you'll get your head blown off for trying to formulate more of the stuff!"

"We, Roger," Jeff corrected. "It's gonna take both of us to come up with that formula. And I guarantee you they won't come after us, not after they missed us the first time. They can't afford that kind of coincidence. It would only incriminate them on the first count."

"You want to put that in writing, man?"

Jeff pounded the table in frustration.

Hillman, watching this exchange, could see the viewpoint of each. The danger Roger feared was real enough, even if the stakes were monumental. In the end there was only one thing he could add. "Maybe we owe it to Nancy."

Jeff said nothing, but the look on his face conveyed his thanks to Hillman.

Roger spoke quietly. "All right, man. Order up the mice."

"Right, first thing in the morning," Jeff managed as he turned away to hide his gratitude.

"Which brings up the second part of this agenda," Hillman said. "What's the status on Nancy?"

Jeff took a deep breath. "I spent two hours this morning with the cops. They won't take a Missing report till tomorrow. It's that lousy telegram. They assume it's genuine. They tell me they have no reason to suspect foul play. If, after forty-eight hours, the people closest to her insist they're concerned, they'll take a report and go from there."

"I see." Hillman nodded, preparing to leave. "Well, I'll put my two cents in. For whatever it's worth, I'll call the police."

"I wish," said Jeff, "I could call everybody who knows her. But you know something? I don't even know who her friends are."

For Nancy, the day seemed distorted, surreal, as though she were looking at it through the wrong end of a lens. She tried to keep a foothold on her fury but her captors made even that impossible. They treated her with courtesy, with the utmost respect, as though the kidnap were a source of embarrassment. She could almost believe she was here on vacation, such excellent care did they offer.

Clyde turned out to be an excellent cook. He was happiest when he was in the kitchen. Swathed in an apron and the ridiculous stocking mask, he had puttered in there for the better part of the afternoon over a simmering pot of beef Bourguignon. Nancy had to confess it was the best she'd ever eaten, and she watched the small man puff up with pride.

Bonnie, whose powerful arms had dragged her bodily over the backseat of her car and who'd thought nothing of pointing a gun in her face, was extremely polite and solic-

itous. When she realized how different her captivity might
have been, Nancy felt flooded with relief. She had already
taken to calling them by those ridiculous names as though
it were altogether natural!

Within the little house, with its blue chintz sofas and
maple tables, Nancy was given free rein. There were books
in the bookcase and playing cards in the cupboard. The
windows were sealed, Bonnie told her pragmatically—as
she had already discovered in the bathroom—to spare her
the humiliating failure of trying to make an escape. As long
as she remained within their view, she could do exactly as
she liked.

All of this Nancy accepted with good grace, reminding
herself that things could be worse. She grudgingly conceded that the telegram ruse had been a master stroke in
their scheme. And she spared herself frustration by ceasing
to ask about her kidnap or the terms of her release. That
she had been victimized for her interest and belief in 6BW
seemed almost certainly the case. She knew now her con-
victions about the marvelous capabilities of the drug must
certainly have a basis in fact. But who was responsible for
her kidnap and what they hoped to gain by her absence was
a puzzle whose solution eluded her. She kept her sanity by
reassuring herself that whoever it was apparently didn't
want her dead.

Now, as the evening wore into night, twenty-four hours
since her capture, she impatiently tossed her magazine onto
the coffee table. "Do you mind if I turn on the news?"

Bonnie and Clyde looked toward each other. "Suit yourself." Bonnie shrugged.

Nancy tuned the television set to where KBLA should
have been and sat casually on the sofa. But the call letters
she saw were from Northern California. She was out of her
studio's range. Even so, she listened intently for an announcement concerning her mysterious disappearance from
Los Angeles the night before. It never came, and she gave
herself up to bitter disappointment.

Midway through the telecast, the anchorman brightened.

His demeanor was not unlike Judd Rohrbach's. "There's more proof tonight," he began, "of the miracle of the drug called Metastaban and a hope for the end of cancer."

The picture dissolved to a public-health clinic in a downtown area Nancy didn't recognize. "This scene is typical of what has been happening today in hospitals and clinics across the nation. It reflects public reaction to last night's announcement of a possible cure for the disease. Cancer victims and their concerned families have literally besieged the medical community in an effort to secure the miracle drug."

Nancy bolted forward in her seat, hardly daring to breathe. She glanced briefly at Bonnie and Clyde, but she could tell nothing from their masked faces, and their bodily postures seemed impassive.

"Metastaban," the newscaster went on, "was researched and developed by Camthon Pharmaceuticals. It has been approved by the Food and Drug Administration and is available by prescription only. Speculation continues to grow that Metastaban may, in some way, be responsible for the so-called serendipity syndrome we've heard so much about."

Nancy felt a sudden constriction in her chest. She fought to keep from showing any emotion as she clamped her teeth together and listened over the roaring in her ears.

"Officials of Camthon," the anchorman intoned, "declined today to be interviewed. They stated only that they were pleased to have been in the forefront of the discovery and would remain dedicated to advancing medical science. However, by arrangement with KBLA News, Los Angeles, we bring you an exclusive interview with physician Dr. Paul Fairfield, who claims early successes with the drug."

Before Nancy's astonished eyes, the familiar aquiline features of Paul Fairfield dominated the screen. The doctor's face registered calm and intelligence. His voice was carefully modulated. "I became aware of Metastaban," he told the interviewer, "at about the time it received FDA approval several months ago." The camera angle widened to include Judd Rohrbach as the physician continued speaking. "As you may know, Judd, Metastaban is chemotherapeutic in nature. And chemotherapy, while it does kill cancer cells, is, in a sense, a poison. It cannot discriminate between afflicted and unafflicted tissue. Therefore, in the process of destroying cancerous cells, healthy tissue is poisoned as well. That's why we hear so much about unwanted side effects like loss of hair and the like."

"I see," responded Rohrbach. "In other words, Dr. Fairfield, the intent has been to find a chemotherapeutic drug which could distinguish between healthy and cancer-ridden cells."

"Yes," agreed the doctor. "That's it exactly, and I believe Metastaban is such a drug. I began using it three months ago on a fifty-year-old patient with advanced cancer of the stomach. Her condition, under normal circumstances, might have been considered hopeless. When I suspected what was happening, I opted for surgery in order to assess her condition. Sure enough, I discovered the spread of cancer had been halted. She is in a state of total remission today."

"What you're saying," Judd prompted, "is that this patient was cured by Metastaban."

"There's no doubt in my mind," the doctor agreed, smoothing back a lock of silver hair. "She is gaining weight; other signs of degeneration are reversing; and she is, at this moment, in good health."

"Amazing," exclaimed Judd with perfect awe. "And she owes her good health to Metastaban."

"Let's say," replied Fairfield, "there seems no other way to explain Kathleen Riley's recovery."

"One more question, if you don't mind, Dr. Fairfield." Judd was properly respectful. "We've heard a great deal about a serendipity syndrome supposedly sweeping the populace. Is it possible Metastaban has anything to do with this incredible phenomenon?"

"Well," said Fairfield, "let me say first that I don't personally believe in serendipity. There's no room in science for miracles, you see. If people have been cured, there has to be an explanation. I will say that as I have been using Metastaban, physicians elsewhere have been using it, too. Possibly, they have experienced similar successes as other cancer victims have been cured.''

The picture tightened to a head shot of the doctor. ''What I think may have happened is that as the media got hold of those first few recoveries, the whole thing was blown out of perspective. It is not surprising that hysteria took over and people began attributing so-called serendipity to a number of real and imagined cures.''

Fairfield bestowed on the viewing public a paternal, encouraging smile. ''I sincerely hope the hysteria will pass, and that, before they become more seriously ill, patients will seek proper treatment.''

Among the millions whose eleven o'clock news broadcasts brought similar clips of Fairfield's interview, none was more mesmerized—more fiercely proud—than RN Vera Presti. At last her Paul, as she had begun to think of him, had the recognition he deserved.

Only one jarring note marred her happiness—Paul had said on television he'd been treating Mrs. Riley with Metastaban for the past several months. Presti could have sworn it was just last week, *after* surgery, that he first introduced the medication. . . .

Chapter Eleven

"Althea?" The voice was soft, hesitant.

Althea smiled into the telephone. "Michael! How are you?"

"Fine. I'm fine. I saw the news last night. I'm glad to know your mother's really well."

"Thank you. I didn't know it was on the news, but yes, she's fine and I'm to take her home today. As a matter of fact, I was going to call you. I was wondering— Well, I don't drive, you know, and I thought—"

"What time do you need me?"

"Eleven o'clock? If that's convenient—"

"I'll pick you up at the convent."

"Thank you. And Michael—" But there was nothing else to say. "Nothing, Michael. Just thank you." She stood holding the receiver long after he'd hung up.

On the patio off the rose garden, overlooking the canyon, Ruthie Hillman poured her husband's coffee. "Louis," she scolded, "I asked if you want grapefruit."

Lou Hillman looked up from his paper. "What? Oh, yes, Ruthie, grapefruit would be nice. I'm sorry, I was— reading this story."

Ruthie expertly sectioned the fruit. "Metastaban. Is it really what they claim?"

"I don't know. I don't think so." He pushed aside the paper with impatience.

"I never did like Paul Fairfield. And I don't think such a big shot on the Camthon Board of Directors should be speaking as a doctor about their product."

Hillman regarded his rosy wife. "Fairfield, a big shot on the board? Okay, oracle, how do you know?

Ruthie calmly buttered toast. "I'm not such an oracle. I invested in them once. I went to meetings."

"My wife the investor. You never told me."

"You're not the only one who has secrets." She shot him a look, but he chose to ignore it, so Ruthie forged ahead. "When my father died, he left me that money. You said I should do what I wanted with it. I decided to invest it. I figured, as a doctor's wife, why not pharmaceuticals? Camthon is big. So I went to them."

"And?" said Hillman.

"I didn't like it. I especially didn't like Paul Fairfield. He's a major stockholder in the name of his own corporation. He's the one who got them into clinics."

"Clinics?" asked Hillman.

"Chemotherapy clinics. They must have several hundred by now. Then they started pushing this new line of drugs. I remember, Metastaban was one of the ones they invested heavily in. But they never said then it was a cancer cure. It isn't a cancer cure, is it, Louis?"

Her husband shrugged. "I don't think so."

She looked at him levelly. "Did you take it?"

"Me?"

"When you were sick. It's not such a secret. You can't hide things from me, after all these years. I'm asking you, Louis." Again, the look. "Did you take any of this Metastaban?"

"No," he confessed, after a long moment.

"But you're better."

"Yes."

"But how?"

Hillman sighed. "It's a long story."

"Tell me," Ruthie said.

"I have patients waiting."

"Then they'll wait. Please. I want the truth."

The doctor reached over to take his wife's plump hand and then he told her everything he knew.

Nancy Rafferty had slept little since her capture. It would have been difficult in any case with Bonnie or Clyde outside her room all night in shifts, playing a radio very low and surreptitiously pushing open her door to reassure themselves she was still there. As if she could be anywhere else! All the windows were indeed sealed shut. She'd tried them again to be certain. And if she entertained notions of another means of escape, they were dashed by the certainty that Bonnie, for all his belated affability, would not hesitate to use the gun he carried.

To make matters worse, she was kept awake by relentless and restless energy. The telecast she had seen last night had galvanized her senses, put the day back into focus and girded her for a battle she was helpless to fight. Her kidnap, she realized, had accomplished two purposes: it had defused the momentum of the serendipity syndrome and, more important, cleared the way for Metastaban.

Metastaban, the unknown medical quantity for which Fairfield had tried so hard to gain Nancy's support! Well, he'd certainly found a willing ally in her co-host, Judd Rohrbach! The two of them had to be in league, each with an ax to grind. As long as the Girl Scout was out of the way, they could peddle their own brand of cookies!

But the Girl Scout would not be out of the way forever, not unless—they actually planned to kill her. She clung to the knowledge that they could have done that instantly. Why bother to keep her safe and well-fed? Why bother, in fact, to send that wire to Callahan unless they planned for her eventual return? Or were they keeping her alive for simple expedience—in the event of some contingency she could not fathom?

Who was it out there deciding her fate? She ruled out Bonnie and Clyde. She knew they were lackeys, neither complex nor motivated enough to concoct such a scheme. And it wasn't Judd. He didn't have the guts.

Fairfield? How great was his stake in Metastaban? Enough to murder? And kidnap? Or was there someone high in the Camthon hierarchy, someone who knew about 6BW? The one thing Nancy was sure of now was that 6BW had started the syndrome. Was there someone at Camthon who knew it as well and decided not only to destroy the drug but to claim its success for Metastaban?

Nancy walked to the useless window. Where in the name of heaven was she? How far from Los Angeles, from Jeff— Oh, God, Jeff! Are you in some blue-chintz prison too? She scanned the landscape in the early morning light as though it might provide a clue. Forlorn, anonymous brush and some stands of scrubby trees, sunflowers growing wild at the roadside.

She jumped at the loud, sudden knock on her door. "Good morning!" It was Clyde. "Breakfast's ready!" Well, whatever happened, she wasn't likely to starve. She supposed that was some consolation.

"Did I miss the unmasking?" Nancy asked. "Or do you and Bonnie eat with those things on too?"

"Now, now," Clyde soothed. "Don't you fret about us." He led the way to the kitchen. He served her sausages and toast with strawberry jam. "Sorry. No fresh eggs so this will have to do. But the freezer's well stocked. We'll get by just fine. I already have the dinner menu planned."

"Really?" said Nancy. "And what if I said, 'Sorry, but I have other plans'?"

"Don't be testy. Eat your breakfast like a good little girl and you'll be home in no time, won't she, Bonnie?"

Bonnie seemed to be staring at the sausages. "Yeah," he muttered. "No time."

Nancy shoved her plate across the table. "You eat it. I'm not hungry. And don't tell me to be a good little girl! What are you, my mother? You're a kidnapper!"

Clyde cocked his shrouded head to one side. "So I am. And you'll do as I tell you. If you don't want your breakfast, you can follow me. There's something I want you to do."

In the makeshift lab installed on the fourth floor of Reese Fowler, Jeff poured liquid from one beaker to another.

"Easy," urged Roger. "Take it easy."

"You do it," said Jeff, handing him the beaker. "I'll take notes. What time is it, anyway?"

"Almost two."

Jeff rapped on the counter. "Eight hours. Maybe the cops'll listen."

"Don't get your hopes up." Roger poured the liquid into the other beaker. "They'll take a report. That's no biggie."

"I won't settle for that," snapped Jeff. "They've got to put out a bulletin. Circulate her picture, ask questions."

"Yeah," intoned Roger. "Seven milligrams. Write it, Kohner, seven milligrams."

Jeff made the entry. "I think it was seven. Yeah, I'm sure. It was seven."

"Then we're just about there, man. Bring on the mice. Let's see what we got in this potion."

Jeff made his way slowly through the makeshift lab. It was littered with supplies hastily assembled, much of it delivered just this morning. He stared at the mice languishing in the cages. "Damn it, do it!" he swore.

The mice were infected with various diseases—meningitis, hepatitis, pneumonia. A few were cancerous, and the hope was that each group would respond favorably to the newly formulated 6BW.

The two young doctors had spent the better part of the night—from the time Lou Hillman left Jeff's apartment—closeted in the makeshift fourth-floor lab. They had compared notes, argued, hypothesized, drawn up lists for immediate order. For Roger, it seemed an exercise in futility; that he'd agreed to take an active part in the project was a tribute to his friendship for Jeff. For Jeff, it was as much to keep his mind off Nancy as it was a commitment to the mission.

The onus, however, rested uneasily on Jeff's tired shoulders. He had formulated the chemical twice on his own, and was alternately confident and utterly despairing as to how much of the process he'd memorized. It struck him, as he watched the debilitated mice, that he was almost afraid to find out.

Roger had several syringes prepared and was watching his friend stare dourly into the cages when the phone rang, startling them both. He picked up and quickly gestured to Jeff. "For you," he said. "Callahan at the station."

Jeff's expression did not change. But his pulse raced as he crossed the room.

"Dr. Kohner." Callahan sounded relieved. "I just heard from Nancy. She's fine." No response. "She called from somewhere up the coast. Said she'd be back in a day or two."

Jeff listened to the clamoring in his chest. He found himself unable to speak.

"She apologized all over the place," Callahan went on. "Guess that's it. I thought you'd want to know." He paused. "Listen, you asked me to call! Oh, and by the way, some nun called—Sister Althea from Saint Agatha's convent. She was asking for Nancy—and a Dr. Hillman too. What the hell am I, a message center?"

"You're a prince," muttered Jeff, finally. "You're sure it was Nancy?"

"It was her," said Callahan. "Jeezus, don't you think I know her voice? . . . Well, listen, you're welcome!" He slammed down the phone, stared at the silent instrument. What he didn't tell Kohner was what Rafferty had said just before she hung up. "Give my love to Judd," she'd said sweetly, and Callahan was puzzled.

Nancy, some four hundred miles north of Los Angeles, wondered why she'd said that, too. She looked into the barrel of Bonnie's revolver. It had been a plea, of course, she realized as Bonnie moved slowly away. A desperate if somehow inept attempt to send her producer a clue. *Something's wrong,* she'd been trying to say, in the only words she could think of. She counted on the fact that Callahan knew of the animosity between Judd and her. But whether he'd caught the subtle plea was another thing altogether.

Too subtle, Nancy cursed herself silently, looking away from her captors. If only they'd not caught her so off guard, if only she'd had time to think. Surely there was something more pointed she could have said, some unmistakable cipher she could have sent him. Callahan was hardly a master of subtleties. Damn it, she'd blown it again!

But Bonnie and Clyde were apparently pleased with the quality of her performance on the phone. "Put the gun away, Bonnie," Clyde demanded. "Miss Rafferty's done well enough, indeed. As for you, Miss Rafferty, you may have earned yourself a one-way ticket home."

"When?" Nancy's green eyes flashed at her captor. "I've done what you wanted. Now, when?"

"Soon," replied Clyde. The words were muffled, but the attempt to reassure her was clear. He tried a smile through the distorting mask. "I should think it will be very soon."

Chapter Twelve

"I have the oddest feeling that something is wrong at home," said Miriam Phillips. She sat at a table overlooking the harbor at Charlotte Amalie, picking desultorily at a salad.

Her husband squinted at her, comical in the sunlight. "Miriam. Everything is fine," he told her and smiled.

"Probably," she admitted, reaching for his hand. "I suppose I'm just a worrywart. I want you to know this time away with you has meant more than I know how to tell you. I'll thank you forever, Zan, for making me see what—what was happening to our lives."

Zan covered his wife's hand with his free one. "You don't have to thank me. I love you, Miriam." He started to rise. "And because I love you, I'll humor you. As long as we're here on land this morning, I'm going in and call home."

Miriam watched his broad back disappear. She gazed out over the harbor at the ship. She tried to pick out their tiny stateroom just above the waterline. It had been a haven for some of the most incredible lovemaking she'd ever hoped to know. A delicious shiver snaked down her spine. She smiled and went back to her salad.

Zan was back in minutes, sliding in across from her. "I told you, everything is fine. Stevie's in school, he won third place in a spelling bee and he's eating like a trucker, Grandma says."

Miriam gave him a dazzling smile. "Okay. What did the phone call cost?"

"Never mind," said Zan. "I'll take it out in trade. Oh. There were a couple of messages. Sister Althea wants you to call when we get back. So does Dr. Hillman. Nothing urgent."

"What do you say we skip the window-shopping and catch a little nap before we sail?"

"My, my," sighed Zan. "I never knew a lady so eager to pay her debts." He tickled her playfully under the chin. "First one in bed calls all the shots!"

Paul Fairfield had the heady feeling he was in total control. He felt like a maestro—sensing, guiding, drawing from a gaggle of ragtag musicians a symphony of consummate excellence. Camthon, Rohrbach—all of them, in fact, dancing to a melody he created. He had never known such joy, such power! It galled him a little that there was no one to appreciate the intricacies of his orchestration.

The clinics, all three-hundred of them nationwide, were filled to capacity with patients eager for Metastaban. Waiting lists were neatly computerized, the likes of the Rileys having been hastily discharged to make room for the better-paying guests. Hospitals, if this morning's papers could be believed, were filling with equal rapidity. The serendipity syndrome, if indeed 6BW had spawned one at all, had just about sputtered to a satisfying end.

What fools these mortals be, thought Fairfield, fingering his sterling silver paperweight. Tell them they were well and they fell all over themselves trying to prove it was so. Tell them they were sick and that there was a cure, and they lay down in droves for you to heal them! Well, healed or not, they would get what they paid for: a dose of the wonder drug Metastaban. Of course, he didn't plan to stay around until anyone got suspicious.

There were plenty of places where a man could disappear, could live out his life in quiet luxury. Places where no one cared where the money came from. He planned to find himself one of them. Let Kohner and Rafferty and all the rest of them struggle. It was enough for him to have rendered them impotent, if only for a lucrative little while.

At the thought of Rafferty, a new thought surfaced. He must keep the brass section in tune. She had served her purpose. If she'd listen to reason, she would now be permitted to play. He lifted the receiver, made one brief call and replaced it, satisfied, in its cradle. He had barely done so when the instrument rang, interrupting his thoughts.

Reese Fowler was on the line, his receptionist told him. Was Doctor coming in to make rounds? "No," snapped Fairfield. "Doctor is busy. Wait—" He allowed himself a smile. "Tell them I'll be there in half an hour." He smoothed back his elegant silver hair.

It would give him great pleasure to march unannounced into the office of the Chief of Staff. There he would tender his resignation, effective as of that moment. He had no further need of the hospital's aegis, its cloak of shabby respectability. This afternoon, he would call his lawyers, set up an untraceable Swiss account. Then he'd make plans for an imminent departure. The prospect gave him great glee.

He sailed into the corridors of Reese Fowler Medical Center, looked in on patients, gave a few perfunctory orders and was finally ready for the confrontation with the Chief of Staff. He was on his way to the bank of elevators when he was hailed by a breathless Vera Presti.

"Dr. Fairfield," she gushed, her mountainous breasts heaving, "I saw you on television. You were wonderful!"

"Thank you, Presti." He smothered his distaste. "May I say it's been a pleasure to work with you."

The bovine eyes widened in comprehension. "Whatever do you mean? Are you leaving?"

Fairfield instantly regretted the gaffe. "No, no. I simply wanted you to know." He started to back away.

"Oh," said Presti, much relieved, her fleshy face folding into a smile. "Doctor, it's always been my pleasure."

She felt herself emboldened by his compliment. "I've been wondering," she fumbled, "I've been meaning to ask—"

"Yes?" snapped Fairfield, his patience dwindling. "What is it, Presti? Well, speak up!"

In a prettier woman, Presti's expression might have been taken for coyness. "Will you do me the honor of coming to dinner? At my house, any night at your convenience. I'm really a wonderful cook, Dr. Fairfield—"

But Fairfield's largesse had reached its limit. "My dear Miss Presti"—he spoke with infinite courtesy as he stepped into the opened elevator—"forgive me for declining your gracious invitation. I would as soon have dinner with a cow!"

The doors closed noiselessly, leaving Vera Presti to stare at them in openmouthed astonishment.

Kathleen Riley was discharged from Sunnyvale Clinic at a few minutes past noon. Althea quickly packed her mother's belongings and had Michael stow them in his car. The elegant clinic was a beehive of activity, beds being moved everywhere. There was so much going on that Althea thought she could have packed the flowered drapes, had she been so inclined, without being too much noticed. As Mrs. Riley was wheeled out through the corridor, Miss Norton's pursed lips and arched eyebrows all but said "Good riddance!"

Mrs. Riley was so delighted to be leaving, she scarcely noticed the young man navigating her wheelchair. She was ensconced in the backseat and five miles from the building before she thought to ask her driver's identity.

"This is Michael Kelly," Althea said, trying to keep her voice neutral. "He belongs to Saint Agatha's parish. We work together in social services. Michael, my mother, Kathleen Riley."

"I'm pleased to meet you, Mrs. Riley," Michael said. "And I'm happy that you're feeling so much better."

Mrs. Riley scrutinized the back of his head. "Hmph," she snorted at length.

Home was a small, stuccoed box of a house where Althea had grown up a few blocks from the convent. In it, the old woman took command as though she had never left. "Young man, put the plants there on the windowsill," she ordered, "and the vanity case here in the hall. Althea, put my radio by my bedside—and don't slouch so, you look like a penguin!"

The young people did as they were told, skittering about like drops of water on a hot griddle while Mrs. Riley, sitting on the living-room sofa, watched with a disapproving air. When they'd completed everything to her satisfaction, Althea faced her mother timidly. "Welcome home, Mother," she smiled. "Shall I put up some water for tea?"

Mrs. Riley regarded her daughter and the young man dwarfing her living room. "No," she replied, her black eyes narrowed in the way that sent shivers up Althea's spine. "You may go." She waved an imperious arm. "I'm tired. I want to take a nap."

Althea did not hesitate. "Very well." She brushed a kiss against the old woman's cheek. "Call me if you need me. I'll see you soon." She nodded to Michael who stood, mesmerized, watching the first act of Althea's young life play itself out before his eyes.

"Uh, again, nice meeting you, ma'am," he managed to say. "Perhaps I'll be seeing you again."

The only response was another "Hmph." He somehow didn't think it meant "Thank you." He followed Althea out to the car, started the engine, pulled away. He watched out of the corner of his eye as the young woman visibly relaxed.

"I'm sorry, Michael. My mother was rude. She might at least have thanked you."

"No need," said Michael. "I did it for you. Now, can I buy you some lunch?"

"Yes!" she decided, startling them both with the hint of gaiety in her voice.

Since the incident at Sunnyvale when she'd put Judd Rohrbach and his film crew out of her mother's room, Althea had been courting the giggles. She'd surprised herself, even more than Judd, at the strength she'd managed to display. How glorious it was to make a decision, act upon it and be done with it!

She stole a glance at Michael, who was staring straight ahead as he drove. "I've made a decision," she announced to his profile as they sailed along the boulevard. "I'm going to get better at making decisions." But that was all she would say.

They lunched at a seafood bar Michael knew, chatting about caseloads and placements. Althea was animated, wanting to know everything that had happened in her intermittent absence. Later, in his office, she was brisk and funny, sending the secretaries into peals of laughter with a pantomimed account of an office skit she'd seen on late-night television.

Michael watched her with bemused incredulity, as though he'd never seen her before. He found neither a hint of the tortured nun nor a clue as to what had set her free. Althea giggled at his visible confusion, drunk with the power she possessed. She wilted a little when they reached the convent, but she stepped smartly to the curb. "Thank you, Michael." An indecipherable smile. "I'll be ready tomorrow morning at nine."

Mother Regina hailed her as she came through the door. "Sister, there's a phone call for you."

"Yes?" she answered, picking up the phone. "This is Sister Althea. May I help you?"

"Sister, this is Dr. Jeffrey Kohner. I'm a friend of Nancy Rafferty's. Her boss, Ty Callahan, said you'd been trying to reach her. I wondered what it was about."

"Oh, we had an appointment. She was coming to see my mother. But she didn't show up and I wondered why. That was the reason I called."

"Your mother?" asked Jeff.

"Kathleen Riley. She was Dr. Fairfield's patient at Sunnyvale Clinic. Miss Rafferty said she wanted to see her . . . something about—a rash."

Jeff instantly recognized the name of Fairfield's famous patient—the cancer victim who'd recovered. Thanks to Metastaban, as Fairfield claimed? Or thanks to exposure to 6BW? "So Nancy had an appointment but she never showed."

"No, and I thought that was odd. Her office said she was on vacation. Is she on vacation, Dr. Kohner?"

"I don't think so. I don't know where she is. But I think she may be in some danger."

"Oh dear," said Althea with a puzzled frown. "Is there anything I can do?"

"Yes," said Jeff, "maybe there is." He didn't know who Nancy's friends were, but he needed all the help he could get. Anything that would indicate that Nancy's disappearance was not what it seemed to be. "Call the LAPD." He gave her a number. "Ask for Detective Vickers. Tell him what you just told me—that Nancy had an appointment she didn't show for. And since it was important, you have reason to suspect that something unusual must have stopped her."

Althea considered the strange request. The doctor sounded so desperate. It seemed her decision to make decisions was going to be tested already. She promised herself she would think it through and make up her mind by morning. . . .

Jeff hung up mildly encouraged. He knew he was grasping at straws. But if he could follow up on every phone call Nancy got at the studio, document every shred of evidence he could that a vacation at this time was unlikely . . .

"Hey, man." Roger Howell nudged him. "How about we go home and get some shut-eye?"

"You go ahead. Thanks for everything, Rog. There's no more you can do until morning."

"What about you?"

"Nah, I couldn't sleep. I'm going down and fight some more with Vickers."

"Good luck," said Roger, glancing at the cages where

the inoculated mice now slept fitfully. He shook his head. It still made no sense. Even if the animals recovered. Yes, 6BW was a powerful antigen—he had no argument with that. If he and Jeff had done the job, maybe they'd see results. He rapped on one cage. Effective against cancer? Maybe. But able to float in the atmosphere somehow? Effecting recovery without inoculation? He shrugged off his lab coat, threw it in the laundry. Jeezus! Science fiction!

Chapter Thirteen

Detective J. D. Vickers was a reasonable man. He prided himself on his patience. But the red-haired young doctor badgering him now would have even tried the patience of Job.

Under normal circumstances Jeffrey Kohner would not have seen the detective tonight at all. He would have been put off by the night duty officer and urged to come back in the morning. But the young man's earnestness—and that the lady he insisted was missing was a celebrity—had given the duty officer pause. He had hailed Vickers on his way out of the building and requested a few minutes of his time. It made for Kohner an encouraging start and for Vickers a very long day.

The young doctor continued to astound him with the most bizarre allusions: chemical chicanery, violence, mysterious disappearance—until Vickers felt his patience quotient snap. He mashed a hand against his stubby nose, slid it up to cup his freckled forehead. "Listen, Dr. Kohner, it boils down to this: we have to have sufficient reason to suspect foul play. How can we report Miss Rafferty as missing? The woman sent a telegram to her boss. She phoned to assure him she's okay, and there's no reason to assume she's not okay. Unless you or anyone close to her can convince us her actions were unusual, we have to assume she really is on vacation!"

"Unusual! Jesus Christ, I was waiting for her at her

apartment! She gave me the key, said she'd be there by midnight! Isn't it unusual that she never showed up?"

Detective Vickers shook his head. "I sympathize with your disappointment. Maybe the lady changed her mind—decided to go away and think."

Jeff raised weary eyes to the ceiling. "Look," he said, trying to sound reasonable, "I'm not the only one who was knocked for a loop when Nancy disappeared. Talk to Dr. Hillman. Talk to Sister Althea. They both know Nancy was on to something. Talk to Callahan, he'll tell you it's not like her—she's responsible! She had a job to do!"

The detective glanced at the list of phone numbers Jeff had meticulously listed. "All right," he agreed. "I'll check 'em out myself—first thing when I get back in the morning."

"In the morning!"

"Yes, doctor. You want me to call them now? Hell, it's nearly ten o'clock at night!"

"Yeah," argued Kohner. "You don't understand. If I'm right, Nancy's life could be in danger. I know you don't believe all this stuff about 6BW. You don't tie it in with the explosion. But Nancy believes it. And someone else knows that. I'm telling you, there's a connection!" He shoved his hands in his jacket pockets to keep them from shaking.

Vickers was not about to get him started again. "Okay, okay, I'll check it out. Why don't you go home and get some sleep, doc? One of us might as well."

RN Vera Presti felt like a thief. She had no reason to be back at Reese Fowler. It was hours past the end of her shift—and she had no authority in Medical Records. What would she say if someone questioned her? She could think of no reasonable explanation. Still, it was something she had to do. She had a point to prove, if only for herself. Paul Fairfield had likened her to a cow. Did he think she was stupid as well?

She rifled through the "R"s in the recent discharge file:

Rigby, Rigowski, Riley! Her shaking fingers extracted the
file. She eased her bulk into a chair. And there it was, in
her own precise hand, just as Dr. Fairfield had dictated.
"Institute Metastaban, thirty milligrams daily as a chemotherapeutic." Only, the word *institute* had been whited out,
and the word *continue* penned in, in a different hand.

Her fingers traveled up the page, found an entry dated
three weeks earlier. Squeezed into a narrow space between
two other entries was the single word *Metastaban*. And the
initials, a hasty flourish in the margin: "P.F., MD."

Sloppy, sloppy, Dr. Fairfield, thought Miss Presti, nar-
rowly stifling a giggle. A naughty third-grader altering a
report card would do more careful work than that! But then,
of course, the naughty doctor never thought the file might
be examined! She allowed the stifled giggle to escape, her
lower lip quivering with glee. Then she was stopped by a
sobering thought. What on earth was she going to do now?

Judd Rohrbach had no time for soul-searching. He was
sick of Callahan's attitude and told him so. "You got more
viewers watching KBLA at eleven than any other station
on the tube!" He shoved the ratings into the producer's
face. "You've got me to thank and don't you forget it!"

"How could I forget it?" Callahan was calm. "You
remind me every hour on the hour."

"Because I did it with news, Callahan—good, hard news,
not some half-cocked, screwball syndrome!"

"It's beginning to sound like sensationalism to me."

Judd flushed. "Sensationalism, my ass! I'm only reporting what's happening. Medicine is back in business. People are screaming for Metastaban."

"Maybe," countered Callahan, "because you over-
stated its case. Touted it up to be a miracle. What proof
do you have that it's really a cancer cure, besides what
Fairfield told you? The FDA's come out with a statement
that it can't back Camthon's claims. There's a good chance
the drug will be pulled from the market until further studies
can be done."

"So what?" Judd shrugged. "Let 'em do what they want. Meanwhile, we're selling a lot of airtime."

"And you're number one. The Metastaban Messiah." The producer shook his head. "What about ethics?"

"Ah, yes, responsible journalism! You and Rafferty know a lot about that! Well, before you start preaching, I've got a show to do." Judd straightened his tie and strode out.

He wondered if he ought to stop by Makeup and powder the gloss on his forehead. Confrontations made him perspire. Damn Callahan for his rotten timing!

Jeff Kohner found it impossible to sleep. He kept replaying his session with Vickers. The detective was understandably wary. What could Jeff have said to convince him? Realizing the futility of that line of thought, another conundrum rose to plague him. Why wasn't 6BW working after direct inoculation into the mice? If he couldn't get it right through inoculation, how was he going to prove it could float?

He prowled his apartment, clad in his underwear, unrefreshed after a long, steaming shower. He decided he was hungry and opened his refrigerator, but the neat row of eggs reminded him of the omelets Nancy had made after their lovemaking. He slammed the door shut, took a box of crackers and a jar of peanut butter from the cupboard and sat down in front of the TV.

For very different reasons, Sister Althea also found it difficult to sleep. On the one hand, she was buoyant, ethereal almost. She could not keep her head on the pillow. For the first time in her life she was guilt-free and absorbed with the weightlessness of her body. Out from under the crush of sin, she hugged herself to keep her limbs from soaring off, from floating out the small, high window into a place reserved for God's rejoicing children.

Oh, she had cowed a little under her mother's domination this morning, but she had certainly met Michael and

his cohorts on an equal footing. She'd enjoyed their camaraderie, been a part of it too, without the heavy mantle
of guilt. It filled her with peace, and she could hardly wait
to see Miriam Phillips and thank her for that shred of truth
from which Althea was building her new self.

On the other hand, her concern for Nancy Rafferty
nipped the perfect circle of her happiness. She'd heard fear
in the voice of that nice Dr. Kohner, and it heightened her
own uneasiness. Althea had expected Miss Rafferty to come
and visit. Why had Nancy left so suddenly?

She would telephone the police in the morning as Dr.
Kohner had asked. It was another decision made. Sighing,
robbed of all desire to sleep, she rose from her bed, perched
on the edge of it and turned on the portable television set
on her dresser.

In the pale blue bedroom overlooking the canyon, Ruthie
Hillman lay with her dark head nestled into the crook of
her husband's arm. "Somehow," she said, "it's very funny
that Nancy Rafferty should take a vacation just when all
this hoopla's going on."

"Mmm," agreed Louis, fumbling for the control box,
turning up the volume for the news.

Judd Rohrbach spoke in stentorian tones, a guest in millions of households. "We welcome this era of scientific
breakthrough, heralding the end of cancer. It is based on
fact. And with it, we say good-bye to the fantasy of a
serendipity syndrome."

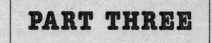

PART THREE

Searches

Chapter One

From the bustle in the admitting office and the crowded conditions of the patient waiting rooms at Reese Fowler Medical Center on the morning after Judd's dramatic pronouncement, it appeared the news telecaster was right. Paul Fairfield would have been the first to agree that medicine was, indeed, back in business.

People who, weeks ago, would have closed their eyes to a lump in the breast or ignored a burning sensation while urinating, were now convinced that an ingrown toenail surely marked them with cancer. In light of the readily available wonder drug, they clamored for their share of Metastaban.

What was a doctor to do? Turn these patients away? For every physician who would not prescribe the drug, there were dozens more who would. Why risk losing faith with a patient who had put his trust in you for years? Metastaban was a chemotherapeutic and relatively harmless in small doses. It made sense to fulfill the patient's request and then go on treating him conventionally.

Camthon struggled to step up production as demand for the drug increased. Investors in the corporation, as Lou Hillman teased his wife, were literally making a killing.

Ruthie was indignant. "I wouldn't take a nickel from those greedy, lying *gonifs!* They're playing on the fear of misguided innocents, and mark my words, Fairfield is responsible!"

Her husband was far too busy with patients to allow himself time to philosophize. It took all his energy to deal with parents who thought Metastaban would cure their leukemic children. But he promised himself, at his first opportunity, to check back with Kohner and Howell.

The two young doctors were equally swamped in the ill-equipped fourth-floor lab. Routine requests for cultures and blood counts and biopsies multiplied with alarming regularity. Extra staffers were sent in to assist, and still it was difficult for Kohner or Howell to steal time for their private objective.

To make matters worse, the inoculated mice showed no sign of marked improvement. They were sluggish and fevered, and if the rate of viral infection had slowed, there was no remission evident in the cancerous group. There wasn't a hint of the idiopathic rash Jeff checked for as frequently as he was able. The error was not in the dosage, Jeff was sure. That much was easily recalled from his memory and confirmed by Roger. The failure was—had to be—in the composition of the formula. But try as he might in the moments he stole, he could not seem to pinpoint his mistake.

Each time the phone rang, he jumped for it eagerly, expecting, if not Nancy, the police. But time after time it was only some doctor who wanted preferential treatment on his lab work. Jeff bit his tongue and tried to be civil, to do the job he was paid to do. But each disappointment left him more frantic. How would he ever find her?

Detective J. D. Vickers tilted back his chair and blew smoke rings up at the ceiling. Reasonable evidence of the possibility of foul play. Maybe there was that, after all. The doctor had a key to Rafferty's apartment, given to him an hour before she split. Their relationship was new—the prime of passion, so to speak. It had not had sufficient time to pall.

The woman had been excited about an investigation she was making in her line of duty as a reporter. That much was corroborated by Hillman, who'd volunteered to help her research. The nun confirmed an appointment she'd had, to which Rafferty never showed up. The appointment centered on the same investigation Rafferty was so keen on completing. The boss, Callahan, had a telegram in hand which could have been sent by anyone. The phone call? Under duress? Callahan doesn't think so, except for the zinger at the end. Why, the boss wonders, would she send her love to Judd when the two of them couldn't stand the sight of each other?

Then there was the fact that the nature of her investigation involved the explosion at Reese Fowler—a puzzle which, to date, neither the bomb squad nor the guys in Major Crimes had been able to piece together. They knew the method and they knew the means, but the perpetrator was a blank and the only "why" was that weirdo theory of Kohner's, a theory Kohner attributed to Rafferty and insisted was the reason for her disappearance.

Lastly, Rafferty was something of a celebrity, and her friends were a reputable group. Reputable enough that you took their concern with more than a grain of salt. So thinking, the detective unfolded his feet from the desk and squashed out the butt of his cigarette. He was a reasonable man with reasonable evidence. He was going in to talk to his lieutenant.

"Good news, Nancy." Clyde hung up the phone. "Your vacation is almost at an end."

"Really?" exclaimed Nancy. "Gee, what a shame. Just when I was beginning to enjoy it."

"Now, now." Clyde attempted another gauzy smile. "There's no need for sarcasm, is there?"

Nancy shot him a look, started to speak, thought better of it and turned away. There was nothing to be gained by antagonizing Clyde. She'd learned as much the other day. Bonnie, for his part, was consistently surly. Nancy's attitude didn't faze him at all. But Clyde was something of a sensitive, reacting to Nancy's moods and responses with a swiftness that was dizzying.

He'd been angry when he demanded that she call Callahan—angry because of her outburst over breakfast. Yet after she'd made the call to his satisfaction, he'd become almost instantly contrite. "Wonderful, Nancy!" He'd clapped his hands. "You ought to give up news broadcasting for the stage!" And he'd left her, quaking, to disappear into the kitchen, humming softly through the damned stocking mask! As Nancy stared at Bonnie's bulk, his pistol eased back into its holster. She decided, then and there, there were no points for backtalk, none for shouting, nor for witty, barbed remarks. In the back of her mind she saw herself bound and gagged, completely at the mercy of these two. Better to be docile, praise the food and try to be cheerful if it kept Clyde on an even keel.

As it was, in penance for her outburst, her television privileges had been revoked. When she wasn't gazing out a window trying to decipher the landscape or devising brilliant but impossible escape schemes, she was overcome with anger and frustration. She was burning to know what Judd was up to in his timely quest for power. It was not surprising that he'd seized on Metastaban and dangled it, like a plum, before his public.

Nancy moaned audibly, saw Bonnie watching her as she rose and began to pace the room. The more she thought about it, the more sense it made that Fairfield knew everything about 6BW. He chose to steal its thunder in order to promote Metastaban—had the gall to arrange a kidnap . . . and a murder.

Clyde appeared in the kitchen doorway, cleared his throat to get attention. "Lunch is ready," he announced. "French onion soup. With Parmesan."

Nancy tried to clear her head of the thoughts she could not act upon. Perhaps if she were nicer to Clyde—would that get her out of here any faster? She smiled broadly. "Goodness, Clyde, you're going to make me fat."

But Clyde saw through the dazzling smile. He patted her

shoulder as she passed. "It's going to be all right," he told her. "Trust me. You're going to be just fine."

Nancy peered at the stockinged face, tried to see the features within. To her utter amazement she found herself thinking, *In another set of circumstances, I'd like him! He's a sweet man, if just a little paranoid. Perhaps that's an occupational hazard.* Aloud, she said, "Why don't you take off that mask and join me, for once, at the table."

"I'd like to do that," he responded. "But no, we'll have ours later."

Yes, she thought, growing bitter again. *When I'm safely locked away in my room.*

Lunch, for Jeff, was a cold ham sandwich brought in from the hospital cafeteria. He chewed it absently while marking slides, adjusting the stage of a microscope. His mouth was full when he answered the phone. "Kohner, lab," he said tersely.

"Dr. Kohner, this is Detective Vickers."

Jeff swallowed quickly. "Yes?"

"We're issuing a bulletin on Nancy Rafferty. I thought you'd want to know."

Chapter Two

In his modest office, the young grant writer stared once again at the accumulation of lab notes and materials he had taken from Rolf Pederson. He still couldn't believe the chemist was dead, killed in that explosion at Reese Fowler. Jeezus, thought Karl Fredericks' nephew, what a way to go. And Pederson had made it clear those notes were confidential—to be delivered into no one's hands but his. Martin wondered for the umpteenth time if the chemist had left a will. If so, there had to be an executor. Perhaps the notes should go to his estate.

He debated calling his Uncle Karl. Nah, why would he know a thing like that? An attorney, that was it. Any attorney could tell him how to find the executor. After what Uncle Karl had told him, Martin doubted that anyone would covet the seemingly useless notes. Still, he had an obligation to fulfill. He reached for the telephone directory.

Ruthie Hillman, expecting her guest, answered the doorbell at seven-thirty. She liked the tall young man immediately, saw integrity in his wide-set brown eyes. There was a gentle warmth in his tired smile that would have lit up an ordinary face. He reminded her of Louis as he'd looked thirty years ago, ringing the bell on her parents' porch—blinding her forever to men of finer features or more graceful, elegant airs.

He reminded her very much of Louis. Except, of course, for the red hair. She extended her hand. "You must be Dr. Kohner. I'm Ruthie Hillman. Please come in."

Jeff Kohner stepped into a mirrored entry, was led into a small, charming room. It was furnished in coral and dusky blue and it overlooked the lights of the city. The unmistakable aroma of pot roast reminded him that he was starved. "This is nice," he told Ruthie Hillman. "No wonder Dr. Hillman is a homebody."

Ruthie smiled. "It's comfortable," she said. "Where else should a man be comfortable if not in his own home? Are you married, Dr. Kohner?"

"It's Jeff," he said. "No, I'm not. Not yet. But I hope to be—" He stopped. A flicker of apprehension crossed his face and did not go unnoticed by his hostess.

"Forgive me for being a Jewish mother, but a man like you should have a wife. Ah, here's Louis. He was upstairs changing. Why don't you both have a glass of wine? Dinner will be ready very soon."

Louis kissed his wife on the cheek and watched her leave the room. "A very Jewish mother, my Ruthie. Did she ask you yet if you were married?"

Jeff grinned. "As a matter of fact, she did. That's okay. It must mean she likes me."

Louis gestured to a coral wing-backed chair. "Sit down, sit down, I'll get the wine." He poured it and, raising his glass, he said, "To Nancy's safe and speedy return."

"Amen." The grin vanished from the younger man's face. "Things are looking up, at least on that score. The police issued an APB. The bulletin went out this afternoon. They're keeping it quiet—no hint to the media. Better for her safety, they say. But every law enforcement agency in the state will have her picture and a description of her car."

"They'll find her," Louis assured him.

"I hope you're right. And soon. God, she could be anywhere by now."

"And how are you coming along in your research—trying to reproduce Pederson's chemical?"

"Not good." Jeff grimaced. "We don't know what the hell is wrong. We've tried everything we could think of, but so far, nothing."

Louis refilled their glasses. "It's extremely difficult to try to duplicate someone else's work."

"I know, I know." Jeff got up and began to pace. "But I've made the stuff before. I had it in my hands!"

"Using his formula—that's not the same thing. Stay with it. You'll do it, I know you will." Louis studied his younger colleague. "You still think whoever wanted Nancy out of the way was responsible for the explosion in the lab."

"I do," responded Jeff. "I'm convinced of that, even if the police won't make the connection. Whether or not Nancy is right about how the syndrome began, somebody out there thinks that she's right. Enough to want to blow 6BW away and turn the syndrome around to his own advantage."

"Metastaban."

"Metastaban. The timing is too coincidental for it not to have a connection. And the whole thing could only be carried off if—if Nancy were silenced."

"What about you?" Louis asked quietly. "As Roger pointed out, the two of you could be considered a threat—by reproducing the chemical in the hope of advancing Nancy's theory."

"I know that," said Jeff, sinking back in his chair. "I have the strangest feeling we're being watched in the lab. But I think they're counting on one small fact. They've got the upper hand because they've got Nancy. Even if we could manage to duplicate 6BW, there's no way we'd put her life in danger. So how in hell are we ever going to prove that the chemical could have started the whole damned syndrome?"

"You said at one point that Karl Fredericks at Camthon knew about 6BW," Louis recalled.

"Yeah, but I don't know how much he knew about it— or guessed from Pederson's lab notes. Rog is right. It's pretty nebulous stuff to try and pin him for kidnapping and murder."

Louis rose. "There's somebody else who has a lot to lose if 6BW really is the wonder drug. That's why I asked you here. I wondered if you knew."

Jeff looked up expectantly.

"The man has a major stake in Camthon and Metastaban—owns hundreds of chemotherapy clinics. Somebody in particular, right at Reese Fowler—"

Ruthie appeared, announced that dinner was ready. "First, the pot roast," she said firmly. "Then we'll talk about somebody in particular."

Paul Fairfield proffered a glass of sherry. "Take it, Karl. You look as though you need it. And for heaven's sake, relax!"

Fredericks didn't want sherry or platitudes. He set the glass down roughly on the desk. A few drops splashed on Fairfield's fine mahogany, but Fredericks neither saw it nor cared. "Damn it, Paul, you don't seem to realize what a serious situation this is! Things are getting—very warm. That's why I needed to see you."

"Well, here you are." Fairfield sounded annoyed. He mopped up the spill with a linen handkerchief and placed a pewter coaster under the glass. "Why don't you tell me what you mean?"

Fredericks closed his eyes. Where to begin? "For one thing, the FDA is putting on the screws. They're threatening to recall Metastaban from the market until Camthon can justify its claims that it's curing cancer. The advertising council is getting on us, too—and some attorneys for the AMA. So far, the directors at Camthon are sitting tight; they're busy counting their money. But sooner or later, the shit will hit the fan. How much longer can we keep this up?"

"As long as possible," barked Fairfield. "The FDA

moves like a turtle. Take my word, it will be weeks, at least, before Camthon is called upon to prove itself. No one else will move until the FDA does, and by that time, you are going to be fabulously wealthy.''

''If,'' retorted Fredericks, ''I don't die of apoplexy when the whole thing blows up in our faces.''

''Never fear. What about Kohner and Howell? Are they making any progress in their experiments?''

''Not that we can tell. They're knocking their brains out, my sources tell me, but with very little to show for it.''

''Well, then . . .'' Fairfield hefted his silver paperweight and weighed it for a moment in each hand. ''I think you are making mountains out of molehills.''

''Molehills, eh? What about Rafferty? Our friends up north are getting a little nervous. In case you've forgotten, they're holding a woman who can't be 'on vacation' forever!''

Fairfield smiled frostily. ''I haven't forgotten. You may pass the word along she's to be released. At eight A.M. day after tomorrow, she's to be deposited somewhere in the middle of Los Angeles—unharmed, just as we agreed—but *encouraged* to stick to her story.''

Fredericks blinked. ''Day after tomorrow?''

The silver-haired doctor nodded. He put down the paperweight, paused for emphasis, enjoying his friend's consternation. How could the likes of this simpering fool ever understand his stroke of genius? But he would explain. He picked up his glass, twirled it and sniffed its bouquet. ''Had you been able,'' he said at last, ''to rouse yourself from your petty self-absorption, you might have realized, Karl, old friend, I've not exactly been idle. I came to your rescue once before. I'm about to do it again.''

Fredericks, suspicious, raised his glass and took an anxious sip. He stared at the man through narrowed eyes. What in the hell was this?

''I've been making arrangements to ensure that both of us enjoy the fruits of our labor. You've worked hard,

Karl, and you've done very well. Now it will all pay off.'' Fairfield summarized a series of expediencies involving Swiss bank accounts, travel arrangements and clandestine accommodations that left Fredericks with his mouth agape. "All of which means,'' he concluded airily, "that by the time Rafferty returns to the city, you and I will be gone. If you're as anxious to extricate yourself from all of this as you say you are, be prepared to leave tomorrow night."

Fredericks swallowed. "Take off without a fare-thee-well? Without a goddamned backward glance? To live like hermits on some goddamned island? Paul, have you lost your mind?''

"*Hermits*, Karl, is hardly the term." Fairfield smiled at him. "I assure you the island is well populated with a charming mix of people. Social, if less than scrupulous types who'll make your new life a pleasure." His mouth formed a contemptuous smirk as he glared at the porcine Fredericks. "As for your fare-thee-well, considering your penchant for extramarital peccadilloes, I wouldn't have thought you'd find the good-bye's quite so heart-wrenching.''

Fredericks sat back and closed his eyes, reeling with the impact of what was happening. Leave? Just like that? Surely there had to be another way. Fairfield was clearly mad! Perhaps he could claim he'd been coerced by Fairfield, forced to go along in order to protect his company. But Camthon would be ruined in any case, even if anyone believed him. And in the end, it was *his* contacts, not Fairfield's, that had set the wheels in motion. Explosions, murder, kidnap, Jeezus! What in hell had he been thinking of? He had not expected it to come to this. Or had he, after all?

Fairfield watched his contemporary with impatience. He was offering the man a new life. He hadn't originally planned to include him in this; Fredericks ought to be grateful! "Come, come, Karl." He sat forward in his chair. "This is no time for dramatics. Sooner or later, as you so crudely put it, the shit will hit the fan. Either you join me on that flight tomorrow night or you'll have to ride it out and take your chances!''

Fredericks gazed dully into his friend's blazing eyes. ''I guess I have no choice. I'll be there.''

Chapter Three

When Judd Rohrbach attempted to reach Paul Fairfield, neither the physician's office receptionist nor the staff at Reese Fowler could tell him where the doctor was. It was not that Judd was especially worried about being implicated in the disappearance of Nancy Rafferty. He knew absolutely nothing about where Nancy had gone or why, and he told Detective Vickers so, unequivocally. But he was shaken by the interview.

"Nancy was under a lot of pressure," Judd intimated to the police detective, who listened with an impassive expression. "She was trying to make a case for something she couldn't prove. This . . . serendipity syndrome, people getting well for no apparent reason." He shook his head sympathetically. "She knew she couldn't keep up the momentum and it wouldn't be too long before her credibility was severely damaged. Hell," he added, hoping he sounded convincing, "I'd get out of town, too, if I realized I'd made a fool of myself and my career was about to go down the tubes."

"But you had no idea," persisted the officer, "that she didn't plan to show up for the broadcast on the night of April nineteenth?"

"No." Judd's face reflected his bafflement. "In fact," he added truthfully, "I saw her as she was leaving the studio late that afternoon and the last thing she said to me was, 'I'll be back in plenty of time.' Until that wire ar-

rived, I admit I was frankly worried." The newsman emitted a ragged sigh. "Poor thing, she must have been more
upset than anybody realized."

"Mmm," mumbled Vickers, looking at his notes. "And
in view of the—ah, close relationship you had shared with
her in the past, did it strike you as unusual that she chose
not to share her anxiety with you?"

Judd smiled sheepishly, and looked down at his open
palms, one beleaguered man to another. "What Nancy and
I had, Detective Vickers, was a brief little fling. She was
a wide-eyed kid from Nebraska who was grateful to me
when she landed the spot on my show. I'm ashamed to
admit it, but . . . I suppose I took advantage of that gratitude. She's extremely beautiful, as you know, officer, and
really quite intelligent."

"And then what happened?"

"After a while I grew tired of her . . . naiveté, I guess
you'd call it." He succeeded in looking sincere. "I tried
to warn her she was going too far with this serendipity
thing, but—well, I suppose when the time came, she was
too embarrassed to admit I was right."

Detective Vickers nodded. "So you have no idea where
Nancy Rafferty might be at this moment—or whether she
might be in danger?"

"In danger?" A look of horror crossed Judd Rohrbach's
face. "Why on earth would she be in danger? She's a good
kid, Detective, a little naive, as I said, but why would
anybody want to hurt her?"

The ship docked at Puerto Plata in the Dominican Re-
public, the last shore excursion before the *Song of Norway*
set sail for home. Miriam Phillips, clutching a wide-
brimmed straw hat, held her husband's hand and, buffeting
the warm wind, walked briskly to keep up with him in the
stream of debarking passengers.

"The amber market's up there on the hill," Zan said.
"You can see it, it's within walking distance."

"Good," said Miriam, not bothering to look. "God

knows we can use the exercise. If we keep eating at the rate we have been, we'll have to be rolled off the ship.''

"Oh, I don't know." Zan kissed the back of her neck. "Seems to me we've been getting enough exercise. 'Course, if you think we ought to step up the pace—''

"Oh," groaned his wife, "Zan, really!"

They crossed the harbor area into the business district teeming with tourists and peddlers. "Let's go this way." Zan veered toward a side street. "Out of the flow of traffic." They walked through a park with a ramshackle bandstand and benches badly in need of paint. At the corner, they found they could not cross the narrow street. Their way was blocked by a large group of mourners.

Zan assumed they were mourners, for they were dressed in black and there was a good deal of sobbing and moaning. Directly across from them was a small wooden church, its warped, peeling doors thrown open. The wailing grew louder and Zan craned his neck to see a procession of pallbearers who entered the church supporting a small white casket, the kind that could only hold a child. A woman followed, sobbing pitifully, and the mourners pressed forward to support her.

Zan turned to shield his wife from the sight, but she had already seen the small casket. She shuddered visibly, her eyes filled with tears. Zan held her tightly. "It's all right."

"I know." She tried to stop her trembling. "I'll be okay. Just hold me."

In moments, the mourners had filed into the church; the doors swung precariously shut. The street was quiet. Zan stroked his wife's face. "Please. Don't let it spoil the day. We have nothing to mourn, only things to celebrate."

Miriam allowed herself to be led up the hill into the crush of the marketplace. The building was a sprawling modern edifice, in contrast with the town. It was packed with tourists and hawking peddlers, their arms strung with tawdry amber jewelry. Miriam found it depressing and vulgar, but Zan was strangely entranced. "Look." He pointed to a carved sailboat fitted with amber sails and masts.

"Stevie would like this, don't you think? How much?" he demanded of the wizened vendor.

Before the man could answer, they were jostled apart and a small boy tugged at Miriam's sleeve. "Too much, lady." He grinned up at her from a dirt-streaked face. "I sell you cheaper. Come."

The wizened vendor lashed out to club the child, but Zan grabbed the surprisingly strong arm. "Let's get out of here," he said to Miriam's stricken face as the boy darted off into the crowd.

In their stateroom Zan tried to comfort her. "It's a way of life. There's so much poverty."

"I know," she replied. "I think I was upset by that funeral. I'll be all right in a little while."

"But you'd rather be home."

She looked at him sadly. "Not for the reasons you think. I have the oddest feeling something is happening, something Stevie is a part of. I can't seem to shake the feeling that for some reason we ought to be home."

"Miriam." Zan stroked her hair. "Just a few days and we'll be home. Let's try to make the best of them, huh? What can happen in a few days?"

Four days, Nancy Rafferty thought idly. I've been a hostage now for four days in some godforsaken dollhouse with a pair of misfit kidnappers named Bonnie and Clyde. Who'd believe it?

The two continued to treat her with respect, assuring her the ordeal was nearly over. She wanted to believe them. She took it as auspicious when Clyde offered her the use of the washer so that she could wash her rumpled clothes. Clad in an oversized terry robe, she had forced herself to watch him cook spaghetti sauce while she waited for her wash to get done.

She studied Clyde now, seated across from her on a quilted blue chintz love seat. His wiry frame was hunched over a magazine which he read through the ever-present stocking mask. "Clyde," she asked, "do you like what

you do? Have you always been a part of—the underworld?''

Clyde turned the page. "It's a job. I do okay. Why? Are
you being a reporter?''

She suppressed a smile. "No. I just wondered. Have you
ever been a chef? You're really an excellent cook.''

"Thank you," said Clyde. "I appreciate that. But I'm
afraid I'm not excellent enough. Not for an important restaurant or hotel. None of the best would ever take me on.''

"You've thought of it, then.''

"Sure. I've thought of it." He seemed to measure her
through his mask. "I've even thought of—opening my own
place. Something small—maybe Continental, where the
food would be the best in the world.''

"What a lovely idea," Nancy smiled. "Why haven't
you ever done it, Clyde?''

He seemed embarrassed. "I don't know. I guess I never
thought I'd be good enough. Besides, I've got a life, you
know? Whatever it's worth. I mean, it's not easy to stick
your neck out.''

"No," said Nancy, "it isn't easy. I guess I know about
that, too." She looked straight at him and wished again
she could see the little man behind the mask. "You're
okay, Clyde—for a kidnapper, I mean. I suppose I should
thank my lucky stars." She glanced at Bonnie, asleep on
the sofa. "But I still want to know why me? Who wanted
me kidnapped?''

Clyde picked up his magazine, suddenly aloof.

The telephone shrilled a raucous intrusion. Bonnie
jumped to attention. But Clyde was the one who picked
up. His responses were terse. Afterward, he turned to Nancy. "Well," he announced, as though it were his decision,
"it seems you are ready to go home.''

Nancy stared. "Now? Today?''

"Very soon." He beckoned to Bonnie and the two of
them held a whispered conference, Nancy sitting forward
in her seat. Bonnie surrendered his gun to Clyde, sauntered

out through the kitchen. In a moment she heard the unmistakable sound of her Volkswagen engine starting up.

Clyde handled the pistol with obvious distaste, but he trained it on Nancy, nonetheless. "Sorry," he said. "A precaution, you see, while Bonnie is arranging transportation."

"I'm actually going?" Nancy sputtered. "You really are going to set me free?"

Clyde cocked his head as though his feelings were hurt. "I promised you, didn't I? That you'd be safe? By tomorrow morning you'll be back in Los Angeles. Now it really wasn't too bad, was it?"

Nancy sat back, stunned. It was all so incredible. She started to speak. She had so many questions. But it was obvious Clyde would not give her the answers. Instead, she looked out the window at the now familiar landscape and tried to convince herself it was nearly over. Would she walk out scot-free? Could it be that simple? And if it were, what then?

Detective Vickers stubbed out a cigarette. "Dr. Kohner, I'm trying to be reasonable. We're doing everything we can to locate Miss Rafferty, checking out every lead. But how can you ask me to go after her abductor when we're not even sure she's been kidnapped?"

"I'm telling you Paul Fairfield has the motive and the means."

"And I'm telling you, you read too many thrillers!"

"He's heavily tied to Camthon. Camthon knew about 6BW. Who was it who led the campaign for Metastaban? For Fairfield, 6BW meant the end of chemotherapy—the end of his empire, for Pete's sake!"

"They only knew what Pederson told them. You told me that yourself. What reason did they have to feel so threatened?"

"The serendipity syndrome!" Jeff exhaled deeply. "They saw the drug working. They knew that Nancy was onto it. They had to have her out of the way in order to capitalize on their own worthless product!''

"Speculation," Vickers said. "Even if I believe it, we can't support it. Paul Fairfield is a reputable physician. We don't harass citizens on speculation."

"What would it take to convince you," Jeff asked, "that he needed the explosion and the kidnap?"

"A suspect, for one thing. The perpetrator of the explosion. We still don't know who did it."

"That's your job. The suspect. What the hell are you guys doing?"

"Losing time talking to you. The best thing you can do, doctor, is go back to your lab. Prove there really was a 6BW. Prove there's a miracle drug that can do what you claim. Then you've got a motive, not before. I already stuck my neck out in assuming she's been kidnapped. As for the suspect, you're right. That's our job. Now get the hell out of here so we can do it."

He walked the doctor to the elevator, and started back to his desk. Then he walked across the hall, strolled into the Major Crimes unit. Pierce, on the bomb squad, was dictating notes. Vickers took a seat at his desk. "Nothing new on Reese Fowler?"

Pierce put down the mike and shrugged his square shoulders. "I don't know. Could be. We got a tip on a torch we never heard of. On the street they call him Blowjobber. We're checkin' it out, but who the hell knows? It's a little early to tell."

Vickers nodded. "Gotcha. Listen, if anything does turn up—call me, will you? Day or night. I want in on this one."

Chapter Four

Nancy struggled as the blindfold went on. "It's too tight."
Clyde obligingly loosened it. But her hands were cuffed
behind her back. She was caught between outrage and tears.

"I'm sorry, Nancy." Clyde's voice was gentle. "There
simply is no other way. We'll be driving back together,
just you and I. It wouldn't do for you to know the route."

"What if I just start screaming?"

"You won't," warned Bonnie. She was lifted to her
feet, shuffled along like an invalid. A car door opened. She
was helped inside. The voices of her captors became in-
audible. Nancy sat back in the smooth interior. It wasn't
the interior of her car. She breathed deeply, determined to
stay calm, already regretting her outburst.

Bonnie had returned at just after dusk, duly masked and
more subdued than usual. Clyde had quickly handed back
the gun and set about preparing Nancy's dinner. She had
picked at it in silence, aware of their tension, wavering
between impatience and apprehension. "Are we going in
my car?" she asked to break the tension.

"No," replied Clyde. "Bonnie will drive yours home.
You'll be reunited with it in Los Angeles—when your 'vacation' is over."

Nancy looked at him but she said nothing. She continued
to chew in silence.

"And it was a vacation. That is your story. I strongly
urge you to stick to it."

"You can't be serious." Nancy stared in disbelief. This could be the story of her lifetime! How could she not report it? "What makes you think—?"

"You have no choice." The threat behind his words was clear. "We know where you are. We know who your friends are. What a shame if someone should meet with a dreadful accident."

The softly spoken words hung in the air like shards of shrapnel, impotent until they found a target. A shiver of fear snaked down Nancy's spine. Her protest froze in her throat.

The hours had passed in silence. There was nothing more to say. Nancy huddled, waiting, on the chintz settee. It was Bonnie who, near midnight, approached her so casually, pinning her arms behind her back. Then there was the blindfold and the unfamiliar car. And now, powerful hands gripped her ankles.

"No!" she protested, wrenching away. She never even felt the tiny pinprick. But she heard Clyde's voice from a distance as she drifted. "Poor Nancy. I really am so sorry. . . ."

Roger Howell inspected the contents of a beaker, checking its clarity through the light. "Could be in the cooking," he murmured, squinting. "Doesn't look right to me."

"There's nothing wrong with it!" Jeff snapped. "Dammit, that's Pederson's formula!"

"Then bring on the rodents and we'll give it a go. Hey man, you know it's close to midnight?"

Jeff threw down his pencil, shoved aside his notes. "I know we've done everything right!"

"Then maybe we'll see some results in the morning." Roger was filling syringes.

"Go on home, Rog. Go on. I can finish it up."

Roger chuckled. "You're a regular Boy Scout."

Officer Ian Connelly, California Highway Patrol, had two hours left of his shift. Traffic was light on this section of 101 at this hour of the morning. There were a few big

rigs hauling produce from Salinas and a small but steady
stream of pickups. Most folks doing the serious driving
south were over on the Interstate 5, an anonymous stretch
of flat gray highway, duller than dishwater but fast.

It was also a speed trap. An alert CHP could pick off
speeders like fleas. If, thought Connelly, chuckling to himself, he didn't die of boredom first.

Officer Connelly preferred the bustle along 101, a mot-
ley collection of sleepy little towns, itinerant farm workers
and cheerful, sweating tourists in the summer. Tonight,
though, it was quiet and he was thinking seriously of
swinging over to the Laurel Inn Coffee Shop for a ten-
minute break in the monotony.

He had decided to do so, and was guiding his motorcycle
toward the Laurel Inn exit when he noticed the big rig just
ahead. It slowed dramatically, then picked up speed and
proceeded to pass on the left. The vehicle now in Connelly's vision was a beat-up yellow Volks plodding along at
a steady fifty-five and reminding Officer Connelly that he'd
promised his kid to go look at a used Volks when he was
off duty in the morning. Connelly shook his head. The kid
had cars on the brain.

He had slowed on the off ramp and was weighing the
merits of apple pie against lemon when something flashed
into his head. A yellow Volks. Hadn't he seen a report
requesting information on such a vehicle? There were a lot
of yellow bugs on the highway, but maybe it wouldn't hurt
to have a look. He swung left on the access road heading
back to 101. All he wanted to do was check the plates.

He caught the Volks easily, noted the license number
and a male Caucasian driving. The driver paid him no mind
as he paced the vehicle and finally swung off at the nearest
off ramp. It struck Connelly as odd. Most drivers, spotting
an officer in the rearview, slowed their speed instinctively
whether they'd been speeding or not.

"Marty," he said to the dispatcher by radio, "check the
computer for a missing yellow Volkswagen, might be a

report from L.A. Give me a description and a plate number, will ya?''

The dispatcher's voice crackled back. ''Yellow VW, seventy-three, small dent in the left rear fender. License John Charles Victor four-four-three. Wanted in connection with a possible Missing Person. The registered owner is Nancy Rafferty, female, Caucasian, age twenty-six.''

Connelly paused. ''Yeah, well, the vehicle's traveling south on one-oh-one five or six miles south of Salinas. Driver is a male Caucasian taking it nice and easy. Look, I'm gonna pursue and check it out. Send me some backup, will ya?''

''Roger, you got it, right away. Trask's in that neck of the woods.''

Connelly revved the powerful engine, swung back onto the highway. He picked up speed until he spotted the VW maintaining fifty-five in the middle lane. The driver wasn't going to be stopped for speeding, that much was for sure. But anybody who maintained fifty-five on an open highway at this hour of the morning was a little bit suspect in Connelly's book. As the backup patrol car loomed into view in his rearview mirror, Connelly drew up alongside the Volks. He indicated to the driver that he wanted him to pull over. The driver did so without hesitation, looking surprised but not flustered.

''Morning.'' Connelly sauntered to the driver's window as the patrol car pulled up behind. His right hand rested lightly on his service revolver. ''May I see your registration and driver's license?''

The driver did not hesitate nor indicate concern over the presence of three police officers. He reached into the glove compartment and drew out some papers which he handed over to Connelly.

Connelly inspected the papers wordlessly, careful to take his time. He liked to allow for a disquieting interval into which most drivers plunged with an anxious question or explanation. Often, Connelly knew, you could learn a lot before you ever stated your business.

This driver, however—identified by his license as James Peter Simmons—showed no inclination to plunge. The photo fit; he was 48 years old, address somewhere in Los Angeles. He sat quietly while the officer flashed his penlight from one document to the other.

"Sir, this vehicle's registered to a Miss Nancy Rafferty," Connelly stated finally. "Are you any relation to her?"

"No, sir." Simmons' face was noncommittal. "No relation. I'm just a friend."

"I see," said Connelly, flanked by the other officers. "Does Miss Rafferty know you're driving her automobile?"

"Sure does," said James Peter Simmons truthfully. "I'm driving it back to L.A. for her. She gave me her keys. See, here's her key ring." He drew the key from the ignition and handed Connelly a ring full of keys caught by a heart-shaped, rainbow-hued ornament.

"Where is Miss Rafferty?" Connelly asked casually. "Some reason she can't drive it herself?"

"No, sir. She's on her way back to L.A., too. But she's driving down with another friend."

The officer hesitated, but only briefly. "Sir, would you mind stepping out of the vehicle?" Simmons immediately did as he was asked, a burly fellow, barrel-chested, seemingly light on his feet.

"Now turn around slowly, put your hands up over the car and spread your legs a little, if you would." Again, Simmons did as he was asked and Connelly frisked him efficiently. He came up with a wallet containing three twenty-dollar bills, a Union Oil credit card in the name of James P. Simmons and a scrap of paper containing what appeared to be a phone number with an L.A. area code. "This your phone number?" he questioned the big man.

"What number is that?" asked Simmons innocently.

Connelly moved it into his vision. Simmons paused. "It's a friend's."

Connelly exchanged glances with his fellow officers. There was an imperceptible nod of heads. "All right, sir, you can turn around now," he informed Simmons. He faced the driver squarely. "A Miss Nancy Rafferty is now listed as a missing person by the Los Angeles Police Department, sir, and this vehicle is being sought for information. I'm afraid we're going to ask you to come with us, Mr. Simmons, until we can check out your story."

A flicker of surprise showed briefly on the suspect's face, quickly replaced by a grin and a hearty laugh. "A missing person? Nancy? Officer—"

"Connelly."

"Officer Connelly. She's been up here on vacation a few days."

"Maybe so, sir. We'll check it out as soon as we get to the station."

Simmons chuckled. "Nancy missing? Like I said, she's on her way back home. Ought to be there by six or seven A.M."

"Well, good. She can corroborate your story."

Simmons was led to the waiting patrol car, still chuckling and shaking his head.

"Meet you there," shouted Connelly to his fellow officers. "I'm just gonna flag this little bug and have a look around inside."

In Los Angeles, Paul Fairfield drove at a leisurely pace to Los Angeles International Airport. It was only two A.M. and he had four hours until flight time; but he'd been ready, and sleep was out of the question. He would pick up his ticket, make do with an airport breakfast and meet Karl Fredericks on schedule.

A heavy mist hovered over the city, turning to fog as he neared the airport and swirling in the beam of his headlights. It was a damned nuisance, but typical of the season. It was difficult to imagine that in just a few hours, the sun would burn through the mist. But it would, as it had every morning this week, bathing the city in harsh, glaring sunlight by the time Fairfield reached his club for breakfast.

As he drove, Fairfield had no misgivings about leaving,

no second thoughts at all. It had come as something of a rude awakening that there was no one whose company he would miss. Not the hospital, certainly not the nuns nor the boredom of his own private practice. All he required was comfort and solitude; and both of those would be plentiful where he was going.

It seemed ironic that he was leaving the city within hours of Nancy Rafferty's return. He hadn't planned on the closeness of timing, but he found a certain keen excitement in the well-timed execution of his plans. And while he was glad to be leaving the city, she would be grateful to return. Grateful enough, he was reasonably sure—and frightened enough—to keep her mouth shut. He wondered whether she would piece together his part in the Metastaban phenomenon. No matter. Regardless of how gutsy she was, he would be long gone.

He guided the Mercedes into a parking stall and realized, with a little pang, that he would miss it. But automobiles were easily replaced. He decided, as he got out his briefcase, that he would order another just like it. He locked it anyway, out of habit. Looking around and turning up the collar of his London Fog coat, he strode toward the Pan American terminal.

If he had misgivings, they were held in check, though he was worried about that simpering fool, Fredericks. He hoped the man had enough of a backbone under all that poundage not to fall apart in front of his wife. As he entered the terminal and glanced around nervously, he wished he had Fredericks safely aboard the plane.

Chapter Five

Karl Fredericks had passed a sleepless night. As Fairfield had surmised, it had been difficult to separate from Mary, far more so than he had anticipated. He had spent a good part of the afternoon charming her over lunch at the Bistro, alternately touched and flattered by her joy in the unexpected tryst. "Why, Karl," she had murmured, coy as a girl, "it's been years since you asked me to lunch!"

She had bubbled on and on with enthusiasm about the success of Metastaban, about how proud she was to be the wife of a man associated with the miracle. It had been almost too easy to convince her of his desire to spend a few days alone with her, "a quiet little rendezvous, just the two of us."

He'd neglected her, he lied, because of the commotion at Camthon. He was happy she truly understood. Now he wanted to make it up to her; would she go on ahead and open the house in Newport? He would join her on Friday for an entire week—what did she think about that? And Mary Fredericks—who had not spent so much as a weekend at Newport with her husband since the last of their sons had gone off to school and who was quite aware of Karl's penchant for young and beautiful women—blushed like a virgin bride. She would leave early this evening, she decided, air out the house and lay in a stock of groceries.

Later, waving to her as she backed out of their Beverly Hills driveway, he was stricken with the enormity of his loss. It was inevitable, even fitting, that Paul Fairfield should chide him, take him for a sentimental fool. He'd been a bastard to Mary for years and—he had to admit to himself even now—he did not regret a single minute of it. But he hoped when he was gone that Mary wouldn't hate him; that in her struggle to preserve the shreds of her dignity she would know, if that was possible at all, how grateful he was for her loyal support.

He turned back to the house in the lingering dusk, blinking back the shocking sting of tears. *I never meant to disgrace you, Mary. I wish there were some other choice.* He started up the stairs, paused to study a portrait of his sons along with Martin, his nephew, as children.

He was halfway up the stairs before a realization stunned him. Martin had been working on Pederson's grant proposal. He likely had a copy of his files! Not that it mattered whether 6BW ever surfaced again—it had served the purpose Fairfield had envisioned, had made them very wealthy indeed. If there was anything to it, if it really was a miracle drug, it was as much of a legacy as he could hope to leave.

Yet he felt something akin to satisfaction that it was he who had discovered the gaffe and not his silver-haired colleague. He could call Martin now, contrive to see the files, offer to review the material in deference to the scientist who was dead. He was breathless by the time he'd mounted the stairs. He sank heavily into a chair by the telephone and waited for his breathing to return to normal. It would give him pleasure, if anything could, to reveal his coup to Fairfield.

Sheriff Roy Orloff, in Salinas, California, reread the bulletin from L.A. He had inherited the suspect, James Simmons, from the CHP; and though he had personally questioned the man for an hour, he knew no more about the whereabouts of Nancy Rafferty or how Simmons had come into possession of her car than Simmons had revealed to the patrolman.

But he'd booked him for suspicion of Grand Theft Auto,

and damned if the computer hadn't turned up matching fingerprints belonging to a John R. Maxwell, said Maxwell implicated in a possible kidnap in Texas in '77, suspect released for lack of substantiating evidence. And this Nancy Rafferty, some kind of local L.A. celebrity, was listed as missing under mysterious circumstances, possibly the victim of a kidnap.

Further, though the fact meant little to Orloff, the Major Crimes unit of the LAPD was considering a connection between the possible perpetrators and an unsolved bombing and murder. What mattered to their case was that the sheriff in Salinas was in possession of the alleged victim's automobile and was holding a man for possible auto theft who had a record of suspected kidnapping. Therefore, Orloff's next step was clear. He picked up the telephone, checked the officer's name at the bottom of the report, and though he seriously doubted he would reach this Vickers at three in the morning, he dialed the Los Angeles Police Department.

Detective Vickers, as it happened, was on his way to Parker Center, the vast downtown complex where police business was conducted day and night. Having left word that he was to be contacted at any hour regarding anything related to the Reese Fowler bombing, he'd been roused from his bed half an hour ago by a colleague with a startling bit of news.

"Blowjobber," alias Arthur Harris, had been picked up and was ready for questioning. The elusive arsonist had been fingered by a nervous hospital employee in return for a promise of protection. A search of a storage unit rented by Harris, supervised by a properly aghast night watchman, revealed a sizable cache of explosives, among them the anesthetic cyclopropane. Did Vickers want to be present at the investigation? Vickers was on his way.

He had no more than stepped off the third-floor elevator when the phone call came from Salinas. Among the things Orloff passed on to the detective was the presence of a single misshapen nylon stocking in the glove compartment of the VW—and a Los Angeles phone number in possession of the suspect.

"Check out this number," Vickers ordered a round-faced young underling; and, concluding his business with the sheriff in Salinas, he headed for the interrogation room where Blowjobber Harris was being questioned.

His attention wandered for just a minute while he contemplated the significance of the simultaneous custodies of Blowjobber Harris and James Simmons. Could be there was no connection—that Kohner's theory was a myth. Or it could be one of those incredible coincidences that happened in police work all the time. Nancy Rafferty, Vickers guessed, would call it serendipity: finding paydirt in an unlikely manner at a time when you least expect it. But seventeen years of putting puzzles together had made a believer out of Vickers. You plodded along and you did your job and you pushed around the pieces. And sometimes you counted on a little luck to make the pieces fit.

Chapter Six

Karl Fredericks decided the fates must surely be conspiring against him. By four A.M., he had still not reached Martin. Pederson's files would likely remain in Los Angeles after all, and it would fall to Fredericks to point out to Paul Fairfield what could be a regrettable oversight. To make matters worse, he had heard on the radio that the fog showed no signs of lifting. The airport was socked in, no flights in or out, and no one could say with any certainty when normal air traffic would resume.

He had tried to reach Fairfield without success, and assumed he was en route to the airport. There was no way to reach his contacts up north who were undoubtedly now, at his direction, on their way back to Los Angeles with Nancy Rafferty.

Fredericks did not put as much faith in the likelihood of Rafferty's enforced silence as his friend apparently did. He felt it was imperative that they be airborne by the time Nancy Rafferty was released, and the dreaded flight to South America now took on an urgency that chilled him. But there was nothing he could do except proceed on schedule and hope to hell the goddamned fog would lift.

He picked up his briefcase, felt for his car keys in the pocket of his raincoat and the reassuring bulge of his wallet. He fought off the desire for a last look around, and trudged resolutely down the stairs. Fairfield was right about this much at least: it was best that they travel without luggage. Anything they wanted could be easily purchased once they reached their destination.

At the bottom of the stairs he tried, one last time, to reach his nephew. But there was no answer and no point in fretting over it. He had, quite simply, run out of time.

He backed the Cadillac out of the garage, cursing the fog and cursing himself for delaying as long as he had. He did not see the vehicle that followed him, inhabited by two surprised young officers who had only twenty minutes earlier taken up their vigil in Beverly Hills.

Nancy Rafferty drifted into consciousness with reluctance. She had the eerie feeling that something prevented her from complete, alert awakening. It was many moments before she remembered that she was blindfolded, stuffed like baggage in the rear seat of a car she could not describe, careering down a highway with a capricious madman who might or might not release her in Los Angeles.

She tried to change position, to ease the cramp in her upper torso and the dull headache that had settled at the base of her neck. Apparently, the motion did not go unnoticed, for a familiar voice floated back to her. "Good morning, Nancy. I trust you slept without too much discomfort. I do apologize for the accommodations. As I said, it could not be helped."

Nancy didn't answer, hoping her silence might prompt her driver to say more.

"We are very nearly at our journey's end," Clyde told her. "I'm happy to say we're right on schedule."

Nancy's curiosity surfaced despite her. "Tell me what would have happened, Clyde, if you'd been stopped for a traffic ticket with me bound, drugged and blindfolded right here in the backseat of the car."

His response was pragmatic. Nancy longed to see his face. "I am a courteous and defensive driver. I have never, as a matter of fact, had a traffic ticket in my life. But I'm beginning to see that sometimes, in life, you have to take chances—be willing to put your neck on the line. As a matter of fact, I owe you a debt for making me see that these past few days."

Nancy slowly shook her head, puzzled. Would she ever understand someone like Clyde? "Where will you be—taking me in Los Angeles?" she decided to ask at last.

"Are you familiar with Olvera Street?"

Nancy had heard of the old Mexican business district in the heart of downtown Los Angeles. It was a colorful bazaar near the newly restored historical plaza, a busy mecca for tourists. But in the two years she had been in the city, Nancy had never been there.

Clyde, however, did not wait for a response. "It's fascinating if you haven't seen it. It's a little early for the tourist bustle, but then again, we hardly want a crowd. We'll rendezvous with Bonnie who will hand over your car keys, and then you'll be free to go."

"Free to go," Nancy repeated dully. "Free to go about my business as though this had never happened. Free to pick up my life again—as long as I keep my mouth shut."

"As long," echoed Clyde, without the slightest trace of menace, "as you accept what you cannot change. You may tell your friends about your little vacation as though it had really happened. And have the good sense to protect them—and yourself—from any further incident."

He had no sooner finished this speech when Nancy felt the car slowing and then a change in their direction. A hammering began in her chest along with a curious inability to swallow. In moments, they stopped. It was eerily still. Nancy felt the need for a bathroom.

"Odd," Clyde commented, as though they were meeting for a picnic. "Bonnie should have been here long ago. No sign of him, though, and I don't dare wait. I have another engagement. I'm sorry about your car. Perhaps he'll turn up soon. That is, if you care to wait."

She heard the front door of the car slam and the rear door open. Smooth hands untied her wrists and reached over to untie her ankles. She lay still, afraid to move, the hammering loud in her ears. Clyde helped her up to a sitting position, patted her shoulder gently. "Nancy, it has been my pleasure to know you. I truly regret the circumstances. I apologize again for the indignity you suffered—and I wish you the best of luck."

She heard the words, the grave sincerity, but she hadn't the faintest notion what to say. Finally, he took her by the hand, led her carefully out of the car. She stumbled against him, fighting for balance; and instinctively she put out her hands. She felt the cold resistance, the roughened pocking of what she decided was brick.

"Stand where you are," Clyde commanded softly. "You are facing against a wall. In a moment I will take off your blindfold. Count to twenty before you turn around."

The big man with the bulging briefcase hurried to the Pan American counter. He elbowed his way through a knot of milling passengers, nearly unseating a sleepy child perched on the edge of a suitcase; he engaged a young man behind the counter in a short but heated conversation. He then stuffed an envelope into his left breast pocket and lumbered down the carpeted corridor, his raincoat billowing around him.

Wordlessly, his surveillants parted, one to follow the portly man and one toward the clerk at the counter. "Excuse me, sir," said the one approaching the desk, briefly displaying his shield. "Police business. May I see you a moment?" The man behind the counter looked annoyed.

The portly man had, according to the clerk, picked up a one-way flight ticket to Buenos Aires previously paid for by credit card. He had checked through no luggage and had been upset over the delay in departure of the flight, scheduled for thirty minutes hence. The clerk had not been able to say when the flight might actually board. He guessed, for the benefit of the plainclothes officer, that it might be within the hour.

The officer asked the clerk to verify the name and account number of the card that had paid for the purchase. He thanked him for his cooperation and sauntered down the corridor where his partner lounged casually near a bank of telephones. "Buenos Aires," he said. "One way. I guess I'd better call it in."

His partner nodded, keeping in view the rotund fellow with the rumpled raincoat and the tall, elegant, silver-haired guy with whom he was engaged in conversation. "Got any idea why we're tailing 'em?" he asked.

The first officer shrugged. "Beats me," he said. "The surveillance was ordered by Detective Vickers."

Detective Vickers took the phone call with ill-concealed excitement. Blowjobber Harris, during the course of his interrogation, had implicated a man he called "Fred" as his contact for the Reese Fowler blowup. For all his belief in policeman's luck, Vickers had difficulty grappling with the idea that "Fred" might be the same Karl Fredericks under surveillance at LAX.

Things were starting to fall into place. The man at the airport had a one-way to Buenos Aires, no luggage but a thick leather briefcase, and a distinctly disquieting air —and his phone number had been in the pocket of some clown in Salinas who'd been driving Nancy Rafferty's car.

Dawn was insinuating itself through the fog-shrouded city when Vickers tossed down the last of his coffee and left Parker Center for the airport.

Nancy Rafferty could not guess how long she had leaned against the cold, damp brick wall, trembling in the misty half-light. She could not have counted to twenty had her life depended on it, so paralyzing was her fright.

She heard the engine behind her churn to life, the car glide noiselessly away. She clung to the wall out of tenacity, determined not to faint again, aware of the starkness, the cold, the support, blinking to bring her vision into focus. When she finally stepped away, testing the ground beneath her feet, she was seized with uncontrollable shivering. Too numb to sob, too breathless to cry out, she hugged herself with icy fingers and peered around at her surroundings. She found herself in a narrow alleyway cluttered with overflowing trashbins. It seemed barely wide enough to accommodate the car from which she'd just been delivered.

She began to breath deeply, great ragged gasps filling her lungs with damp air. The shivering stopped, giving way at first to a steady chill and then to the heat of her fury. How dare they reduce her to gelatinous mush, incapable of action, of thought! She galvanized her legs to march out of the alleyway, her footsteps bleakly echoing her resolve.

She saw that she was at the entrance to Olvera Street, across from the now-deserted plaza. It was shrouded in fog, but she knew where she was and she turned south toward Los Angeles Street. She took off her shoes and began to run, mildly aware of the spectacle she made with no jacket, no handbag, no shoes on her feet and a wrinkled dress she'd been wearing for days. She glanced over her shoulder once at the sound of a car, almost fearing yet wishing that Bonnie had somehow materialized at the curb in her Volkswagen. But it was only a rattletrap Ford puttering by.

She could barely see it in the cloying fog, but she knew the building was there. She had covered stories there often enough, on the walkway of Parker Center.

From the moment she'd gained control of herself, there had been no doubt where she would go. Clyde and his pointed threats be damned, she was going straight to the police!

Detective J. D. Vickers pulled up his collar and pushed open the heavy glass door. He found himself looking into the drawn white face and incredible green eyes of the reporter Nancy Rafferty.

Chapter Seven

He recognized her at once. There was no mistaking the well-defined features of the much-televised face behind the mask of exhaustion. "My God," he muttered. "Nancy Rafferty."

Nancy closed her eyes, felt the surge of adrenaline that had propelled her subside; she sagged against the man who had recognized her. Vickers supported her, led her through the door and, seating her on a bench in the outer corridor, began to examine her closely.

"Are you hurt?" he began, checking her pupils for signs of concussion, noting the absence of bruises. Her clothes were a mess, her mane of hair was disheveled; but apart from a chafing at her wrists and ankles she appeared to be unharmed.

"No," she replied. "I don't think so." Her breathing had slowed, her voice was steady. She reached down to rub her ankle. "I ran here from Olvera Street, where I was dropped off from a car by a man—who abducted me several days ago." An uncertain frown crossed her face. "Are you an LAPD officer?"

Vickers produced his identification. "We have a missing bulletin out on you."

"They set it up to seem as though I'd gone on vacation. They jumped me from the backseat of my car." The words came quickly to her now.

"Do you know who they were?"

Nancy shook her head. "I knew them only as Bonnie and Clyde." She hesitated, peering at him, feeling foolish. "That's what they told me to call them."

Vickers noted her dilating pupils, the agitation verging on hysteria. "Let's get you inside. Can you manage?" he asked, attempting to help her to her feet.

She nodded, moving slowly, limping a little. Her left ankle was beginning to swell, but she gripped his arm, determined to walk, determined to tell her story.

"I'm going to have you talk to another detective," said Vickers, pressing a button in the elevator. "I'll get back as soon as I can. I was on my way out on something else. Something that may be related." He looked directly at her as they emerged on their floor. "Does the name Karl Fredericks mean anything to you?"

Nancy shook her head. "No, I don't think so."

Vickers allowed himself a grimace. "Do you have any idea—any guess at all—who might have been responsible for your kidnap?"

"I'm reasonably sure the men who took me hostage were only doing a job. That they may have been hired by someone at Camthon Pharmaceuticals. Or by Dr. Paul Fairfield."

The elevator doors opened and Vickers led her through another door into a large room partitioned with glass. He seated her in a vinyl chair. "I'll be back in just a minute."

When he returned he was followed by a woman, tall, slim, unquestionably feminine even in an austerely tailored suit. "This is Detective Vale," Vickers informed her. "She knows all about you. She'll take your story."

The pretty detective smiled and extended a hand. "I'm happy to meet you, Miss Rafferty. Can I get you something first? Coffee? A sandwich?" Her smile became a rueful grin. "I'm sorry. I wish I could offer you a hot tub and an hour and a half to soak."

Nancy managed a wan smile. "I'll settle for a ladies room."

* * *

The fog was lifting by seven-forty when Vickers entered the Pan Am terminal. He noted the boarding gate number for the Buenos Aires flight and strode quickly down the corridor.

" 'Bout time," he was greeted by the younger plain-clothes officer strolling up to him through the crowd. "If you want him, you better go get him now. That plane's about to board." He nodded in the direction of two men moving with the flow of the passengers. "The fat one's Fredericks. He met his friend, the one who looks like a snotty Cary Grant, just after he picked up his tickets."

The detective melted into the crowd and positioned himself directly in front of Fredericks. "Karl Fredericks?" he asked. The man stared at him, wide-eyed. "Detective J. D. Vickers, LAPD."

The fat man's mouth worked but no sound came out. He looked as though he might faint. Vickers continued. "I'd like to talk to you. And to you, sir," he said to the silver-haired man who had stepped off gingerly to one side.

"I'm afraid I have nothing to say to you." The silver-haired man's tone was haughty. Then someone shrieked, and the crowd pressed forward as Fredericks slumped slowly to the ground.

"Your name, sir?" pressed Vickers, meeting the steely blue eyes of Fairfield, ignoring the man at his feet.

The man drew himself up to his full height and glared at the detective. "I am Dr. Paul Fairfield. And unless you have adequate reason to detain me, I'm afraid my flight is about to board."

"Implication in an alleged kidnap. Sir, I'm afraid you're going to miss that plane."

Nancy repeated her story twice with as many details as she could muster. Then she begged to be allowed to go home for a long, hot bath and fresh clothes.

"We'll need you later this afternoon," said Vickers, who had just returned from the airport. "But Detective Vale can take you home at least long enough to do that."

In her apartment she paused for a minute, as though it were all somehow new to her. Then she proceeded to the telephone where she promptly dialed a number and waited. "Laboratory, please." She sat on a sofa. Detective Vale watched her closely. "Jeff? It's Nancy. I'm home. I'm all right." The beautiful face began to crumble. "Yes. Oh, please." Her eyes filled with tears. She hung up, put her face in her hands.

In a moment she straightened, wiped away tears, her eyes luminous and determined. She inhaled deeply, composed her features, picked up the phone and dialed again. "Callahan," she greeted her producer, her voice firm and steady. Detective Vale watched in fascination. "It's Nancy. I'm home." She threw back her head. "And have I got a story for you!"

She was bathed and dressed when the doorbell rang, her damp hair cascading in ringlets. She flew to the door, opened it wide and stepped back slowly from the threshold. A clean-cut young man with carroty hair stepped into the room, touched her cheek. Detective Vale felt compelled to look away from the shameless joy of their embrace.

Chapter Eight

The following morning several stories competed for space in the headlines: "Kidnap Plot Bared," "Physician Interrogated," "Executives Implicated in Explosion." And the one that gave Nancy the most satisfaction—"Metastaban: A Fraud?"

In the fast-paced hours of the preceding afternoon, a number of things occurred. Nancy forcefully clung to her theory about why she'd been kidnapped and by whom. It was 6BW, she maintained, that had accounted for the wave of serendipitous recovery. And it was Fairfield, with his accomplice at Camthon, who had conspired to destroy the drug and silence Nancy in order to promote the sale of Metastaban.

James Simmons, who had been picked up driving Nancy's car in Salinas, was transported to a Los Angeles jail. He was identified by Nancy, based on body build, clothing and voice inflection, as the kidnapper known to her as Bonnie. Simmons, in an unsurprising bid for a deal, identified Clyde as Lloyd Parsons. The pair, he admitted, were hired by "Fred" to accomplish the abduction of Nancy Rafferty. Lloyd Parsons, or Clyde, was previously unknown to local authorities and was, regrettably, still at large. And although James Simmons could not positively identify Karl Fredericks as his telephone contact, it turned out the corroboration was not necessary.

Karl Fredericks, coming around from his inglorious faint

at Los Angeles International Airport became, to the ever-lasting contempt of Paul Fairfield, a blubbering, penitent spokesman.

He related what he had learned and subsequently guessed about the remarkable capabilities of 6BW. He related that he had innocently shared this information with Fairfield, and became a victim of greed and circumstance. It was Fairfield, he asserted, who had engineered the plans for both the explosion and the kidnap. Fairfield had coerced Fredericks into locating and employing first the arsonist and then the kidnappers. In his haste to explain his proficiency at locating such underworld professionals, Fredericks—in an unforeseen bonus for the authorities—implicated Senator John Evanson.

Paul Fairfield remained disarmingly cool, and staunchly denied these allegations. He maintained it was Fredericks who had hatched the plan, acting on behalf of Camthon. He himself had no ax to grind with regard to the sale of Metastaban. Vickers, and later the district attorney, marveled at the doctor's gall in the face of a flood of damning testimony—much of it unsolicited—by a host of well-informed witnesses.

All in all, by the time Jeff Kohner accompanied Nancy back to her apartment, she was both exhausted and exhilarated. She was desperate for sleep, and yet she was too keyed-up by the rapid chain of events to be able to put her mind at rest.

Jeff traced the dark circles under her eyes. "God, I'm glad you're back. I missed you so. I kept imagining the worst kind of danger—"

"Hush," said Nancy. "I'm fine. Believe me, love, it could have been worse. In a way, I was very, very lucky." She told him about Clyde, the gentle little man who was a gourmet cook and who, in his frequent rational moments, clucked over her like a mother hen. "Honestly, Jeff, when I think how it might have been, I count myself one fortunate hostage!"

"And you had absolutely no idea where you were."

"None." She shook her head. "I knew I was up north, but I didn't know the terrain well enough to recognize it. And then, when we made the trip back home, I was not only blindfolded but drugged."

Jeff held her close, caressed her face, her hair. She tilted her chin to look up at him. "And speaking of drugs, my darling, what about 6BW? You and Roger have had no success at all?"

Jeff held up his fingers to form a circle and his tone changed. "Zero. I don't understand it. I've tried everything I know, racked my brain till it hurts. Even Roger got caught up after it finally became obvious to him that you must have been on to something. The guy never sleeps; he lives in the lab; he's convinced it's a simple, stupid error. But no matter how many times we redo the calculations, we can't seem to see where we've gone wrong."

"You'll do it," Nancy murmured into his chest. "I know you will. You're brilliant." Against her will, she allowed a yawn. "I guess I'm tired, after all."

"Let me get you to bed. Would you like me to leave?"

She looked stricken. "Are you kidding? No way!"

He put her to bed determined not to arouse her, though he ached to mold his body to hers. Instead, he began a gentle massage, coaxing every muscle into relaxation. He spent a lot of time on the bruised swollen ankle injured in her run to Parker Center. Willing strength into his fingers, he stroked her calves, and then the silky flesh of her thighs.

He hesitated, then moved up to her belly. "Hey," she exclaimed. "You missed the good part." Grinning, he placed his hand over her pubis. She arched her back and slowly began to writhe. He made no move to help her, kept his palm firmly anchored, allowed her to manipulate herself to orgasm. When she shuddered and moaned, he slipped a finger into her moistness and brought her to another trembling climax. He soothed her with his lips, caressed her with his tongue, until she gripped his shoulders and cried out. Then he lifted himself so their eyes could meet and he fitted his body to hers.

When at last they slept, it was the rest of fulfillment, each sustained by the other. Neither of them saw the clear, rosy dawn that ushered in the morning nor noticed that the plaguing fog had simply slipped away.

Ruthie Hillman, on her canyon patio, thoroughly enjoyed the clear morning sunshine. She read every word of the stories beneath the headlines while her husband now and then refilled her coffee cup. "I knew it," she clucked. "I knew it all along. That *momzer*, Paul Fairfield, is guilty."

"Hold it," said Louis. "He's not convicted yet. An arraignment only means he'll go to trial."

"He'll go to trial, all right. And he'll be convicted, too."

"Ruthie, my sweet, you should have been a lawyer."

"It doesn't take a lawyer to pin this on him. He and that Fredericks from Camthon. They knew what they were doing, they were perpetrating a fraud. Using people's tragedy to make a fortune."

Louis considered. "What they did was criminal. Explosions. Kidnaps. Okay. But what they were selling was chemotherapy, Ruthie. Chemotherapy is still a respected form of treatment."

Ruthie was furious. "But look at what they destroyed! Not only a man but a future!" Her expression softened. "Look at you, Louis. There's no doubt 6BW cured you. And Stevie Phillips and God only knows how many, countless others."

"If Nancy is right, the serendipity will continue. There are carriers. That's how it spread in the first place."

"Slowly, Louis. If Nancy is right. But think what might have been. A universal cure for viral disease—up to and including cancer."

An impish grin lit up her husband's face. "Then I'd have to retire. I'd be out of business."

Ruthie swatted him with a section of the paper. "So you'll work on a cure for old age!"

* * *

Vera Presti digested the news over waffles at the coffee shop she frequented. She had called in sick—the first time in twenty years. She had a lot of thinking to do. To her self-disgust, a part of her still cherished the fantasy of the silver-haired doctor. But her choice was clear. She must tell what she knew. She would show him she was not a stupid cow. She dipped the last of her waffle in a pool of syrup. She finished her coffee and dabbed daintily at her mouth. She was going to the district attorney.

Martin Jennings read the news in his office and the grant writer was overcome with shock. His Uncle Karl had practically raised him! As he regained his senses he was struck by two thoughts. One, he must call his Aunt Mary. She was a docile little thing, so in awe of her husband. She'd need a lot of support to get through this.

The second thing he realized—not without relief—was that he now knew what to do with Pederson's papers. After his conversation with his Uncle Karl, Martin tended to believe those papers were worthless. Still, with the unassuming chemist dead, he supposed they ought to go to his estate. He would turn them over to the DA's office—let them take it from there.

He reached for the phone to call his Aunt Mary. He could drop the papers off at the DA's on the way to her house.

St. Agatha's convent reeled with disbelief. Not Paul Fairfield, their respected parish doctor! It had to be a mistake! He could not have done such things—not a man of such noble and charitable character! The telephone rang incessantly. Mother Regina moved about the convent all day, reassuring parishioners and soothing the anxious sisters.

Sister Althea retired to her room directly after morning prayers. She would speak to Mother Regina at her first opportunity. First, she had to contend with her private feelings. She'd been numb with shock when she heard the news, though not entirely for the same reason as the others. Dr. Fairfield had lied to her, that much was clear. He'd not had a thing to do with her mother's recovery. If anything, he'd subjected her to needless chemotherapy without regard to the suffering it had caused her.

Nor was it the hand of God that had made her mother well. The bargain Althea had tried to make with God was, once and for all, invalid. If anything had restored Mrs. Riley's health, it was the new drug, 6BW—the chemical Nancy Rafferty had spoken of—the one that had caused the rash. Althea shuddered to think what Nancy must have suffered during the days of her kidnap. And if there was the slightest chance that Dr. Fairfield had been responsible for that, he deserved to suffer for his crime. Althea knew she must speak out against the doctor. Parishioner or not, he'd been despicable. She knew firsthand the depths to which he'd sunk out of his own lustful greed. Whether or not he'd had a part in the hospital explosion or in the abduction of Nancy Rafferty, he had lied to Althea and used her mother to further his own ends.

She roused herself and peered down the stairs. She must speak with Mother Regina.

Chapter Nine

Ty Callahan could not remember ever being so furious. Not only had Judd Rohrbach manipulated the news to his own advantage—in itself defying every rule in the newsman's book—but he must have had some awareness that Nancy's mysterious disappearance was more than a lucky break for his career. "Damn you, Rohrbach." He kicked a wastebasket across the room. "How much crap do you expect me to believe?"

He grabbed up a sheaf of papers, hastily assembled—test results on Metastaban, censures against Camthon, disclaimers made by the giant corporation—and shoved them menacingly in the reporter's face. "You knew this stuff was garbage, Rohrbach, you knew it when you touted it! You bought it to get a step ahead of Rafferty!"

"How the hell was I supposed to know it was a setup?" He glared at the producer, squaring his jaw.

"Because Fairfield never gave you proof, you opportunistic son of a bitch, and what he did give you, you never bothered to check out! As far as I'm concerned, you're as guilty as Fairfield of perpetrating a fraud on the public." He sent the wastebasket sailing again. "And you used my show to spread your lies!"

"It's my show, too, Callahan! So I made a mistake! Jesus Christ, it's not the end of the world!"

The producer glowered. "Oh yes, it is! And it's not your show any longer, buddy boy!"

Judd fell silent, but Callahan wasn't through. "I know this much. You'll have your day in court. You can try to dazzle a jury with your fancy footwork, maybe even convince them you were duped. But you'll never convince me you didn't suspect that Rafferty disappeared for your convenience!"

"Come on, Callahan . . ." Judd fished for words. "What do you think I am, some kind of demon?"

"No," roared Callahan. "You're a glory-hungry fool! And you're through at KBLA—as of now!"

By nine P.M., Deputy District Attorney Steven Wishnofsky decided to call it a day. Since eight this morning when the Fairfield/Fredericks thing was dumped in his lap, he hadn't had a minute to himself. He thought he remembered a sandwich at lunch, but he sure couldn't prove it by the gnawing emptiness roiling around in his gut. He sat back in his chair, braced his hands behind his shaggy head and gulped a couple of deep breaths, hoping to fool his metabolism into giving him another hour of concentration. But all that happened was a button popped off his gray, pinstriped vest and he realized that he really ought to quit.

As it was, he'd accomplished a lot—some because he knew what he was doing and some because he just plain got lucky. Apart from the media people breathing down his neck, he'd had half a dozen solid phone calls from potential witnesses and nearly as many uninvited walk-ins. Everybody and his dog, it seemed, had something to buoy the case against the defendants. Most of it was damaging and much of it was useful. Wishnofsky had no doubt he had a case.

Damn, he'd forgotten to call the murder victim's assistant—Pederson's second in command at the Reese Fowler lab. Wishnofsky had no idea what was in those files the kid delivered, but he guessed that . . . Kohner, Jeff Kohner, that was it, might want to have a look at what they contained. He glanced at his watch. It was too late now. He'd have to call him first thing in the morning.

Meanwhile, he'd content himself with the fact that he had a case. Now, he was going to get himself a steak.

Zan Phillips turned on the small TV in their bedroom while Miriam started to unpack.

"Honey, turn it down," Miriam whispered. "There's no point in waking the whole house now."

It had been past nine when their plane landed in Los Angeles. Late enough for Stevie to be in bed. Probably Grandma too, and there was no point in waking them. They'd have to wait to see them in the morning.

In light of this, Miriam was persuaded to prolong the trip with a candlelit dinner for two. They had blissfully consumed a huge Italian dinner with "last fling before tomorrow's diet" abandon and, sated and weary, cabbed it home to the dark and quiet condo in Westwood.

Now Miriam insisted on "sorting out a few things," systematically emptying their bags. Zan stood, puzzled, before the TV. "Hey, look." He stepped aside for his wife. Nancy Rafferty spoke animatedly into the camera. "Where's Rohrbach?" Zan sat on the edge of the bed.

"Both Paul Fairfield and Karl Fredericks," Nancy announced, "are scheduled for indictment tomorrow morning. This reporter," she added with a meaningful inflection, "will be there to see it happen, you can be sure."

"Fairfield," said Miriam. "He's that doctor at Reese Fowler. Sister Althea's mother was his patient."

Zan shrugged. "What the hell is he being indicted for?"

"Sshh." Miriam joined him on the bed.

"In other news tonight," Nancy went on, "researchers at Reese Fowler Medical Center are continuing their efforts to reproduce the ill-fated chemical, 6BW—and to understand how it worked. The chemical is now considered by many to have been the cause of the serendipitous syndrome of recovery which began to sweep the nation weeks ago.

"Victims of major illnesses who believe themselves to have been cured by otherwise unexplainable means, especially those who were left with a benign red rash—and physicians of such patients—are asked to contact the Special Studies unit under way at Reese Fowler in order to assist with research.''

Zan frowned. ''What's this all about?''

''I don't know.'' Miriam stared at the black-and-white screen. ''But I'm calling Dr. Lou first thing in the morning. That 6BW saved more than Stevie's life. In a way, it saved ours as well.''

Chapter Ten

Lou Hillman received the message from Miriam as soon as he reached his office. "Good morning," he greeted her as he returned her call. "Welcome home. Did you have a good trip?"

"Wonderful, thank you. But a rather sleepless night. What's been going on while we were gone? I know you tried to reach us, and my mother-in-law briefed us some. On the news last night—"

"Miriam, it's a long story." He brought her up to date as quickly as he could on the tumultuous events of the past week: Nancy's abduction, the Metastaban fiasco, the vain attempts to reproduce 6BW.

Miriam listened with growing concern. "What can we do? Is there anything?"

"Well, for one thing, I need to see Stevie. I wasn't able to do that without your consent. I'm heading up a Special Studies unit at Reese Fowler in hopes of learning more about how 6BW worked. Since Stevie made one of the first known recoveries, there's a good chance he may provide us with something valuable. There's an outside possibility some patients may be carriers. Do you know what I mean by that?"

"I think so," said Miriam. "When do you want him? He gets home from school at two-thirty."

"Bring him in whenever you can. It's a twenty-four-hour operation in the lab these days. The tests could take several hours to complete and he may need to be seen more than once.''

"I understand. I'll bring him in this afternoon—Dr. Lou, did Mrs. Riley have that rash?''

"She did, and in fact, she's already been seen. And there's another thing you can do. Would you call Sister Althea? She's been very distraught. She's been asking me when you were coming home.''

"I will," said Miriam. "Right away. Dr. Lou . . . thank you for everything.''

"Don't thank me. I haven't done a thing. Let's hope we can find out more about 6BW.''

"I'll keep good thoughts. I'll even say a prayer. And I'll see you this afternoon at Reese Fowler.''

"You won't believe this," Jeff told Roger Howell. "That was the DA on the phone.''

"Some guy in Caracas found all the answers. We can go take a very long lunch," came the sarcastic reply.

"Be serious, pal. There's a special messenger on his way over here now. It seems before he died, Pederson hired a grant writer. The writer had a box full of notes.''

"Pederson's notes?''

Jeff nodded. "You got it. I don't believe it myself.''

Roger paused. "Not the formula, man. You don't suppose we'd get that lucky?''

His colleague shrugged. "We'll know soon enough. But what else would he have left with a grant writer?''

Sister Althea was stunned and hurt. She could not believe what she'd been told. To believe in the doctor's innocence was one thing. To withhold information was quite another. Mother Regina had been her usual solicitous self, even in the face of such disquiet. She had listened attentively while Althea spoke, without interrupting her. When the nun finished, it seemed a long while before the superior responded.

When Mother Regina finally came around from her desk,

it was to cup Althea's face in her hands. "Sister, you've been through a trying ordeal. You're understandably upset. But before you make the decision to speak out, I would like you to consider this." She moved to the window, and looking out, spoke in a calm, quiet voice. "Dr. Fairfield, like all physicians, must make terribly difficult decisions. The course of treatment they ultimately prescribe is based on a number of factors. I think we both know Dr. Fairfield well enough to believe he chose what he thought best. How can you be certain he did not act in good faith when he prescribed this Metastaban for your mother?"

"I can't be certain, but—"

"Then, Sister Althea, why are you so quick to pass judgment?"

"Because he lied about the time he first prescribed the drug, and in light of what's happened since—"

"What, exactly, has happened since? Your mother has made a satisfactory recovery."

"Yes," said Althea. "But—"

"Then praise the Lord. And the decision that Dr. Fairfield made."

"But Mother, Metastaban may be a fraud—"

"That has yet to be proven. And in the event it is less than what was hoped, you cannot fault Dr. Fairfield. He chose to use it out of the best of his medical knowledge."

Althea persisted, surprised at the vehemence with which she stated her case. "I don't agree. I think my mother was better before he prescribed it. He subjected her to needless chemotherapy. Her recovery, I now believe, was caused by another drug. And if Dr. Fairfield knew about that drug, if he had anything to do with the explosion at Reese Fowler or the abduction of Nancy Rafferty—"

"Sister, Sister." Mother Regina turned to face her. "You are putting the cart before the horse. To the best of my knowledge this country still adheres to the principle of innocent until proven guilty. It would be a mistake for you to add to his indignity by publicly questioning his ethics."

Althea stared in disbelief at the fragile old woman,

straight-backed, indomitable, sure. "You're telling me I am not to go forward, even believing as I do."

"I think it would be in no one's best interest for you to make a spectacle of yourself. Certainly not in the church's best interest for you to accuse Dr. Fairfield."

"Suppose," ventured the nun, "I decide to go forward with or without your approval?"

"I remind you, Sister, of your vow of obedience. You would do well to remember your place."

It was Althea's turn to walk to the window, gaze out at the world beyond the gates. There it was again. Remember your place. Only first, she had to find it. . . . Althea sighed, pained to realize that she now faced another crossroads. Since those first euphoric days after the incident with Judd Rohrbach when Althea had discovered her own will, she had gathered every ounce of her strength and begun to formulate a plan.

She loved Michael Kelly, there was no denying that, but she was not ready to renege on her commitment. She'd thought of leaving the restricting walls of the convent, taking an apartment with some other sisters. It would give her the chance to try her wings in the world; to discover, at last, where she belonged. Now she wondered if that kind of freedom was anywhere near enough.

Slowly, she climbed the stairs to her room. There could be no halfway measure. The ties that bound her must bind forever—or be forever cut.

Nancy burst into Callahan's office. "The date's been set for trial."

Callahan looked up with mild surprise. "They aren't waiving time?"

"Not only aren't they waiving time"—Nancy sat across from her boss and smiled broadly—"but Fairfield's indicating, through his attorney, that he wants to 'clear the air' as soon as possible."

"I can't believe his attorney would go along with that.

He knows the more time he can get to elapse, the better the chances for his client.''

Nancy shrugged. "Apparently, Fairfield is adamant. Somehow or other, believe it or not, he's managed to convince himself he's innocent. He's blaming Fredericks, who can hardly wait to tell his side, and the DA's just been sitting back and grinning like a Cheshire.''

PART FOUR

Serendipity

Chapter One

"In a way," proclaimed Ruthie Hillman, turning to her husband to indicate she needed zipping up, "in a way, this is your party, too."

She turned again to inspect herself in the full-length mirror in their bedroom and paused to swat disparagingly at her hips. "It's been six weeks since little Stevie's recovery, and it's six weeks since your recovery, too! Do you see what I mean, Louis? It's your party, too. Are you listening to me?"

Louis smiled at his wife. "Yes, I am listening, and as usual, you are absolutely right. And by the way, there's nothing wrong with your hips. I happen to like them the way they are."

Ruthie met his glance in the mirror and bestowed on him a wicked, sexy smile. "Then get it together, as the kids would say. I can see that you're nowhere near ready. And I guarantee you'll not get me back in this bedroom until after the party is over."

Louis picked up the hand-drawn invitation from the blotter of Ruthie's desk. It had come from the Phillipses a week ago today, and it read on the front, in scrolled blue letters, "In Celebration of Serendipity . . . And Good Friends." Inside was a map to the Phillipses' home and the date and time of the party. He tossed it aside, began to knot his tie. "I guess," he admitted softly, redoing the knot, "I'm just not in the mood for a party."

Ruthie reached up, took the tie from his fingers and expertly knotted the silk. "I know," she agreed. "You've been absolutely grumpy for four out of the last six weeks."

"Well, what do you expect?" He sat on the bed. "It hasn't exactly been fun. The Special Studies project hasn't turned up a thing except to verify a few carriers. The process is slow and very spotty, and nobody knows how it works. We're hardly seeing an epidemic recovery; and with the whole 6BW thing stymied at this point, the prognosis doesn't look very good."

"That's the part I don't understand." Ruthie sat next to her husband. "When that grant writer turned up with Pederson's files, the formula was there in black and white. It should have been easy to reproduce the chemical exactly the way Pederson had."

"Except for some reason it hasn't worked, and nobody seems to know why. Kohner and Howell have had help from some pretty high-powered minds these past few weeks, but nothing they've done has sparked a syndrome. I'm beginning to think it wasn't 6BW at all, just a figment of our own imagination."

"Figment, my foot!" Ruthie hooted. "You had a tumor and it's gone. Damn that Fairfield, he should burn in hell."

"First, I'd like to see him convicted."

"He will be," Ruthie nodded. "Mark my words. With Karl Fredericks testifying on behalf of the state, he doesn't stand a chance of being acquitted."

"Mmm," muttered Louis. "Probably not. But I'm still in no mood for a party."

Ruthie rose and took up a hairbrush. "Nonsense, it's just what you need. You've been working too hard. Every one of you has. Miriam Phillips knows it, too. That's why she's giving this party, Louis, because you've all been working too hard."

"For all the good it's done—"

"Stop that, Louis. Your navy suede jacket is in the closet."

* * *

The face in the mirror stared fixedly back at her as she brushed her short hair to a coppery glow. She turned her head to examine the result from as many angles as she could. Her glance traveled down to the softly ruffled bodice of the new aqua shirtwaist dress she wore. "Althea Rose Riley," she thought aloud. "Yes, you look perfectly fine."

Althea Rose Riley. It had been five years since she'd tried the name, but it rolled off her tongue with ease. There was something to be said for that, she decided, and she placed the hairbrush just so in the tidy arrangement on top of her dresser, with the matching comb, two pale lipsticks and three small bottles of cologne, the gifts from the girls in Michael's office on the day they had taken her shopping.

She picked up the invitation to Zan and Miriam's party, noted the time and realized with dismay that she was ready far too early. She walked around the small bedroom, touched the silky peach of the coverlet and the frilly shade of the lamp on her bedside table. She counted six steps into the tiny kitchenette with its tinier bathroom off to one side. It was nothing more than a guest house, really, situated behind a modest family home and not designed for the comfort of long-term tenancy. But it was inexpensive and within walking distance of the social services office where she would begin work on Monday. Best of all, it was filled with tranquility, a private place exactly suited to her tenuous self-assurance.

She was very lucky, Miriam said, to have found the apartment so quickly. Miriam had listened to Althea's account of her separation from the convent with a face that betrayed some misgivings. Zan still regarded the former nun with an awkward, respectful distance that made her feel uneasy and equally awkward. Althea had chosen not to tell them, or anyone, of her decision until it had become an accomplished fact.

Even now, she could hardly believe the swiftness with which it had been done. She had felt no shame, no sense of betrayal; the act was not a reflection of her failure. Her choice was accepted at the convent with a calm that surprised her and in no way robbed her of her dignity. With the signing of a few papers and a hasty review of her new status, she found herself liberated from her vows. She felt a growing sense of rightness and an undiminished reverence for God.

Only after she had obtained the small apartment, unfamiliarly dressed in a sweater and skirt, and hired a taxi to move her few belongings from the convent, did she lie in the middle of the strange new bed and wonder what on earth she would do next.

She finally decided to tell her mother first, because she knew that would be the most difficult. As she expected, Mrs. Riley had neither pleaded nor accepted. She had simply glared at her daughter with unrepressed malice and ordered her out of the house. Strangely, this did not pierce Althea's heart as it might have done in times past. On the contrary, it left her resigned to the fact her mother could never love her for herself alone and filled her with feelings of compassion she had not known she possessed. She had written down the phone number of the family from whom she rented the apartment, and after tucking it under a clock on the mantel, firmly closed the screen door behind her.

Then, without thinking, she had boarded the number six bus for Westwood and appeared in the Phillipses' doorway. Shaken but welcoming, Zan and Miriam had talked with her for hours and helped her to analyze her situation—so that by the time Zan drove her back to her apartment, she had a list of things to do: a plan of action. She also had a check—a loan, they assured her, which Althea accepted under duress.

She had gone, the next day, to the employment office of the Department of Social Services and registered to take the examination. It was offered on Wednesdays, two days hence; and, yes, if she passed the exam, she would be offered employment on the basis of her experience and her interview.

She had stood on the steps of the county building and watched the procession of smartly clad people moving with purpose and direction. No one paid her the slightest attention; she was anonymous in her sweater and skirt. She remembered the night she'd worn Miriam's coat, how she'd longed for that kind of anonymity. Now she wondered, with a queasiness in the pit of her stomach, how she would blend into this strange new sea without being swallowed by the tides.

She opened a bank account, shopped for groceries, even purchased some underthings, a nightgown and a loosely belted dress, though the watchful eye of a solicitous saleswoman made her nervous and unaccountably indecisive. Finally, dressed in her newly purchased clothing, three days after her separation from the convent she forced herself to walk into the East Valley office of the Department of Social Services where she'd spent so many of her working hours on behalf of the church. "Good morning, Helen," she greeted the gray-haired receptionist. "I wonder if Mr. Peale might have a moment to see me this morning." She swallowed, hoping to slow the tattoo in her chest. "I think he should know there's been a—change in my status. I will no longer represent Saint Agatha's."

Helen, to her credit, never missed a beat, though her startled eyes missed not one detail of Althea's new demeanor. "Of course, Sister," she replied, in her customary manner. "I believe he's just back from a meeting." She buzzed the director, spoke briefly into the telephone, her eyes never leaving Althea. "You can go right in." Her smile was hesitant. "And Sister . . . you look very nice."

"Has the order dispensed with the habit?" Helen could not resist asking as Althea marched stoically past her.

"No," replied Althea with a trace of a smile. "It is I who have dispensed with the order."

Her interview with Mr. Peale was brief and reassuring, the genial director a model of restraint except to inquire how she wished to be addressed. "As a social worker," she replied with a feeble attempt at humor. "If Althea Riley passes the examination." Mr. Peale assured her heartily that, of course, she would pass, and that he would

welcome her to his unit. He would put in a request for her
as soon as she was eligible.

Encouraged, she wandered finally into the familiar partitioned room where Helen, as she expected, had preceded
her. A Catholic girl from the parish excused herself, making a tight-lipped exit. But the others clustered around her,
welcoming, and she let herself be questioned, hugged, assured. She was aware of Michael, on the fringe of the
group, his expression wary, anxious, for she hadn't told
him either. Finally, he took her hand, kissed her lightly on
the cheek, suggested they have lunch and she accepted.

Over salads, haltingly, she told the story: how she'd
questioned, argued, finally understood. She was Catholic
still, but she could no longer accept the strictures that the
order heaped upon her. Her small hands fluttered. It was
important to her that he fully understand. "It was not for
you," she concluded at last, "but for me, that I made this
decision."

He had taken her hands, held them firmly. "If you're
happy, Althea, then I'm glad. I'll always be your friend,
I've told you that before. My love for you implies no obligation." His eyes had filled with mischief; his mustache
began to twitch. "Of course, if you happen to grow in my
direction—"

Althea had laughed and finally cried, out of relief and
exultation. She was suddenly overcome by what she'd
done.

"This is your party, too," Michael told her last Sunday
when she showed him the invitation after mass. "In celebration of serendipity—and good friends."

Now she brushed a speck of lint from the skirt of her
ruffled aqua dress. It was her party, too, and she meant to
enjoy it. He would be there any minute to escort her.

The special messenger left her office, and Nancy turned
the creamy envelope he'd given her over and over in her
hand. There was no return address, just her name on the
front, and she felt the chill of apprehension. She laid it,

unopened, next to the Phillipses party invitation propped against the nameplate on her desk. She stared at it, wishing she'd refused to accept it. She would not let it spoil this party.

The trial was in progress, going as expected. There seemed little doubt of the outcome. It was a question, Callahan assured her, of sorting out the charges, assigning the burden of guilt. To the last, unbelievably, Fairfield maintained his innocence, even in the face of damning testimony. He'd become a pathetic figure to the press and to the public, a tragicomic villain to despise.

From the arsonist and from Bonnie—James Simmons, Nancy corrected herself—the link had been firmly established: first to Fredericks and then to Fairfield in a way that left no doubt. From unexpected sources came a dozen willing witnesses, the prosecution's roster swelling daily. And finally from Fredericks, who turned witness for the state and gave the unexpurgated version of the truth. There wasn't a jury who could acquit Paul Fairfield of the crimes he'd engineered.

Only the stubborn failure of the new 6BW made Nancy's vindication incomplete. That, and the absence of the kidnapper known as Clyde, who had seemed to vanish without a trace.

Nancy's glance returned to the thick, creamy envelope resting unopened on her desk. A threat against her life because she chose to disobey, because she went to the police with her story? A threat against Jeff? Clyde was unstable; was he unstable enough to harass her?

Whatever it was, it would wait until Monday. She would not open it now. She'd come through danger once. If it was coming back to haunt her, she'd just as soon pretend it didn't exist. Tonight, there was the party. She intended to enjoy it. And she'd better get a move on, it was well past five. If she knew Jeff and Roger, they'd still be in the lab. It would be up to her to haul them away.

Her gaze fixed on the damnable envelope, she threw a few things hastily into her purse. Callahan, smiling broadly, appeared in her doorway. "Congratulations, Nance—it's now official."

He tossed a letter onto her desk. "This just came down from upstairs. Beginning Monday, you're the official anchor for KBLA *News at Eleven.*"

Nancy picked up the congratulatory letter, read it slowly, savored every word. "Tell me," she said, sticking out her chin, "do I get to have a say on the co-host?"

Callahan laughed. "You're one tough lady. Yeah, now go on, get outta here. Enjoy your party." He regarded her fondly. "In a way now, it's your party, too."

Nancy wasn't smiling. "Callahan, stay a minute, will you?" She reached for the dreaded envelope and tore it open. She extracted a card, scanned it quickly and looked up at Callahan, wide-eyed. She read it again. She started to giggle, collapsed into helpless laughter in her chair.

Callahan, smiling against his will, took the card from between her trembling fingers. It read, "Celebrate with us the grand and glorious opening of Clyde's Cafe Americaine in Algiers." It gave an address in the Algerian capital and was signed, in bold black curlicues, "Your friend, Clyde."

"Jeezus, I don't believe it!" Callahan's smile faded. "Not Clyde, your friendly gourmet kidnapper?"

Nancy nodded helplessly, almost prostrate with laughter, tears beginning to roll down her cheeks.

Callahan watched her. "You know you have no choice. You have to pass this on to the DA."

"S-sure," said Nancy, trying to control herself. "For all the good it will do."

"Huh?" responded Callahan, clearly puzzled.

Nancy put her chin in her hands. "Clyde's no dummy. Nobody can touch him. Not while he's in Algiers."

"Holy mackerel, you're right." Callahan nodded. "The U.S. has no extradition treaty with Algeria!"

"Bingo!"

"So now what?" He waited for an answer, but his anchorwoman dissolved into mirth.

* * *

Roger Howell removed his lab coat. "Hey, man, it's party time, Nancy'll be here any minute. Come on, enough for one day."

"Yeah," Jeff said. "Be with you in a minute. I just want to run these tissue samples through." He adjusted the scope, bent over the lens. "Nothing, dammit. Absolutely nothing."

"Could have told you that. If there'd been any eczema, you'd have seen it with the naked eye, you didn't need the scope."

"True," muttered Jeff. "But there's always the hope—"

"Yeah, we'll start hoping again on Monday."

Jeff picked up a beaker of the colorless chemical. "What in the name of God did Pederson do?"

Roger shrugged. "Maybe not a thing. Maybe it was pure serendipity."

Jeff held the liquid up to the light. "No, he had to have done something. Or somebody did. It wasn't just luck that started that syndrome." He stared at the chemical, willing it to speak, to whisper to him a hint of its hidden secret. But the liquid was still, silent and placid. And he found himself struck by a weird idea. With deliberate will he opened his fingers, let the beaker slip from his grasp. It splintered on the countertop, glistening shards of glass, the liquid dripping, pooling at his feet.

"What the hell?" Roger rushed to his side. "Man, you are crazier than I thought!"

"Maybe," muttered Jeff. He was thinking of a night—two nights, in fact—when he'd done the very same thing. He'd sent a beaker of 6BW crashing after a late-night session with Alana McNeil. "I was wondering," he explained to his astonished friend, "if the answer is in the nature of its volatility."

He started to explain about impact on the chemical, changing it to a vapor, a floating gas. A vapor capable of floating on the air, upward through the vents of the lab and into the wards. The theory he advanced was remarkably similar to the one Karl Fredericks had patiently broached to Fairfield.

Roger listened, momentarily swayed. Volatility? . . . Maybe. Then a new thought surfaced. "When the lab blew up with that much force, why wouldn't the vapor have escaped?"

Jeff shook his head. "I don't know . . . the heat! The heat of the fire could have destroyed it. Look . . ." He rushed on with mounting excitement, but Roger's face was closed and Jeff's excitement dimmed. "Nah," he decided. "Fantasy, huh? Okay, let's get ready for this party."

Epilogue

REESE FOWLER MEDICAL CENTER

"I am going to fall asleep," the woman chastised herself, "if I don't find something to keep me awake." She considered the television bolted to the ceiling, but decided she couldn't take the chance of disturbing Ed, even though the nurses claimed it wouldn't. She rose from her chair to peer at the man in the bed. He looked exactly as she'd always known him. Except, of course, for the tubes in his nose and mouth and the IV seeping soundlessly into his hand.

He was a good man, Ed, the best she'd ever known, even if he'd never gotten around to marrying her. He was kind and he was proud and he'd be damn well upset to find himself a burden to her now. Well, she wasn't going to cry. Ed would hate it if she did, and even if he was asleep, she didn't want to upset him. But if, as the doctors said, he could slip away at any time, then she wasn't about to let him go alone. It was the least she could do, to keep him company at the end. She wiped a maverick tear from the corner of her eye.

She sniffled once and went to the window, fumbled with the slats of the blinds. It was nearly daylight. In the courtyard below, she saw milk being delivered into the Reese Fowler Kitchens. In an hour, the drone of construction would begin—the noisy, mechanical task of replacing the basement. Well, that noise wouldn't disturb Ed either, not if the nurses were right.

She dropped the blinds and moved again toward Ed. When she thought she heard him moan, she looked over at him quickly but he was still. She was relieved that he was getting decent care. It was amazing, she thought, after that horrible explosion, how the hospital just went on about its business. For the hundredth time she wondered if that miracle drug, the real one—the one that was destroyed—might possibly have saved Ed's life. But she found no comfort in this deliberation. If anything, it made her want to cry.

She wondered if the newspapers had been delivered to the nurses' station. Having something to read would keep her awake. She got as far as reaching for the doorknob when she heard a sound that froze her in her tracks.

"Franneh?" The word was muffled, but it sounded like her name. Then it was more distinct: "Frannie, 'on't go."

Frannie turned, hardly daring to breathe. Ed's eyes, fully open, seemed to be pleading. " 'on't go," he begged again, raising one freckled hand as though to tear the tube from his mouth.

"I'm here, Ed," she whispered, taking his hand to keep him from doing any damage. But he slowly raised the other, the hand with the IV, and clutched at the collar of his hospital gown. "Itches," he mumbled, as he began to squirm in discomfort.

Frannie removed his hand and carefully reached beneath his head to undo the ties of the gown. She tugged at the fabric as gently as she could and frowned at the blotchy, reddish rash.

"I'll be right back, Ed," she told him, her heart hammering in her chest. "I promise. I'm just going to call the nurse. . . ."

The Provocative National Bestseller

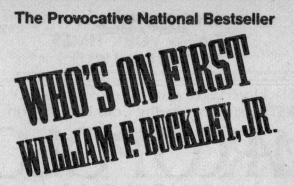

WHO'S ON FIRST
WILLIAM F. BUCKLEY, JR.

"Timeless thriller ingredients: murder, torture, sex...
Soviet defection, treachery. And there in the middle of
it all is good old Blacky: charming, insouciant,
escaping one dragnet after another without rumpling
his trenchcoat." *Boston Globe*

The cunning and sophisticated hero Blackford Oakes is
back in a new adventure involving a beautiful
Hungarian freedom fighter, Blacky's old KGB rival,
a pair of Soviet scientific geniuses, and the U.S.-
U.S.S.R. space race.

"A fast-moving plot.... As in all good espionage novels
there is thrust and counterthrust....Mr. Buckley is an
observer with a keen wit and a cold eye."
Newgate Callendar, *New York Times Book Review*

"The suspense is keen and complicated....Constantly
entertaining." *Wall Street Journal*

"A crackling good plot...entertaining."*Washington Post*